A Rebel's Path

The Enchanted Isles, Volume 3

I.L. Cruz

Published by Bosky Flame Press, 2022.

This is a work of fiction. Similarities to real people, places, or events are entirely coincidental.

A REBEL'S PATH

First edition. October 3, 2022.

ISBN: 978-1732547162

Written by I.L. Cruz.

Brandice,

I'll miss you...

Prologue

The first thing Cat noticed was the air. It was clean and crisp with just a hint of the sea. He'd missed the way it felt against his fur. When he finally opened his eyes he glimpsed familiar stars. When he'd left Canto so abruptly all those years ago it had been midday.

Breathe in. Breathe out.

He remembered it all. In fact, he was so lost in the memory that he failed to notice the woman less than six feet away. She sat across from a humble fire and in her hand was a fiddle that shone silver in the moonlight. A haunting tune reverberated under the careful ministrations of her elegant fingers. Without conscious thought, his tail began to sway in time.

When he finally registered her presence, he stood transfixed watching her graceful and deft fingers holding the bow like a lost love. If he had been any other audience, he would have been moved to tears.

But he wasn't just any other audience.

Instinctively, he recoiled. His muscles tightened and an involuntary hiss escaped his mouth. The player faltered on a note, but quickly recovered. Yet it was just enough time to slow his breaths.

He took a step forward and the playing ended abruptly. The woman lowered the bow and the fiddle but kept them near at hand. She wasn't familiar. Her figure was hidden by a voluminous cloak and the surrounding darkness. *How long had he been gone?* From behind her she withdrew a horn, the color of the sky at dusk, making him stop his approach. She smiled.

"Now that we understand each other," she began, "perhaps we can work to each other's benefit." Her voice, rich and resonant was a surprise to him. He didn't know how long it had been since he'd heard a human voice.

He smiled back, displaying razor-sharp teeth and appearing untroubled by this current wrinkle. He took another step forward, his tail undulating with the breeze. His long whiskers twitched and for a brief moment he wondered if he still knew how to talk. When he last walked the paths of Canto he had been feared, so either this woman was very powerful, or her desperation was great. Either way, he intended to find out.

One thing was certain—she was powerfully, desperately foolish. Teaching her that lesson would be an added bonus to his unfinished work. His smile widened and he was gratified to see the woman look momentarily alarmed.

"Shall we begin?" asked The Cat, who executed a mocking bow before taking his fiddle.

Chapter 1

I stood in the bay watching the shore of Canto. The icy pool enveloped my near naked body and wisps of air escaped my lips.

Warm...warm...warm...

I'd said it repeatedly for the past ten minutes in my mind, but my body knew better. Getting my Powers under control was more urgent than ever. Since accepting Zavier's proposal over a month ago, I'd had too many close calls that could have revealed my illegal magic.

A stiff wind made ripples on the surface of the water.

Warm...hot...scalding...

My fingers told the real story, turning blue and losing feeling—along with the rest of me. It would have been so easy to give in to the feeling and float away. No more worries about Mythos discovering my magic. Or the royal house. Or Zavier. I wouldn't be indebted to the hidden market anymore.

Warm...hot...fire!

Nothing was working. My breathing was ragged, and I imagined small ice crystals forming on the inside of my body. The chattering of my teeth made my jaw ache. It made the reality of my situation sink in. I didn't have the luxury to turn my back on my responsibility to my Powers, my family or to Canto. I redoubled my efforts.

Warm...cold...ice...really cold...I'm so fu...

"Time to get out," said a voice, rich and female. I bit back a response while the towing of my body through the icy waters felt like a thousand knife points piercing my skin. It was a relief when I reached solid ground and hot breath tried to thaw my hands through excruciating pain. I looked up to see the pink and purple swirls of the Mist House overhead.

"I don't understand. She's done it before," said Viktor Lake. Her voice was once again disguised as male. Her hood was up, covering her silver-white hair and obscuring her sex. I was sure neither Rowley or my mother knew Viktor Lake was a woman and I'd yet to learn why she insisted on the ruse. It was only because of the magic in her home that she could continue the deception.

Shivering on her floor, I envied her disguise, if only for the added warmth. As if reading my mind, Mamá threw a blanket over me. She had flawless skin, but even now I saw the beginnings of the lines that would etch her face. Lines I'd caused, no doubt.

"She was fighting for her life then. Deep down she knows we're here and we'll save her," barked Rowley. I knew he was right.

His response was harsh, and each word was tinged with impatience. My progress had stalled. In past attempts at getting me to feel warmth in the frigid water, he'd cast a warmth spell over me afterward. This time he didn't bother. His one cloudy eye softened the hint of reproach in the other. His black fur shimmered in the mystical light of Viktor's home.

"Are you suggesting we leave her and hope she won't die?" asked Mamá, her words clipped and precise. Her hands chafed mine through the blanket. It was both an agony and a balm. Mamá said she came to these sessions to help, but I wondered if it was really to protect me from Rowley and Viktor's expectations. Her jaw tightened when Viktor draped a coat over my shoulders.

"Perhaps we should—" Viktor began.

"Perhaps you should just leave her alone!" yelled Mamá.

"Do you know the kind of fire I had to put out, Filomena?" snapped Rowley. Few people talked to my mother the way Rowley did. Although she never expected the deference due to her by her right as a duchess, at that moment she loomed over Rowley like he was a peasant.

"I can-can h-h-hear you," I said, feeling left out of the conversation. My three teachers were clustered around me, their truce slowly breaking down. They were talking about me again like I wasn't even there. Just a vessel. I understood their panic because I shared it. The fire Rowley had put out had been a literal fire I'd started in my home with my erratic magic. The memory of it was humiliating and beyond frightening.

My chattering eased and I pushed myself up to a sitting position. I looked to Rowley, knowing he would agree to my demand.

"Again," I said. Rowley nodded.

"*Nena*, no. It's starting to snow. You need food and some rest," said Mamá. The snow drifted down in front of the entryway to the Mist House. It gathered close enough that it looked lit up by the swirling lights. It was a beautiful reminder that there would always be a reason to put off practicing my erratic magic. This Power was given to me by generations of my family, hoping that I would return magic to the Enchanted Isles.

So far all my magic had done was kill a queen from Faerie, trap a man in a shell and start a fire in my home. It had done good things, too, but rarely on purpose. I had to learn to control my magic before I destroyed anything or anyone else.

"No, she's right Inez. We'll start practice again tomorrow," said Rowley grudgingly. Viktor was conspicuously silent. She had helped me convince Mamá and Rowley that I had to speed up my progress and had suggested the water test. The bay in winter was just short of freezing and my will to shut out the cold was supposed to trigger my Powers. So far that approach had been a dismal failure.

"Yes, tomorrow," said Viktor without making eye contact. I felt her disappointment in me as keenly as I felt the cold that had seeped into every pore. I couldn't argue with all three of them and gave a short nod before standing up. Dry clothes were waiting on a nearby stool and despite my fumbling frigid fingers, I refused any help. I may not have been able to will myself warm, but I sure as hell wasn't going to be dressed like a baby.

I heard their hushed squabbling and started to feel like half the problem I faced was keeping my teachers from bickering amongst themselves. A flare of heat went through me and just as quickly retreated. Rowley's head turned and I knew he was scenting the air for magic. Annoyed, and frankly frightened what that would lead to, I stalked off to the woods.

The woods were a haven for me.

They asked nothing of me other than to tread lightly and even that was more of a suggestion. I'd walked its secret pathways since I joined the hidden market. Searching for enchanted eggs filled with wild magic to sell while avoiding the long arm of the King's Men was my only test.

That was until my inherent magic awoke and it was revealed that I was the Ternion, the one person who would bring magic back to Canto and all the Enchanted Isles. Rowley, Viktor and even my mother believed in the prophesy and it was the only point they all agreed on although how to prepare me for it was still up for debate.

My smuggling of enchanted eggs might have ended but being back in the woods where I'd plied my trade for so long was a comfort. After the Egalitarian Ball and becoming Zavier's intended, I thought my days working for the hidden market were at an end. And they were...except for the deal I'd made with Áliz, the feared Jabberwocky.

It was risky for me to be seen connecting with her or any other market activity. At least in the open. Ever since the Jabberwocky had changed my role in the market from smuggler to spy, I'd had to resist the small pockets of magic tugging at my own coming from the contraband eggs. The enchanted eggs were ripe for the plucking and more lucrative than ever since the season was coming to an end.

The lloras that laid the eggs full of wild magic had already gone underground for their seasonal hibernation. They wouldn't emerge until mid-spring and who knew what I'd be doing by then.

So much had already changed since discovering my inherent magic and the burdensome destiny attached to it. By now I knew I was less likely to cause irreparable damage this deep in the forest if I had a sudden burst of Power. No one would notice a few singed trees in all this wilderness. Anyway, I felt closer to my grandmother, Lita when I walked the forest paths.

It was funny I still thought of her as Lita when her real name was Sabrina. My young and inexperienced tongue couldn't produce the word *Abuelita* clearly and Lita she remained. I smiled at the memory. She and my grandfather, Beval, searched for plants to bring back to her herbal room until he died and then I walked with her. We had many deep conversations about my future on those walks.

And yet she had kept my magic a secret, just as Mamá had done.

My future was just as uncertain now as it had been when I fretted about not inheriting the family title. I hadn't known then, I had an even bigger title to inherit, that of the Ternion, the person who would return magic to all of the Enchanted Isles. But the prophesy hadn't said how I would achieve that lofty goal.

Getting my own magic back had been easy—if dangerous. I suspected getting everyone's magic back would still be dangerous and far from easy. I also suspected it would involve an inordinate amount of destruction. Who would I hurt and who would I lose along the way?

These were not the questions I'd been able to pose to Lita. She'd always said I'd find my purpose and I had, but it was a lonely realization that my purpose was safeguarding illegal Powers with little guidance and a very real threat of exposure. Even I didn't know if revealing my Powers would lead to imprisonment, exile or worse. Lita would have understood. Then again, who was to say that she would understand me any more than the other people in my life? Would she have been cautious like Mamá, guarded like Viktor or impatient like Rowley?

I continued to trudge through the damp leaves, weaving through the dense growth of trees.

The chill in the air matched my self-pitying mood. But I wasn't so lost in thought that I missed the signs of someone approaching. The steps were light and the gait distinctive. Without turning around I remarked, "You're losing your touch, Jacque. Is money making you sloppy?" His inheritance was still new, but Jacque always moved like a thief.

"Is being a princess making you slow? You should have picked me up fifty steps ago," he said, a smirk in his voice.

I had a momentary scare. What if he'd watched my practice at the bay? He'd be yet another person who knew about my illegal Powers. *No, I did hear him approaching*—his comment was just to goad me.

"I'm far from a princess. Taking a stroll?" I asked.

Jacque fell in step next to me as the path cleared. He cocked his head and raised his eyebrows at my clothes. I was wearing a riding suit and not my normal smuggler garb. Since becoming the official girlfriend of the heir apparent I had to marginally look the part. What I was wearing was better than what Queen Hortensia had originally insisted on, full court dress.

Mamá had acquiesced for a time before realizing how impractical fancy clothes were with my magic practice. I offered no explanation to Jacque other than to mutter, "Royals," and after a few moments Jacque shrugged.

"Speaking of royals—the *Empress* would like a word," he said.

"And how does she propose I do that?" I asked. "I've been barred from the hidden market to keep the KM—the King's Men—away."

"About that—there's a secret I've been keeping," said Jacque.

"Join the club. What is it?"

"I have to show you." Jacque led me to his old house. Since coming into an inheritance from Delaware Humphrey, he'd bought a place closer to the more fashionable part of town.

"Why are we here?" I asked. In response he opened the door and sitting in an ornate chair was the Jabberwocky.

Chapter 2

I looked around the room to give myself a moment to compose myself.

The windows of Jacque's old house were boarded up from the outside—not unusual in this part of Canto—but inside was a cozy den with a roaring fire in a newly refurbished fireplace. Thick carpets covered the floors and while sparsely furnished, the chairs, table and tea set were opulent enough for the palace. It was quite the step up from when Jacque lived there.

The bigger shock was seeing Áliz outside the hidden market. To my knowledge a Jabberwocky never left the confines of the underground. Her graceful fingers drumming against the arm of her white peacock chair were the only sign of her impatience.

I could imagine what I looked like to Áliz. My clothes were sticking to my skin from the moisture that still clung to it. The tips of my hair were fragile icicles from where they'd touched the water. I couldn't prove it, but from how cold I felt I was sure my lips were a purple-blue color. And as Jacque had noted, I wasn't wearing my usual hidden-market clothes.

"Have you decided to become an honest citizen, or have you been kicked out of the market, too?" I asked, taking a seat before she offered. A single eyebrow arched on her lined face.

"Neither, although I hear great things from the world above," she said gesturing around the room. "As I understand it, even a smuggler can become a princess." She held a smile and I returned it with as much grace as I could muster. Conversations with Áliz had always been dueling matches, but they were even more fraught since we'd struck our bargain.

A few weeks ago, I'd promised her access to information from the King's Men about possible raids on her smugglers and procuring magical objects from the royal palace in exchange for her releasing the KM in her pay without murdering them. I also promised to be her personal smuggler but to stay away from the hidden market. It was a deal that benefitted both, but I'd yet to deliver any substantial results. I assumed this impromptu meeting was to take me to task.

"Ladies, don't fight. I'd hate for the neighbors to overhear you," said Jacque, casually leaning against the wall. For a moment I'd forgotten he was there. From her reaction, so had Áliz.

"Nonsense. I've had that taken care of. All the houses on this block are now empty. I've decided it was in my best interest to have an above ground presence from now on," replied Áliz. "We are alone."

The way she said it made me uneasy. The hidden market was a place for smugglers and vendors to sell illicit magical merchandise and while the KM didn't like the trade, they mostly tolerated it. And then a visiting queen from Faery died in a magical battle and I had been involved. Soon after other magical crimes disturbed the relative peace of Canto. The result of the uptick in magic had been increased vigilance of the illegal magic trade. My Powers hadn't been discovered yet, but it was a daily fear of mine.

Áliz setting up on Canto's streets was brazen at the best of times and these were far from the best. As if reading my mind, she waved her hands in dismissal.

"Not that my new home will be about the hidden market. Everything I do in this house, and the surrounding ones, will be above board. Except, of course, my dealings with you. Your Grace," she said with a nod of her head. Her being here was more about a threat rather than my working for her.

"Áliz, if I'm seen coming here too often someone will get suspicious. At the very least they'll think I'm spending too much time with Jacque," I reasoned.

"Not if you're visiting his grandmother, who is sadly housebound and hard of hearing, which sometimes makes it impossible for her to answer the door. You're looking in on her as a favor and don't royals need to be seen as charitable to their subjects?"

My eyes darted to Jacque, and he shook his head.

"Don't look at me," he said. "She came up with the story and no one knows my grandmother anyway.

"How'd she get here?" I challenged.

"A transport from the outer territories," said Áliz. Jacque shrugged.

"Not the story you tell other people. How did you leave the hidden market without being noticed?"

Jacque was about to answer, but a look from Áliz silenced him.

"Some secrets are my own. The details of my comings and goings are not your concern. What is your concern, our mutual concern, is the deal we struck. I've yet to see any return on that investment. I was promised information and priceless magical objects. I believe palace clouds were mentioned. Where are they?" Her tone was light, but the way she gripped the arms of her chair told me she wasn't taking the delay lightly.

"I need more time," I said simply. I was proud to hear how calmly I said it. "I haven't been called to the KM since the ball—"

"Since you became engaged to the crown prince," she interjected.

"I'm not engaged," I admitted, reluctantly. Even though Zavier and I had shared the betrothal dance at the Egalitarian Ball, Queen Hortensia would have the last word, which she would withhold until absolutely necessary. The need for her approval rankled even as I worried about the implications of hiding my magic from a man I was supposed to share my life with. "I've been recognized as Zavier's girlfriend. And as Jacque can tell you, it isn't easy stealing from the royal family."

A few months back Jacque and I had stolen rummage stones from the palace, and it hadn't gone smoothly. I'd made it out, but Jacque had been caught. Somehow he'd managed to avoid any punishment from the KM and Áliz, which he still hadn't explained.

He'd even maintained his membership in the hidden market, despite the fact others with lesser offenses had been expelled, or worse. I looked over at Jacque who kept his face blank. *What does he owe her?*

Áliz sat waiting.

"It just so happens that I know exactly how hard it is to steal from the palace, so don't waste my time." Áliz paused as though considering something, but I didn't fool myself into thinking she hadn't thought out whatever she was going to say well in advance of my arrival. "My new home has me feeling generous—the same kind of generosity that allowed you to make this ridiculous deal with me."

"Áliz, you and I both know you made the deal because it was too lucrative to dismiss," I said.

"Lucrative remains to be seen. No, I have no doubt you will eventually get something from the palace that is valuable enough to warrant my kindness toward the wayward KM you made me spare. In the meantime, there is a little smuggling job I have, uniquely suited to your placement and talents." Áliz reached into a pocket hidden deep in her voluminous dress and removed a slip of paper and handed it to me.

The texture was rough and only had five words I read hastily before it disintegrated. It wouldn't be hard to remember, and I assumed she wrote it for me, to avoid saying it in front of Jacque. I wasn't thrilled at the prospect of getting this particular item.

"Consider it done. Where should I bring them?" I asked, happy I kept the irritation out of my voice.

"You can hand them off to Jacque. Work it out among yourselves, but the job has to be done by you, alone."

"Or course," I replied. There was no way I was bringing Jacque along on a job to Green Gardens. Not with Meiri being involved.

Jacque and I left Áliz in her cozy home, but neither one of us were at ease with the situation. Even so, we did not voice our concerns. There was no need—we knew the risks of the Jabberwocky being above ground. Áliz doing business out in the open meant risk of exposing the hidden market and its dealings. If she were caught, someone else would have to take over the market and the power struggle would cost a lot of lives.

"Did she ask you about the Faery border?" Jacque asked suddenly.

"No; why is there something good coming through?" I asked.

"I don't know, but the market's been warned off any traffic close to the border. Security's gotten tighter since that queen from Faery died at the Academy and it's getting worse. But I don't have to tell the princess that, do I?" he said good-naturedly.

"I'm not a princess," I said with more venom than I intended. His casual mention of Queen Celeste unnerved me. Only four people knew about my involvement in her death and Jacque wasn't one of them.

"About that, why did you tell the Empress you're not engaged? I think we all know you are, even without the formal announcement," he said.

"It's a process," I replied and managed to keep from sighing. Queen Hortensia had been reluctant to make my relationship with Zavier binding. She never came out and said she didn't want me to marry her brother-in-law and future king of Canto, but she'd done her best to make her feelings known that I wasn't right for the role of queen. Since the ball, she'd found precedent after precedent to block Zavier's and my wishes.

Mamá had made it her second career countering every hinderance the queen threw at us, doing as much research in the library as she had when she thought she could bind my magic.

In truth, I was almost as reluctant to make the engagement official as Hortensia. I still hadn't told Zavier my biggest secret—that I had magic. More importantly I was the mythical Ternion, a mage able to wield Power in all three magical disciplines and was tasked with restoring magic to all the Enchanted Islands—against Mythos' wishes. Zavier's not knowing about my magic made it necessary for me to lie to him on a regular basis. It wasn't ideal for starting a life together.

"So, what are we stealing?" asked Jacque. He walked with me to the center of town. All the shops were closed for the night and no one else walked the lanes of Canto, but I still shushed him.

"We are not stealing anything. I have a job and you get to be the go-between once it's done. Trust me, you'll want no part in this," I replied. The problem was, neither did I.

Chapter 3

"You'll just have to eat a little crow and call on Meiri yourself," said Zavier. He spoke like someone who'd had to apologize to Meiri more than once and that was not a surprise because they were cousins, but he'd never had to steal from her on behalf of the Jabberwocky. This would be my second time.

Zavier's voice was a rumble under my cheek as we lay on the couch. Mamá had converted one of the many libraries in Árbol Real into a sitting room for Zavier and me. It was one of the many concessions we'd made to accommodate Hortensia's sense of decorum.

I didn't relish the idea of spending time at the palace and the queen was horrified by the idea of Zavier spending all his time off in my bedroom. In response to Hortensia's concerns, Mamá had offered this solution. Hortensia needn't have worried. It was a rare day when Zavier didn't have KM or royal duties that kept him from spending time with me. We were taking full advantage of our free time and the excuse of a cold day to stay warm with each other indoors.

"Maybe you could pave the way for me with Meiri? You are related," I said with my head resting on his chest. He still had a slight smell of horse, but it was mostly pleasant on him.

"You seem to think that means something. I know she misses you because when she and the rest of the Verdants came over for dinner the other day she asked about you," he replied rubbing my back in lazy circles.

"She did? What did she say exactly?" I asked, lifting my head to meet his gaze.

"Are we in school? I'll pass her a note between classes," he said with a laugh. I slapped his chest lightly.

"Fine. I don't want to know," I said.

"Very mature. Okay, she asked if I'd seen you and if you had asked about her," he said, and I could almost feel him rolling his eyes.

"And I'm the one who's immature? Dammit, I need to talk to her, don't I?" I asked, propping myself up to a sitting position. Zavier reluctantly joined me.

"Is that such a bad thing? Unless you like talking through me," he said and added a light kiss. "Where is your mother?"

"Not here," I said and kissed him back. It was a slow lingering kiss that I relished despite my predicament with Meiri. He ended the kiss too soon.

"Are you ever going to tell me what you argued about?" said Zavier, his hand brushing my hair back. I shook my head, pulling away from his reach.

After all that had happened at the Egalitarian Ball with Rex and Betlindis, I knew more than ever that magic was best served away from the seat of power—for now. I couldn't tell Zavier in the same breath that I had thwarted a magical coup and then say it was my magical birthright they used to try and take the throne away from his family.

At the very least he'd have to report the whole affair to Mythos, our magic-embargoing overlords. At worst, he'd have to turn me in, for Goddess only knew what kind of punishment. And he'd hate me—hate me the same way he hated whoever had wielded the magic that had killed his parents. Telling him about my Powers was out of the question for me.

Not so Meiri. After all that had happened she thought I should tell Zavier about my shells, the prophesy and my magic.

"Are you insane?" I'd asked Meiri incredulously. "He's officially the heir. He'd have to do something about my magic."

"He loves you, Inez. He stood up to Hortensia, Mythos, and all of Canto to let you decide. A man like that would not slap you in chains and ship you off to Mythos," she replied calmly. Her serenity irked me. Her problems were trivial compared to mine and for a moment I forgot we were friends.

"You're clinging to some vicarious romantic fantasy because you aren't brave enough to go with Jacque and he won't risk being with you." I regretted it even before I'd finished uttering the words, but the damage was done. The look in her eyes was cold fury.

"Mother was right about you," she said and then walked away. We hadn't spoken since.

Zavier prompted me, caressing my cheek with his hand and bringing me back to the present.

"The argument was silly," I replied looking down. To talk about it would bring up too many questions that I still couldn't answer. I pushed down a lingering bit of guilt and let Zavier put his arms around me.

"Well, you should cut her some slack. Her homelife isn't ideal. Aunt Eugenia is...formidable," he said with a mock shudder.

"So am I, and you live with a very formidable woman, too," I replied.

"Yes, but she's not my mother—just my sister-in-law," he said. He was quiet for a minute, and I knew he was thinking about Queen Hortensia and his brother, King Xander.

"How is that going? Home, I mean."

"Home is just another place that I work. All my spare time I spend with you," he said, leaning in for another kiss. I wouldn't be swayed.

"Really, Zavier. Is everything okay?"

"It's fine, I guess. After the Ball, when Hortensia realized I wasn't going to pick Angelien, she moved on to other things. She has a lot on her plate," he said and then hesitated before he continued. "There is a situation brewing with Mythos," he said, crossing his arms.

Our cozy afternoon was becoming chilly. After our announced pre-engagement there had been a flurry of visits from Mythosian officials. It was even rumored the Arbiter of Mythos had taken an interest as well. I was privy to none of it because Mamá and Zavier had formed a wall of silence about the whole thing. I presumed no one in Mythos was happy with the idea the daughter of the most vocal peer for magical return was marrying into the royal house. I didn't want to press him.

"How is shadowing Hortensia?" I asked. I knew part of being the heir apparent meant learning all the duties of being the reigning monarch, including council meetings and creating favorable connections with agents from all the Enchanted Isles—especially Mythos. It should have been Xander's role to mentor Zavier as his brother and the king, but we all knew Hortensia ran Canto.

"Interesting, despite having to follow her around. I still don't know all the issues she deals with, but there's been a lot from Faery. Something about extradition treaties, but she kept me out of that one," he replied. "You'll have to start shadowing her too once the engagement is official." I cringed at the thought.

"Promise you'll never leave me alone with her? She's liable to push me out a window," I said.

He pulled me in close. "On my honor as a King's Man, I will keep you safe from the queen," he joked.

"I'll hold you to that," I replied, turning to face him.

"You can hold me to anything you want, so long as I can do this," he said, following with another kiss. It started to grow warmer as the kisses deepened. His hand cupping my cheek moved down to my back, crushing me to his body. My arms wrapped around his neck. Breathless, he stopped after a few minutes.

"I think you're the only guy who would stop at a time like this," I said, taking a deep breath.

"Not to take away your belief in my gallantry, but I think I heard the door," he said, and I reluctantly sat up with his assistance. I was so busy straightening my shirt and smoothing down my hair to be presentable, that I didn't notice Meiri standing in front of us with a bloody gash on her arm.

"Inez, I think I'm in trouble."

Chapter 4

I rushed to Lita's herbals room with Meiri and Zavier following closely behind. He'd wrapped his handkerchief around her arm. The clean cream fabric was slowly turning dark red. The sleeve of her coat and sweater were sliced through and I had to wonder how big and how sharp whatever it was that got her. Meiri's eyes were still wild, wide and unblinking, but now they were also clear and dry.

"Meiri, what happened to you? What do you mean you're in trouble?" asked Zavier.

Zavier sat Meiri down on the cot Lita would use when she worked through the night. It still released a strong lavender and mint scent when anyone disturbed it. Meiri remained closed-mouthed and I thought she was gritting her teeth against the pain of her injuries. Zavier crouched in front of her, removing the handkerchief and awaiting her response. Her lips pressed together and her gaze slipped away from his.

"I... I saw...The Cat," she said in a whisper. Her eyes darted around the room as if she thought he could be hiding in one of the corners of my sitting room.

"What cat? *The* Cat, do you mean *The Cat*?" I asked.

"Did you say The Cat? Meiri that's just a—" started Zavier.

"I saw The Cat! I saw him with his little fiddle," she shrieked. The vehemence of her response did nothing to lessen the absurdity of her statement.

"Meiri, The Cat isn't real. It's just something adults tell children to keep them in line," he replied. Meiri sprang from her seat as though ready to do battle with Zavier. I quickly stood between them and coaxed her out of her coat. The ragged slit in her arm would have been much deeper if she hadn't been wearing it and her thick sweater.

Even so, the damage was extensive reaching from an inch above the wrist to nearly an inch from her elbow. It was lucky the gash was on the top side of her arm, or she could have bled out before getting to my door. She winced as I cautiously touched the outside boundaries of the wound.

"Why do you think you saw The Cat?" I asked.

Meiri tried to pull away, but I guided her to the workbench. "Zavier, find clean bandages and the small scissors in the drawer over there." He quickly found the things I needed and I had no problem finding Lita's wound medicine, a tincture of red sage and meadowsweet. I carefully cleaned the wound the way my grandmother had taught me and was glad it wasn't as deep as I'd originally thought. What did surprise me was the light thread of magic I felt running through her injury. I looked over at Zavier, hoping I hadn't revealed anything in that unguarded moment.

Zavier watched quietly as I dressed the wound, a smile forming on his lips.

"You have access to KM records. Have you ever seen anything about The Cat?" asked Meiri, directing her question to Zavier. It was a children's story and a portent of doom, but The Cat was based on something real—an attack over a century ago that nearly erased Canto from the Enchanted Isles.

Since then, The Cat had become the veritable hidden monster under the bed or the horror waiting in a darkened closet, something whispered about around campfires. When someone did something wrong or out of character it was blamed on The Cat, who supposedly had the Power to control the thoughts and actions of others. Seeing him was considered a bad omen.

"The records from when that supposedly happened are from so long ago they may not be reliable. You'd be better off looking in library archives. But as far as I know, it's just a story," said Zavier. I was inclined to agree, but I couldn't explain away the gash on her arm.

"It doesn't matter. What matters is that I've seen The Cat and now something terrible is going to happen to me," she said with a shiver.

I would have argued that something had already happened to her, clearly. Over a hundred years ago Canto was almost inundated by a large wave. The wave was preceded by strange happenings like livestock bounding as high as the moon and inanimate objects coming to life. And there were some who swore a cat had been the cause of it all.

Most people reasoned that if something of the sort had happened, Mythos would have stepped in.

"Okay, where did you see it?" asked Zavier fighting the incredulity in his voice. He failed.

"I *did* see it, by the edge of the woods toward the Fae Range," she replied.

"What were you doing there? Where were you going?"

"If you must know, I was coming here," she said looking at her shoes. She sat down heavily on the bed. Bits of brambles still stuck to her hair.

"Here? Why?" I asked. The words just slipped out.

"I was coming to see you," she said and looked at me with sad eyes. "I had cabin fever being cooped up in that house and I knew the only person I could talk to was you and..." The words just trailed off into the silence and stilled. The moment stretched on.

"I should probably go," said Zavier. He stood up to leave.

"You don't have to go," I said, reaching for his hand. He smiled and looked down at the top of Meiri's head. "I have patrol in less than an hour. Walk me out?"

I closed the door behind us and left Meiri in the room. Zavier already had his coat on with his bag slung on his shoulder.

"Didn't you say you had to talk to her? Here she is and she just made a huge admission saying she wanted to see you. Meet her halfway at least," he said. He dropped his bag and pulled me in for a quick passionate kiss. "I'll look into The Cat thing. See you later?"

I nodded with a ridiculous smile and watched him leave. Before I opened the door, I heard Meiri quietly sobbing.

"So, The Cat, huh?" I asked, hoping to lighten the mood. She just kept on crying. "Did you sneak out of the house just to see me? Please don't tell me you jumped from your window again," I said with a chuckle. The memory of Lady Meiri Verdant jumping out of her second-story window onto a pile of trash wasn't one I'd soon forget.

"I didn't jump. Mother barely acknowledges my presence since the ball. That's not what caused this," she said, looking at her arm. I held it and felt my magic rising to the surface of my fingertips. I dropped her arm, not knowing what my Powers would do.

"After I saw...what I saw, I ran out of the woods, but somehow *it* still caught up with me and did this before I escaped. I didn't stop running until I got to your door," she said, looking at a spot beyond the cozy confines of the herbals room.

It took her a moment to refocus her gaze on me. "I came to say I'm sorry. I've never had a real friend who was willing to speak as frankly as you do. I didn't mean to say... I mean, I didn't mean what I said."

"Yes you did, but it wasn't untrue. I have no right to scold you or Jacque for your relationship. I know it's more complicated than just wanting to be together," I said, holding her hand. "How's that feel?"

She gingerly touched her bandages and winced.

"Fine," she said, and gave a tentative smile. "Oh, I'm sure it will feel fine. Are *we* fine?" she asked. I nodded and we hugged awkwardly because of her arm. I knew things would be okay—even if a tad strained for a while. I judged it best not to broach Áliz's request just yet.

"So, what are we going to do with your cat?" I asked. She pulled out of the hug and her look of panic returned.

"I didn't tell you all of it because I didn't want to say it in front of Zavier. Someone else was there," she said in a whisper.

"Someone? Do you know who it was?"

"I don't know, but whoever it was wore a heavy hooded cape, like the kind Viktor wears. I don't trust him Inez," she said. It took me a moment to realize she was still referring to Viktor as "him." I was the only one who knew he was really a she who disguised herself as a man.

"This is an old argument. I know how you and Toman feel about Viktor," I said with a heavy sigh. Nobody trusted Viktor and I wasn't an exception. In addition to the fact that she hid her gender from everyone for reasons unknown, she was also the only person in Canto allowed to have known magic. No one knew why Mythos had been lenient with her and hadn't taken her magic or left her exiled on one of the Outer Isles without her memory. She did live in a prison of sorts, the Mist House, which was the only place she could use her magic. It was a unique arrangement and both Meiri and Toman thought it added to her untrustworthiness.

Anyone who could convince Mythos, the ones who stripped us of all our inherent magic, to keep their magic, was formidable. Meiri and Toman's feelings were also in line with Rowley, Mamá and if I were honest, with mine.

"As someone who just admitted that friendship means getting messy and angry, let me just say I'll never trust Viktor Lake. I know he has magic, and he wants yours," she said, grabbing my wrists.

"Having magic doesn't make a person evil, and Viktor already knows my secret. He knew before I went to see him, so isn't it better to keep him close instead of wondering? Lita trusted Viktor," I said defensively.

"I hope he's worthy of it. So now what?"

"There are only two places where records go as far back as the founding of Canto, the library and KM records. Maybe searching the KM records will get us more information about The Cat or whatever it was you found in the woods," I said.

Smugglers had stories about all sorts of creatures that had inherited our magic and lived in remote areas of the forest. Sadly their knowledge had become harder to access since the day I was barred from the hidden market.

"Okay, that means going to KM headquarters for the files," Meiri said. And then I remembered that the oldest KM files were kept at the library.

"No, they're not there. Zavier was likely right when he said those records are in the archives. That means a trip to the library. Betlindis Hart requested access to them awhile ago for a 'personal project' I think," I said with trepidation. "She's researching to find out more about sudden disappearances and memory loss. It's related to her father, Rex."

"You mean when you disappeared him and erased her memory?" asked Meiri.

"Yes," I replied, the knot in my throat making it hard to swallow.

MEIRI LEFT WITH THE promise she'd return the next morning to search the archives with me. The shock of her arrival and news of her encounter with The Cat—or whatever had caused the gash—was enough excitement for one day.

Quiet moments were rare for me. When I had them, other than spending time with Zavier, I hungrily read the book left by my grandparents. There were stories passed down orally until Lita and Beval committed them to the page as well as words of Power. The words had been passed down through the generations from even before we raised the Enchanted Isles from the ocean.

Mostly I worked on memorizing the words of Power. My ability to access words in my head that I didn't understand scared me. I couldn't risk using the wrong word and causing another inadvertent death. So many of them sounded alike. *Gwei*, to live and *gwhen*, to kill or strike. *Ag*, to move, draw or drive and *aug*, to increase. Others were close in definition, but with different shades like *mori* and *akwa*, meaning body of water and water, respectively. There were dozens more that could stand on their own or combine with others to create a new spell. At times I marveled that so few words could accomplish so much, and other times I wished there were even fewer to mangle.

I opened the book to the list of words and let my fingers graze the raised ink on the parchment. There was a rare annotation next to one of the entries: *Wrad: branch, root. Used primarily with bheu to grow plants and trees but may also have equally useful application to send magic in many directions at once. (Cus. Mar. & Abs.)*

The handwriting was unfamiliar to me, but certain letters reminded me of Lita's hand. Many parts of the annotation puzzled me. While most words had no annotations, the ones that did, indicated the application that may be used. This one had that, but also indicated that it had been used. *By Lita? By Beval?*

Lita's primary resource had always been herb lore. *Had she used this to help her plants along? And if so, how had she done it?* She had no active magic that I knew of. Words of Power required a magical source.

I pushed my questions aside because the entry had inadvertently given me a way to fulfill Áliz's latest request, without involving Meiri.

"WHAT IS IT?" ASKED Áliz, her greedy hands grabbing for the small urn I held before she even knew its purpose. I'd trudged out to her new home after sundown. There was a teapot waiting with two cups as if she had been expecting me. I took another look around Jacque's old house and was impressed by the homey touches. When Jacque had lived here it had been little better than a flop house. The walls were covered with tapestries and the fireplace was outlined with blue and white ceramic tiles, creating a checkboard effect. It was like the market above ground.

"A lagri-copa," I replied, holding it just out of reach. She furrowed her brow at my explanation.

"A lagri—you mean a tear cup? Those are a myth," she scoffed.

"How's the saying go? 'Myth is as real as the place up the coast just missing the O.' We deal in the mythical, remember?" I reminded her.

"You're telling me that sad bud vase can capture a person's sorrow and what? Hand it off to an unsuspecting drinker? I've never understood the purpose of such a thing. A waste of magic and not what I asked for," she said. While she'd asked for the firefly chandelier from Green Gardens, the thought of having to steal from Meiri so soon after making up seemed inappropriate. I hoped a more valuable magical object would assuage her greed.

"Maybe so, but I know at least five clients who have commissioned to have one found. Imagine the bidding war?" I said. Áliz's eyes lit up in anticipation of the potential profits.

"True. No doubt some scorned lovers looking for revenge or some such." She looked at the cup in my hand with an appraising eye. It was translucent and cobalt blue with an uneven rim and an indent at the side of its base.

"Shame it doesn't look better," she said and poured two cups of steaming tea that smelled of pine needles and fruit.

"It's not about the packaging—just the strength of the magic," I said, keeping the defensiveness from my voice. I'd made it myself as an exercise to practice my magic. I knew from Lita and Beval's stories that one existed in the palace. And their annotation for *wrad* allowed me to create a spell that existed away from me. I'd imbued it with magic I didn't have to activate. I was proud of the endeavor, but also wary. I knew my spell had worked, but it was a delicate thing.

Use of the lagri-copa could lead to loss of empathy if the user abused it. I consoled myself with the notion that whoever used it made their own decisions. Almost.

"Consider this a down payment on your debt to me," said Áliz, who extended her hand. I reluctantly handed it to her. "Lovely. Want to share how you got one? Will the queen miss it?"

"Áliz, you know better than to ask. I'm just good at what I do," I replied.

Chapter 5

The library had a new name. A new plaque adorned the outer wall of the library along with a small likeness of the plaque's subject, Delaware Humphrey. Flora Humphrey had shaken the dust off her grieving and gone on a donation and endowment spree. Her first dedication had been to the library, now the Delaware P. Humphrey Library. It was an interesting choice as was Flora publicly embracing my mother at the unveiling. Naturalists, who frowned on magic and the magical returners weren't known for their displays of public agreement and it hadn't gone unnoticed by Queen Hortensia.

No matter what it was called, the library was no longer a haven for me. What used to be a place of comfort and family was now a minefield of thwarted dreams and lost souls. Evelien had hoped Zavier would choose her sister instead of me and Betlindis had an even bigger grievance against me.

As I entered the nondescript square building, I felt a knot forming in my stomach. Even with Meiri's presence, I felt alone in this feeling of unease. I scanned the open space for faces I hoped to avoid and breathed a little easier for not seeing either of Mamá's assistants.

I'd forgotten about the aisles.

"Well, Your Grace, can I help you find anything?" asked an approaching Evelien. Her half-bobbed curtsey ended in a thinly veiled sneer. Our chilly relationship was practically frigid after Zavier chose me over her sister, Angelien, at the Egalitarian Ball.

"As a matter of fact you can, Lydia. Where can we find Betlindis Hart?" asked Meiri. I laughed at Meiri's obvious use of the wrong name for my nemesis.

Evelien's jaw tightened. Meiri managed to look down on Evelien despite being shorter than her. I would have to learn that skill if I ever wanted to deal with life at the palace. For now, I managed to smile at Evelien's obvious discomfort.

"My name is Evelien...Your Grace. She's in the archives, behind the stacks," she replied. "If you need anything else..."

"I'm sure Betlindis and Inez are more than capable. Thank you, Lydia," Meiri said and walked away. I followed with a choked laugh when I overheard Evelien grumble her name again.

"I need to bring you here more often." I stole a glance back at Evelien. She looked ready to spit nails.

"Serves her right for her bad manners. Did you know she's telling everyone that he chose you because you're pregnant and can't imagine abandoning his unborn heir? Like he would ever have chosen her low-bred cow- of-a-sister," she whispered with vehemence.

"I don't exactly have a title either, Meiri," I reminded her. She stopped cold at that and faced me.

"Just because you won't inherit your title, doesn't bring you down to a level with her. You would never stoop to a slanderous whisper campaign. Besides, it takes more than royal affiliation to bestow good breeding. You're more than Zavier's equal and don't get me started on Aunt Hortensia," she said forcefully.

We found Betlindis sitting at a long table with stacks of files next to her and in front of her. She was taking feverish notes, referencing one file and then another. Her concentration was such that she didn't hear our arrival or react when Meiri cleared her throat for the fourth time.

I saw nothing of the woman who'd bewitched an entire party of men while wearing her enchanted dress. What was more curious was everyone's complete loss of memory about it. Even Mamá, Meiri and Toman had forgotten until I told them. Something in the spell of the dress had caused everyone to forget, as though they'd collectively overindulged and had no recollection of it. That included Betlindis. She had a genuine grievance against me, and she didn't even know it. I'd fought Rex, her father and only family. I'd used magic and I banished him to a cowry shell. The knot that had eased with Meiri's defense of me suddenly tightened back into place.

"Betlindis? Do you have a minute?" I asked sheepishly. Meiri noticed my demeanor and threw me a quizzical look, which I ignored. Betlindis shook her head as if she could erase the imaginary cobwebs that surrounded her area. When she looked up, her expression was unreadable, but I thought I saw unguarded hostility that was quickly replaced by nonchalance. I must have been wrong because she jumped up from her seat and grabbed my hand with a smile.

Before the disappearance of her father, Rex, Betlindis blended into the background like uninteresting wallpaper. With the loss of Rex's domineering influence, she looked more alive. Her color palate, which had been beige on beige was still monochromatic, but now tended to the rich browns and deep yellows. That reminded me of the eyes of fever patients Lita tended—bright, but unhealthy.

"Inez, hello. How are you? I've been thinking about you lately...especially after the Ball. I have some more questions for you," she said earnestly. The knot in my stomach shot up to my throat and started to choke me. A coughing fit saved me from any response.

I'd yet to tell her that her father wasn't missing. Fighting for control of the cowry shells that had awakened my magic, he'd been forced into one of the shells. I didn't dare try to remove him because I didn't know how. Three of the four shells still had all their magic intact and I had no reason to open any of them, other than to gain more Power.

Seeing Betlindis so obsessed with Rex's disappearance was the only thing that made me consider risking the absorption of so much magic.

"Inez, sit down and have some water. It's so dry and dusty back here, it's no wonder," Meiri said. She spotted a small desk with a pitcher of water and poured me a glass. I was too startled to argue. I drank in gulps, grateful to avoid talking and to ease my discomfort.

"Ms. Hart...Betlindis, we know that you have taken an interest in some KM files and we were wondering if we could borrow any related to...well, the...The Cat legend," Meiri said in a whisper.

Meiri couldn't help herself and her eyes darted to the corners of the room. Betlindis quickly transformed into a librarian again, efficient and curious. The frenzied look left her eyes, replaced by bemused wonder. A professional challenge was enough to reorient her attention.

"The Cat and the Fiddle? An interesting subject. In the library it's stacked in both the historical section as well as the myth and legends department, besides having a section in the KM archives. There's so much speculation as to whether it really happened or if it's an old wives' tale. As for the KM files, I seem to recall seeing something about it in the archives I've been researching," she said, sifting through the clutter.

Betlindis' movements were direct and purposeful, more so than in the past. The loss of her father had made her more self-assured. I wondered if she realized that. That positive result of what I'd done didn't take away the guilt, but it did ease the feeling enough for me to find my voice.

"How long ago was that?" I asked. I could feel Meiri's stare at my change in demeanor.

"Yes, a very interesting case. I was just reading it for...personal reasons. I assume this is for your new position with the KM? The King's Men lent me the key to read through the archives. Sorry, but I'm not quite done with them," she said. In my mind, I planned a late-night break into the library whereby I'd use my Pandora key to open the archives, but I wasn't sure if she had taken any files home.

"Betlindis, Inez is Zavier's intended, who is a King's Man. I don't think it should be a problem to let us borrow one case out of all these," Meiri said without hesitation. Name dropping with Betlindis was not the right approach. Funny enough we would have had better luck with Evelien for that tactic. Betlindis didn't look convinced, but Meiri plunged ahead.

"Betlindis, I can't imagine you're looking at all the files at the same time," said Meiri.

"Well, that would be true, but research like this often requires cross-referencing," said Betlindis. Despite it being an inconvenience for me, I was impressed with the way Betlindis wasn't backing down from Meiri. And yet I knew the only way to give Meiri peace of mind was to know more about The Cat.

"How about a compromise?," I offered. "Betlindis is the best researcher in the library besides Mamá. Maybe she can take notes regarding anything related to The Cat and send it to us and that way she can keep the files in order." I looked from Betlindis to Meiri. They looked reticent and frustrated, respectively.

"We saw something that we can't explain and we want to make sure it's not something harmful. It's the not knowing that really bothers us. You understand, right?" I asked, hating myself for drawing any parallels to her situation and mine. I was both thrilled and tormented when I saw it was working.

"No one likes having unanswered questions," she said in a quiet whisper. "I can do that. When do you need it?" asked Betlindis.

"Today," said Meiri at the same time I said, "As soon as possible." Meiri gave me a withering look and I shrugged. It was Betlindis' turn to look between the two of us.

"I can send notes over tomorrow morning. I should warn you there are some files even I can't access. They only exist at KM HQ," said Betlindis. Being the official liaison between the KM and the royal house gave me an advantage, but any files would be under the distrustful eyes of Podkin. I smiled my agreement and pulled Meiri along and out of the library.

Chapter 6

The walk back home was silent. I stayed a few steps ahead of Meiri to avoid answering any uncomfortable questions. We returned to my sitting room empty-handed.

"I don't know why you feel so bad about Betlindis," she said softly.

"Let's see...maybe because I killed her father?"

"You didn't kill him, Inez," she replied.

"No, I just imprisoned him in a shell. Let's see was Mamá has at the house about your Cat?" I said, not wanting to continue that discussion.

We spent the next few hours reading through anything in the libraries at home and taking notes. All we found was a book called Canto Confidential, which was clearly written with sensationalism in mind. The stories revolved around random incidents in the early 1800s. It quoted small blurbs from the *King's Men Blotter* normally hung in the Cup & Board and then went on to state wild theories. Only two stories mentioned The Cat.

"Listen to this," I said.

"A sighting of an orange and yellow cat wearing boots and plucking a small fiddle was reported. In a related incident Haro reported seeing a cow jumping over the moon and stated another witness was present for that event. Further investigation revealed the other witness was a dog."

"How old is Mrs. Haro?" asked Meiri.

"*Shhh*! There's more." There was a footnote at the bottom of the page directing the reader to a story called "Arco Twin Agony."

"J. and J. Arco were questioned due to a recent rash of tricks found to be caused by the pair. Deeper investigations are expected as well as any connection to their household cat." There was a squiggle in the margins that had been crossed out, but I could tell it had been a caricature of a woman who looked unhinged. *Why did Mamá have a book like this?*

"So, you see? The Cat is just a trick that was pulled by two kids. You probably just thought you saw it," I said. Meiri just rolled her eyes at me and kept reading the sections where the author made the case for something nefarious. "...Or maybe they had latent Powers." There were a small number of Canti who had retained a fraction of their family magic. Those that Rowley could get to were protected by Birthright, the organization he ran that secretly hid or housed the small percentage of Canti that manifested small amounts of inherent magic. The others were rounded up and sent to Mythos never to be heard from again.

"Here's something to change your mind," she said. "Update: J. and J. Arco were found dead, the apparent victims of a fall down Green Hill. Efforts to remove them from the site proved fruitless. The bodies were somehow stuck in place."

"What? No mention of the dish running away with the spoon?" I asked.

"That was probably added later to make it into a convincing rhyme. How do bodies become stuck?"

"Maybe it was cold and they were frozen together," I said.

"It says stuck, not frozen. Well, I guess we'll have to wait for Betlindis' notes and maybe talk to Old Haro," said Meiri.

"Sure," I said with little hesitation. "She should have lots of information. If my mother wasn't chief archivist, Mrs. Haro would be a great choice. She's more of a historian than my mother is," I said.

"Who's more of a historian?" asked Mamá. She walked into the sitting room with her arms full of papers. They were sticking out at weird angles, and I jumped up to help her put them down. Her eyes swept over the tawdry book clutched in Meiri's hands and gave an indulgent smile.

My relationship with Mamá had practically gone back to normal since the Egalitarian Ball. I no longer felt the need to hide my magic from her, which eased our conversations.

"Thank you. What's all this?" she asked, pointing to the stack of books left out of order on the floor. I gave her an apologetic shrug.

"We're not sure yet. Meiri swears she saw The Cat—"

"I did see hi—"

"So, we're waiting for Betlindis to send us notes about it. In the meantime, we were searching through the home library for anything of value," I said, ignoring Meiri's protest.

"A curious line of research. I think I can find some books about it upstairs, if you girls would like to look," she said. scanning the titles of books we'd thumbed through. Her interest was unusual.

"It'll be nice to do something with you that's not... That's research related," Mamá said. I knew she was thinking about our last "tutoring" session in magic at the bay. My near-case of hypothermia was not a good memory for me either.

"I'll go upstairs and pull down some books." Mamá retrieved her stack of papers and left.

"That's nice. Your mom wants to help," Meiri said, wistfully.

"Speaking of moms; shouldn't yours be demanding the KM find you?" I asked, looking at the coming dark.

"She probably hasn't noticed my absence yet. It could be days," she said with false mockery. I was about to reassure her about her mother's concern, but I couldn't be sure that would be true. Lady Eugenia wasn't the warm and fuzzy type.

Just then there was a knock at the door. I muttered something about "speak of the devil" and left to answer it, but I didn't know for sure Arch would be there, so to speak.

Yet, Meiri's brother, Arch, stood in the doorway wearing his KM uniform, which he managed to keep spotlessly clean. There had been a time when I considered Arch a viable option as someone to date—he was handsome and flattering—but lately our meetings were strained.

"Hello Inez. Is my sister here?" he asked in clipped tones.

"Yes I am. What are you doing here?" asked Meiri.

"Well, someone's been away too long. Mother sent a messenger to KMHQ to find me so I could find you. I sent him back with a message that you were already with me, but I'm going home now so you should come with me to preserve the lie. Did you sneak out all by yourself, baby sister? I'm almost proud of you," he said with a grin.

"Why did you cover for me?" asked Meiri. She squinted at him and crossed her arms.

"I don't know, actually. I guess I felt sorry for you. Don't worry, it'll pass. Inez, you look wonderful. Being engaged to a prince obviously agrees with you," he said though something in his tone rankled.

It still irritated me that Zavier's and my relationship needed official permission. We were grown adults and yet on the word of Hortensia or some faceless representative from Mythos, our freedom to be together as a couple would all end. Too much of my life now was dependent on the sufferance and discretion of others. With that thought, my mask of tranquil indifference slipped, giving Arch an opportunity to pounce.

"Oh, do I detect discontent?" he asked. His smile grew wider.

"I'm not engaged," I replied, feeling slightly rebellious. Arch had that effect on me.

"I'm glad to hear it. Whenever you get sick of being with the good boy, let me know," he said with a smirk.

"Archibald don't embarrass yourself," sneered Meiri.

"Who knows what could have happened if Meiri hadn't interrupted our date. Rain check?" he asked, ignoring Meiri. He brought my hand up to his lips and kissed it.

I knew exactly what would have happened on that date. Nothing. Despite his good looks and charm, I felt nothing when we'd kissed. Arch was adept at making a woman feel special, until another woman walked by.

"Inez, I'll take this book and stop by the library tomorrow morning if you visit Old Haro," said Meiri, collecting her things. Our combined notes were rather thin, so I wondered how much more we could possibly learn. I was happy that I wouldn't have to think about going to library and running into Betlindis any time soon.

"How are you going to do that? I covered for you today, but my love only goes so far," said Arch.

"Oh, you'll cover for me or I'll tell Mother about finding you and Delicia in Father's bed," she said.

"You wouldn't." Arch had the sense to at least look shamefaced about Meiri's revelation.

"I still have her corset. Now let's get going in case we run into...anyone," she said. Her eyes betrayed a little of the fear they held when she first showed up after her cat sighting. Arch grumbled but hurried after her out the door.

"Who was that? Did Meiri just leave?" asked Mamá.

"It was Arch taking her home," I replied.

"That doesn't sound like Arch," she said, balancing a stack of books.

"I'll explain later. Are all those books about The Cat and The Fiddle?"

"Yes as well as information about the whole Arco family. It's a fascinating piece of Canto history," she said with a twinkle. Mamá really enjoyed her work.

"Well, this should be enough to get started. Thanks," I said and hugged her for trying to help in any way she could.

"I know you don't like going down to the library. I want to help, if I can." Her words hitched in her throat as she squeezed my shoulder to reassure me.

"You did. You do. Are you okay?"

"Well, I know we haven't spoken about it for a little bit, but I wanted to make sure I had all the facts before I told you any more," she started.

"What are you talking about?" I asked with concern.

"I promised to tell you more about your father," she said.

"I remember, but then you stopped and said you needed more time," I said.

"I wanted to make sure I could give you more than just a story. I wanted you to meet him so we could tell you the story together," she said with shining eyes.

"Okay. You want to introduce me to my father?" I asked.

"I did. But that might be difficult because I just learned he's dead," she said.

Chapter 7

I'd only seen my mother cry twice. The first time was when Beval died. The second was when the KM came to our door and told us Lita had been killed in a mirror transport accident. This was only the third time in almost three decades.

"Are you sure?" I asked, not knowing what else to say. Her only response was to nod and continue crying silently.

There's something wrong with parents crying. Years of going to them with bruises, scrapes and heartaches makes it uncomfortable when the tables are turned. A parent comforting a child works because we have complete faith in our parents when they tell us it will be okay.

Now, with my mother crying more than I'd ever seen her cry I couldn't say those words to her. I didn't know if it would be okay. A knot formed in my throat seeing my mother in pain and for a person I'd never know and was still connected to. How could I console her about a man and a relationship I knew nothing about? I swallowed, blinking back tears for what we both lost and fell back on what was comfortable for me. Curiosity.

"What was he like?" I asked. Mamá had given me basic information when Viktor insisted I learn more about my father. I still didn't know why she wanted me to have the information, and she hadn't asked me to reveal any. I knew his name was Rahd, a Mythosian with martial magic who had inherited a diplomatic position in the government. Other details were scarce because Mamá wanted me to form my own opinions about him. That wasn't possible now.

"Stubborn. Arrogant. Romantic. Where do I start?" she said with a chuckle, her tears subsiding.

"The beginning always works," I replied.

She started her story—halting at first, but soon she spoke with the fluidity of a natural storyteller at her craft. Like bedtime when I was a child, I saw the pictures her words painted. A girl with wild, raven hair and a boy with formal, yet colorful attire ran hand in hand through the streets, in the woods, everywhere. They reminded me of Toman and myself. I watched them grow and change. The boy was sweet, guileless and a little sad. The girl was what I wanted to be, fearless and kind as she brought him into her adventures.

One day the way he looked at her changed and he wanted more, but she was unsure for once. Then it abruptly ended with a letter and an apology. Her best friend was gone. It was the biggest blow of her life and for weeks she wore her heart on her sleeve until an opportunity presented itself.

"What do you mean?" I asked when the story stopped.

"A climbing expedition up Fae Range," she said, startled out of her revelry.

"Is that the picture?" I asked, pointing to a picture. It was my favorite of my mother. Her smile was unrestrained, and her hair was loose, which was how she never wore it.

She stood and crossed to it.

"A lifetime ago. Yes, that was the day before the ascent and two days before the accident," she said with a sad smile. A pale comparison to the one she held in her hands.

"Accident? What accident?"

"Oh, so many mistakes. So much... Well, the short answer is I fell off the mountain."

"What?"

"*Nena* please," she said, putting down the picture. With a deep breath, she loosened her bun and parted her hair. A thin, faded line ran all the way down her hair line. "This scar— It's from the fall and that's how I met your father."

"Explain."

"I was climbing a lot faster than everyone else. Delaware and I had been climbing rocks for ages, but rocks aren't the same as a mountain. I was careless and I fell. I don't remember anything except a flash of red and then darkness." She absentmindedly ran her finger over the faded line on her head.

"And?"

"And I woke up in a place that was...different. It had a roof and a floor, but no walls. Just columns holding it all together. There was a fire pit next to my bed and I was covered in quilts and furs, but I was still cold. A man stood there when I opened my eyes and he looked...ancient yet intimidating.

"There was also younger man next to him and the look he gave me was...well, let's just say I didn't expect to become friends.

"The older man explained that I had fallen, and he had found me and brought me to his home to heal me. He also said it would take some time before I could go home, but that I would be fine," she said.

"You fell off a mountain and he said you would be fine? That's it?"

"No, that wasn't it. He left, but the younger man stayed. He asked all sorts of rude questions, like did people in Canto hunt for food or live in trees?" she said with a laugh.

"Some of us. We are surrounded by trees," I replied.

"Yes, that's not what he meant, but it got me wondering where I was and he told me I was in Mythos," she said.

"But you were climbing Fae Range. How did you end up in Mythos?"

"His father and he were traveling between Mythos and Faerie. So, I asked him questions about Mythos and over the course of my recovery we learned as much as we could about each other. You have the same kind of curiosity as Rahd," she said wistfully and I realized it was the first time she'd said my father's name since the last time they'd spoken of him.

"After I got better, he walked me to the border, and even though I'd hoped, it was still a surprise when he kissed me. We both knew that being together would be challenging, but I was in love and didn't really care. For a whole year we wrote letters and had secret meetings, before your grandparents found out."

"A whole year? Lita must have been hysterical," I replied.

"She was, but Beval talked her down. And I knew I had to be careful. I started my library studies and on weekends I would go to see Rahd. It only felt like an hour or two. Those hours were like magic," she said with a smile I'd never seen. She looked twenty years younger and radiant as she thought of it.

"He was traveling back and forth with his father to Faerie, and we were making plans." Her smile dimmed and I knew the tone of the story was about to change.

"Could you do that?" I asked, but I already knew the answer.

"No, but I didn't know that at the time. Canti and Fae weren't really welcome in Mythos. He wouldn't move to Canto. We argued and made up, but we knew our time was over.

"Rahd had to take over for his father soon thereafter and in that position, his attachment to me wouldn't be looked on with favor. After my fall, the range had been closed to travelers. We said goodbye right before he left for his posting," she said, looking off into the distance. I could imagine seeing the young lovers parting and knowing it was the last time.

"Did he know...about me?" I asked.

"I didn't know until well after our parting. By then I was angry at him for not having fought back for us, but it was a little of the anger I still felt about Delaware and me. I knew by then that his mother didn't want us to be friends and now Rahd's father didn't want us to be together. It was too much, especially after hearing about how Beval was so courageous when he left The People to be with your grandmother," she said. "You don't know how lucky you are that Zavier knows his own mind." I didn't mention that Zavier still didn't know about my magic and I had no idea what his mind would decide to do with that knowledge when he found out.

"Did you ever see him again?"

"No. Relations between Mythos and the rest of the Enchanted Isles were never very cordial, but they worsened for a time. It wasn't until Xander and Hortensia took the throne that affairs improved.

"But my fa... Rahd? Why didn't you tell him about me later?"

"Who knows? I always thought there would be time, but now it's too late," she said with a heavy sigh. She gave me a kiss on the forehead and patted my shoulder before getting up.

"You have his smile, you know. So, I never really lost him," she said and walked out of the office. I sat there in silence, considering all she had said, looking out the window. I'd never sought to find my father, but now even the possibility was closed to me. I stared out the window, looking toward the silhouette of Fae Range. The crescent was bright, and it was with almost no astonishment that I saw a cow crest the glowing orb of the moon.

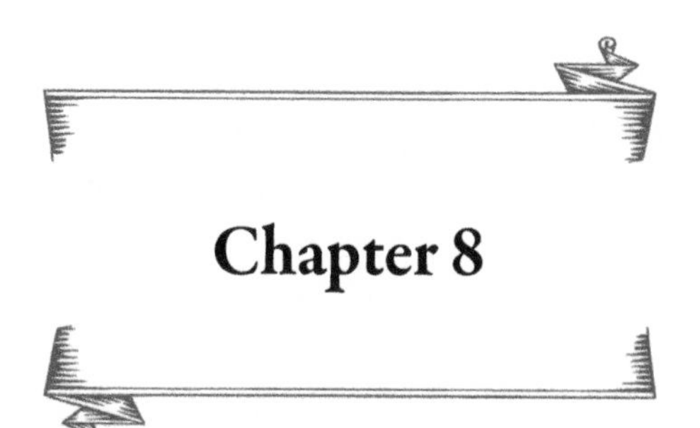

Chapter 8

The appearance of the cow jumping over the moon was almost a relief. It meant Meiri wasn't crazy and something *was* going on. That relief didn't last long. Could it have been someone other than The Cat trying to scare all of Canto? Or was there a simple magical reason. Canto and all the Enchanted Isles were born of magic: Didn't it stand to reason that random magical occurrences were always a possibility? And those considerations still didn't explain Meiri's sizeable injury.

All the questions and justifications were meaningless without investigation. I wanted to run out into the night and track the cow, but I knew I would have to wait until Mamá went to bed. She'd been through enough today learning about Rahd's death and revealing their love story. I didn't need to have her worrying about me as well. I grabbed all the materials from Meiri and my search as well as the books from Mamá and went to my room.

While I waited, I waded through the books Mamá had provided about The Cat. On further inspection they were really histories about all the Isles at the times The Cat had been reported. From what I gathered The Cat was blamed for many things even after the tidal wave scare. Some were mentions from obvious hidden marketers claiming The Cat bewitched them into carrying illegal magical goods. Others were from those who were suspected of having Powers explaining any magical workings. But those mentions seemed to be isolated incidents, unlike the original sighting which occurred over several days. One history noted with interest the uptick of patrols before the appearance of The Cat and the subsequent interference from Mythos. The evidence of the Cat being an agent of Mythos was thin at best, but I marked the page, nonetheless.

After reading until I thought my eyes would cross, I slowly opened my door and looked down the long hallway to Mamá's room. Years of practice with the market made it possible for me to walk across the landing knowing which spots would creak. I made it to her door without a sound and fished a recent purchase out of my pocket.

The glimpse glass was another ingenious item from Anselmo and for not the first time I wondered if he would have become a revered magical inventor if Mythos hadn't prohibited magic in Canto. Instead, he worked in the hidden market and at any time could be caught in a raid, betrayed by a fellow marketer, or worse.

I held the simple lens against Mamá's door and rubbed the side facing me counterclockwise. Slowly a murky picture formed revealing Mamá's darkened bedroom. She was asleep in bed and looked as though she wouldn't stir until morning. I quickly put the lens away after rubbing it clockwise and went back to my room to prepare for a cold night outdoors.

THE RUSH OF WINTRY air brought tears to my eyes. A waxing moon hung over the landscape like a beacon, lighting my path through the woods. My buttons were difficult to fasten with my numb, fumbling fingers. I hadn't counted on how cold the night would be. The damp smelled of snow coming and the lighting pink sky confirmed it.

I heard the fading strains of a fiddle up ahead, but there was no sign of a cow. The frigid air robbed me of my momentum—each inhale tickled my throat. I tried to concentrate on my lessons at the bay and willed myself to get warmer. The tingling in my fingers and toes was more mundane than magical.

I should have brought some gloves.

Concentrating wasn't helping and I could almost hear Rowley chiding me, saying I couldn't only use my magic when I thought I would die. At the moment, it felt like I was dying, but my magic clearly thought differently.

The music was growing fainter, but I knew it hadn't moved. It was more like the piece that was being played was coming to its conclusion.

Ahead of me the clearing revealed a fence. Suddenly I knew where I was headed.

After so many years of being abandoned, the old trail to Fae Range looked desolate and forbidding. Someone had written their own take on the posted No Trespassing sign adding Enter if you Dare for dramatic effect. The silence that pervaded was more chilling than any sign or cold winter's night could achieve.

Looking over the fence to the path I saw in my mind's eye the echo of a girl with windswept hair and a carefree smile egging her classmates on and running ahead. I wondered whether that girl would have run so far and so fast if she knew what was to come. *Would she accept the inevitable heartache in her future along with the love that preceded it? Or would she stay close to her group and make careful decisions to avoid the hurt? I suppose if she had, I wouldn't be here. Who would have been charged with protecting the shells or was I just as inevitable as my mother's broken heart?*

These questions, I couldn't answer, but I was starting to believe in Meiri's Cat. I followed the fence away from the mountain path, hoping to find hoof prints or even the whole cow and prove Meiri right. The music was long over, but maybe the cow and The Cat were together.

The silence of the clearing was starting to put me on edge. Footsteps startled me and I whirled around quickly, and a flash of magic left my hands, lighting a branch of a nearby tree on fire. Out of the corner of my eye I saw a deer scamper away. I exhaled a breath I hadn't realized I'd been holding. I wasn't as cold anymore but each time I used martial magic it left me a little more drained.

Does magic leave everyone drained? Rowley had a theory that my magic was unbalanced because I'd yet to absorb the Power from the other three shells. I realized with some shock that the one person who might have the answers was now dead—Rahd.

I'd never given much thought to my father, but knowing he was a marital mage brought up all sorts of questions. Would he have turned me in to the authorities if he knew I had magic or would he have insisted on training me? Could we all have lived in Mythos together? Deep down I already knew the answer to that one. Besides, I wouldn't have traded knowing Toman, or Mrs. Haro, or Zavier or even Meiri for all the magical know-how in the world.

I kept thinking of all the things I could have done in Mythos—out of hiding—but that only paralleled my complicated life in Canto. Could never replace it. All the lies and intrigue were exhausting, but at least they were of my own choosing. Rahd had to leave my mother because of his career, but I wouldn't have to make that choice.

Or would I?

That question brought me up short as I reached the end of the fence. There was no cow and without snow there wouldn't be any hoof prints to track. I was ready to turn around when I heard more rustling from the wooded side of my path. This time my magic only dimly responded with a flash of cold in my center and then it was gone. I didn't have time to puzzle out what that meant.

Crouching down low, I waited to see who...or what would emerge. My nerves were more settled and my fingers barely tingled.

I pressed them to the ground to keep my balance and heard whispering ten feet in front of me. It should have been impossible to hear, and yet I did.

"You're becoming careless. Too many people could have seen that ridiculous stunt this evening," said Hortensia. I recognized her voice immediately. Even low-pitched and urgent, it sounded haughty. Her face was hidden in the shadows of the Fae Range and her companion had their back to me. She had forgone her usual court dress and looked more like someone who worked at the hidden market.

"Our envoy has been careless, not me. You requested this type of help and were warned it was unpredictable." The voice was vaguely familiar, but I couldn't supply a name or even a face. Hortensia responded to his—because now I knew it was a man—by putting her hands on her hips. Even without being able to see her face clearly I knew she was fixing him with the same stare she used on me whenever Zavier took my side. "And now it cannot be undone," he said.

"I would believe you if you hadn't been the one to cause all this," said Hortensia. She was no longer whispering furtively. Most people would have flinched from her tone, but her companion made no sign that he was at all discomfited by her statement.

"No madam, you brought this about with your ineptitude," he said, and I saw Hortensia wince. She wasn't accustomed to being contradicted. "This should have been handled years ago and instead you held on to some absurd hope that it wouldn't be necessary. Do not contact me again," he said, turning from her, and then vanishing into thin air.

For her part, Hortensia didn't look surprised by her companion's sudden departure. She signaled to someone I couldn't see, and I heard an approaching horse. Hortensia rode off in the direction of the palace.

Although I'd only seen his face for a moment, I finally recognized the man to whom Hortensia was speaking—the representative at the ball, the man from Mythos.

Chapter 9

The world grew silent as I approached the path. There was no sign of a fence or any warnings as a group of hikers checked their backpacks and re-laced boots. One girl stood slightly apart from the others. Soon the group began their trek and I followed as the girl took the lead. The group started humming a tune. It was familiar and although I didn't know the words, I hummed along until I heard it echoed on a fiddle...

My emergence from sleep was challenging. I opened one eye, stretched and took my bearings. It had been a while since I had a real dream. After the series of bad sleeps I'd had, I was diligent with my Dreamless Sleep tea. There were times I wondered if I would ever dream again, but I still kept taking it. My eavesdropping on Hortensia and the Mythosian representative had brought me more questions than answers. I'd taken the opportunity to read over the notes Meiri and I had taken about the previous sightings of The Cat and must have dozed off.

I wondered how many times The Cat had appeared without being reported. Could he have been on Mamá's hike all those years ago? The idea of a malevolent cat, spreading doom, always seemed silly to me in a world that had real dangers like the King's Men, Mythos, or the Jabberwocky but after all I'd seen I couldn't discount that possibility any longer.

Was the stunt Hortensia referred to, the cow jumping over the moon? And if so, did that mean she was responsible for The Cat returning? As far as I knew Hortensia didn't have any magical Powers, so she would have had to ask Mythos to help. But to what end? And who was this envoy the Mythosian mentioned? Could it be Viktor? She was essentially their magical prisoner considering she only had access to her Powers in the Mist House they constructed and controlled; was she also their agent? Or could it be Áliz? I didn't like the coincidence of her choosing to come above ground just before The Cat made an appearance. Jacque and I had stolen those rummage stones for her and although I didn't know what their Power was, I suspected they could trap a magical being. I'd worried it was me she wanted to catch, but was all this really for The Cat?

I considered going back to sleep and pretending none of this was my problem. If Hortensia had somehow gotten Mythos to summon The Cat, she could likely get them to return him from where he came.

Except the representative already refused.

His exact words came back to me in a rush, "You requested this help and were told it was unpredictable and now it cannot be undone."

Was that true? Did even Mythos have no way to contain The Cat? Or did they want The Cat running loose in Canto? The first time he'd surfaced, Mythos had been forced to intervene more directly in Canti affairs.

It was early. Too early to contemplate the schemes of realms. I patted my pillow longingly and sighed heavily. The sun had the dull shine it reserved for dawn or preceding serious storms. Going back to bed was pointless so I made my way downstairs.

I was glad to find the kitchen empty. With the demands of work and her internal clock, Mamá was normally up for hours before I found my way to the kitchen. Today I'd beaten her to it and once there, remembered the last time I had:

While looking around for the teapot and the pans, I'd seen a small smudge on the wall. It was a scorch mark. The spot felt brittle and soft. Closing my eyes, I almost smelled the wood burning. I've always liked the aroma of a wood fire—an odd affinity for someone who lives surrounded by trees—but on that day my fears were realized—losing control of my magic—in the normally comforting scent of kindling.

I was in a rush that day and wanted to eat and go, but I couldn't find the pots. Hindsight being what it is, I can now say my experiment wasn't something I should have tried when I was already frustrated. I'd been studying the words of Power that morning, meant to focus my raw magic. The unbidden voice that came to my head when I tried to use my magic, muddled my thinking. What should have been *Hengwa* Akwa—calling boiling water from thin air—became *Gwapehwr*—a bonfire.

Flames had licked the walls, consuming anything in its path. It was lucky Rowley had come when he did and saved the day. He literally barked the fire out of existence. Then he barked me to shame.

I couldn't help feeling a little persecuted by his reprimands. It wasn't all my fault. Maybe if I had known about my magic sooner, I'd have been more controlled. Or maybe I had too much Power.

Back to the present, I started the new pan, purchased the day after the blaze, and poured myself a cup of strong tea. I needed a clear head to think about last night's events.

Why would a cow jump over the moon and what did that have to do with The Cat? I was skirting the most glaring question, but it pushed itself forward anyway. *Why did Hortensia want The Cat causing trouble in Canto?* It was with more than a little dread that I realized I was likely the reason. She wasn't being discreet with her opposition to me and Zavier. Was she so desperate to get rid of me that she would allow Mythos to control Canto even more? If they did Mythos or Hortensia could negotiate terms like an arranged marriage for Zavier. I wouldn't put that past Hortensia.

And what about Viktor? It wasn't so long ago I'd caught Viktor working with Rex and Yvette to try and get the shells away from me. Mamá and Rowley assumed Viktor was helping with my magic because we all had the same goal—the return of magic to all the Isles.

That was only partially true. I still hadn't told Mamá or Rowley about Viktor's demand for one of the shells. Or my agreeing to give her one in payment for help with my Powers. I reasoned that once my magic was under control I could combat anything Viktor planned.

And Áliz? The Jabberwocky craved money and influence. Who better to supply that than Mythos? With that, an even more troubling thought came into focus.

A possible alliance between Áliz and Viktor.

Áliz had years of experience working in the criminal underground and Viktor had Powers. The possibility that either of them was somehow involved with The Cat appearances was troubling.

I was stirred from my musings by a knock on the door. I put down my cup of tea and answered it. A royal messenger, discreet enough not to react to finding his future queen in her nightgown, handed me a note on Zavier's stationary.

"Done with overnight patrol—I have the day off... After a long nap and ice ball practice can I see you?"

I groaned before I could stop myself. The messenger kept his face professionally blank. Ice ball was now in season, which meant that the already limited time Zavier and I spent together would be cut in half by practices. Games were only played on the nights after it snowed and stuck, so planning them was erratic. I gave the messenger a verbal "yes," the only easy answer I'd have today.

MEIRI HAD YET TO COME by the house with information from Betlindis about The Cat. It was just as well because I needed to ask someone who might remember the first sighting, years ago. I happened to know someone who fit that description and whose family was mentioned in at least one book referencing The Cat.

The snow, which had been just a hint in the air last night had come and gone, leaving a blanket of white in its wake. I trudged through drifts and wondered idly if tonight would be the first ice ball game. Zavier would have to cancel our plans.

I watched a couple walking toward me hand and hand and I sighed. Would we ever get quiet moments like that? My musings were cut short when I overheard a piece of their conversation.

"...I'm sure you think you saw—" said the older woman. She looked at him indulgently, but he shook his head, emphatic.

"I'm telling you; it was a cow!" he yelled and then looked around. They both saw me and hurried past. Hortensia was right. Other people had seen the same as I had, a cow jumping over the moon.

It was clear that I was one of the first people to venture out toward The Cup & Board, Canto's own lost-and-found and gossip grapevine.

I picked up the pace in anticipation of warmth.

The Cup was oddly quiet without its usual complement of nosy readers by the boards, especially after hearing I wasn't the only one who saw the cow. The tinkling of a spoon tapping a teacup to alert Mrs. Haro of visitors, echoed in the empty space. Ever since the KM had raided the Cup & Board for illegal magical goods, business had been slow.

The punishments for contraband had become more stringent and even consorting with a suspected trader in illicit magic had been enough for the KM to pay a visit.

"Hello? Mrs. Haro...Rowley? Hello?" I shouted.

I was greeted by an echoing silence. It was the first time I'd found the place unattended.

Knowing there was a potential threat out there in the form of a violin-playing cat, I started to feel anxious. A cold feeling in the pit of my stomach rose to my throat. Something about the sensation made me pause. It was the same feeling I'd had last night when the deer startled me. I didn't know how, but my body was shielding me from the inside out. It gave the world a filmy quality like I was trapped inside a soapy bubble. Was this panic, or a coping mechanism?

I couldn't be sure. A quiet rustling, coming from the opposite end of the shop, intensified the feeling.

I wasn't sure if I could walk with this strange protective bubble. The bubble itself felt fragile and flimsy, but sticky in an insistent way.

Rustling continued, punctuated by little yelps and whimpers. With an effort, I lifted my foot deliberately and stepped through the film that surrounded me. I waited for a popping sound or something, but the film clung on for a few more steps before dissolving away. It left me woozy. a little nauseous, but I pushed that down as I approached the sounds from the back room.

"What did I do with...? Oy! Rowley I don't know what happened to them. Maybe over... Sorry, did I step on your paw again? I'll go... Oh Inez, dear," crooned Chavah Deena Haro, proprietress of The Cup & Board. She swiped an errant strand of hair from her florid face and straightened up her wrinkled blouse. Her smile made her look at least ten years younger than her admitted seventy, but I thought she was closer to eighty.

"Thank goodness. I couldn't leave this place without someone to watch the door, but poor Rowley's bowl is empty. As bare as the top of Fae Range. I'll have to step out to get some food. Be a love and watch the counter while I'm gone. Rowley will keep you company," she said, pushing a hat down over her hair. Today the wisps were a deep red with streaks of white for the coming Yule celebrations.

Her small, round frame spun about the office collecting anything else she needed. Before I could object, she was wrapping her shawl around her shoulders and sliding into a down coat.

"Sure...um... Do you think we can talk when you get back?" I asked. I was more anxious about my recent manifestation of magic than running the Cup & Board.

"Did something happen? Is it your mother all right...or that nice man Toman? I heard *his* mother isn't doing well. Would soup help? Or maybe some of my pound cake?" She prattled on. I was surprised that Dottie's condition was becoming common knowledge. I needed to check in on Toman.

"No, nothing like that. And I'm not a KM anymore." Technically. I still had my liaison duties to finish, at Queen Hortensia's insistence. I had access to the KM but no authority.

"Meiri and I decided to look over a few cold cases and we came across The Cat and the Fiddle. We read one of your relatives saw it and I know you have a family history somewhere in here," I replied.

"Oh. Yes I did have a...relative who saw The Cat. When I get back I'll dig up the journals. Be back in two shakes," she said, collecting her bag. A few moments later I heard the teacup tinkling and I turned to see Rowley staring at me intently.

"Yes?" I asked.

"You reek of magic. Do I have another fire to put out?" he asked, sniffing the air with distaste. "I smell a protection spell with other magics mixed in. What have you been up to?"

"Nothing."

"Your magic is getting stronger." He growled.

"Good. It's what we wanted, right?" I said with growing unease.

"Not if you can't control it. Too much power and not enough control could destroy all of us," he said, and I couldn't help but roll my eyes. I stood silent however, as he paced. "I have a friend—"

"You have friends?" I quipped. I couldn't resist.

"...who lives in Faery. He could take you in and continue your training..."

"Wait! Leave Canto? That seems a bit extreme. The shells are here and so is Mamá and all my friends. I won't hurt anyone—you wouldn't let that happen," I said with more conviction than I felt. The startled deer last night could have easily been a person who saw me light that tree on fire. I was also aware that the tree could have easily been a person I blew a hole through.

Rowley ceased his stalking of the room and seemed to consider my words.

"I'll admit your sudden absence would raise questions, especially with Zavier. Well...we'll have to increase your training times. I'll talk to Viktor and see—"

I decided on the spot not to share my suspicions about Áliz and Viktor, especially if he had plans to send me away.

"Maybe it could just be you and me? I mean...Mamá can't get comfortable with all the chances I take, and Viktor and you don't really get along. I'll see Viktor myself—that way, you don't have to fight in front of me," I said reasonably.

"Faery may not be the best place for you now, anyway," he said, seeming to follow my train of thought. But the way he said it told me he was holding something back.

"Why not?" I asked, curious.

"Why did you use a protection spell?" he asked, ignoring my question.

"I didn't. At least I didn't mean to," I replied, slightly flustered. "I heard the rustling and yelping and Mrs. Haro is never away from the front... I don't know; it just—happened."

"*Hmm.* What about the other spells? Were you practicing on your own?" I couldn't tell if the prospect pleased him or worried him.

"Not exactly. I was startled while following a lead for a friend," I replied.

"What lead? Which friend?"

"Meiri. She thought she saw The Cat and I—"

"The Cat! Do you mean this is more than just looking at cold cases? Cat sightings are not infrequent and usually false," he said.

"I thought so too, but last night I saw the cow jump over the moon," I said. Rowley looked around the room abruptly, reminding me of Meiri and her new manic habit. He paced and sniffed the air and his growing agitation was feeding my own.

"You saw the cow? Is that why you came to talk to Mrs. Haro?" I'd thought he was going to be dismissive of the whole thing, hoped for it in fact.

"Yes," I said, my sense of unease growing.

"You're going to need more than a protection spell. If The Cat came back then I can't help you. May the Goddess protect us." Calling on the Goddess was not something I'd ever heard Rowley do, even at my most exasperating. I'd never known him to put his faith in anything but hard work. Whatever this was, it couldn't be good. My feelings were confirmed when Rowley's hackles rose.

Chapter 10

"There are only two things that really frighten me," Rowley began. He had led me to his hidden room behind the Cup & Board. In the past he'd used it as a retreat whenever one of the Birthright sanctuaries had been discovered. Birthright was one of the many secrets Rowley kept, a loose organization that protected Canti and who had managed to retained small bits of their inherent magic.

At least it had been until Yvette's treachery with Rex and had made it impossible to continue.

Too many of the members thought Yvette had a point and magic had to be returned to the Isles even if it meant using violence or overthrowing the royal house. Others agreed with Rowley and wanted to continue hiding until it was safe to reveal their magic.

Trust was lost and the climax to the fracturing of Birthright had been finding Yvette dead not far from one of the organization's havens. Each side blamed the other. The infighting became so belligerent that Rowley had been forced to end Birthright in Canto. Rowley was able to send a few of them to Faery and others to the ungoverned Outer Isles. I thought of all of this as Rowley began his story. His eyes had the same tired, haunted look they'd had when he told me about the end of Birthright.

"I fear your growing, undisciplined Powers and the Cat with his fiddle."

My feelings of compassion lessened with that comment.

Rowley then added: "I'm sure you've guessed I am considerably older than I appear."

"I figured at least a hundred but who can tell on a dog," I retorted a little stung by his lumping me in with something as dangerous as the Cat.

"Miss Garza, if you were to spend as much time and energy on your magic as you do your wit, my list of frightening things would lessen dramatically."

"I get it. I'm a huge disappointment—move on," I said with an edge. The tingling of my fingers was my warning.

"If you just applied all that anger and frustration—you should be *asking* to practice more, not... Take a deep breath Miss Garza before you destroy Mrs. Haro's shop," he said sniffing the air again. The tingling and tension in my fingers were seeping into my hands. His constant berating made it difficult not to want to light him on fire. But the thought of only having Viktor as a teacher squelched my anger. I also couldn't bear telling Mrs. Haro her companion was now barbecue. I flexed my hands and sat down on them, letting the power ebb away.

"Thank you. As I was saying, I came across The Cat at another low point in my life. Please, no questions yet. As that unfortunate episode with Rex taught you, I haven't always been a great judge of character, but my estimation of The Cat was different."

His reference to "an unfortunate episode" Rowley epitomized his characteristic penchant for understatement. He managed to describe the results of him telling Rex about my shells—which nearly brought down the monarchy. I would have pointed this out, but I was too interested in the story he was prepared to tell me.

"I was going through a resentful period. One only needs to be a dog for so long before one realizes the drawbacks—especially regarding one's treatment at the hands of humans. The Cat understood that." Rowley's eyes took on a faraway, haunted look, stopping his story. “I found out, despite all my skill and intelligence, he is still more powerful than I ever was or could be.”

“Someone more powerful than you? I would love to see that,” I mumbled.

“Then look in the mirror. You have no idea the gifts you have. You’re more powerful than you’ll ever know.” The comment brought me up short. He hadn’t said it with malice or even frustration. It was the first time I’d heard Rowley sound awed.

“You’ve had what? Centuries to learn. I have had only months. And fending off the barrage of people you’ve told about the shells has broken up the time between tutoring sessions,” I sniped.

His jowls drooped and he sighed.

“I’m not unsympathetic to the way this was thrust upon you. Believe me, I understand what it is to be given a task that seems impossible.” I looked at him expecting impatience and prepared to give him a cutting reply, but his expression stopped me. A new look was in his doleful eyes. It looked like regret and maybe a touch of compassion. His eyes took on such a human quality I could almost see the depths of him but that passed away too quickly.

“There was a time when discipline and responsibility were not my main concerns. I knew I had a mission, but all I could do was wait for you to appear. At the peak of my impatience, I met The Cat,” he said. “Cat had a philosophy about our lot. He believed that if humans gave animals their power, animals should make use of them.”

“That doesn’t sound so bad,” I replied.

“He meant use them on the humans. His home life was...difficult. The woman who took him in was indifferent and he was really there only for her children.”

“The Arco children,” I said. Rowley shivered at their mention.

“They were frightful children, to say the least. Mischievous tricksters with a mean streak. Cat bore the brunt of it until he ran away. He was free...from responsibilities, from cares and it was...

seductive," he said, his voice taking on a wistful quality. Strange that I saw a small twinkle in his eye before they hardened into something flinty, angry.

"What did you do?" I asked.

"What did *we* do? At first, little pranks, harmless really, but it wasn't enough for him. I should have known he was plotting his revenge. He'd found a fiddle that washed up on shore with the body of an Outer Isle pirate. It had the power to drive mad any human who heard it," he said simply.

"What do you mean?" I asked with dawning realization.

"The player constantly longs to hear the tune. Cities could burn and the victim would continue to play. But in The Cat's hands—the listener constantly hears the tune even after it's stopped. In Cat's hands, he could make the listener do anything he demanded, enchanted by the tune. He used it on the Arco children and then led them to their deaths on the hill. And an enchantment he learned from me rendered them frozen."

"From you? How did the Haros get caught up in this...?

"Mrs. Haro's grandmother was at Mrs. Arco's when Cat came back to play," he said and lapsed into silence. I heard a small whimper escape him before he continued. "Despite my disaffection, the Haro's had always been good to me. It was because of them I was no longer a stray and I owed them a lot. What Cat did... Well, after that I knew I shouldn't, couldn't follow The Cat. I told him the fiddle was too dangerous, but he wanted to use it some more. We fought, but there was an outbreak of insanity before he was stopped. People were unable to control urges that weren't even their own." Rowley growled and the hackles on his back rose again.

"How did you stop him?" I asked, but the look of defeat already imprinted on his face told me more than I wanted to know.

"I didn't. At least not without help. It was the horn that did it."

"The horn? What horn? Not the El Niño Amoratado horn? Only someone related to El Niño can play it, right?" The El Niño Amoratado horn was one of those rare magical objects that not even smugglers and thieves tried to sell. Everyone knew it only played for someone related to El Niño Amoratado, an infamous pirate of the Outer Isles who earned his name from supposedly taking multiple beatings, feeling nothing and then beating all his rivals bloody. He was king of the pirates and so were his descendants.

"But his descendants haven't been seen in years. Or the horn."

"I know," he snapped then subsided. "After Blue, one of El Niño's wayward sons, used his horn, everything went dark for a bit. I was unconscious for a day and when I woke up I was alone in the woods. The Cat, Blue, and his horn were gone. If The Cat came back, I don't know how he did it or more importantly what we can do to stop him."

The silence in the room was deafening as I took in all the information Rowley had given me. I tried to think back to my time in the woods and I felt a tightening in my chest.

"Why don't I hear the music in my head?" I asked feeling the tendrils of worry start to take hold.

"As I have mentioned, you're very powerful. Your protection spell must have guarded you from its effect," he said, but my mind had already moved to another sickening dread which had half-formed when he started his story.

"What about Meiri?"

Chapter 11

My heart was beating in my ears. Frantic and panting, I searched the ice ball field in a panic. The layer of snow slowed my steps. My run to Green Gardens just got me a polite dismissal from a Green Girl, but no confirmation as to Meiri's whereabouts. That's what brought me running at full tilt to the field where I'd just spotted Arch. For his part, he was milling about the outskirts of the pitch, likely warming his feet.

Ice ball is a game of, as Lita would explain it, *Visteme despacio que voy de prisa*, or more haste, less speed. The game requires precision with bursts of speed from one person to another and timing is everything. The ball is made of ice with a thick outer layer that is constantly melting while protecting a smaller ball dyed red. Each team is trying to keep the ball on the other team's side because whoever's side the ball is on when it finally melts and releases the inner ball, loses, but only if the last player to kick it was also from that team.

I flagged him down like a demented ref and ignored the laughter of the other players.

"What a wonderful surprise. To what do I owe the honor, gorgeous? Taking me up on my offer?" asked an amused Arch.

"Have you seen Meiri?" I asked, breathless.

"Despite what you or my mother think, I'm not my sister's keeper," he said pursing his lips. His face changed suddenly back to one of amusement, and I realized, belatedly, Arch was in the mood for mischief.

"Hey, I thought we were seeing each other tonight?" asked a newly arrived Zavier. The difference between them couldn't have been more pronounced than it was now. Unlike Arch's crisp and clean uniform, Zavier was filthy with mud and melted slush all over his shirt and pants. He was completely unconcerned with the smudges of dirt on his face while Arch was wiping away imaginary specks of dirt from his shirt.

"She's not here for you, Captain. She's here for me," he gloated.

"Why's that?" asked Zavier with furrowed brow as he faced Arch.

"Maybe she's finally come to her senses and realized she chose the wrong man," he teased, facing Zavier squarely.

"Then she definitely isn't here for you. Inez—?"

They both stared at me—Zavier with confusion and Arch with growing relish at Zavier's discomfort. Arch saw an opportunity to bait Zavier even more.

"You look worried, Cousin. I would too, especially if my fiancé said she wasn't really engaged—didn't you Inez?"

I yelled: "I don't have time for this. If you guys want to fight, go pee on the ball. Zavier, I need to talk to Arch." By then the team was looking in our direction with heightened curiosity.

"Inez, did you tell Arch we're not engaged?" asked Zavier.

"Yes, but that's not what I meant..."

"Oh, I'll leave you two alone. And Arch hurry it up. We still have practice," said Zavier and stalked away in a huff.

"Zavier!" I called but he didn't look back. Then I turned to Arch, fists on my hips, "You really had to do that?" I asked.

"Serves him right for thinking of abandoning us. Dating a commoner is excusable if it's you, but for him to consider playing for them..." He shook his head.

"What are you talking about? Is this about ice ball?" I couldn't imagine a more asinine reason for them to fight.

"Yes. He wants to join the KM team. Of all the—"

"Arch, where is your sister?" I asked through gritted teeth. At this point my hands were almost shaking with the effort to keep my Powers at bay. It wasn't just fighting for my life that triggered them now. Anger and frustration went a long way with magic. Something in my face must have alerted him that I was not playing around anymore.

"She mentioned the library," he said soberly.

"Thank you," I said and ran before he or Zavier could drag me into their silly game squabble.

MY FEAR FOR MEIRI OUTWEIGHED my new aversion to the library. I ran there as though The Cat were chasing me with his enchanted fiddle.

Thinking about that brought me back to Rowley's story. I couldn't imagine a carefree Rowley, laughing as his friend brought dishes and spoons to life and helped set them free. Would I become brusque and world-weary after a year of this? Even now it all sounded so fanciful with flying cows and an animal revolution.

I would have found this exciting not too long ago. Now I had to worry if my friend was being driven mad.

Rowley's parting words echoed in my mind. "This is what you were meant for, Inez, just as I was meant to teach you. Now, more than ever we need to work together."

It was gratifying to hear Rowley admit I was needed—that I was meant for important work. He needed me, but the look of fear in his eyes made it hard to gloat. I felt that fear now creeping closer, pursuing me. As I arrived at the door of the library the cold feeling from the pit of my stomach spread throughout my body, making the world filmy again.

My temper was rising as I entered the library looking for the very person who made this place so much harder for me to visit. But first...

"Oh, it's you. And you're not with your new royal pet?"

"Not now Evelien!" I shouted and saw a row of books collapse to the floor. It was all I could do to keep my temper under control. She turned, startled and saw the books. Her eyes narrowed before she bent to pick them up.

"Aren't we imperious today? Well, you're not queen yet so don't—"

"No time," I snapped and quickly left her on the floor. I searched the archives for Betlindis. Unfortunately, she found me first and startled me.

"*Oww*. This cold weather. It causes the worst static electricity," said Betlindis rubbing her hand.

My protection spell intensified, making me swallow down the threat of bile.

"Have you seen Meiri?" I moaned, stepping back from Betlindis.

"I'm sorry to mention this, but you're rather loud...and you look green. Are you sick?" she whispered.

"A little maybe. Have you seen her?" I said, wrapping my arms around myself.

"As a matter of fact, she was here bright and early to collect my notes and with a million questions about the KM archives. I gave her everything I found," she said with a frown. She pointed to a neat stack of handwritten notes, which Meiri clearly hadn't taken. "And did you know I have had other enquiries into The Cat? At least three different people have come asking about it."

"Perfect. Where is Meiri?" I asked, my frustration growing. I seized the notes and tucked them away for later.

"Sorry. I came to check on her about thirty minutes ago and she was gone," she said.

"Dammit! I need to..."

"Wait, Inez. I know we've talked before but can we...?"

"I'm sorry Betlindis, but I have to find Meiri," I said, turning, striving to hide the panic in my voice.

"Oh, of course. I know what it's like to feel that urge to search. Especially for someone important to you," she said with such a sad sigh that I turned back. Her eyes suffused with unshed tears brought up enough guilt in me that I stayed.

"I have a few minutes," I said, trying to tamp down my anxiety. I hoped I wouldn't be too late for Meiri.

"Thank you," she said with a slight catch in her throat. "I spoke to a few people that were at the Ball. They remember you leaving for a bit and my father and I following you. All I remember is getting to the Ball in a pretty dress and getting more attention than I'm used to. Then I remember the prince's announcement and I think I danced with your friend Toman. I'm guessing we left sometime in between that?" Her earnest entreaty was almost more than I could bear.

I was the only one who remembered Rex, Betlindis and her enchanted dress and its effects. Even Zavier only remembered my arrival and then our dance and he'd been the target of the dress.

"Um...well, you needed help with your dress and your father asked me to help you. He said he would see us back in the ballroom and...and that was the last I saw of him," I said. The lie came so easily that I was afraid it sounded rehearsed. It almost kept me from feeling guilty. Almost.

"Is that when I ended up in your mother's dress?"

"Yes. She wanted to go home and knew you were—uncomfortable in your dress," I said. Uncomfortable was an understatement. The enchanted dress turned every male's head in the room, including Toman who usually reserved his sly looks for Zavier.

Her father, Rex, hoped the dress would convince Zavier to engage himself to Betlindis and wrest power from the royal house. My Power was able to stop him and trap him in one of the shells, I thought. On bad days, when the guilt of lying to Betlindis threatened to overwhelm me I'd assumed I'd killed Rex. "After that it's all a blur."

"Me too, but I suppose your reasons are a lot more pleasant. Such a handsome man and such a romantic gesture. I don't know if I would have been able to breathe knowing I would be married to the future king," she said, and I laughed nervously thinking how close she came to realizing that.

"Sorry. I'm still in shock myself, I guess. I have to go," I said, sensing my Powers taking over.

I still have more questions—"

But I already felt it happening.

"Betlindis, I *have* to find Meiri. I need to know where she is." I ran through the stacks and out the door. I got myself behind the building where I hoped it was secluded. I could feel my Powers trying to carry me away to find Meiri. I wasn't sure Betlindis hadn't seen me fading out.

Chapter 12

My eyes were squeezed tight, but I couldn't deny that I was no longer hidden behind the library. The air was crisper and the snow drift where I stood was at mid-calf—something that wouldn't happen in the city center.

It was only the second time I'd accomplished a displacement spell. I was relieved that this time I hadn't passed out from the experience. Last time I had to bring two people and a dog with me, so maybe that made the difference. It was a concern that I'd done it spontaneously. My Powers were growing and expanding, and I still had little control over them.

I finally opened my eyes and confirmed what I already knew. I was in the woods. And spinning in front of me, near the edge of a cliff, was Meiri.

"Meiri...Meiri! What are you doing?" I asked trudging toward her. The depth of the snow made it difficult. She stopped spinning at the sound of my voice but swayed dangerously close to the edge.

"*Hmm*? Inez where did you...? Do you hear that music? It's so... I have to dance and... I was somewhere else, wasn't I?" Meiri's clothes sported dead leaves and it looked as though she'd rolled around in the snow. If she'd left home with a coat on, it was nowhere in sight. Her swaying was punctuated by the odd tremor of chill. I reached out for her. She recoiled. I stopped moving.

"Yes. You were at the library," I said, trying to sound nonchalant. I made my movements deliberately small, hoping she didn't notice me advancing while we both spoke, but each time I paused she got closer to falling over the edge. I knew at the bottom were jagged rocks and the bay. I couldn't bring her back from that were she to go over.

"Betlindis said she gave you some notes and then you were gone. Are you...okay?" I asked, struggling to sound calm. The icy cold feeling was starting in the pit of my stomach again. The protection spell wrapped me in a filmy embrace that was oppressive. I realized with a start I could hear the music, too. The Cat was somewhere close by.

"I feel like... Have you ever had a song stuck in your head all night and...it doesn't leave...?" she said, rubbing her temples with increased agitation.

Her eyes cleared for a moment, but then the music accelerated. It sounded like a reel, moving faster in a circle of melody. Beval used to play songs like that while I kicked up my heels and spun until, dizzy with excitement, I fell to the ground.

I could feel my insides churning. Within the grip of the protection spell the music didn't affect me. My spell was making my movements jerky. Each step was more labored, but Meiri was just an arpeggio away from her doom.

"Meiri...Why don't...Why don't we go to m-my house. I have a piano... We can figure out the...the tune together." I concentrated on my goal—not letting Meiri fall—and felt myself adjusting to the cocoon I was in. It was enough to allow me to get close to her. "When I have a song in my head," I said calmly, to reassure her, "it helps to know all of it so you can...get to the end!"

I grabbed her wrists hard and several things happened all at once. The protection spell burst. Meiri's eyes widened with clarity and fear. I heard The Cat hiss as the music ended and I felt the earth give way under us. But before plummeting to the forbidding rocks below I thought I heard laughter that sounded like a *purr*.

"INEZ, ARE YOU IN THE shower?" I heard Mamá call.

"No, I'm in here," I said from my room. I was looking for a clean shirt.

"Then who...? *Nena*, what is this mess and that smell?" Her eyes surveyed my room. Aside from the usual detritus of shoes, books and chinchilla bedding that escaped the confines of the cage when Cochi was in a particularly acrobatic mood, there were bloody bandages and a pile of wet, muddy clothes.

My rescue of Meiri had been both dramatic and messy.

"You're a grown woman, engaged to our future king. Please tell me you don't bring him up here to this mess," Mamá said, picking through the debris.

"Not without warning," I said, slipping on a clean sweater I found under the bed. I rubbed my still-tender stomach.

"Who's in the shower, then?" she asked with a sigh. I could see her hunting around the room for the smell she'd detected a moment ago. She stopped in front of Cochi's cage and grabbed it by the handle, sending the chinchilla scurrying for shelter. More bits of chinchilla bedding drifted to the floor.

"Meiri. She's getting cleaned up," I replied, handing her the coat I had been wearing. She sniffed it gingerly.

"Should I ask?"

"Do you really want to know?"

"Yes," she replied, but I heard the slight hesitation in her voice. Mamá was still torn between wanting to know everything I did and knowing that more information wasn't necessarily a good thing.

"I threw up on Meiri after we jumped off a cliff," I said with a shrug.

"What?"

"Actually, it happened as we were jumping, but the good news is I got us here without passing out and I don't think she's crazy anymore."

"*Nena*...I—"

"I'll give you details later, okay? I need to check on Meiri," I said. In truth, I was still pretty shaken from the whole experience. I wasn't ready to let Mamá see my fear. I wasn't even ready to address it.

"No, I'll go. Zavier is downstairs and he looks upset," she said, taking my coat and the pile of soiled clothing.

I heard the shower turn off as I reached the landing. Zavier had clearly come straight from practice. His uniform was still a mess, and his face was covered in grime. The look on his face was what really held my attention. It was the same look he gave the opposing team during a match.

Before I could say anything he stepped inside.

"Is he here?" he asked with folded arms.

"Is who here?" Still firmly entrenched in my ordeal, I thought he meant The Cat.

"Arch—the one who knows more about what's going on than me—*that* he," he replied.

"Are you serious? Look, I'm sorry I had to run off, but that's no reason to start imagining things."

"Your mother said someone was upstairs in the shower and Arch hinted... Forget it," he said uncharacteristically flustered. I could see the turn his mind had taken. Arch rushing over here after practice and washing up. I could have laughed out loud.

"That someone is Meiri. She's cleaning up after...a fall," I managed to say. *Who needed guilt about another guy?* I had enough lies to keep me remorseful for a lifetime with Zavier. "I should get back to her."

"Of course. I hope she's okay," he said, but he still sounded too cool.

"She is and don't let Arch bother you. He's all flash and no substance. I need real depth," I said, planting a kiss on his nose. "And I didn't say anything that isn't true. We're not engaged according to your sister-in-law, who is the queen and the only one who can make it official. You can hardly blame me for complaining a little."

I was slightly annoyed that I had to justify anything I said and shocked at how easily Zavier had lost faith in me. Something in my tone caught his attention and he took my hands in his.

"As far as I'm concerned, we're engaged—no matter what Hortensia or all of Canto and Mythos thinks. And you chose me, remember?" he said with a nervous chuckle. His comment was more question than statement.

"Do you think I would leave you for Arch because he's somehow easier?" I asked.

"He has no strings attached," he muttered.

"I would call Eugenia a rope with an anchor." I laughed. I could see he still wasn't convinced.

"But he doesn't have to worry about being heir apparent. I know how you feel about the 'royal' thing. That wouldn't be a problem with Arch. He could easily walk away."

"Zavier, I would be lying if I said I was...comfortable with the idea of being your queen, but I would take you over him any day. Of course he could walk away. The uncomplicated pretty boys only care about themselves. Do you think Arch would come to my door reeking of sweat and covered in mud because he was scared his girlfriend was with someone else?"

"Well, when you put it that way," he said taking a discrete sniff of his shirt.

"You know what I mean," I said taking his hand in mine. I heard Mamá calling me upstairs, but I needed to make sure he understood. I smiled at him willing him to smile back. He laughed when I made a face—Mamá was being rather insistent. "I should really..."

"In a minute," he said as he wound his arms around my back. I gave him my cheek as he came in for a kiss. He pulled back with a quizzical look on his face.

"Sorry. I threw up before," I said, covering my mouth with my hand.

"Are you okay?" he asked with touching concern.

"Yes it... Something disagreed with my system. It's why Meiri's in the shower. She got the brunt of it," I muttered. At least it wasn't a complete lie and I wondered how long I would have to keep this up. Half-truths and flubs would soon wear thin.

"If you're willing to put up with my sweat and mud, I'll take my chances." He pulled me in gingerly and kissed me breathless. "I'll come by later tonight after I've cleaned up," he said and kissed me again on the cheek before leaving. I stood there smiling for a minute before Mamá's voice bellowed through the house again, calling me back to my responsibilities.

MAMÁ, MEIRI AND UNSURPRISINGLY, Rowley were standing in Mamá's bedroom. I could just imagine her not wanting to show guests my mess even though they'd both seen me at my worst. It was funny and irritating all at the same time.

"Is everything okay with Zavier?" asked Mamá.

"Yep. There was a misunderstanding about Arch," I replied.

"Arch *is* a misunderstanding," replied Meiri. She looked pale but lucid. Her hair was still damp from the shower, and I saw that Mamá had given her a pair of pajamas. I noticed that Meiri's eyes kept darting around the room just as it had the first time she told me about The Cat.

"Yes, yes. You can have a girl talk later. Right now I need to know what happened. I can smell most of it," yipped Rowley. *Was he smelling the magic or the vomit?*

"I went looking for Meiri and my magic found her in the woods dancing near the edge of a cliff," I replied.

"That was a specialty of Cat's. Although he never actually let them fall off the edge before," mused Rowley.

"Well, that may have been my fault. I grabbed her because I thought she was going to fall, but the edge gave way and we fell anyway. I concentrated on us not falling to our deaths, so I think that's what brought us here." I was proud of the control I'd had. Last time I used that much magic I'd passed out. I might be shaky now, but I was still upright.

"I take it the protection spell grew too tight? I can smell the result of that, too," Rowley quipped. "That will lessen once you trust your magic more. Right now, it just wants to protect you and it leaves very little room for anything else to get in. When you're truly adept, the barrier will lessen. Your magic will be confident you can protect yourself."

My pride was slightly wounded at that, but I still felt smug at all I had accomplished. "If you used the rest of the shells—"

"We've talked about this before. I can barely control all the Power I have now. If I take all of the magic in—"

"It would balance it. Inez, really I think the reason you have such bad physical reactions to excessive use of magic is the lack of balance. As the Ternion you have access to Abstract, Custodial and Martial magic, but we don't know in what percentage that first shell awakened those abilities. I'm willing to bet each of the other shells are a magical discipline. I know a couple in Faery who better understand what discipline mixing does. If only you were willing to go to Faery," he said and made a sound that in a human would have been a *harumph*, but in a dog was more of a soft bark.

For me it was a nonstarter. I knew taking in all that magic had the potential to drive me insane before it "balanced" my Powers, as Rex optimistically opined. And going to Faery likely meant staying in Faery with friends of Rowley, who had proven to be an unreliable judge of character at best.

"Meiri's safe and that's all that matters now," I said, looking in her direction. She still looked uneasy, but who wouldn't after the shock she had?

"Not yet. Filomena was looking through her notes and found something interesting about The Cat's fiddle," said Rowley. Mamá had a large book on her lap opened to a page with her scrawling handwriting. I recognized it as one of the books that inhabited her private collection.

"This was the journal I kept of all the things I learned from Beval," Mamá said wistfully. He told me to keep a chronicle for you, with the condition I never give it to the library. "The fiddle originally belonged to The People but was lost on one of their many migrations. There's a notation about tamp root that can lessen the effects of the madness the fiddle music causes. Taken over time it can erase them completely."

"Perfect. Wait, hasn't tamp root been wiped out?" I asked.

"Not entirely," she said. "There's a note to see the Jabberwocky."

"Wonderful," I said. I knew from experience that the tamp root had been systematically eliminated by the joint efforts of Birthright and the hidden market. I'd searched for some shortly after discovering my Powers in the hopes of suppressing them. I should have known Áliz or one of her predecessors would have kept some. I was already in debt to the Jabberwocky. Asking her for a favor would not only make my situation more difficult, but it would also make her suspicious.

"I saw some at Viktor's when we were practicing your magic by the bay," said Mamá.

"Much as it pains me to say this, we'll need her help. If anyone has herbals, and illegal ones at that, it'll be Viktor," grumbled Rowley.

"About Viktor—" Meiri began.

"Meiri, I already spoke to Rowley about Viktor and we decided that I should go to lessons with Viktor on my own," I interrupted. I didn't want to have the conversation about Viktor yet. I still wanted to give her the benefit of the doubt. And if I was wrong, I didn't want to send Mamá or Rowley out there to fall under The Cat's spell. "I'll run over there and be back within the hour."

"No, you need to use the mirror," said Rowley. "With The Cat out there, he's a danger even with your protection spell. Besides, he could be tracking Meiri as we speak, and I can't hold her here indefinitely." As he said it, I could perceive what he meant. An invisible barrier was surrounding Meiri.

"You're doing that?" I asked.

"Yes, and it's not easy. We don't have much time," he said. There was no exertion in his movements, no difficulty in his voice. I hoped that magic would come that easily to me some day.

"*Nena* I know how you feel about the mirror," Mamá said sympathetically.

"What are you talking about? I'm fine with the mirror. I just like to walk, that's all," I said defensively.

"Good, then you can get going. Walking around the woods, searching for the Mist House would take too long as I'm sure the drifts by Viktor's are at least a foot deep," said Rowley. "Don't tell Viktor, but I've devised a way to track the Mist House using the mirror. It should work now."

I looked at Meiri again, who was swaying slightly to music no one else could hear. "And ask Viktor for a masking herb too. We should make sure Cat can't sniff Meiri out."

I agreed with a stiff nod and left for the mirror room. My dislike of the mirror had increased since my Powers had awakened. The last time I'd used one, the mirror cracked. I squeezed my finger and felt the still imbedded sliver of glass. Mirrors behaved strangely with my magic, and knowing that kept me from using them. At least that's what I told everyone and myself, too. What really made me cringe about the mirror was how Lita had died.

When those KM came to tell us about finding Lita in the woods, they failed to mention that it had been a mirror accident. We didn't learn about that until after the funeral. They were unheard of—mirror deaths. We never found out what really happened, but it was proven that a mirror was the cause.

I imagined all sorts of scenarios, with Lita being trapped and suffocating in the depths of the mirror before being dropped in a heap in the middle of nowhere. I even imagined a mirror monster for quite some time, lurking behind the clear façade, waiting to strike unsuspecting riders. I grew out of my fear of the mirror monster, but not my aversion to the mirror.

As I reached the doors of the mirror shed, I took a deep breath and tried to reassure myself that nothing would happen to me. Meiri needed medicine more than I had the luxury of being afraid, so I entered with brittle confidence, hoping to trick myself into being brave.

"She approaches," a voice said. It was barely a whisper, but the sound was distinct. It reminded me of a stone skimming the water's surface. The sound of a mirror.

I hesitated. Of all the things I'd had come to terms with, believing in a talking mirror was never on my list. Enchanters had used mirror transport for centuries. I'd never thought of them as living.

"Hello? Who said that?" I asked, holding tight to my mirror deflector. The ridiculousness of me trying to carry on a conversation with a mirror was not lost on me. Questioning the viability of a sentient mirror and defending myself with a weapon made of glass, essentially another mirror. *Would it even work? Would they gang up on me?*

"Did you hear me child?" asked the voice from before. It sounded as incredulous as I felt. Ripples appeared on the calm surface of the mirror, echoing the words spoken. I stood, watching the interplay, transfixed.

"Are you the mirror?" I asked, not knowing what else to say.

"I am its guardian. And you are the descendant of the maker, twice removed," it said. I supposed since Beval was my grandfather and he made the mirror, that was true.

"Yes. Inez. And do you have a name?" I asked, fighting the urge to stroke the surface of the mirror.

"The mirrors have decided to refuse you transport. They claim you committed a mirror murder."

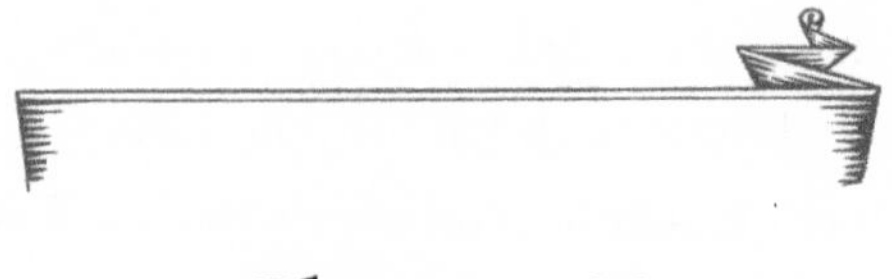

Chapter 13

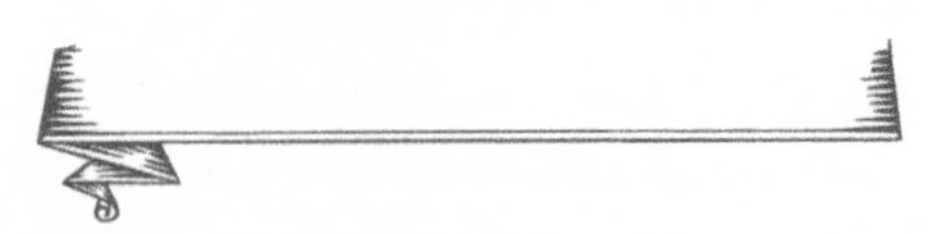

"Mirror Murder? Are you serious? Is there really such a thing?" I said, perplexed. All feelings of fear had evaporated, and a sense of foreboding had replaced it. When Meiri, Toman and I had traveled through the mirror to Piar Farm, I'd heard the cracking of glass, but when I inspected the small fissure it had vanished. What had perplexed me at the time was I'd seen a much bigger crack before I touched the mirror's surface. After the disappearance of any damage, I wondered if I had imagined it all. My only clue had been whatever hard, sharp object had lodged itself in my finger. Did I really kill a mirror? Were mirrors living things? Another death attributed to me.

"Your comments betray your ignorance, but the very fact that you can hear me means you're guilty," said the mirror, as though it could hear my thoughts.

"What does that mean?" I asked.

"It's rare, but someone with magic can sometimes hear us if they retain any of the glass from the shattering. The result is the same. You killed a mirror and the other mirrors have refused you service.

"I didn't know. I'm sorry about that. But it wasn't maliciously done." I knew he meant my cracking of the mirror at Piar Farm. The sliver in my finger seemed to vibrate in response. "Did the mirror have a name?" I asked, fully aware that it still hadn't disclosed its own.

"Arkaitz. They claim you shattered him on purpose. Some are even saying it was reckless endangerment because you have wild magic and blame me as well for allowing you passage," it replied. "Because I knew you had magic, I should have warned them."

"You know I have magic?" I asked tensely. "Does any other mirror know?"

"Just a few, but mirrors are known gossips. Still, they are all refusing you transport... Not that it makes any difference," it replied, sounding slightly bitter.

"What do you mean?"

"We are officially named as furniture and therefore have no rights, especially to say 'no.' We find ways around that by making the trip less than comfortable," he said with a ripple I recognized as a chuckle.

"So, they have to transport me? No matter what?" I asked, still thinking about the merits of using my own two feet. Remembering Meiri and how she swayed before I left, told me I had no choice. The idea of a bumpy mirror ride made me shiver and I felt the beginnings of the icy chill in the pit of my stomach.

"Yes. I have no means to stop you and neither do they. I would hate to think you would ever impose your will over me or any other mirror for that matter, so I advise against it until I can convince them you weren't the cause of Arkaitz's demise," it said. I couldn't blame them if they didn't want to transport me. My powers were volatile at best, and Rowley was right—they were growing. With my protection spell trying to assert itself now, how could I possibly risk breaking another mirror? Would I even be able to get back from the Mist House? I had to do something. At this very moment, The Cat could be hunting down Meiri's scent.

"I would never want to push my will on you," I said, knowing full well I'd done it before, however inadvertently, "but this is an emergency. Meiri needs medicine desperately and the only place to get it is from Viktor. With all the snow, it could take me over an hour to search for the Mist House. Rowley said he found a way to let the mirror... To let you track the Mist House. I know you can't make the other mirrors change their mind about the kind of ride I'll get, but I'm hoping you'll understand how important this is to me," I said, concentrating on being calm. I didn't just have to convince the mirror to let me travel, but I also had to convince my body that I felt no danger. So far, the former was the easier of the two.

"Of course, Inez. I wouldn't want your friend to get hurt because of some jumpy mirrors. Still, I have to warn you, some of them could get rough and the closest mirror is far enough away from the location of the Mist House that you'll pass through more than a dozen. The one thing in your favor is that this is a time for high volume transportation, so many people will be transporting with you. Mirrors don't want to get a reputation for giving poor service... That'll send their passengers straight to the stables," it said with a sigh.

More than a dozen mirrors? I didn't know which of these mirrors were against me and I could find myself trapped, or worse. I kept thinking of Meiri and how badly she needed the medicine. I shoved my hands in my pockets and hoped the restricted space would keep them in line.

"I understand. Whenever you're ready," I replied, taking deep breaths and closing my eyes. I touched the liquefying pane and stepped through to whatever awaited me.

THE WARMTH OF A MIRROR is like nothing else. It envelops you in a stream of velvety glass the temperature of the perfect spring day. Murmuring voices create a hum like spoken music, letting the rider drift off in thought. It all happens in minutes. At least that's a normal ride when the whole mirror community isn't screaming for vengeance against a passenger who allegedly killed one of their own.

My ride was chaotic. The shard of glass in my finger throbbed painfully. The warmth became a nearly untouchable heat as I was shuffled and shunted from one mirror to another.

At first I only heard my own rasping breaths.

Then the voices of the mirrors started chanting. *"Murderer, Mirror Killer!"* I didn't know if any other riders could hear them, but I never saw anyone else. My ear caught on to a particular mirror voice that was lower and meaner than the rest. Her chant was different.

"You'll die like your grandmother," she said. The fevered, angry sound of her voice and words terrified me. It was my nightmare made real. *Could it be true? Did a mirror kill my grandmother?* The cold pit in my stomach was starting to grow, traveling up my throat. I could hear the wavering of the mirror voices—their confusion, their distress.

The protection spell was making its way up inch by inch, clamping down on me with a strength I didn't know my magic possessed. It was like fighting my own will, but it had two minds. I was wedged between the fire of the mirrors and the ice of my spell, gasping for breath. The voice in my head started to whisper a counter chant to all the chaos around me.

Bher...Bher...BHER...BHER!

I sang it like a descant to the atonal harmony assaulting my ears. I felt myself being pulled from the mirrors. It was more than flying, it was becoming air. Martial Powers were elemental in nature. My trip from the library to the woods had been a reaction to frustration and the fall with Meiri had been sheer panic, a visceral thing, and likely martial magic. This was communing with movement and making it my own—it was abstract magic.

It was exhilarating as I moved on a wintry breeze over rooftops and passed soaring trees warmed by the late afternoon sun. I could skim the clouds and let the sunlight wash over me. Drunk on the power I had, I kept climbing higher, following a flock of geese across the great horizon. Who needed responsibilities and great destinies? To be the air, cresting and falling was purpose enough.

But the voice in my head kept up its chant. *Bher...Bher...BHER*, reminding me that there was a purpose to this flight. I had somewhere to be...didn't I? Someone needed my help and...and what was the rest? Who could need help when there were such adventures to be had? Shaking a tree free of its frost or blowing a crow off course were much more pressing, much more fun.

Bher...Bher...BHER...

Couldn't it wait? Who could rush when there was a snowbank to whip up through a funnel or a cat dragging a fiddle to...*The Cat*? My consciousness registered The Cat with the fiddle slinking between the trees, his little paw prints leaving a trail behind him. Were those boots on his back paws?

The sighting jarred me. A vision of Meiri, twirling by a precipice, like a top about to end its revolution brought me back to myself. *What was I doing?* This time I strained to hear the chant in my head.

Bher...Bher...BHER...

It meant carry. I knew that now from Lita and Beval's book. As air, I could still whisper and did so with a concentrated effort.

"*Bher Viktor*," I said and whisked my way toward the only structure at the edge of the bay made entirely of swirling magic. Circling the edifice, I saw the unmistakable prints of paws and boots at the tree line.

Chapter 14

Reaching the ground was literally a downer. It felt odd to have arms and legs again which moments ago had been wisps on the breeze. Using my powers that way had been heady, intoxicating. It was expansive, being part of everything yet beholden to nothing. Now back on solid ground, I felt the weight of all the responsibilities I had to shoulder. It would have been so easy to stay up there, going wherever and doing whatever.

Usually after using big magic, I felt woozy and weak. Now I just felt empty and trapped. But I had seen that cat and he was headed home where Meiri, Mamá and Rowley were defenseless. They needed me more than ever and I couldn't ignore that call. I squared my shoulders and prepared to face Viktor.

"Hello? Viktor?" I called in the echoing space. It was well lit with a large log crackling away in a metal pit. My favorite smell and worst memory. I suppose that would always stay with me, along with the feeling of complete freedom on the wind.

"Miss Inez, don't you look windswept," Viktor said with wry amusement. *Had she seen me?* I couldn't tell. She lowered her hood, releasing the pale silver waves of hair and exposing her angular, yet clearly feminine face. Her voice no longer had the masking spell that distorted it.

"We need your help. Rowley and Mamá sent me to get some tamp root. Do you have any?"

"You do know that tamp root is—"

"Extinct? Yes, I know, which is why—"

"Which is why you came to me, am I correct? That dog turns his nose up at me, but who does he come to when he needs help?" she said, searching through pots and vials. The smells were overwhelming. I could only recognize a few...jasmine, lavender, pine...but the more exotic ones were a mystery. It reminded me of sitting with Lita as she tied up herbs for drying. I wish I had paid more attention. "And for your information I do the things that need doing. There are rules that need to be broken sometimes. I do it all for the same reason I train you. To bring back magic."

"And why do you need one of my shells to do it?" I asked, feeling slightly light-headed from all the smells. What I wanted to ask her was why I'd seen paw prints leading away from her home.

"If we had more time, I would tell you. I could tell you the next time we have a lesson, but I'm sure that dog would object," she complained.

"Well, you're in luck because we've decided that I should have individual lessons with you and with Rowley at another time. Now you needn't step on each other's toes," I said. I wanted to say that was to keep everyone safe and I felt a small prick of my magic sting my fingers.

"*Hmm*. His paws could use some treading. And I felt that, young lady. Your Powers are growing, did he tell you that, too?"

"Yes, he did," I said, oddly defensive. I might not like Rowley, but I didn't like her saying anything about him either.

"Here it is...This root is very powerful and used for a very specific purpose. Does this have anything to do with your Powers?" she asked with an arched brow.

"Not really. What do you know about the Cat and the fiddle?" I asked watching her reaction to my words. She didn't blink or react, but was that because it meant nothing to her or was she really good at disguising her reactions from me? She'd spent her life pretending to be a man for a purpose she hadn't disclosed. Was it that far-fetched that she could contain her reaction to hearing about The Cat?

"It's a story, isn't it? Nothing more than that," she said dismissively.

"You've told me a few," I retorted. "We saw him. He was...in the woods and he used his fiddle on Meiri. She almost felt off a cliff," I said, getting frustrated. I was almost sure Viktor knew something, and her nonchalance was maddening.

"Well, your mother should know about dosage. I was the one who introduced your grandmother to tamp root although she would have said your grandfather did first," she said with a smile, ignoring my comment. For a moment I could see her as she must have been with Lita—no agenda, no lies. Just two women exploring their craft and enjoying each other's company. *What had happened to change her? Did it have anything to do with what the mirror said about Lita?* I didn't have time to think about that now. I was getting anxious to get back home.

"Thank you for this and I'll be back soon for a lesson," I said, grabbing the bag. Viktor held fast.

"Yes, and the first thing you'll learn is that I don't do this for free. Tell that dog he owes me 500 rhyians. Goodbye Inez and take care," she said somberly. She held my hand a longer than necessary and pursed her lips as though trying to decide if she should say more.

I waited, but she released me and her back turned in dismissal. I would have pressed her for answers, but Meiri was waiting.

I TOOK MY CHANCES WITH the mirrors. Secretly, I hoped it would trigger a repeat of my air ride, but the trip was oddly smooth. perhaps that could be attributed to more passengers. Still, I didn't know if it was guilt about how they treated me or if they had confirmed their suspicions.

I'd used magic in there—did they notice? Who would tell? I decided I needed to get better at self-transportation to avoid another bumpy ride.

My mirror remained silent as I arrived, but I shrugged that off. I had other thoughts on my mind. Rushing inside the house, I hoped I wasn't too late.

I couldn't shake the feeling that Viktor was holding something back. *Did she really think The Cat was just a story?* A few weeks ago, I saw Rex and Yvette emerge from her house and then all hell broke loose at the Ball. I didn't know what she was up to, but one thing was clear, I had to be the one to deal with her especially if she was involved with The Cat. I couldn't risk any of my friends, my family or even Rowley being hurt by her.

Meiri, Mamá and Rowley were just as I'd left them. The strain on Meiri's face was starting to show more, but Rowley had her well in hand. She looked like a child pretending to nap by squeezing her eyes shut.

"Did she have them?" asked Mamá. I brought the bag into view as my reply. "I'll go brew this with the masking," she said and I heard her walking briskly down the stairs.

"Viktor says you owe him 500 rhyians," I said to Rowley. I didn't add that she gave me the masking without being asked. Even I knew I couldn't afford to lose Rowley this early in my training. If Viktor and The Cat were partners, I needed to keep Rowley and Mamá away.

"I owe Viktor a lot of things. Money is not one of them," he said sardonically. "Chief of which would be a bite for colluding with that feline."

"How did you—?"

"Before I had to silence her, Meiri told us her suspicions. I can't prove it, but I have a feeling it's true. And I understand why you felt you couldn't tell us...although it was foolhardy of you," Rowley said. His voice was oddly gentle—as though his reprimand wasn't wholehearted. I thought about the conversation I'd overheard in the woods and the Mythosian envoy mentioning an agent. Was it Viktor, in which case was she working for them under duress?

"Thanks, I guess. I thought I couldn't risk it, but there's something else you should know. Actually, there's a lot you should know," I said. I told him about the wild mirror ride, my flight above Canto as air and how Viktor wanted a shell as payment.

"If that's true and she is working with Cat, we have a bigger problem than I realized," he said in a hush voice.

"More? What now?"

"Cat knows about the shells, too. I told him all those years ago."

MAMÁ AND ROWLEY THOUGHT it best to keep Meiri away from her house tonight, while she was taking doses of the tamp root. Lita figured out a way to distill it and make the dose more concentrated. Working from that recipe, Mamá made a dark brown liquid that smelled something like old socks and from the looks Meiri gave us, tasted worse. Mamá also gave her sips of Lita's Dreamless Sleep tea as a chaser. After three cups and four doses she fell asleep in my room.

Mamá took this opportunity to go to the herbalist and replenish some of Lita's stores of herbs and Rowley wanted to get back to Mrs. Haro. In the meantime, I decided to let Meiri sleep and went downstairs to the sitting room to read and decompress.

Rowley's revelation that he'd told yet another acquaintance about my cowry shells added another dimension to this problem. Celeste and Rex had had access to Power, but not their own inherent magic. Celeste had tapped into her daughter's awakened magic, which was as unsteady as my own. Rex stole the cowry shells but hadn't counted on them being more tied to my will than his demands. Now I had to contend with a cat who had both magical objects and inherent magic with the will and wit to use both. I couldn't see my way to a working solution, but I hoped one of the books Mamá had given us would hold a clue, reveal a weakness we could use. At the very least I needed to find Blue's horn.

My eyes were starting to cross after an hour when I heard the door open.

"Hey, are you busy?" asked Zavier. He looked more tired and a lot cleaner than when I saw him last. His ice ball uniform was long gone and in its place was his KM uniform.

"I thought you had the day off?"

"So did I, but the protestors had a different idea," he replied and walked in. I led him to the office and did my best to clear all the books before he could see their titles.

Ever the gentleman, he helped and skimmed some of the more interesting books. "*The Cat-tastrophe*? What's this? Is this about what Meiri thought she saw? It's like an epidemic."

"Something like that, but don't change the subject. What protestors? What epidemic?" I asked taking the books from him and stacking them on the desk. I was relieved the journal of *The People's History* was upstairs.

"Canti, for Universal Magic, are protesting new measures from the Academy to curb our use of mirrors. There were a few threats, nothing too dangerous, but enough to keep us all on alert," he said, sitting down heavily on the couch and rubbing his face. "I was in royal council meetings most of the afternoon, which reminds me, where was your mom?"

"She had other things she had to do. Maybe next time I'll come in her place?" I suggested jokingly. Zavier didn't respond and I wondered if his silence should worry me. "What's this about an epidemic? An epidemic of what?"

"Can't we talk about something else? I have an hour before I have to head out to my post, and I really wanted to spend it with you. What was your day like?" he asked, pulling me onto his lap.

"Boring...quiet—nothing to tell. What about you leaving your ice ball team?" I asked, averting my eyes. I hated lying to him, but I still didn't know how to broach the subject. Not only was he a KM, but he was a prince of the ruling house. How could I ask him to keep my secret when he felt such a sense of duty?

"Who told you...? Let me guess... Arch, right?"

"Does it matter?" I slid off his lap to the couch and folded my arms. How could he worry about someone as inconsequential as Arch when there was a crazy Cat on the loose, perhaps with the Jabberwocky or Viktor as a partner and Meiri upstairs, coming down from her trip 'round the bend.' Then again, I couldn't blame him for not worrying about things when he didn't know anything about them.

"Sorry. You're right. It's just... Forget it," he said.

"Forget what?" I asked, turning back to him.

"I wanted to have a hassle-free visit... Wait, that came out wrong. I mean I just wanted to spend some time with you away from all the madness out there." If only he knew the madness was in here, too. "But, I'm glad you ask questions and want to be involved. Arch's right... I'm going to join the KM team. After I was named heir, things have gotten...tense at work.

"Podkin never liked me joining the KM and now he's starting to turn some of the men to his way of thinking. It's hard enough being a prince, but throw in future king and it's ten times worse. Some of the KM think it's not my place to put myself in harm's way if it means we'll lose the next ruler of Canto and others think I was never cut out for being a KM in the first place. Now I I'm forced to switch shifts all the time, so I can make it to council meetings and manage my other royal duties... I don't want to be treated any differently," he said with a sigh.

"I hate to point out the obvious, but you are different and when you're different, people are bound to react...differently to you," I said, but it wasn't just Zavier I was talking about.

"Well, I'm hoping that joining the KM team will reconnect me with the KM who I work with and that way I won't be any different."

"But you love being captain and Podkin's son is captain of the KM team. He won't do you any favors," I said.

"Exactly. I'll do well on merit alone. Besides, being captain of the royal team was never that great. Most of the players are like Arch—they don't want to get their uniforms dirty and they leave all the hard stuff to me. Men like that aren't going to miss me, they'll just miss what I got them," he said.

I knew what he meant. Ice ball had no special equipment other than long pants and long sleeve shirts and shoes that protected their feet from frostbite when kicking around a ball made entirely of ice. However, the royal team players, having the backing of royal funds, were given specially made uniforms from Mythos that kept everyone toasty warm. All except Zavier. It was yet another reason I loved him and another example of both Canto and Mythos looking the other way when magic and commerce were involved. I even knew the smuggler who procured the uniforms from Mythos.

"Zavier, one day they'll all be your men...the KM and the 'Arches' and that's what makes you so different," I said. I held his hand and squeezed. He looked so lonely at that moment, and I couldn't tell him that I knew exactly how he felt. He smiled a tired smile.

"Well, so long as you're there to keep me from getting too big for my crown, I suppose I'll avoid most mishaps," he said, squeezing back.

"I'll always do that, no matter what happens," I replied with a laugh.

"What do you mean? Inez, how am I ever going to accept being king if I can't even convince you that you'll be Queen?"

"Zavier, let's not—"

"Stop. You have no idea how much I'm going to need you, do you? You're so brave and forthright and honest. The way you befriended Meiri, how you worry about Toman, and put up with my irrational jealousy. One day you will make an excellent queen," he said and hugged me tightly.

I felt like a fraud. I could only hear what he was leaving out. I befriended Meiri unwillingly and at times ungraciously. I hadn't checked in on Toman and his mother in days. And I was the reason he had something to feel jealous about when it came to Arch. The most damning was him calling me honest. He pulled back and looked into my eyes.

"What's with the face?" he asked.

"What face? Nothing; I'm fine," I replied, shaking my head.

"You need to learn how to take a compliment, especially from me. How about this?" His hand entwined in my hair and he pulled me in for a kiss. It was sweet, delicate and asked for nothing in return. It felt wonderful to allow myself to think of nothing, just to feel. The kiss continued and slowly deepened, like kindling being consumed, bit by bit.

His hands left my face and made their way down to the edge of my sweater. I felt him teasing it away from my body followed by his hand on my bare flesh. We were sliding down, laying on our sides on the couch, facing each other with eager hands and hungry mouths.

I grew bold and let my hand stray between us searching lower and lower as his hands did the same. It was our new dance. Absence didn't just make the heart grow fonder, it made lusts intensify. I couldn't think; I couldn't breathe. I just *wanted* and so did he, which is why we never heard the door open.

But we did hear Mamá standing there, clearing her throat.

Chapter 15

"Good evening Zavier. I understand I missed a council meeting," said Mamá with a face that was unreadable. It innerved us both.

"Lady Filomena... Mrs. Garza... I... I'm sorry. I..." stammered Zavier. Self-consciously he combed his hair with his fingers and straightened his uniform. I thought it was sweet that he chose to stand in front of me while I fixed myself, like a man taking on a firing squad. I almost laughed, but Mamá's face kept me in check.

"Breathe, Zavier. The council meeting?" she asked again. With pursed lips she looked annoyed. Only I knew that meant she was holding back a laugh.

"Um... Yes the meeting. I can send you the notes. It's about the protestors coming tonight," he said still shaken, but gradually regaining his composure. He continued to block my mother's view of me.

"The queen was kind enough to send me that information via messenger and if I'm not mistaken patrols were asked to arrive early. Perhaps you should...?"

"Yes... No... Inez?" He looked back at me with such a look of panic I nearly lost it. If I laughed now, so would Mamá, so I just nodded my head. After a deep breath I was able to mouth the word *go*. "I'll see you later?"

It was a question and with a well of uncertainty underneath. I nodded again and to make sure he was okay, and I gave him a kiss on the cheek. He started but recovered enough to say his goodbyes and leave. Then Mamá and I both laughed.

"That's a nice young man, but really Inez you shouldn't—"

"Mamá, nothing happened," I said.

"I thought so too, but that's before I saw the state of your blouse," she said with arched brows. I had forgotten it was untucked and askew and felt my face redden a little. "You don't want to give Hortensia, Eugenia, or any of the others on the council who disapprove of Zavier's choice—a reason to say you're unsuitable," she said, sobering.

"Mamá, I spend so much time worrying about...about everything. This is the one normal part of my life. Just relax and trust me," I said, fixing the cushions on the couch. "And Zavier and I are adults."

"You are not just normal adults. You're the future king and queen of Canto. I'm sorry *nena*, he can't be here when I'm not," she said fervently.

"You can't be serious? You're constantly away and we see each other little enough as it is... Mamá be reasonable," I said. Mamá had been okay with this just days ago. *What's changed?*

"I know that if something were to...happen, he would take care of you, but do you really want to become that girl he had to marry? Think about Queen Hortensia and the rest of the court," she said, and I could see her worry and knew she was thinking of herself not much younger than myself, unwed and pregnant.

"I'm not... We're not... Zavier is not Rahd and nothing is going to happen," I said and saw the hurt in her eyes, but I didn't know how to take it back. "I should check on Meiri. She's due for another dose." I went upstairs and found Meiri sitting up in bed. My room was unusually neat and had stayed that way longer than expected. I'd learned that Meiri had a tendency to putter.

Despite having a myriad of servants in her own home she'd done a remarkable job cleaning up my room. Even the clods of dirt we'd traipsed in were gone. I now found her trying to sketch my chinchilla. Cochi seemed to like the attention and her small head swiveled to me as if to say, "See, some people know how to appreciate beauty."

"I take it Zavier is gone?" she asked. Her voice sounded normal even if her eyes still had purple smudges underneath.

"You should be asleep," I said, grabbing pillows and blankets from the closet. I intended to sleep in the herbals room to give Meiri some privacy. The teapot was already full of Dreamless Sleep and the jar of tamp root was next to that on my desk.

"Let's just say I woke up... Give your mother a break," she said.

"Meiri, you know me and you know Zavier and—"

"And I've seen the way you two look at each other. Is it any wonder she's a little nervous? Not that I know," she said a little wistfully. "Mother never had a chance to catch me and Jacque and there's been no one since. I've seen the way she's scolded the Green Girls when she catches them with Arch. I hope she never catches me."

Still, she sounded sad as though it wasn't even a possibility. "Your mom was actually rather nice about finding the two of you in a state I can only imagine." I thought about Zavier's clear discomfort being caught and Mamá saying nothing to him or to me about our dishevelment.

"I guess, but can't I have one thing that no one else needs to monitor? I feel like a child," I huffed. I could hear the whine sneaking into my voice and I hated how petulant I sounded.

"Who's Rahd?" asked Meiri.

"Oh...no one. Time for your medicine," I said and turned to fix the tea.

THE NEXT MORNING, I still hadn't heard from Zavier. Mamá must have been scarier than I thought, but I was still annoyed. *How could the man who stood in front of me, blocking my mother's view, be afraid to even send a messenger?* I was frosty to Mamá as she offered to take Meiri through the mirror to Green Gardens.

"Sure," I said with ill grace. "*Ouch*!" Meiri had found the perfect spot between my ribs to poke, and hard.

"Thanks, but I feel fine," said Meiri without a trace of remorse.

"I'm sure you do, but perhaps it would be best if I talked to your mother about why you were here overnight," she replied, stifling a laugh.

"Yea, wouldn't want her getting the wrong idea," I said. I couldn't help the slight sulk that crept into my tone.

"Meiri, whenever you're ready," she said, unfazed by my mood. She left us in the kitchen to our own devices.

"Inez, stop being such a grump," whispered Meiri.

"You have no idea—"

"No, *you* have no idea. Have you even noticed that my mother hasn't bothered to look for me and I've been gone more than twenty-four hours! I would love to have a mother that cares enough to intrude—mine just gives orders," she said, her face a flushed pink.

"*Humph*," I muttered, but softened. Mamá wasn't intrusive, but if I had been gone as long as Meiri had been she would have sent out all of Canto to find me. I was really angry at Zavier for not sending a note or calling on me, but Mamá was available for my hurt feelings and annoyance. "How are you feeling, really?"

"I don't hear music if that's what you mean. Honestly, I'm glad your mom offered to take me. I'm in no rush to face the outside alone," she said. Her pallor had lifted, her coloring was back to normal, but her eyes still had the haunted look of someone who had been chased. I reached out and patted her shoulder. She responded with a watered-down smile.

"We'll figure this out. We always do. I'll go see Rowley and see what he says. At the very least I can get some more practice in," I said. Meiri's fear solidified my resolve to learn as much as I could to keep everyone I cared for safe.

We collected Meiri's medicine along with more of the masking agent. It smelled like green apple candy on its own and Mamá explained that it was a natural animal repellent. Meiri worried her mother would find it offensive and I bit back a remark about female dogs, but I saw how relieved she was to have some sort of defense. Soon after they left, I made my way to the *Cup & Board*.

MRS. HARO WAS DOING brisk business by the time I arrived. It was good to see the cafe returning to normal. Quite a few of the patrons broke off conversations to watch me approach the counter.

I felt an odd tingling sensation rushing up my spine that had nothing to do with my Powers. I got the distinct impression that I was being discussed. That belief was confirmed when I saw mingling looks of pity and anger directed at me. Mrs. Haro saw me and rushed out to embrace me.

"Oh sweetie. I'm so sorry about all of it. This morning I had half a mind to scold you for leaving my Rowley alone to tend the shop, but after hearing about the accident I didn't have the heart. Are you okay? Would you like something to eat?" she asked, still holding me fast to her chest. I had to struggle to break free.

"What are you talking about? Are you talking about Zavier?" I asked in confusion. The mingling customers were listening with bated breath. Mrs. Haro covered the perfect O of her mouth with her hand. I heard whispering behind my back, and it didn't sound friendly.

"Vultures, all of you. We're closed for the next hour. Go gawk somewhere else," she said, shooing everyone out. I heard a few squawks of protest, but none gainsaid Mrs. Haro. In her own way she was formidable.

After turning the sign and locking the door, she brought me over to the cup marked "Breaking News."

"Now I think you should read this without an audience," she said, but stood right next to me as I read the contents:

"Important Item...the peaceful demonstration by the Magical Return Movement at the Academy of Natural Studies has become a riotous mob. The disagreement stemmed from the Academy pushing for more mirror controls in central Canto. The Returners felt it was another ploy to curtail the little magic still allowed in Canto. It is still unclear how the violence was instigated, but confusion took hold, to calamitous effect. Many are reported injured and at least one protestor is dead. Prince Zavier, heir to the Canto throne, was dragged away to the palace by some of his comrades. Eyewitness accounts say he was badly beaten and in need of medical assistance... Other witnesses report seeing a cat wearing boots, leaving the scene, but none can confirm if he was involved or merely passing by... The deceased protestor's identity has not yet been released."

I stood there, stunned into silence. How could I have been so selfish, wondering why Zavier hadn't reached out and knowing he was on patrol last night? I knew about The Cat. Even though I knew it was The Cat's doing, and maybe even Viktor's, I felt responsible. I could have prevented this if I only knew how to control these damned Powers! I didn't trust myself to speak.

"Sweetie, have you heard from Zavier or Toman?" asked Mrs. Haro.

"Toman? What about Toman?" I asked, finding my voice.

"There are other stories from the...last night, and Toman's name was mentioned in one of them. Take a look," she said, handing me another cup, this time from the "About Town" section.

"Some of the demonstrators were available for comment before the chaos, including performer, Toman Tookman, who said, 'I think magic is something we were given, born with, and to deny it is the same as denying a part of ourselves. Not to mention the resources we're denied that could help people. We're here to say we want our birthright.'"

I could just imagine Toman standing up and adding his voice. With all the talk about who should have access to magic, I was sure he was concerned about relations between us and other magical realms that could help his ailing mother. But I also knew he was talking about me when he said it was our birthright. There were more comments from the pro-magic and anti-magic camps that were made before insanity took hold, but the statements were not my concern.

"Does anyone know the dead protestor's name?" I asked in alarm.

"Not yet, but we know the protestor was male," said Mrs. Haro, her words heavy.

I wasted no time and ran out of the Cup & Board, heading for Toman's.

Chapter 16

I hadn't seen Toman in weeks.

After the Ball my life became even more hectic than it had been. I had magic instruction with Rowley, Viktor and Mamá, responsibilities with the KM and working off my debt to the Jabberwocky. I also had Zavier, who had just as little time as I did. It all sounded so flimsy when I factored in Meiri. I'd had time for Meiri and researching The Cat. Why hadn't I made time to see Toman, my best friend.

I thought about what he'd said: "I think magic is something we were given, born with, and to deny it is the same as denying a part of ourselves."

I knew he was talking about me. I had been a terrible friend.

My mind was a jumble of half-thought reproaches and guilt. Even in my decisive movements, in my heart, I dithered. I had to see Toman—make sure he wasn't the one who... I couldn't finish that thought. I forced it back, knowing it couldn't be true. Dottie would have contacted me. But she was sick. Another check on my actions of a neglectful friend list.

The house came into view, but on the horizon I saw the palace looming. Its shadow cast everything in its path in semi-darkness. Bobbing sedately, I wondered at the turmoil within its billows.

He'll be okay... The best healers attend the royal house.

I can't be in two places at once... But even as the thought occurred to me I felt my Powers trying to acquiesce to my dilemma.

No! Not here! Not now! I said that in my head and then out loud. I stood in place, breathing deeply and willing myself to stay calm. The sensation of splitting in two abated, but I knew it was just under the surface. I dashed the last steps to the Tookmon townhouse.

DOORS FOR STAFF AT the palace were recently changed to "recognition doors" by order of Mythos. No explanation was given. The doors only allowed entry to people known by the door and those inside. I considered it unnecessary, but Hortensia was, as ever, happy to acquiesce to Mytho's demands.

When I reached it, the door hesitated to allow my entrance. Even that little dig told me how long it had been since I visited Toman and Dottie. Finally gaining entry, I collided with a new face.

"Whoa...um... Hello? Who are you?" I asked, ready to pick up any object at hand and smash him over the head with it. Standing before me was a tall man, about my age with sandy brown hair and dark blue eyes, one of which had a vivid bruise, who blocked the entrance. A crease formed between his brows before he relaxed his stance and smiled.

"I'm Pablo, Jr. but people call me PJ. You must be Inez. Toman mentioned you tend to be in attack mode," he said, still grinning. Looking down at my hand, I realized I *had* picked something up—an umbrella from a stand.

"Well, PJ, that doesn't answer my question," I replied, tartly. Why did he know me, while I had no idea who he was? More fuel for my guilt fire.

"I'm Pablo Gaitero. My dad runs...ran the Pickled Pepper," he said with a slight catch to his voice. "I guess I'm running it now."

The Pickled Pepper was a bar, which claimed it dealt in holistic spirits. According to the menu, any ailment could be cured with the right drink, although most people who went there had the same problem—too much drinking.

Most healers in Canto discounted the Pickled Pepper's claims and at some point there had been a campaign to shut the place down for "false advertising." It was a Canto institution however, and many people supported its continued existence, especially those who couldn't afford expensive healers.

PJ seemed too young to have been part of that particular fight. None of that explained why he was there. *How did Toman get mixed up with this guy?*

As if he'd heard a cue from off-stage, Toman walked in from the back room. He noticed and studied my stance, still gripping the makeshift weapon.

"I think she's going to need more of the... Inez? So, you two have finally met. Or have you? Inez, put the umbrella down," he advised, walking over. I could see he had an equally prominent bruise on his cheek. He threaded his arm through PJ's and grinned at my blank expression.

Ohhh. Then I understood.

"I really hope that wasn't from the first date," I said, putting the umbrella back in its stand.

"No, that was from last night...at the protest, I mean," he said, just as flustered. "Is that why you're here?"

"I heard someone died and all they were releasing was his gender, but then I read that little blurb you gave the reporter..." I noticed that PJ let go of Toman's arm and walked to the corner of the room. I couldn't prove it, but I thought I saw tears forming before he turned away from us.

"That wasn't me. It was PJ's dad, Pablo Sr." Toman whispered. "PJ stayed here last night after it happened. I've been going to the Pickled Pepper in the hopes of finding something for Dottie and that's how we met. Last night was the first time I met Pj's dad."

"And it'll be the last now because of the KM. My father didn't even want to go to the protest. He did it to support me, finally," responded PJ, bitterly. Toman went to him, but PJ shook him off. "I'll go check on Dottie. You two catch up."

I'd always wanted Toman to meet someone, but I didn't know if I wanted him with someone so angry. Then again, today, the day after his father died, was probably not the best day to judge PJ. I decided to reserve my opinions for another time.

"Sorry about that. He's sensitive about his dad and now they'll never patch up their feelings for each other. PJ wanted to change the way they dealt with healing and Pedro Sr. thought it was just PJ trying to change himself for the palace crowd. PJ is a very talented healer and I think his father was finally starting to acknowledge it. It was a struggle for both of them. It's really very sad. I don't know what I would have done if Dottie had been that way with me and then suddenly died," he said and then I heard the catch in his throat. *How bad was she now?*

"What's going on with your mom? Do you know anything new?" I asked, steering him to the couch. He sat with a sigh, frustration written plainly on his face.

"She's...Dottie. I never know how bad it is because she puts on such a brave face. All I know is that she seems so tired all the time and sometimes she doesn't want to eat. She's just wasting away and no one knows what's causing it. I got so frustrated that I went to see PJ's dad for some 'home remedy' he brewed. It smelled more like rubbing alcohol. PJ thinks he has a better solution," he said with a shrug.

"Are you sure? I remember the healers trying to stop the Pickled Pepper from selling those home remedies," I said. I didn't like the idea of someone giving my friend false hope even if I'd been less than helpful on the subject.

"At least he's trying," he said and the sting of it brought me up short. Something in my eyes must have told him as much and he gave a quick shake of his head. "Not that I'm accusing you of anything. I know you're nervous about using any magic on a person." He whispered the last bit, but I still looked down the hall for any sign of Dottie or PJ.

We'd discussed my figuring out what ailed Dottie using magical means, but I was hesitant. What if I hurt her? What if I killed her? I'd done both inadvertently with my Powers—who knew what intentional magic would do? If I were honest, it was likely the reason I'd been avoiding him. I couldn't stand the disappointment in his eyes. He took my hands in his and squeezed.

"Anyway, what are you doing here? Shouldn't you be mopping Zavier's brow and playing nurse?" he said with almost believable levity.

"I needed to check on you first. Besides, I'm sure Hortensia would love the excuse to send me away. 'Dear Inez, I'm sure you understand but the prince needs rest,'" I said, doing my best imitation of the Queen. Toman laughed which was all I wanted at that moment.

"I'm touched, really. But I'm sure he wouldn't let her send you away. He's the reason I only got this bruise. After fighting off some of his 'friends' he told me he wouldn't be able to show his face at your house if I had been beaten," he laughed.

"Too true. My Toman is precious. Beware anyone who hurts him," I replied and gave him a big hug. It was a relief when he hugged me back.

"I couldn't agree more," said PJ, reappearing. I gave him a look that I hoped conveyed that the sentiment applied to him, too. If he hurt Toman, he would have me to reckon with. His slight smile told me he understood my meaning. "Dottie's sleeping and I should take off."

"No, I'm leaving. Don't feel obliged—"

"It's not that. The store needs tending, and I should get to work on my tincture for your mother. I'll call on you later?" he said, but it was a question as though he was concerned he might get a "no." The notion was touching and all too familiar and all at once, I missed Zavier and wanted to know how he had fared.

Toman walked PJ out and I turned my head discreetly as they shared a quick kiss. I bit my lip, thinking about seeing Zavier and how I would get into the palace.

"I know that look. What are you thinking?" asked Toman, returning.

"Getting up to the palace without an escort," I replied.

"Oh, that's easy. You have a Pandora key and I have a backstage pass, courtesy of Dottie," said Toman with a smile.

IT FELT WRONG LEAVING Dottie alone and taking Toman along for the ride. But he insisted on coming with me. Truthfully, he looked a little relieved to get away from the house and I could sympathize. I'd never taken care of Mamá, but if needed, it wasn't something I would relish.

Even a castle in the clouds made of clouds needed something as mundane as a service entrance for all those men and women who kept the palace clean and working. Dottie was one of those people and while I knew there was a water elevator, I should have known the queen wouldn't have workers using the guest entrance.

Toman brought me to the rear of the townhouse at the basement level. I was surprised to see a retractable iron fence embedded in a brick wall. A slight draft blew in from under the fence. It was a good thing I hadn't known about this at my early days in the hidden market. Toman gave me a pointed look as though he knew what I was thinking. He cleared his throat and did his best Dottie impersonation:

"Ms. Tookman needs the elevator," he said in a passable falsetto into a brass horn that connected to a tube on the side of the fence. A voice crackled to life from inside the horn.

"Today's password?" it asked. Toman frowned and put the horn down.

"You don't know the code?" I asked.

"There's never been one, except on the rare day they lock down the palace," he said. My pulse quickened.

"Why would they lock down the palace?" I asked. Toman shook his head.

"Password?" the voice asked again.

"Foxcart," said a voice from behind us. Toman and I both spun around and saw Dottie on the stairs. Little Dottie, with her rich brown hair and a sparkling smile had always been full of life and fierce. The woman before me was diminished as though all the light had left her. Her frame, always slight, was now delicate in a way that made me gasp. Toman went to her immediately.

"What are you doing out of bed? Do you need anything?" he asked, taking her hand gently in his. He wrapped his other arm around her waist, but she backed away.

"I'm fine. Whatever PJ gave me is working and the password is foxcart," she repeated. "You should go see the prince. The last I heard, he wasn't doing well." Toman came back to my side and Dottie gave a sad smile.

"Toman, you should stay here," I said.

"No, I'm just going to make sure you get in, that's all and then I'll come back. Mom, will you be okay?" he asked.

"I'm not going anywhere. Stay with Inez," she replied and went back upstairs. I felt Toman's hesitation, but before I could encourage him to stay he called back into the horn.

"Foxcart." The whoosh of the elevator descending brought more cold air into the room. Toman lowered the horn and opened the gate. “If anyone tries to stop you, I can say we’re picking something up for Dottie. Let’s go.”

Will they notice our intrusion? Maybe walking in with Toman, a person with a known association with the palace, would be enough. I doubted any guards would challenge me, but there was that possibility.

It was too late for worries now. We were at the gate, but luck was improving. Arch was on patrol.

Chapter 17

It was reassuring to see the gates and a familiar face manning the entrance. But the face wasn't as I remembered it. Arch's left eye was swollen shut and a scab was forming on the corner of his bottom lip. What really left me speechless was the look on that bloodied and bruised face. He was pale and frightened.

"Arch? Are you okay?" I asked. It was a stupid question, but I was at a loss as to how to start our conversation. Usually, he took care of that. The last time we saw one another he was flirting with me and baiting Zavier.

"Hey, how did you get here? There's-s a block on the entranc-ce," he said with an accusatory look. It was hard to take him too seriously with his split lip that caused him to lisp.

"We have a key...or better said, my mother does. It let us in," Toman said hastily. I was still staring at Arch's mangled face and unconsciously reached for his cheek. I caught myself and shook my head.

"Does Zavier look as bad as you?" I asked. He flinched at my tactlessness.

"What she means is, how is Zavier?" fumbled Toman. At that, Arch looked so lost and helpless I ran toward Zavier's apartments.

"Go! I'll stay with him," Toman, called after me.

A CLOUD STRUCTURE ABSORBS sound, but it still felt eerily quiet. I found no one patrolling or challenging my advance. My mouth was dry and all I could think about was how thoughtless I had been to get upset about him not coming by or sending a messenger. I soon found his room and heard voices from within.

"Xander, do you understand what I'm telling you? I need you to pay attention," said an exasperated Queen Hortensia. I could almost see her staring at King Xander imperiously. All I wanted to see was Zavier. I felt my frustration being channeled into my power and a small voice said, *Weid. Weid...Weid...WEID*

My palm started to burn and my vision blurred. I put my hand against the coolness of the cloud wall and was shocked to see through it. Beyond the wall was a clear picture of a bed with a sickly figure sleeping. Standing at the foot of the bed was the queen and King Xander was staring out a window. I yearned to reach out to the shadowed figure in the bed.

"Xander, listen to me! Your brother is dying. The doctors say they can do no more. He needs your help," Hortensia said as though to a simpleton. Despite the situation, the queen held on to her regal dignity. Her gown was less formal than the ones she usually wore when she held court, but no less rich. Lines of worry etched her face.

The king was still staring out the window as though he hadn't heard anything Hortensia had said. I was fighting back hot tears at the thought of losing Zavier. It was an impossible thought. Just moments ago, I worried that my best friend was dead and now my...my...

"Xander! You'll have to use your Powers," the queen said in a shrill voice. Xander spun around as though someone had smacked him. His dull, gray eyes and stunned, open mouth belied what I felt from him—magic. I'd suspected the king had magic since the uncomfortable dinner party at Green Gardens when he made the lights flicker, but it was still a shock to have it confirmed. And by

Hortensia. His face took on a hectic color and his eyes widened in disbelief. He advanced on her in three steps.

"How could you even suggest such a thing? I'm so...so... I should go back to my rooms. You can..." His voice was so muddled. It was like the three steps used up all his strength and brainpower. Xander looked so much like his brother, with kind eyes and chiseled features, but something in the set of his jaw set him apart from Zavier. He always had the look of someone holding himself back.

"Xander, focus. You must use your Powers to save him, or the kingdom will go to that peacock, Archibald. Do you know how Eugenia will strut if that happens? Her precious boy king with her pulling the strings behind the scenes. We can't let that happen.

"Xander, I know you're scared but it must be done. I've sent all the guards away and Zavier will never know," Hortensia said, reaching out for him. Xander flinched, but if it was from her words or her tone I couldn't tell. Her hand rested on his cheek and something in the gesture touched him because he stood a little taller.

"Hortensia, my Powers are...are all wrong. I need...something to make them even," he said clearly, struggling for the words. Even as he struggled, he sounded more lucid than before.

"I know. You can use me," she said, and the look of horror returned to his face.

"I can't. Last time... We lost too much," he said. He sought her hand in reassurance.

"We didn't... It wasn't your fault we lost the baby," she whispered. "We could always try—"

"That's not possible. Not anymore," he said.

I quietly wondered about what I was hearing... if his magic had made her barren or if he worried their heir would have magic, too. I always wondered if the king was mad, now I just thought of him as an unhappy person who chose to ignore life. My bigger concern was what I had just learned.

Xander had magic, too. And from what I could gather, it had driven him to some sort of instability. *Was this the person I wanted using dangerous magic on Zavier?* I felt my custodial magic start to tingle. It was the first time it had responded to someone else's danger.

"Please try, my darling. We cannot lose your brother. Our situation is precarious with Faery and Mythos. Zavier has been forming friendships with their envoys. What kind of help do you think Arch will be? Not to mention, promising Zavier to one of their princesses already."

I couldn't believe my ears. Zavier was at death's door, and she was still trying to break us up. I almost punched through the wall to smack her, but Xander moved toward the bed and placed his hand on Zavier. My protective magic rose at the sight.

"He's fading. We must do this now if he's to have any chance. Hold his hand and mine. This may hurt," he said with a voice full of confidence.

"You almost sound like the man I married," she said with a wistful smile. They stood together and I couldn't deny they made a handsome couple.

"I'm still here," he replied. They joined hands and I swallowed when I saw how limply Zavier's hand lay in Hortensia's. A soft moan escaped his lips, and I held my breath.

I felt Xander's magic being raised. It was different than the shells' or Viktor's or Rowley's magic. It was a ragged thing with sharp edges surrounding pockets of great power. I couldn't explain how I was able to sense that, but it was as real as knowing my feet were attached to my legs.

Xander's power didn't pulse, like my own—it started then stopped then started again.

"Concentrate, Xander. Think of your brother being whole once more. Think of your love for him and how you only want to heal him," she whispered. The power coming from Xander became slightly stronger, steadier. He must be a custodial mage. My own was reacting by raising the bubble. I quickly removed my hands, fearing what a bubble of custodial magic would do to clouds—enchanted or not.

"He's coming back to us," replied Xander. His voice was heavier than before, straining with his efforts. The flow of his magic was lessening as was the seal on my protection spell.

"Can you remove all his ills, including his desire for that girl?"

"Hortensia, be serious."

"I am serious. It would benefit us all if he could—"

"Hortensia, enough! I will not waste my efforts on something like that. Let him be," he replied with authority. She pursed her lips and said nothing, but I had plenty to say.

"I am tired. I am going to rest, and you should let him do so, too," Xander said, his voice losing its forcefulness.

Zavier's color was returning, and I released the breath I'd been holding as I watched the rise and fall of his chest. I was so relieved I nearly missed Xander's movements.

He was heading straight for me.

I RAN HALF-BLIND DOWN the hallway. The spell to see was still fading from my hand, making my vision blurry. Standing behind a tall vase I watched Xander, our king and brother to Zavier stumble like a drunkard down the hall in the opposite direction.

I needed a moment to catch my breath and let the spell recede. I was relieved I wasn't nauseous after the protection spell. Either my body was adapting to the bubble or Rowley was right and I was getting stronger.

That got me to thinking about Xander and Austra for that matter. Were we all doomed to madness because of our magic? It was something I'd thought about idly since the encounter at the Academy, but now I saw it was a real possibility. And so was another.

I'd never really thought about children, but after hearing Hortensia and Xander talking, I started to wonder if that was also part of my fate. Would I be subjecting Zavier to a life without an heir, worrying about leaving the kingdom to Arch and whatever Green Girl he decided to marry? How could I face him with so many secrets between us? My hand stung just as much as the corners of my eyes.

I saw clearly then, in more ways than one.

The walk back to Zavier's room was filled with deep thoughts. I was startled to still see Queen Hortensia sitting at Zavier's bedside, clutching his hand and silently weeping. Fingers pinched the bridge of her nose before she looked up and saw me approach.

"Your Majesty," I said neutrally.

"Inez. How did you get up here?" she asked sharply.

"How is he? What happened?" I asked, avoiding the question.

"Nothing, just some scratches and a bruise or two. You needn't worry yourself and stay," she said, dropping his hand as she stood. *Why was she lying?*

"Then why does Arch say differently and look like death warmed up?"

"He's probably just upset about having to break a date, or some such nuisance. He was put on patrol duty this morning...for as much good as it did," she said, more to herself. I wanted to challenge her with the conversation I overheard in the woods between her and the Mythosian envoy. It was just as much her fault Zavier was in this bed as it was The Cat's. Instead I bit back my accusations.

"Thanks for the advice, but I think I'll stay. If you have other matters to attend to, I would be happy to watch Zavier for you," I said, sitting on the other side of him. "I'm not going anywhere."

"I don't think it's entirely appropriate—"

"Hortensia, could you give me some time with my intended?" asked Zavier. We were both surprised to hear him. His voice was raspy from lack of use, but his eyes looked clear. None the worse for wear from Xander's magic. At least so far.

"Zavier, you need your rest. I can let...Inez know when you're up for guests," she replied, shooting daggers my way.

"I think Zavier can manage one guest right now," I replied, shooting her daggers right back.

"I think Zavier should decide what Zavier would like right about now," said Zavier, trying to sit up. I saw his hand reach for his side and let out a slow hiss. Both of us were on our feet to help him, but he waved us off. "I just want a few minutes with Inez and then we should call the healers. Thank you for all your attention and concern, sister."

"You never have to ask me to look out for your well-being, Zavier. I'll return momentarily," she said. The last remark was for my benefit and sounded more like a warning. I chose to ignore it and took her place as she left the room.

"Well my queen, I think that was very well done," he said with a hint of mischief.

"Zavier, don't start..."

"No, listen. Most people are so intimidated by Hortensia—myself included," he added ruefully. "You were fearless." I wanted to tell him about all I'd heard including Hortensia's plan to marry him to a foreign princess, but too much would have to be explained. Instead, I leaned over gently and kissed him.

"Is that all?" he teased.

"I don't want to break you. I can't take much more of this. First Meiri and her...accident. Then Toman and his face from the protest and now you! You can't get hurt anymore, understand? At least one of you has to be fine while the others are in distress," I said. I was embarrassed how close to tears my little diatribe had pushed me.

"Hey, what's this? I just called you fearless and now...? Don't be afraid for me, okay? I'm feeling a lot better than before. Those healers really know what they're doing. I'll be back on patrol in no time," he said, sitting up some more. I saw his jaw lock, trying to keep the pain to himself. He wrapped his arms around me, and I felt even more ridiculous being consoled by someone who'd almost died.

"I'm fine. Don't move so much. By the way, thank you for keeping Toman safe. He told me what you said."

"It's true. I didn't think I could show my face at Árbol Real if I let Toman die," he said, and I couldn't help wincing a little.

"So, you went and got yourself all bloody. For what? Sympathy?" I joked.

"It's working. You stood up to the Queen, didn't flinch when I called you my intended—and you're in my bed," he teased back. I rolled my eyes, but I blushed.

"Well, not for long. I wouldn't put it past her to call the guards on me. I'll come back tomorrow to make sure you're still in one piece. Please try hard to stay that way," I replied.

Before I could stop him, he leaned in and gave me a kiss no sick man should be able to deliver. I half expected to find myself pushed onto the bed, but we heard a throat being cleared.

"There will be plenty of time for that later, Your Highness. For now, let's get you back to fighting form, shall we?" said an older man with a practical air I could only attribute to someone in the healing arts. "Young miss, I promise to return him to you better than ever." He gave me a smile that spoke of a younger man who enjoyed mischief and pretty girls. I smiled back. Behind him Hortensia nearly snarled.

"I'll see you tomorrow, Inez," asked Zavier, but I knew it wasn't a question and it was for Hortensia's benefit.

"Oh, yes, please do. Nothing works better on an ailing system than a young man trying to impress a girl. It's the perfect medicine," said the healer, good-naturedly. "I'll see you up myself."

"Thank you, Mr. Fell. The patient, please," fumed Hortensia and I had to compose my face into blankness, so I wouldn't crow.

Chapter 18

I left the bedroom feeling pretty smug. It was a minor victory, but seeing Zavier like that—helpless and at their mercy—solidified two things for me. One, I had to work harder on my magic to keep those I loved safe. And two, Zavier was one of the people I loved. I didn't consider myself overly sentimental, but a world without Zavier would lack color. I also agreed with Hortensia, much as it pained me to admit it. We couldn't leave the kingdom to Arch.

That was the only way Hortensia and I could be allies because other than that I knew I was in for a fight.

"Inez." Speak of the Devil...

"Your Majesty." I was proud of the fact that my being startled hadn't risen my protective spell. Determination could make me control my Powers. She walked right up to me, invading my personal space. We were of a height, which I'd never noticed before.

"I don't know how you got up here, but it doesn't matter." Her hand grabbed mine in a threatening grip. Her face came in close, menace barely concealed from her voice. "I'm watching you. I think you're a bad idea for this kingdom and for Zavier. I will do whatever it takes to protect the royal house and no upstart will get in my way—I don't care who your family is or who they think they are. The women in your family tend to meet interesting ends," she said in a dangerous whisper. She was like a cornered animal, but what I saw wasn't fierceness—it was fear. What was she afraid of? I knew I couldn't freeze up or feel threatened by her or my magic would flare and give me away.

"This upstart will be here tomorrow and every day thereafter. As for my family, they raised a woman who the future king wants to marry," I said and then leaned in closely.

"And don't think for a minute you've gotten away with anything," I whispered. "Secret meetings with the Mythosian envoy don't stay secret for long and if the heir had died because of some political maneuvering, more than a few questions would have come your way. Your Majesty," I said as calmly as I could.

Turning on my heel, I silently hoped that my outburst would encourage her to back off and not fuel her desire to be rid of me. As I had said more than a few times in the past few days, I was no princess.

Inside I felt my heart pounding in my ears with each measured step. Another thing solidified. I may not like the idea of being Zavier's queen, but I had better start acting every inch of one in front of Hortensia.

I reached the gate, shaking with fury. Hortensia never liked me, and I didn't care. Threatening my family was a different matter. My face must have betrayed the strain because one look at me and both Toman and Arch jumped up from the bench where they sat. Toman grabbed my hand, still trembling and Arch looked like he'd faint.

"Is it...did he—?"

"Inez, are you okay? What happened to Zavier?" asked Toman. I lowered my head to stop the sudden spinning of the world. What was happening to me was more than just a reaction to confronting the queen.

"Oh no. I can't do this. He can't—" rambled Arch.

"No, Zavier is fine," I said, closing my eyes, taking slow, measured breaths. At another time, I would have congratulated myself on having enough control to keep my protection bubble at bay.

I opened my eyes and the world had righted itself again. Slowly, I lifted my head and saw two faces peering at me intently. One was pale and the other looked on anxiously.

"Then why are you—?

"Hortensia. The queen had a private word with me... Several actually."

"Oh," they said in unison and I laughed.

"What happened?" asked Toman.

"I sort of told her off," I replied.

"Good for you."

"I don't know. Aunt Hortensia is quite formidable," said Arch, color returning to his cheeks.

"Well, I've seen formidable before—I can handle that," I said.

THE NEXT DAY LOOMED large with a sky the color of a dusty white quilt. Bitter cold winds cut through me as I walked briskly toward the palace stables. Morning walks were a holdover from working for the hidden market and I appreciated the moments of solitary peace before the madness of the day took hold.

I'd made myself some promises yesterday, and I was now off to fulfill one. Mr. Fell, the healer taking care of Zavier, had sent me a note last night. All it had was his name, a time and *PALACE STABLES* written on it. I was grateful that he remembered me and was willing to get me in past the queen. After yesterday's confrontation, I wasn't in any hurry to challenge her again.

My other promise would wait until later today. I was meeting Rowley by the bay for another lesson. I told him about Xander's powers and Hortensia's threats. He agreed I needed to take more time with my magic. For once I didn't argue.

In the cold air, the stables almost smelled clean. Snuffling in the stalls produced little puffs of smoke. In one of those corners, nuzzling a horse, was Mr. Fell. He was talking to the horse, like I'd seen Zavier do. Reaching inside a well-worn satchel, Mr. Fell pulled out an apple and fed it to the happy horse. When he finished the treat, the horse nuzzled Mr. Fell's hand.

"Sorry, filly. No more today, but I'll be back. Promise," he said, kindly. Mr. Fell moved away and noticed me waiting.

"Well, now I get to deliver two surprises. Hello Miss Garza. Sorry for the early hour, but under the circumstances I thought you wouldn't mind considering the queen is out this morning on state business," he said, taking my hand. "I know my patient will be pleased."

Mr. Fell had eyes the color of molasses and they twinkled with good humor as he kissed my hand. I realized that my assessment of his age yesterday had been incorrect. His happy spirit made him look a lot younger than I'd thought. I put him closer to sixty or seventy, but I still smiled at the gesture.

He tucked the same hand under his arm. "Shall we?" he asked, and I nodded. "Most people don't know this, but there are stairs that go up to the castle. I use them whenever I can—good exercise. Most people wouldn't dare use them because the view can be unsettling. Even I don't use them on windy days, but you strike me as the adventurous type. Here we are."

Mr. Fell removed a key from his satchel and opened a wall that concealed a cleverly painted door in the stables. The stairs were built in a spiral and open on both sides. Not only that, but there were gaps between each step. They were ample, though, and I was glad that Mr. Fell seemed inclined to walk with me side by side with my arm firmly grasped in his.

Mr. Fell's steps were firm and sure, which allowed me to relax and take in the scene. Standing between Canto and the cloud palace. I could see the tops of the taller trees and it reminded me of my air trip a few days ago.

"A wonderful sight, isn't it Miss Garza? I find it invigorating, but I will admit winter is not the best time to climb. I hope you're not too cold," said Mr. Fell, continuing at a nice pace. He did look happy to trudge along with me and I hoped he was in the mood to talk.

"How is Zavier, really?"

"Well, I won't lie to you Miss Garza. I was more than concerned when I first saw the extent of his injuries. There was a point when we thought... Well, he's fine now. Mostly sore and in need of rest. His body will do the rest of the work on its own. It already did quite a bit. His internal bleeding righted itself and all I was left to do was knit a few ribs.

"The human body is remarkable. But I think seeing you will do more good than I could," he said, patting my hand tucked under his arm. "I made you a promise and I mean to keep it." Something in the way he smiled, his twinkling eyes and even his posture reminded me of someone, but I couldn't place it. He made me feel at ease and in no time we'd reached the top of the staircase.

MR. FELL COMPLETED his examination swiftly and efficiently with a steady stream of small talk with Zavier. I sat in a chair next to the window, watching Zavier's reactions. I saw every quick intake of breath and clenched jaw as Mr. Fell redressed Zavier's bandages. By the end of the exam, Zavier looked slightly pale and sweat dotted his forehead.

"I'm done here, and I think you're healing nicely. I would say another few days and I can take you off bed rest. All that walking worked up an appetite. I think I'll find my way to the kitchens. Should I ask for something for you, Your Highness? Miss Garza?" he asked packing up his tools.

"No thank you, Mr. Fell. And Hortensia isn't here. You can call me Zavier," said Zavier, easing himself against the pillows. His smile was warm, but I could see what all the movement had cost him. His energy was waning.

"Are you sure you shouldn't have something after all that?" I asked genuinely concerned.

"Inez, I'm—"

"Yeah, you're fine. Can you have the kitchen send a sandwich or something? Mr. Fell, doesn't he need food to get better?"

"Mr. Fell, can you tell her that I was able to heal myself without needing a sandwich?" he said smugly.

"I know enough that I am not getting involved. I'll leave you young people to visit...but not for too long," he added apologetically. Discretely, he made his exit, but I saw him chuckle and shake his head as he left.

I tried glaring at him, but the sight of him struggling made me soften. I knew I was no better when I was sick or hurt. Now I knew how Mamá felt when she had to nurse me.

"Now that we're alone, can I have a real hello?" asked Zavier, settled on his pillows.

"I don't know where to touch you. Where do you hurt?"

"Where don't I hurt? My face is fine and so are my lips," he said with laugh. I was reluctant to sit next to him after he had been manhandled, albeit gently, by Mr. Fell. I sat on the corner next to his pillows and kissed his forehead, still damp with perspiration.

"Now I know I'm not dying if I'm getting forehead kisses. My lips are down here," he said. His hand found my face and pulled it in for a repeat of yesterday's kiss. Even with all my hesitation, I couldn't help but respond and I felt his other hand entangle itself in my hair. His kisses were slow and passionate, stirring sensations in me I was finding hard to ignore.

The angle was starting to get uncomfortable and I tried edging away to end the kiss, but Zavier had other ideas. He sat up and I felt the intake of breath from the effort. With both his arms around me, he drew me back down with him. I was scared to touch him for fear I would injure him more. But his kisses were so insistent and made me melt.

We were laying down, facing each other, kissing as though we would drown otherwise. I hazarded a hand on his leg, letting it rest there lightly. His hand found its way under my sweater. It was déjà vu, but this time my mother was not coming home to catch us.

Instead, we were caught by the king.

Chapter 19

The unease I was feeling had nothing to do with where Zavier's hand was placed. That made my mind go fuzzy and want to ignore common sense.

But the feeling was something external. It kept insisting I notice something. I pulled away from Zavier with a sigh.

"What? Sorry, was I being too...?" I looked over Zavier's shoulder and saw a torso with arms crossed over a soft chest. Up close I saw what I couldn't before. A face I loved, but older and with a world-weariness that would stir anyone's pity. It spoke of longing and regret, but the owner of the face was still silent and staring directly at me.

"I just came to check up on you, Zavier," said King Xander with a raised eyebrow. *Did everyone do that?* "I thought you were resting."

"Um...I was. I thought you were with the queen at the council meeting," said Zavier sounding abashed. He pushed himself up with effort and again blocked the view of me while I unrumpled myself. Sadly, there was nothing I could do about my blushing. Now I knew how Zavier felt being caught by my mother.

"No, I...no. I haven't been feeling well. I was concerned you were bored being alone and cooped up, but I can see you are...entertained," he said and turned to leave. I didn't like being referred to as a diversion. My cheeks were hot with more than embarrassment.

"Xander, you know Inez. She was...checking up on me, too. It was my fault you found us like this. I apologize Inez," he said solemnly, facing me. I could see the king fighting back a chuckle, but sobered before Zavier turned.

"Remember Zavier, only we can control ourselves and I would hate for Hortensia to have any more objections to your choice. I can only do so much," he replied, all mirth evaporated. Xander sounded so much more composed than he had yesterday. It wasn't quite the voice of the man who commanded respect from Hortensia, but it also wasn't the man who stared out a window trying to ignore unpleasantness.

"I'll see Inez out while you rest."

The idea of being alone with the king was not something I relished. His moods were so changeable. What if I said something to trigger his Powers? Now I knew why Rowley was so concerned about me. *Had the queen told him that I may have overheard their conversation or seen him use his magic? Or did he know about Hortensia's involvement with The Cat? Did he approve?* I didn't know if I could fight against Zavier's brother and then face Zavier again.

Zavier's face was set as he squeezed my hand. He wasn't cowed, but he understood the sense of what his brother was saying. I could see the king he would become, and I was suddenly filled with a sense of pride.

"I know you have work to do with the KM, but I hope I'll see you tomorrow," he said. It wasn't a question and I remembered reluctantly that I had been sent a summons to appear at KMHQ tomorrow. Had I mentioned it to him or was he being kept informed? With effort and a jaw so tight I thought he might shatter his teeth, he stood up.

"I'll walk her to the elevator." I wanted to stop him, but I knew he was proving to himself as much as to his brother, that he was equal to any task. Stopping him would have hurt his ego, and I wouldn't do that in front of Xander.

We walked slowly and silently. His concentration was completely consumed by his effort. I was glad the floors were made of clouds, which made it naturally absorb the shock of his steps. Little beads of sweat were forming on his forehead regardless, and after ten steps started to trickle down his jaw. He held my hand casually, but I walked closer to his side in case he tumbled.

I was doing some hard concentrating of my own. My Powers were itching to help him and keep him safe. I kept chanting in my head, *he's fine*, but the evidence was walking unsteadily beside me.

We finally reached the elevator without incident. I looked down the long hallway we had just walked and wondered how he would get back to his room.

"Don't worry. It makes you frown," said Zavier. He laughed, but it was a brittle sound. His hand was lightly holding his side and his face was pale again.

I didn't want to leave. I kept imagining him falling, half-way to his room and his brother finding him near death again. He would use his magic and with no conduit he would only succeed in killing Zavier. I felt my panic start to solidify in the pit of my stomach. *Not now, not here!*

"My goodness, the young are remarkable. I thought it would be another few days before you were out of bed. Didn't I say a pretty girl was the best medicine?" chirped a cheerful Mr. Fell. He strode over and smiled at both of us indulgently, and discretely checked Zavier's pulse.

"I think that may be enough for today, though. Let's get you back to bed and then I will make sure this charming girl returns to the ground safely."

"Thank you, Mr. Fell. I can manage on my own, but I would appreciate it if you brought Inez again tomorrow," said Zavier. His voice was weaker, and I had to clench my stomach to keep the protection spell at bay.

"Of course, of course. But I should go back to your room anyway. I need to make sure I brought back all of my instruments. Be back in a jiff," he winked at me. He kept pace with Zavier, chatting affably the entire way. Zavier kept his answers short, but Mr. Fell filled in the silences like a pro. I barely knew the man, but I could have kissed him for his kindness. We both knew he didn't leave anything in the room, but the deception kept Zavier from having to walk alone.

As they entered, I saw Xander leave. He looked down the corridor and stared at me for a minute. His face told me he was considering something, and I hoped he wasn't thinking of talking to me. My queasiness wasn't full blown, but I knew I didn't feel safe yet. If he approached it would be difficult to keep my protection spell away. But then Mr. Fell emerged and Xander took off in the opposite direction.

"Your young man is quite a marvel. But with such an incentive, I can see why he's so anxious to mend. I took the liberty of checking his bandage and no harm was done. I also alerted the kitchens that he needs to eat, so no worries there. Shall we descend from the clouds?" he asked with a chuckle.

His mood was infectious, and I immediately felt better. Without thinking, I gave him a hug.

"Oh, my dear. Thank you for that, but your spell is still lingering a bit." I stepped back so quickly that I fell to the ground. He immediately grabbed my arms and pulled me up. "No harm done. And no need to worry about your secret. Your grandmother and I were old friends. We ran in the same circles because of our healing work and discussed you quite a bit. And, of course, the Society. You remind me of her. Now, shall we go?"

"I CAN STILL REMEMBER her explaining calmly to King Xander's grandfather that she thought it was silly for nobles to disdain having a vocation. 'Your Majesty, would you want to be a useless noble if you couldn't wear the crown?' She was about your age when she started petitioning for all Canti to have an apprenticeship of some kind, no matter how highly placed the person.

"Sabrina wanted to be a healer, like me, but no one would take her on. I let her look at my books and then she started reading up on herb lore and then your grandfather came to town." He laughed at some private joke. "He had no idea what he was in for, but I was glad they found each other. They were such a pair." He smiled, lost in thought and I didn't want to intrude on his memories. It had been so long since I'd heard anyone call my grandmother by her given name. I'd grown used to Mamá calling her Lita as I did.

Mr. Fell's home wasn't that far from Dottie's as were most of the royal retainers' homes. It was smaller than Dottie's, but then Mr. Fell lived alone and didn't seem to need much to be content. In the corner was a picture of him as a young man and he was quite handsome. There was a woman in the picture, too. When I enquired, he told me it was his wife and his smile turned wistful.

"She and Sabrina were great friends. But Sabrina and I were best friends. We understood each other," he said, and I knew just what he meant—it's how I felt about Toman. No one got me the way he did, and I liked to think the feeling was mutual.

We sat there for about an hour while Mr. Fell told me stories about his adventures and misadventures with Lita. I loved to hear about seventeen-year-old Sabrina. I missed her, but now I also missed the part of her I never knew.

"I'm sure you want to know about the Society for a United Enchanted Isles. It ended abruptly when your mother thought it was becoming too dangerous for you. We all agreed, but your grandmother was dismayed that you wouldn't have access to all that knowledge. She wanted you to be prepared for what was ahead," he said and took a sip of tea. Something in the way he moved kept reminding me of someone I knew. “But I promised her that when the time came you would be as determined as she was. I wish she were here now so I could tell her I told you so.” He grinned.

“Well, determination isn’t the problem. It’s more about the ability—but I have tutors, sort of. It’s all getting rather complicated,” I sighed. Sharing all my trials felt like an imposition, but not with Mr. Fell. Still, it was too much to explain.

“You mean Rowley and my sister? They’re a good start, but Sabrina always said your abilities were innate. Remember to trust your instincts, like you did with the king,” he said.

“Your sister? Do you mean Viktor?” I asked. He was the first person I’d met who knew she was a woman and now I knew why his mannerisms looked so familiar. He reminded me of Viktor playing the role of a man, clearly trying to emulate her brother. For a moment I remembered I didn’t know anything about this man other than his connection to Lita and now to Viktor. My time at the hidden market had taught me to question anyone’s motives especially when they so readily offered up unsolicited information. And yet, I trusted my instincts with Mr. Fell.

“Yes, she’s my baby sister. It’s because of growing up with her that I knew the signs of magic on the king. She was taken away when we were both young, but it still left an impression. At least she was spared the imbalance King Xander sometimes displays. I’m sorry to say she’s become cynical and chosen some paths I wish she wouldn’t, but she’s stubborn and convinced she knows what’s right. Her problem is that she feels the ends justify the means. I would be careful there,” he said with sober earnestness.

I could barely believe that this happy-go-lucky man was related to Viktor Lake. Did he know about The Cat and everything that had been going on? I had a suspicion he did.

“What about the king? Do you know why his magic is unstable?” I asked.

"Yes, I'm the court healer. I have to care for him when he has his...lapses. In truth he's a sad man burdened with something he can't handle. In so many ways," he said as an aside. *Did he mean kingship, his magic or something else?*

"As his healer I can't say more, but I would be careful there, too. Inez, you are a remarkable young lady. The prince chose well with you—I fear you both have your work cut out for you," he said. Placing his hand on mine, he smiled a sad sort of smile, and I could recognize the gesture. It was the same one Lita used to give me in quiet moments, but I'd never known what they meant. Now it all made sense. "Have you told him about your magic yet?" asked Fell.

"Speaking of work, I have an appointment with Rowley to practice. Are there any funny stories about him or was he always this dour?" I asked avoiding his question.

"Not as a dog, but maybe when he was a man. By the time we met him, he was very serious. A product of his profession," he said.

"He was a man?" I asked, incredulously.

"Of course. He was another side effect of the Great Working. Someone had to be around from that time who could instruct the one who would solve the mystery of the shells. He was a powerful sorcerer in his day. Didn't he tell you? Well, I get the feeling he doesn't like to talk about it," said Mr. Fell with a shrug. "If you ever need help, I am always here, although I can't help you with your magic."

I covered the hand that a moment ago had covered mine. I wanted to know so much more, but I knew that Rowley would not tolerate lateness. I gave him my thanks and left with a lightness I hadn't felt in days.

Chapter 20

My life settled into a routine for the next few days. I spent my mornings with Zavier, who was being almost formal with me. Clearly what his brother said had made an impact. His feelings for me hadn't changed, and I knew his desire hadn't either. One day I caught him uncharacteristically talking to my breasts. On the upside, neither the king nor the queen made any impromptu appearances.

My late mornings I spent an hour or two talking to Mr. Fell. He told me about the Society for a United Enchanted Isles, its members and anything he could remember that they uncovered. Sometimes he would just tell me stories about the scrapes he and Lita got into when they were kids. He never spoke of Viktor, which was telling in itself.

Afternoons were dedicated to practice with Rowley. In the beginning I spent an inordinate amount of time trying to not think of him as a human being. He barked at my inattention until I asked him about his "other life," but he made it clear that it was a closed subject. After that reprimand, I buckled down for real study.

I tried calling on Toman before the sun went down because he was always with PJ in the evenings. I never realized how annoying it was trying to find your friend only to get a reply that he was about to step out. Mostly I was happy for him, even if PJ had seemed too intense and broody for my liking.

"WHAT'S WITH ALL THE water magic?" I asked, standing at the edge of the bay. It was covered in vapor hanging there like frost.

"Concentrate! Now think of warmth, heat, summer days—the blasted sun for all I care—but get yourself warm," growled Rowley. We'd been doing this for over an hour and his patience was beginning to match my frustration level.

"Maybe if you told me why we're doing this, I could get it faster," I pleaded and hated the way that sounded. He turned in a circle, acting so dog-like that I almost laughed. I didn't know if he was going to take a nap or if I had to get a baggy for clean-up.

"Do you like being cold, Miss Garza?" he asked with controlled vehemence.

"Are you serious?"

"It's a perfectly valid question considering your progress. Do you like being cold?"

"No, as a matter of fact," I said and sneezed as if my body wanted to punctuate the point.

"And why is that, do you think?" he asked patiently.

"Because...because...it makes me feel numb and pained all at the same time. Like I'm trapped in this feeling and nothing I do can make it go away."

"Does it remind you of anything?"

"I feel..." And then I remembered. A flash of a cane. The honeyed voice from a breathtaking face with murderous intent. Being driven to my knees without an ounce of control. The pain and the numbness.

"Well?" he asked.

"Yes," I said and felt the slightest flush of warmth. I could almost wiggle my toes.

"Miss Garza, you are a magical being. It is part of your essence; your soul if you will. And when a magical being faces another its magic seeks to suppress your own. It tries to suppress your soul and it hurts like nothing else. Power is making your will real, and when in combat—"

"Combat? Who said anything about—?"

"You silly girl. What did you think you'd been doing all this time? You've been fighting in battles. And until now your only will has been to survive, but that's not enough in war," he snapped.

"War?" I repeated dully.

"Stop interrupting me, especially with such inane questions. This is a war for your will and for us all. You've been on the defensive, but now you must learn the offensive. Have you never watched your intended play ice ball?" he asked.

"He's not my—"

"He doesn't just kick when a ball is passed his way. He must judge when to strike and when to step back. He must be ten steps ahead in order to control the ball. Perhaps being engaged to a prince has made you think you're just a princess," he growled.

"I know I'm not a princess," I replied, defensively.

"No, you're not. You are a warrior and I have to make you into a general so we don't all die," he said with an odd catch to his voice. He almost sounded compassionate.

"So why all—?"

"Water magic is the hardest magic of all. Water can dilute a spell, so you must reinforce your will to stand up to its Power. Some foolish story from the Mundane has a witch melting, just from a splash of water. Complete nonsense of course, but it has its root in truth. Water can sap you of your will, if you let it. If you can master it, you can master any magic thrown at you. Celeste didn't know you were magical until it was too late. Austra will not make that mistake."

"Austra? She's in Faery with her own kingdom. Why should I worry about her?" I asked.

"If you don't know why you should be worried, maybe you're less of a warrior than I thought," he said, and it stung. My body finally started to produce more heat, enough so I could feel my feet and my nose thawed.

"Good. Now let's try again and this time walk further out," he said.

Hours later, dripping wet and annoyed, I arrived home at least knowing I need not worry about the cold. After hours of practice, I'd learned how to make myself warm with my will. It would be handy for the cold winter nights, but I couldn't think of any other reason this skill would help me against The Cat or others. What I needed was more information.

IT WAS MY LAST DAY performing community service for the King's Men. My semi-engagement to Zavier, suddenly made my time with the KM in that capacity, objectionable. However, Hortensia didn't want to fully acknowledge my new standing at court, so she devised another way to keep me under the watchful eye of Chief Podkin. I was to become the palace liaison to KMHQ.

After so many unpleasant incidents in the community with KM, especially with the Magical Detection Unit, the Crown needed to be seen as more involved with the handling of magical matters. After the beating Zavier had endured at the hands of his comrades during the protest an intermediary was more necessary than ever.

I could have cleared up the whole affair by telling everyone that it was really The Cat's fault, that it was he who was driving everyone mad, but that would lead to more questions than answers.

The liaison position was a thankless job, the kind of job you gave to someone you really detested. From the KM perspective it meant more royal meddling in the safety of the Canti. The more snobbish element of the court saw it as a menial job, and those already opposed to the KM, and the magical ban in general, considered the liaison an enabler to the Crown and Mythos. It was a job for a seasoned diplomat, the kind that knew exactly what to say to soothe ruffled feathers and frayed nerves.

That was not me.

And yet, it was a relief when I was given a new excuse to access KM records and stay current in their policing in general, but my need was twofold. Mr. Fell mentioned that the healers had been busy of late handling cases of "frayed nerves" and reports of a Cat with a fiddle. To my intense relief none of them had complained of hearing music like Meiri, but it meant The Cat had a whole new way to compel people.

I also still owed Áliz information and warnings if any raids were planned for the hidden market. The arrangement was far from ideal, but it was a deal I struck to keep everyone safe and alive.

I opened the door to the Paddock, headquarters to the King's Men. It may have been my imagination, but lately it seemed as though the normal din quieted when I entered. No one made eye contact, but that had also been true when I'd been sent there to do my community service. The only ones who did look in my direction were Cleph Sigrada and Lucas Mixtel, both of whom stared with varying degrees of disdain or loathing. Leonor Abreu, the one who would have been disposed of by Áliz if I hadn't made the deal had left the KM's service for parts unknown.

At the far end of the Paddock there was a group speaking in hushed tones and gesticulating madly. One of them mimed bowing a violin. Another one said, "It was a cat."

I'd left the uniform at home, opting for something I'd wear for a day out with Toman or Meiri. I steeled myself for a coming confrontation, seeing Podkin's solid wood door closed. I would have preferred to look through files for information and stories about The Cat and scurry back out but being unobtrusive was not the way to handle this abysmal assignment. I knocked then turned the doorknob without waiting for a response.

"Did I say...? Oh, *you*. What errand are you on now?" barked Podkin. He was just as chloric as ever, his face a hectic red, his ill-fitting uniform straining at the sleeves, as he sat behind a desk he dwarfed with his heavily-muscled bulk in a room that smelled like a distillery. He didn't frighten me in any way other than concern he might keel over from some fit of pique, and I'd have to revive him. His unrestrained antagonism toward me was unrelenting and new to me.

Hortensia and her faction at court veiled their hostility. At the hidden market, any animosity was usually specific, like a smuggler bested you at a deal, but there was always another deal. Podkin hated me because I was the daughter of a noble, and dating a noble even though I wasn't titled.

I represented a nebulous area he couldn't understand or penetrate. I irked him and no amount of condescending cordiality or gruff bravado on my part would change that.

"Today I start liaising with the KM and the palace and I thought the best way to accomplish anything was to make myself more familiar with your files," I said as pleasantly as possible.

He sneered. "You didn't need to before, so why should you now?" he asked. I could have pointed out that I had started with files, only to be scolded by him that they were none of my business. I tried another approach.

"The royal court is keeping Mythos at bay by promising to share any pertinent information about magical incidents with them as they happen. However, Mythos wants to know when the trouble really started and if a pattern can be detected," I said, smoothly delivering my cover story. "If they don't get something to keep them occupied, they may decide to replace you and your officers with Mythosian agents. Which would you prefer?" I asked, although we both knew it wasn't a question.

Podkin harumphed and threw up his hands in surrender.

"Don't expect my officers to be dragooned into paper pushing while you gallivant with the heir apparent. You want files, you look for them yourself," he said. It was the closest I would get to acquiescence, but it gave me a moment's pause. The last time I'd rummaged through his precious files, he'd been apoplectic. *What's changed?*

"I wouldn't think to presume. I just need a place to look over the files and take notes," I replied.

"Why do you need to take notes?"

"Unless you'd rather I take the files home with me and then take them to the palace and whatever Mythosian representative is assigned to this? Then they can make their own notes," I said. He blanched at the thought.

"I'll find you a room, but don't expect palace finery," he grumbled.

"As long as it's not a prison cell," I said, and he narrowed his eyes as though it had been his exact thought and I'd robbed him of an excellent joke.

A KM-in-training showed me to a cramped room that may have been an overflow holding cell with no windows, the smell of stables and a permanent chill, but it did have a light, a chair and a desk. And I had free access to all the files.

I knew I needed help. Finding information to send to Mythos in order to keep my cover story while I searched for information for Áliz in addition to learning as much as I could about the last time The Cat was presumably involved in Canti affairs, was more than one woman could handle.

I briefly considered enlisting Betlindis' help. She had proven to be a first-rate researcher and had already wrangled files from the KM. I also knew that working with her would be awkward because Betlindis couldn't seem to help herself when it came to asking me questions about the night her father disappeared. My options were limited, as was my time.

A stack of wooden crates was wheeled into the cramped space. Pushing them was Cleph Sigrada of the Magical Detection Unit. He was tall and muscularly built with stern features and a neatly worn uniform. Not that long ago he was on a hit list for the Jabberwocky because one of her paid KM informants had been feeding sensitive information about the hidden market to the KM. Although I'd proven that he had not been the mole, I'd still made sure his debt to Áliz was cleared as part of my deal with her. I'd also learned during my investigation of him that he had a sister, Theoda, who was being protected by Birthright, or had been until they disbanded.

"Thanks, Cleph," I said, and he directed a short nod at the floor. I wanted to ask him about Theoda but asking him here wasn't safe. She was only fifteen and I knew he was very protective of her and her martial magic. "How's... How is your family?" I asked, hoping he understood what I was really asking.

"They're fine, thank you," he replied carefully. His brow furrowed and he pushed the crates off the cart with little effort. He moved to take the top box off the other two but stopped and instead closed the door. "Have you heard anything?" he whispered. His blank mask fell away, and I immediately regretted asking him anything that may have given him false hope.

"No, but I know that Rowley made sure everyone went somewhere safe, especially the younger ones," I said and hoped it was true. Rowley had sent some of the members of Birthright to Faery, where the magic ban was less strictly enforced. But others, with stronger magic, had been sent to the Outer Isles. There, magic couldn't be patrolled, but the region was lawless, and piracy was a way of life for many. I also knew that Rowley had kept every members' destination a secret to protect them and their families.

Cleph shook his head and began to pace, forgetting about the boxes and likely, my presence. He flexed his fingers into fists and then out again. I tentatively reached out and put a hand on his arm and he stilled. I didn't know what I could say to reassure him but was spared from the attempt by a loud crash from the other side of the door.

Cleph immediately shook himself back into professional mode and swung the door open, with me right behind him. A fight had broken out in the middle of the Paddock with a uniformed KM wrestling two civilians out of each other's reach. The group I'd seen speaking in furtive whispers were now yelling at the top of their lungs, each at a KM, and a woman was banging wildly on Podkin's door.

Cleph ran at the woman, and I was surprised to see substantial divots in the heavy wooden door. Over the din I heard the soft strains of a violin and just as suddenly it all stopped. The violin, the yelling, the fighting all ended. For a brief moment everyone stood silent, looking to their neighbor with bewildered expressions.

The silence was shattered by Podkin, barking orders and directing in unsubtle language that anyone not in uniform was to leave or get thrown in a cell. I took my cue and left as unobtrusively as possible.

THE NEXT MORNING STARTED without fanfare. I'd heard nothing about the incident at the Paddock and no mention was made at the *Cup & Board*. My search for The Cat had turned up no sign of him, which was just as well because I had no way to stop him yet. Nevertheless, I'd searched well into the wee hours of the morning and had collapsed, cold and exhausted in my bed.

I was surprised that my body had voluntarily woken up so early. Every part of me was sore from wading in the freezing depths of the bay. I decided my early morning was worth sitting in a tub for a bit to properly thaw my muscles.

I tested out my new ability to warm myself, a skill I had forgotten while tracking The Cat. A pleasant flush spread throughout my body and I ruefully thought of all the cold nights I'd spent hunting for some object for the hidden market—not knowing I had this ability.

Mamá was humming in her room. It had been a while since I'd heard that sound. Not since all this shell business started had she sounded so carefree. It was the perfect moment to pounce.

"Mamá? Are you busy?" I asked, entering her room.

It was a stark contrast to my perpetual mess. A large blaze burner crackled happily in a sconce above her desk, which had been cleared except for a sheet of blank paper and a pen.

"Not at all. You're up early," she replied.

"I'm meeting Meiri this morning and she has a bad habit of starting her day when the sun comes up. I think it's a gardener thing," I said, sitting at the edge of her bed. There were open books surrounding her as she leaned against the pillows. Her jet-black hair was loose and cascading down her shoulders in casual disarray. The scar from her fall down Fae Range was plainly visible.

"What are you researching?"

"I was looking into The Cat thing. Cross-referencing Beval's notes with Lita's and anything else I can find in my library. I think there are some more books at the library, but I have an appointment to speak to an expert this week in Faery. I hope they won't cancel," she said, furrowing her brow.

"Why would they?" I asked. I didn't miss she avoided connection with my eyes.

"No reason. Just thinking out loud. So, what's up?" she asked, with forced cheer. I could tell there was a story there, but I wanted to keep her in a good mood before making my proposal. I'd been talking about it with Mr. Fell for the past few days.

"Well, what do you think about reviving the Society? I know I have the notebook and you and Rowley, and now Mr. Fell, but I think we should be prepared for anything. These days with The Cat and maybe Viktor up to no good, it makes sense to have reinforcements," I said.

Mr. Fell had told me all about the goals of the Society for a United Enchanted Isles. Their charter wasn't exclusive to bringing back magic, but also wanted to have true collaboration between the isles for information. It was something I imagined would have appealed to a librarian like my mother. Her face was set without expression, and I hoped it meant she was really thinking it over.

"The Society is what made this situation so dangerous. Too many people knew about the shells and soon they all would have known about you. We can't take the chance that you'll be discovered, *Nena*. Enough of us are involved to make sure you stay secret. Did you say Mr. Fell?"

"Yes, he's taking care of Zavier and we started talking about...Lita and the Society." I didn't want to mention him knowing about my Powers. I had the feeling Lita told him against Mamá's wishes.

"Do you know who he's related to? Viktor. Did he tell you that?"

"Yes and he seems to like Viktor as much as you and Rowley do. Stop worrying so much. I need to arm myself with information. Isn't that what you've always said?"

"The information I gather, doesn't usually endanger *my* life. I just want you to be careful about what you share with him. *En Guerra avisado, no muere soldados*," she chimed. I wanted to say that plenty of soldiers die in announced wars, but I knew that it was the principle for her. I held back a sigh.

"Exactly why it would be great to have the Society back. More soldiers means it's less likely anyone dies," I reasoned. I could see we were at an impasse. I needed reinforcements and I hoped Rowley would see my side of it. She might relent if he liked the idea.

"I'll think about it. That's all I can promise."

"Better than a no. I should go get ready. I'll be in the tub if Meiri shows up..."

"Inez? Are you awake?" I heard from the hallway. It was Meiri.

So much for my relaxing morning.

THIRTY MINUTES AND an unsatisfying shower later, we were traipsing through the center of town. I'd called on Meiri yesterday to help me sort through the filing mess at KMHQ. She had been reluctant, but braved leaving home in order to learn more about The Cat, namely how to stop him.

Although it was early, it wasn't too early for shops and eateries to be open. However, the streets were emptier than usual. Some of the doors had homemade signs asking patrons to knock if they wanted entry. Meiri darted glances up any alleyway we passed. Her normally buoyant gait was muted and she stood very close to me.

"Meiri, how are you?"

"I'm fine, just fine. What was that?" A door had slammed.

I looked across the lane to a man offering an apologetic shrug.

"Oh, I don't know. People, doors, horses—take your pick. We are walking through the center of town, Meiri," I snapped. And I immediately regretted it. She had every reason to be jumpy. "Sorry, I think I've been spending too much time with Rowley. His personality must be catching," I joked, but I saw her eyes still darting. "How are you, really?"

"I'm fine...mostly fine. It's the first time I've left the house, actually," she sighed. Her body lost some of its tension making that admission.

"Are you serious?" I felt even worse snapping at her. Walking to my house, no matter how close it was, had been a real act of bravery on her part.

"Well, mother decided I should stay in the house after the riots, and I didn't disagree. How is Zavier?" she asked.

"On the mend. He's returning to patrol today in a restricted capacity, but I'll see how much that sticks. I think I was more affected by it than he was. Stop jumping. Maybe he lost interest and moved on," I said. Neither one of us needed to elaborate on who *he* was.

"You're a terrible liar, Inez," she replied.

"Oh, yes? How long before you knew I had Powers?"

"Even you can't make that lie stick," she said and indicated the half-empty streets and darkened businesses. Two men walked by us quickly, more quickly than was necessary for a leisurely morning. "He's out there, lurking, waiting..."

"You're going to scare yourself. Anyway, I've been practicing and I'm getting better at making my magic happen deliberately," I offered.

"Really?" she asked, incredulous. I tried not to take offense. "Have you figured out how to get rid of him?"

"No, but I can keep myself warm in cold weather," I replied. Meiri's reaction was less impressed than I would have hoped. "Rowley said the last time he defeated The Cat he used the horn of El Niño Amoratado."

"But that's lost, correct?"

"Yes, and it's a shame because I need something that can amplify my Powers. Rowley seems convinced I'm strong enough on my own," I said, moving to the right to avoid a slushy puddle.

"If Rowley says that, he's probably right," she replied. "He doesn't strike me as the type to throw around compliments."

"I hope so because I think the riot was The Cat's doing," I said casually.

"What? The Cat caused the riot!" she shrieked. I quickly clamped my hand over her mouth.

"Want to say that louder, or maybe share with the world that I'm a magical fugitive?" I whispered and removed my hand.

"Sorry. Inez, are you sure?"

"I read the cups and some of the witnesses mentioned hearing music."

"That's it. I'm moving in with you," she said and stopped dead in her tracks. The Paddock came into view, but it wasn't the reason Meiri had grabbed my wrist so forcefully.

I followed her line of sight and at the end of the street was Jacque and he wasn't alone. He'd also spotted us. After the scene Meiri had caused at the Egalitarian Ball, albeit at my urging, I assumed Jacque would turn the other way. Instead, he headed in our direction. Meiri turned her back and spun me with her, but we didn't move.

"What's the plan here, by the way?" I asked genuinely curious as to how this would all play out. I'd already noticed that the woman in Jacque's company was the same one from the ball.

"I... There isn't... Oh, h-hell," she stammered and turned right back around just in time to nearly collide with Jacque. It was odd seeing Jacque in the daylight, like an owl that got lost. He was still scruffy, but with a dancer's grace—ideal for the acrobatics he employed for his day job and his night one too.

His eyes deliberately stayed on my face, but it was comically apparent to everyone present who he really wanted to look at. Meiri plastered a banal smile on her face and avoided looking at Jacque or his lady friend, the effect being that she had to stare at me.

The lady in question also avoided looking at Meiri so I had three sets of eyes watching me intensely and no way to extricate myself from the situation.

"Hello, Inez. I was hoping to run into you. There's a piece of music stuck in my head and I think it would be perfect for my next show. Could I see you later and work on the timing?" he asked, saying the phrase we used when we needed to talk hidden market business around those who weren't marketers. The phrasing was unfortunate, considering Meiri's over anxiousness about The Cat and his diabolical fiddle playing.

"Music? What music?" asked Meiri, forgetting that she was supposed to be ignoring Jacque. He forgot as well and addressed himself to her directly. His date grimaced.

"Sometimes Inez helps me with my music for the shows. And it's a strange one this time—4/8," he said and I knew it meant four hours after the market opened at the Remembrance Tree. Meiri looked puzzled but said nothing.

"Are you okay?" he asked with such earnestness that I was surprised he hadn't reached for her hand or caressed her cheek. His date noticed.

"That sounds good. Meiri and I have an appointment to keep," I said and dragged her away with as much dignity as I could give her. Meiri didn't struggle and she didn't look back. I felt Jacque's eyes on us nonetheless.

"That was...something," I said, not knowing what to call that interaction. Meiri took a deep breath and straightened her spine.

"If only I had known how all this would turn out, I think I would have avoided Jacque altogether," she said with little conviction. I patted her hand.

"But you can't. I know it's a touchy subject for you, but I think you two should try again. It's almost as good as going back in time," I said and the flash of an idea made me stop. Meiri stumbled at the suddenness.

"Well, that's not entirely true," she quipped.

"And the events can't really be revisited unless...unless you revisit them."

"What? What are you thinking, Inez?"

"I'm thinking I know exactly what I need Rowley to teach me next."

Chapter 21

We arrived at the Paddock with me brimming with unconcealed smugness and Meiri looking perplexed by my demeanor. It was with a shock that we both nearly collided with what looked like a wall of KM standing outside KMHQ. Despite their uniforms and thick wool coats, none of them looked pleased or warm. One grim-faced officer stepped forward with a raised hand.

"No visitors today," he said. He took in both our appearances and smirked. My previous buoyancy vanished, knowing I was going to have to argue my way through with Meiri at my side.

"Lucky for us we're not visitors," said Meiri. I inched in front of her, hoping she wouldn't continue her thought. I knew any minute now she would inform the officer that I was not only the prince's girlfriend but also the liaison, neither of which would endear me to him. As it happened, she was beaten to the punch.

"That's Inez Garza—you know," said another officer, stepping forward and loudly whispering in the first officer's ear. The second officer gave me an apologetic shrug when the first one shushed her. I wasn't in the mood for this.

"Look, tell them I hit you when you weren't looking," I said to the patrolman and simultaneously grabbed Meiri and pushed through the line of KM to the door. I swung it open before anyone had a chance to protest and then Meiri, bless her heart, pushed it closed.

The inside of KMHQ looked relatively normal other than fewer people were present. I attributed that to the line of officers standing guard. There was only one sign of the previous day's disruption, and that was Podkin's battered door. It was being replaced by another door that leaned against the wall next to it, but that also meant Podkin was overseeing the installation. Or he had been, until we walked in.

"This is not a café or a museum. We don't have visiting hours here," he snapped as he stomped in our direction. Meiri remained calm, but I sensed her tense at his tone. I kept my acerbic comment to myself not wanting Meiri to bare any of the repercussions. He had no power over her, but she was jumpy enough as is.

"You told me none of the officers could be spared for my assignment and the number of files I have to review is more than I can do alone. My friend, *Lady* Meiri, was available to assist. The faster I get this done and leave, the better. Don't you agree?" I watched him react to my using Meiri's title. His face at first betrayed his annoyance, but he shoved that aside for terse resignation.

"That may be, but we are not prepared for outsiders to be here today," he said, his tone oddly conciliatory. I looked at Meiri and briefly wondered if I could always take her with me when I had to speak to Podkin.

"Did something else happen yesterday? After those people—" I began, but was stopped by Podkin's glare.

"Nothing happened yesterday other than a few suspects becoming unnecessarily agitated at the thought of being detained. It was a minor matter," he said with a smoothness that sounded like he'd had to say that more than once.

"So it had nothing to do with The Cat and his fiddle?" I pressed and felt Meiri stiffen next to me. Podkin clenched his jaw before taking a deep breath.

"There is no cat or fiddle or anything else. Just. Agitated. Suspects," he said. "Now please leave."

"I left some things here yesterday before the something that never happened happened. I'll just get them and we'll leave," I lied. It was easy, but just to make sure he didn't question me, I grabbed Meiri again and moved swiftly to the back room. Before I could close the door, Lucas Mixtel pushed his hand against it.

"I'm here to make sure you leave quickly," he said and stood, keeping the door open with his body and crossing his arms. I hadn't really thought about him much since I was able to get his debt to Áliz paid. From the way he glowered at me I knew he still blamed me for his daughter, Damaris, who now went by the name Dam, getting mixed up in the hidden market even though I had effectively saved his life.

I ducked behind the desk and retrieved a few odds and ends from my bag and made a big show of finding them and replacing them in my bag. Meiri stood by the crates and lifted a lid before Lucas slammed it back down.

"I don't know why they think we need a liaison. We already sent tons of files to Mythos," he said, staring Meiri down until she backed away from the crates. I vaguely remembered that Lucas Mixtel was a KM file clerk. He mostly handled the front desk and took statements from people, so of course he knew about the papers I was researching.

"What do you mean?" I asked, with dawning comprehension.

"Some liaison you are. The order we got from the royal house was to send all those files directly to Mythos. Anything that mentioned magic and was more than fifty years old. What more do they want?" he asked, but it wasn't a question. Meiri and I left under the watchful eyes of Lucas and Podkin.

"THE RETURN OF THE CAT was Hortensia's doing. And Mythos helped her, but I don't know if they did it officially or if she convinced someone from Mythos to help her," I said without preamble to Meiri. As I walked her home, I noticed that the streets were even emptier of patrons but they'd been replaced by patrols. For someone who said there was no cat, Podkin sure had a lot of people out searching for something.

"What do you mean?" asked Meiri. The patrols seemed to make her less jumpy, but her eyes retained that haunted look. I told her about the conversation I'd heard in the woods between Hortensia and the Mythosian envoy—and my suspicions that Mythos would benefit from uncontrolled magic in Canto causing the royal house to ask for help from Mythos.

"Of course the files are gone. She sent them to Mythos the second she decided to ask them to use The Cat. Then nothing could link her or Mythos to the event," I said and lowered my voice as a patrol passed us.

"What about the files Betlindis has? Wouldn't she take those too?" asked Meiri.

"No, it would look suspicious if everything related to The Cat disappeared. What Betlindis found was mostly assumptions and half-formed ideas about The Cat and his mischief. The confidential KM files are the important ones with real information," I said. I was sure I was right. Hortensia was many things, but stupid wasn't one of them. She'd sent the files away and now I had nothing to learn from them. Knowing that, strengthened my resolve.

"YOU WANT TO DO WHAT?" asked Rowley, but it wasn't a question—more like appalled incredulity.

We were in the kitchen practicing one of my many words of Power. Even Rowley admitted it was too cold to practice at the bay, but I thought it was more for his benefit than mine. Today was *bheid,* to split and *gleubh,* to tear. I'd been using *gleubh* to crack the eggs and *bheid* to divide egg yolks from egg whites. Rowley said it was an excellent way to practice precision and control and even laughed at his own pun. He wasn't laughing now.

"I want to go back in time and find out what happened to the horn. I've done it before," I said reasonably. I didn't add that it had been the cowry shell that had taken me back to the past to meet the architect of the spell that helped me regain my inherent magic because he already knew that.

"Correction, the shell did it before and for a very short while. It's not as easy as you think. Do you remember how hard it was for you to control a heat spell in the water?"

"And now I can boil water if you ask me. Didn't you say water magic was the hardest? And that I was very powerful? I can do it, I know I can and I'll bring you with me so I'll know what to look for on that day," I said. I'd thought this out carefully. I could just go back to the time The Cat first started up with his fiddle, observe what happened to the horn and thus know where to start my search in the present. It made perfect sense.

"It's a terrible idea. Besides, I can't go with you," he said with bitterness. "I am a being of borrowed time and cannot tamper with it. If I go back to that time, I may get stuck there. I don't know how someone like me would disrupt time." He said it as though it were an argument he'd had many times with himself. I wondered if he'd considered going back to the day he was turned into a dog.

"Well, I'm not on borrowed time. I can still go and—"

"You don't understand time spells, child. Going back or forward is borrowing time that wasn't yours to have. It means you'll have to pay for it later. At your age you see your whole life ahead of you, but what if you were meant to die before your next birthday? Whatever time you spent outside of your own time would be taken from you at the end of your life. You spent minutes in the past last time. Who knows how long you would have to stay in the past to ascertain where the horn fell.

"It was a long time ago and I don't remember the exact day I confronted The Cat. That time you borrow may be the time you need to finish something we're starting now. It's too risky and time travel should only be used in extreme emergencies."

"I think we're almost there. Meiri can't leave her house without an escort. Toman was almost pummeled, and Zavier nearly died because of The Cat's interference. The streets are empty, and people are scared. We both know he came back here for a reason. I can't stop him without the right tools and I'm not strong enough yet. We don't have the time to waste," I pleaded.

I could see the idea taking root in his mind and he was fighting it. He knew I was right even if he didn't like it.

"Miss Garza, impatience will be your downfall or the downfall of one of us," he said, but it was half-hearted. I saw the refusal flicker and dim in his eyes. "But some of what you say is true and it may be worth finding the horn. I need to prepare a memory spell so I can give you as exact a time and location as possible. I should warn you that memory spells are rarely foolproof and more fool I will be for trying it, but it's all we have."

"Are they dangerous?"

"In a sense, but not the way a time spell is. Memory spells are subjective because they're based on a person's mind—which isn't precise. In those days I was a bit of a...let's just say precision was not my goal. It works better when you have multiple people who had the same memory because then the spell can infer what really happened from many minds, but besides The Cat, I'm the only one with a memory of that day. And El Niño Amoratado." Then he muttered something I didn't quite catch.

"What did you say?"

"I said, I'll need your help. And then I can help you with your time spell," he said grudgingly.

"Sure," I said with surprise. "We're partners."

"Miss Garza we are far from being partners, but I begin to believe that you are my pupil."

"TAKE US WITH YOU," said Toman. His face lit up at the prospect. With his fading bruise, he looked rakish. Clearly almost getting beat up agreed with him in a way I hadn't anticipated. It also worried me. This had to be PJ's influence. I'd only met Toman's new love interest once, but the impression PJ gave me was someone who liked conflict. Toman seemed to be feeding off of that. Both he and Meiri had come by after my lesson and were happily helping me make *merenguitos* with all the egg whites. The egg yolks I set aside for a *flan*.

"No thank you. I know better than to go traipsing through the woods at night. Especially, to see *her*," chimed in Meiri. She refused to mention the Jabberwocky by name. Somehow Meiri and Toman had converged on my house and we were baking and drinking mugs of hot chocolate while I told them about the past few days.

I also told them about my plan to travel back in time and that I needed a particular something from the Jabberwocky to do it. While Toman had perked up at each twist and turn, Meiri looked as though she wanted to hide and forget her part in any of it. Frankly I was surprised she'd even left the house.

"Don't worry Meiri, I'm not taking you, or Toman so you can forget it," I said, looking pointedly at Toman. Downing my last sip of cocoa, I collected their mugs. I frowned and looked at Toman. "Didn't you hear Meiri's story and everything that's happened? It's not safe."

"No kidding, which is why you shouldn't go alone," replied Toman.

"On this I have to agree, Inez. You shouldn't go by yourself," opined Meiri. When the two of them got together it inevitably ended up with them ganging up on me about something I shouldn't do on my own.

"I'm not going alone," I replied, keeping my back to them. I knew that wouldn't be the end of it, but I hoped no one would ask my plans. That hope lasted only a moment.

"Rowley is a good choice, but I have a feeling you mean someone else," said Toman.

Trust him to read between the lines.

"I'm going with Jacque," I said, trying to avoid Meiri's eyes. Nevertheless, it was impossible to avoid her reaction.

"Did you not want to tell us because of me? I am well aware that you and Jacque have a relationship. I am concerned that you'll have to use magic in front of him," said Meiri. She crossed her arms reflexively and I didn't know if she was protecting herself from my mention of Jacque or her mention of magic.

"I didn't mention it because it's not worth mentioning. I appreciate all the support you both give me, but this requires someone with my skill set. And the only magic I'll need is the kind all smugglers possess, a keen eye for opportunities."

"What are you getting from the Jabberwocky, anyway?" asked Toman.

"A peer needle," I replied.

"What is a peer needle?" asked Meiri.

"The only way for me to see Rowley's memories from the past and pinpoint where to go is by looking directly at his memories. A peer needle lets me do just that." Rowley had explained the mechanics of using a memory spell and the more he explained the more I knew it wasn't enough. It required time we didn't have and effort I wasn't comfortable making. Instead I told him about the Jabberwocky's prized possession.

"It sounds painful," remarked Meiri.

"It's not pleasant. I've only seen it used once by the Jabberwocky, but that time it was used on an unwilling participant. I'm hoping Rowley's experience will be less so," I said. I did worry I would hurt him, but he'd agreed it was the only chance we had to stop The Cat from continuing to terrorize Canto. The murmurings that, at first, were easily dismissed as fanciful—how often does a cow jump over the moon even in magical realms—were growing louder with small pockets of unexplained violence gripping Canto. The King's Men were spread thin and the streets were emptier than usual. I already had a set meeting with Jacque and I could guess what it was about, so it felt like kismet to take care of both problems.

Meiri and Toman said their goodbyes only after I promised to let them know how it turned out. I munched on some *merenguitos* after they left, knowing it was going to be a long night and the sugar was welcome.

JACQUE WAS WAITING for me by the Remembrance Tree at two in the morning. The tree grew in the center of Canto and was also the place that marked where all the residences attached to the royal house ended and average Canti houses began. The further south one ventured from the tree, the poorer the citizens. Jacque had lived on the outskirts of town, but now lived just opposite the tree—a sign that he'd come up in the world.

To anyone watching, our meeting would look like one woman stopped to look at the tree and a man walked away. Nothing to comment on.

With my new notoriety as the future queen of Canto, I had to be more circumspect in my movements. I'd dressed the way I did when

I worked for the hidden market and walked in the opposite direction of Jacque, disappearing into the night. Or into a magic hiding place.

There was one that existed near the tree and was connected to another near Jacque's old home. It had been one of the many places the hidden market had resided. It had been the Jabberwocky's idea to move the market periodically to keep the KM guessing as to its whereabouts. I walked the tunnel, breathing in musty air and searching the delicate walls for cracks. Jacque had assured me it was safe, but he threw himself off buildings as part of his legitimate work. Our definitions of "safe" were vastly different.

I arrived at the other end alive and hopefully not followed. Jacque was just up ahead.

"This is going to get awkward when you're installed in the palace," remarked Jacque. He closed the opening, which melted into the ground without a trace. I felt the tug of magic from the simple exercise.

"*If* I'm installed in the palace. Many more nights like these and I might not make it to the altar. Zavier will realize marrying a smuggler is not good for the realm and you and I will go back to digging up enchanted eggs for bored nobles." I said it as an afterthought, but the truth of my statement caught me off guard. There had been so many close calls and just as many opportunities to come clean with Zavier.

"I'm counting on you getting a crown so when I'm eventually caught you can save me, so don't talk crazy," Jacque said with a little nudge. "I also figure you're good for a title, should I wish one," he said with mock seriousness. I laughed.

"What do you need a title for? You're already rich and famous. Don't be greedy," I replied.

"I hear they come in handy," he said. It was then I realized he wasn't entirely kidding. With just money and fame, he hadn't been able to marry Meiri. *But with a title?* I didn't know if it would be enough for Lady Eugenia, but she was shallow enough to at the least consider it.

"Is the Jabberwocky at home?" I asked, changing the subject. Jacque nodded.

"She doesn't stay all night. Usually, she heads down to the market hours before daybreak to make sure she's seen. The natives might get restless if they think their Empress is away," he said. She keeps the choicer trinkets in her office. If she does have a peer needle, it's down there."

I considered my options. It had been years since I'd seen her use it. She could have sold it off or even decided to keep it on her person. For all I knew it was with Pao, her enforcer, to use on unsuspecting marketeers. There were so many possibilities and yet this was my only option—to hope I or Jacque could get our hands on it.

"Did you ask if anyone else had one?" I asked.

"Yes, for the hundredth time. No one's seen a peer needle on the market for over a decade. She has one. I've checked the house and it's clean."

"Remember when we thought stealing from the Cloud Palace was madness? This is ten times worse. What are we doing?" I asked.

"I seem to recall us getting out of that situation. And we're doing nothing. You're meeting with her topside so she can call you to task, and you're coming with something so juicy she can't resist coming herself instead of sending someone, while I poke about her office looking for the needle. It's your plan and it's a good one. Is palace life making you skittish?"

"It's making me realize I've been damn lucky so far and any day now it's going to run out. But you're right—it's a good plan."

"So, who's this client you're willing to stick your neck out for?" he asked. I'd told Jacque I had an interested buyer, not because I didn't trust him but because I didn't need all the questions about why I needed it. Also, getting him involved on any other level was a bad idea. Too many people already knew about my Powers.

"You know better. Anyway, it's a contact in Faery and that's all you have to know."

"And the information you're passing on?" he asked.

"The only kind the Jabberwocky can't refuse," I replied. Jacque whistled.

"You know someone with Powers?" he asked, but it was more of a statement.

"Not just one. I'm going to sell her the list for Birthright."

"YOU'VE FOUND A TREAT?" asked Áliz. Treat was the term used for a person who somehow retained some of their magic, despite the treaty with Mythos that had stripped us of it. Treats were a rare find and the most lucrative commodity at the hidden market. Their trade was also despicable. It was the only smuggling I refused to do—putting vulnerable people under the control of other smugglers for money. Anyone exhibiting Powers had to be turned over to the King's Men and then Mythos. The lucky ones found Rowley and were protected by Birthright. The others were easily blackmailed into working for those who could afford to buy them from the smuggler who found them.

"You know about Birthright?" I asked, taking a careful sip of tea. Steam rose up my nose, tickling the inside with notes of spearmint and rosehip.

"Birthright is the worst kept secret in Canto, short of the hidden market," replied Áliz. Her tea stayed cupped in her hands, warding off the chill. The fire crackling in the fireplace had yet to spread its warmth past the grate.

"A better secret is they are my clients. I know hiding places, names and Powers for quite a few of them," I said, holding the cup in my hands against a chill that had nothing to do with the temperature of the room. I had a moment of satisfaction when I saw the look of surprise on Áliz's face. It wasn't every day someone surprised the Jabberwocky.

"Indeed. And now you're willing to tell me about them? Inez, you've made it very plain that you're against the treat trade. Why the change of conscience?" she asked. Her eyes twinkled in the firelight.

"Some time ago I gave you a peer needle," I said and took another sip. Áliz's rich laugh echoed in the space.

"What would Lita say? *Nadie sabe lo que hay en la olla más que la cuchara que la menea,* or something to that effect. You have hidden depths Inez. You're willing to sell me the names of Birthright for the peer needle? I think I can arrange something—"

"I didn't say I'd give you names. I only need the needle for a short while and that entitles you to one name," I said, rising from my seat. If I'd played my hand right, I wouldn't be leaving. I headed for the door, entreating the Goddess for Áliz to call me back or for Jacque to have found the needle by then. My plan was a house of cards—if anything didn't go to plan I was in trouble and part of my plan was Áliz being too greedy to turn down the chance of a treat.

I reached for the handle and turned the knob.

"Inez, I think I can accommodate you. Give me the name and tomorrow I'll send you the merchandise."

"Áliz, one of the first things you taught me when I joined the hidden market was negotiations are fine except when it comes to a treat. Those are never expected and are priceless. Send the needle and I will send you the name. I can even give you her location. It should be a simple matter of contacting the pirates. And Áliz, this is a one-time offer. I still don't like this," I said, not turning away from the door.

"Don't sound so superior. You aren't any different than any other client who explains away any misdeed to get what they want. The difference is, you know how the sausage is made."

I opened the door, still unwilling to meet her eye. "It'll be at your home tomorrow evening." I knew the promise of a treat was too good to pass up, but it gave me no pleasure to save Canto this way. I left before I lost my nerve.

"EXPLAIN TO ME HOW THIS worked again," said Jacque. He handed me a small case. I opened it and ran my finger over the enclosed needle, feeling the magic touching my own.

"Asking for the needle means she'll look for it and when she comes up empty, she can't blame me. I was with her and would hardly ask for something I already have in my possession. And having it means I don't have to worry about her asking what I needed it for." I didn't need to add that alerting Áliz to the existence to people with magic in Canto meant she'd start to hunt them soon.

"And I don't get to know either?" asked Jacque.

"You get to have the needle in a year's time. She's liable to check you for it first because of our past partnership. Thank you for this, Jacque. Really."

Chapter 22

The walk back home was an uneasy one.

Had the plan gone too well? Was this the con that would finally get me caught?

There were few things in this life that scared me and for all the sparring I did with Áliz, she was one of them. No one stole from the Jabberwocky—no one who lived. I still remembered Squirrel taking her rummage stones, which I stole from the palace. When the body had been recovered, I saw the mess Pao, Áliz's enforcer, had made of his face. It was a warning.

I backtracked through the woods—a place that was like a second home to me—but I couldn't relax. I startled at the sound of my own footsteps and retreated from the shadows made by the trees. One tree was particularly terrifying with a clump of leaves creating an odd shape in its recesses. I sidled by it and swore I heard breathing coming from all corners of the wood.

My protection spell snapped into place after I felt a sharp pain blossom across my arm. The gash welled with blood. I gave up all pretext at that point and with the spell ebbing and flowing, I ran. The sleeve of my coat grew wet and cold.

I finally stopped running when my house came into view. The nausea and tightness had receded, but fear was just under the surface. As I drew closer I saw the outline of someone waiting by the door. This time I was ready to let my Powers have full reign, but then the figure turned.

It was Zavier at my door in the hours before dawn.

I stumbled to the door and his smiling face changed to one of concern.

"What happened to you?" he asked taking hold of my hand. It was shaking and bloody.

"I was in the woods and I—got spooked," I said with a weak laugh.

"We have to check on that," he said, pointing to my arm.

"I'm fine. What are you doing here?" I asked more sharply than I intended.

"I have a double patrol and won't be around for a couple of days. I wanted to see you before I disappeared. Let's get you inside and clean that up," he said. I didn't resist, but I hoped he couldn't feel the residual from my spell.

We found a first-aid kit in the herbals room, but the gash was deep. Instead, Zavier found a roll of gauze and wrapped my arm from wrist to elbow. It stung, but I managed to stay quiet.

"You know, it doesn't look like a branch scratch. Maybe it's The Cat," joked Zavier.

"The Cat? What cat? What have you heard?"

"Relax, I was just kidding. Wow, Meiri's really got you believing this stuff," he said, putting the finishing touches on my bandage. "One of you must have blabbed because now everyone's talking about the return of The Cat. That's why I have patrol duty. Everyone's gone nuts. I'd blame it on the moon, but it's not full."

"No, it's a lurking moon."

"What?"

"Nothing. Do you have a partner? You're not going out there alone, are you?" I asked with growing unease.

"We always go in pairs. My partner's Arch now. A little joke by Podkin—thinks I'm missing my old teammates. Anyway, I'll be fine.

This is just cabin fever run amok. People have been cooped up too much."

"You're still trying out for the KM team?"

"If they hold them. When the patrol is over I have tryouts, but with everyone pulling double shifts the whole season may get canceled. Still, I have hope," he said, massaging my arm. His hand strayed down to my waist and he looked at me intently. Our connection was electric, but just as suddenly he stepped away. "I'll earn his respect."

"Wait, you're going to play gladiator two days after recovering from a beating that put you to bed for over a week? Now I see what you mean about everyone going nuts," I said in shock. And they thought I took too many risks!

"I can't ask for special treatment. The queen asked if I could be taken off the rotation and I still haven't heard the end of it," he said with a shrug.

"Well, where's the tryout?"

"You want to come and see? Really?" he asked incredulously.

"I figure if you're going to die from an internal hemorrhage, I should be there to say my goodbyes," I said with a roll of the eyes. "I'll also need a kiss before you leave, if it's going to be our last." He laughed and crossed to me, but all I got was a peck on the cheek.

"I should go," he said, his voice husky. I wrapped my arms around him, refusing to budge. He pushed against my arm and I winced. "You're hurt."

I wanted to remind him that he hadn't minded when he had three broken ribs and pulled me into his bed.

"When do you go on patrol?"

"In an hour, but I have to go pick up Arch and you know how long it takes him to primp," he said, stepping back. He was talking to my breasts again. Zavier's control was becoming an annoying habit. Xander must have said something to get this reaction.

"I know what your brother said got to you, but you don't have to be this guarded with me," I said, moving forward. "I miss you."

Zavier stopped moving backward. The look he gave me held an intensity I'd never seen. It was conflicted. His eyes kept straying to the cot. I could see him caught between his desire for me and his desire to live up to expectations. I thought the latter would lose, but then we both heard something upstairs. It broke the trance.

"I should go. I'll let you know when we have the tryouts," he said, taking my hand. He was so controlled, it was infuriating. I shook his hand.

"Good night, Your Highness," I said and left him in the room. He had enough pride not to call me back and I had enough anger not to look over my shoulder.

I REGRETTED THE TENOR of our parting almost immediately. If he only knew how much time he was wasting worrying about what his brother thought of him. What if he met with The Cat and he got hurt or worse? Knowing our last words were so chilly, it would hurt more than my arm.

Magic was draining, especially when I had to keep it from Zavier. There were times I wanted to blurt it out and other times when I wished I'd never been given my Powers. I felt my energy ebbing.

Maybe Lita had some kind of fortification tea I could start taking. I'd moved all her papers back into the herbals room, and was surprised to find the door open.

Mamá was sitting on the floor, flipping through yet another book and nibbling on an apple.

"I thought I heard Zavier's voice," she said, not looking up.

"Don't worry. Nothing happened," I replied.

"You sound disgruntled—want to talk about it?" she asked turning the page.

"Not really. What are you looking for now?" I asked, taking a seat next to her. I didn't bother to tell her the time. When Mamá found a subject she wanted to know more about, she was relentless.

"Just more of Beval's journals. He kept them even before I was born. I was hoping to find something about the horn. The fiddle belongs to the People—maybe the horn does, too. There's not a lot that's here from Beval's family, but I found an inventory. He had to account for what stayed with him when he broke from the People."

"That's so weird. How come?"

"Oh, they have strict rules. Beval wasn't the first to leave them, but it was still rare to do so. The idea is The People hold things in common and therefore he couldn't keep anything from traveling that wasn't specifically made by him.

"He didn't have much. He had a restless spirit that he resisted when he fell in love with your grandmother. You have some of that, too. What happened to your arm? Did The Cat...?

"No, it was a really dangerous tree that didn't feel I should run past. Can we talk about it some other time? I was hoping to get a look at some of Lita's recipes. Did she have something for—I don't know...building up strength?" I asked, trailing a finger across some book spines.

"A tree? Inez I...I won't ask. What do you mean about building up strength?" she asked with a heavy sigh.

"I don't know. Sometimes when I use magic, it makes me so tired. I can't afford to pass out every time I have a confrontation. It's worse when I have to suppress my Powers. Can you think of anything?"

"I might have something. Actually, it's from Beval's journals. He was an amateur herbalist. When he and your grandmother got together it was a real meeting of minds," she said wistfully. "They were fun to watch when they debated the efficacy of this or that plant."

"Why didn't you become an herbalist?" I asked.

"Why aren't you training to be a librarian? I liked something else. Herbs were okay, but I wanted to know about everything. What better place for a person like that than in a library?"

"I guess, but it's so—"

"Boring? I know it is to you. I felt the same way about herbs. They could spend days hanging bunches, grinding them in a pestle, using the augmenting lens..."

"An augmenting lens? We have an augmenting lens?" An augmenting lens was a rare find. It had to be used in conjunction with another magical object amplifying its efficacy, but I'd never heard of it used with a living thing. It was one of the highest-priced items requested at the market. I knew one was used at the palace to keep the clouds from dissolving, but even smugglers stayed clear of that one because bringing down the entire Cloud Palace would bring too much attention.

"Don't even think about it. Beval and Lita only used it when someone was seriously sick and needed the brew to steep faster. I wouldn't recommend it for your Powers. Plus it's gone missing," she said, getting up from the floor. She dusted herself off and put the book back on the shelf. Removing another, Mamá flipped through another tome.

"Here it is... 'To strengthen the body magic.' It's a simple mixture. I'll whip some up for you tonight. It needs to mature for eight hours. For now, go to bed *Nena*. You look exhausted."

I felt exhausted and didn't argue. I gave her a quick peck and thought ruefully of Zavier before taking myself off to the bedroom.

I WAS IN THE FOREST at daybreak.

In front of me was a brightly colored caravan ambling by. Wagons and carts were pulled by ponies, donkeys and mules. And the music was amazing. I heard instruments playing, voices raised in song, and even the conversations were in rhythm. It made me smile and I wanted to join them. But then a man with a concerned look on his face detached himself from the train.

He was handsome, tall and muscular from a life lived moving on two feet. His jet-black lank hair fell over his face obstructing my view of his eyes. But he moved like a dancer, in time with the music, and his dance was one of confusion.

"What are you doing here?" he asked me.

I don't know. Where I am?

"Can you hear me? What are you doing here?" he asked again slowly, careful to enunciate every word. But I couldn't respond. My eyes relayed my distress and he reached out for me. His hand, strong and callused just missed me, as though an invisible barrier kept us apart.

"The train is leaving, Beval. We have to go," I heard a woman's voice call.

Beval?

Now a woman was approaching and her lithe movements swayed with the music. She wore a smile that spoke of home and comfort, but it changed when she saw me and then her expression mirrored the man's. The man she had called Beval. My grandfather.

"What is she doing here?" she asked in confusion.

"I don't know. I don't think she's really here. I can't hear her and I can't...I can't touch her," he said and demonstrated. The woman frowned, but looked relieved.

"Good. That means she's not really here. Inez, listen to me. I know you're confused, but you have to go back. It's not time yet. Goddess willing, it won't be for a long time. Fight, child," she said with a kind smile.

But I wasn't listening. The music was so beautiful. It rose and fell like breathing and a pulse, like a heartbeat, drove it on. I saw two boys kicking a ball back and forth, laughing, happy. Everyone in the train looked so unafraid. Peaceful. Why couldn't I join them? It would be so easy.

"*Inecita*, listen to me. You must fight this. I know it's so tempting, but it's not time. You have a road you have to travel and it's... I know it's hard," her voice broke a little when she said it, "but you're a fighter, my love. And Filomena...your mother needs you." She dropped to her knees and placed her hand on the invisible barrier. An entreaty—a plea.

I recognized her face. High cheekbones, a nose like my own, chestnut brown hair. She was regal, but approachable. The man wrapped his arms around her shoulders and his hair fluttered away from his eyes.

Coffee brown. Eyes like mine. The eyes of my grandfather. I knew his face, too.

"My little Mother Goose. Return to your mother. Tell her... Tell her she's stronger than she knows. That you get your strength from her," he said with a sad smile. I knew that smile and I had to return it. I felt a stinging in my arm and felt my eyes fill in response.

"That's it. Remember *Inecita*, we love you and we're proud. Go back," said Lita. I felt a small tug at my back. It pulled me away by inches, but I didn't want to go. I reached out, hoping to feel my grandmother's hand—my grandfather's strength.

Eyes like mine. Restless eyes. Eyes with determination.

I kept reaching out and yelling in my head. *Beval! Lita! Wait!*

The stinging in my arm blossomed into fiery heat, blooming throughout my body. I was far away from the train, but I could still hear the music. It was fading, calling, reminding me of home.

"Beval! Lita! Wait!" I screamed and felt hands grab me, pushing me down. Their touch made me grit my teeth.

"I think the fever broke," said a voice. "She'll be okay."

That was the last thing I heard before the world went dark.

MAMÁ TOLD ME I SLEPT for three days before the fever broke. She was in and out of my room and filled in the gaps. My arm had become infected. They knew something was wrong when I hadn't woken up by the following night. I was burning up with fever and didn't acknowledge anyone in the room. She told me all of this over the course of two days, while I slipped in and out of sleep.

On the fifth day, I was thirsty. I stared up at the ceiling and concentrated on water. I shaped the word in my head, pronounced it with my mind and saw a glass fill with crystal-clear liquid. It was in my hand, but when I tried to sit up and drink from it dropped to the floor and shattered.

"Inez? What happened?" asked Mamá as she burst into the room.

"I'm thirsty. Do we have any water?" I said with dry lips and a parched tongue. She poured water from a pitcher into a glass and helped me sit up.

"What's this mess on the floor?" Did you get up?" she asked, fluffing up my pillows.

"No. I wanted water and—I made it appear, but I couldn't sit up—"

"*Nena*, no magic while you're recovering."

"I didn't do it on purpose. I just, it just..." My thoughts trailed off. *How had I done that?*

"Don't worry about it. You scared me," she said with a shaky voice.

"It is just a broken glass. I'm fine," I said, taking another sip. The cold water was biting but welcome. It reminded me I was really there and not in *that other place*. I felt oddly comforted and calm.

"I don't mean the glass. I mean, this—magic. Your arm. We almost lost you," she said in a tearful voice. "It's all too dangerous out there..."

"Mamá, I was cut by a tree. This could have happened anytime," I replied. But had it been just a tree? I thought back to Meiri coming to my door and her arm cut with something sharp, which left a ragged gash. Zavier had said it looked like the same cut when he bandaged my arm.

Zavier in the woods...

"But would you have been running through the woods if it weren't for all this magic and The Cat and who knows what else?" Her mention of the woods triggered a memory.

"I was in the woods," I whispered.

"I know. Seeing Áliz—I could wring Rowley's neck," she said, dabbing at her eyes. My eyes. The eyes of my...

"No, I mean afterwards. I saw Beval...and Lita. They were young and happy. I wanted to be happy with them," I said softly.

"*Nena...*"

"But they told me I couldn't stay, that it wasn't time yet. It was so nice there," I said and heard my mother taking a big breath. "Wait, I need to remember this. I can almost hear the music. I think they were with The People and...and...Beval told me to tell you that you're stronger than you know—that I get my strength from you. Mamá, you have to be brave," I said, grabbing her hand and squeezing as hard as I could. My grip was weak, but she looked down at our entwined hands and then wept.

Chapter 23

Toman and Zavier burst into the room. Their faces were flushed and they looked as though they were going to fight to be the first one inside. They both saw Mamá sobbing into my shoulder.

"What are you two doing?" I asked. "Do you want to break the door?"

"We thought...we heard...your mother..." said Toman and Zavier in turns. I laughed a little at that.

"They thought your mother was crying because you'd died," said Meiri from the doorway. She said it casually, but her face was paler than usual.

"I've seen all of you looking pretty bad and I've never said anything like that," I joked. Mamá dabbed at her eyes furiously and poured me more water.

"She's fine. I already feel put in my place," said Toman, but he held my hand as though I might slip away.

"She's getting better, but you guys shouldn't be here. You'll tire her out," replied Mamá.

"We won't stay long," said Zavier, rooted in place, looking pained.

"Okay. Just a few minutes. *Nena*, I'll make you some oatmeal," she said, and slipped out of the room, still sniffling. But she was smiling.

"Is this payback for the scares we've given you? Because I don't find it at all funny," said Meiri. She sat by my feet, unable to get Toman to relinquish his place.

"How's the arm?" asked Zavier, his jaw tight. He was wearing his patrol uniform and it looked as though he'd slept in it for days.

"I want to cut it off, but other than that it's fine. How are you?" I asked and our eyes locked. I could see all the fear and pain that still hadn't receded. But I could also see relief and something else I couldn't name.

"He's how we all are. Ecstatic that you're still in the land of the living," said Toman.

"Well, I did take a short trip to the land of the dead, but the food's better here," I joked. They didn't find it amusing. "Relax, I'm fine. But I have a bone to pick with a certain tree out there."

"Get in line. We all have words for it and I'm thinking of borrowing the family axe," said Meiri. I'll come by tomorrow to fill you in. So will Toman. But we should go now," she said, nudging Toman.

"What? Oh...yea... I'll see you tomorrow. Glad you're back with us," he said and kissed my forehead. He and Meiri made a discreet exit and closed the door. Zavier still looked rooted to the spot and his eyes shone with emotion.

"Is this where you say I told you so?" I quipped. But I knew he was thinking of our last meeting and how abrupt our goodbye had been. *What if it had been our last?* I knew Zavier well enough to know he would have carried that guilt for a long while.

"This is where I say don't ever scare me like that again. I was... I was insane with worry. Useless at my job and my duties. I have half a mind to move you into the palace and keep you under armed guard," he said with ire. And he was angry. No, he was furious, and I didn't know what to say. I had expected a lot of things, but not this. He was still standing in the same spot, his eyes burning and his fists clenched. I needed to make him understand.

I lifted the blanket, and he saw I meant to get out of bed. That sent him into action.

"What are you doing?" he asked, rushing to my side and covering me again.

"Giving you a hug because it's the only thing I can think of before I throttle you. You have no right to be angry with me any more than I have a right to be angry at a damned tree! How can you—?" And he stopped me with a kiss so tender I nearly cried.

"I'm not angry with you. I'm angry with...well, lots of people really, but also myself. Losing you would end me. I know I can't make you stay home and be still—I wouldn't do it either—but please be careful," he said and kissed me again. And this time there was no restraint. All politeness was over. I broke away from the kiss.

"I'll try," I said breathlessly.

THE NEXT DAY I FELT better than I had a right to feel. But even I knew I needed a little more rest. I wondered when the parade of visitors would start again and then I had my first one: It was Mr. Fell on loan from the royal family.

"By order of his Highness, Prince Zavier. I am to attend you until you leave this bed, but clearly I'm not needed. You look glorious." He beamed.

"Thank you. Should you really be here?" I asked.

"Oh, yes. The young prince moved mountains *and* the queen to make sure I watched over your recovery. Although I can take little credit for it," he laughed.

"What do you mean?"

"Although in public I have taken pride in my ability to snatch you back from the brink, it was all you."

"Me?"

"Yes. You healed yourself and that was no mean feat. When the fever started your mother and I worked around the clock trying to find a way to reduce it, but we were thwarted at every turn. I quickly realized that it was you. You weren't ready to come back to us, my dear," he said with the same wistful expression Mamá had given me. I swallowed the lump in my throat. "So, I made the controversial decision to do nothing and wait for you."

"Sorry I took so long," I said.

"Your return was miraculous, but I know you had some help," said Mr. Fell. He was quiet for a moment with a thoughtful expression on his face. "I heard you call their names. How are they?" he asked, smiling.

"Happy," I replied and couldn't help but smile, thinking about them.

"And proud of you, I'm sure," he replied.

"Yes, but I don't know why."

"My dear, what you did was incredible even for a person of your Powers. And while I could attribute your return to the natural pull of youth, I think it's more to do with a well-developed sense of duty," he said, patting my shoulder. "And we do need you."

"That makes me sound nobler than I feel. Right now, I feel stupid for being felled by a tree branch. Why do you need me?"

"The Cat has indeed returned. We need to get you back to full strength to face him. I don't think a tree caused this trouble. I haven't told your mother—that's for you to decide—but I think The Cat knows you're against him."

I lowered my head, not wanting to hurt such a nice man.

"I...I think your sister had a hand in his return," I said with regret.

"I don't doubt it. I feared her involvement from the first. That was why your mother disbanded the Society. Most of our number were also a part of the Magical Return movement, but I, your mother, and your grandparents left the organization when they started advocating violent measures. And then you were born, and your mother saw the danger. The Society would have made you into a weapon and she wanted better for you. My sister didn't agree."

"And the queen. Hortensia did this, too. Maybe we can convince her to beg Mythos to fix this," I said, but with little faith. If Hortensia came forward now, she would likely lose her crown and Canto would lose the last bit of sovereignty left to it by Mythos. Mr. Fell's gaze conveyed all of that as though he'd read my mind.

"But that's why we have to get you strong. Your mother left this tea for you. You drink and I'll tell you about the madness that has gripped our fair Canto.

Acts of vandalism and violence were on the rise. The KM could barely contain the increase and the council was considering sending in reinforcements from the other isles. Zavier had been on a thirty-six-hour rotation and the palace guard was supplementing them, on Zavier's orders.

"It's all anyone can do to keep the KM in order, too. Some have been accused of misconduct. People are picked up daily for trying to destroy property or fighting with their neighbors," he said between sips of tea.

I drank my own slowly, disliking the bitterness of whatever herb Mamá had put in it to speed my recovery. I felt much better despite my aversion to the remedy. Another sip brought a thought to mind.

"Why haven't the royals called Mythos? Even in a royal capacity, without admitting to anything Hortensia has the right to ask?" I asked. I'd hinted as much to Zavier, but he'd evaded my questions deftly.

"Perhaps it is better to wonder why Mythos hasn't stepped in yet?" replied Mr. Fell. He watched me intently, as though he was teacher hoping his pupil would connect the dots without him. And I agreed: Why hadn't they stepped in yet?

"They did in the past, from what I've read," I said, slowly. Mr. Fell stayed silent, letting me puzzle it out for myself. "And it wasn't long after those events that Mythos decided there should be Mythosian monitors in Canto. And now?" Then I thought about all that had happened. The Cat appearing. The upheaval in Canto...

And the engagement. The royal family then had a daughter on the verge of being engaged. After The Cat had appeared and Mythos had intervened—albeit not with The Cat directly—they had given their suggestion as to who the princess should wed.

"Did Mythos bring The Cat the first time?" I asked.

"That I can't prove, but it would be quite the coincidence if it happened all over again. The prince is engaged to you," he said with a raised eyebrow.

I couldn't imagine Mythos taking the chance of an uncontrollable magic cat wreaking havoc on the Canti, but then again perhaps The Cat wasn't so uncontrollable to people who had magic and the ability to use it?

"That is just a theory. I'd rather talk about what you're going to do about our current cat problem. Rowley says you have a plan, but I've heard it and I'm dubious," he said with seriousness.

"After this, I understand the risk, but we can't risk not trying," I replied. Rowley explained how time magic robbed the caster of her own lifetime and the dangers of meddling in the past. It couldn't be helped.

I tested my arm and felt a dull throbbing pain but I could manage.

"Rowley agrees and surprisingly, so does your mother."

"I'm not surprised. Beval could always talk her around," I replied and Mr. Fell smiled.

"THIS ISN'T WORKING," I fumed. I was tired of being berated for my shortcomings. I'd only gotten out of bed three days ago.

"No, Miss Garza, you're not working. We are running out of time. Try again," Rowley barked. We were in an outbuilding next to the *Cup & Board*. I threw myself down on the floor and rubbed my mended arm. I refused to meet his eye.

Canto was in serious danger. The Cat was using his magic and his fiddle to cause violence and destruction. The royal family would have no choice but to ask Mythos to intervene, which would tighten their hold on Canto. Mythosian interference would lead to greater scrutiny of the hidden market, anyone with Powers and possibly the end of what little sovereignty Canto had left. It had to be stopped. I was growing more worried about Zavier being out there as our first line of defense against an enemy he didn't even believe in. Selfishly I also knew Mythos would end Zavier's and my relationship in favor of someone more aligned with Mythos and their zero-magic policies. I was highly motivated to work on my magic, but the toll of recovering after the Cat's attack on my arm was still something I was getting over.

"What can I do differently?"

"Your mother tells me you've been calling things to yourself," Rowley replied.

"Yea—glasses of water, a towel, and things like that."

"And how do you do that?" he asked patiently.

"I don't know. I just do it."

"No, you don't or you would just do what I'm asking. Tell me your process," he demanded.

"It's stupid," I said, looking away.

"I'll be the judge of stupid. Tell me what you do," he replied.

"Okay. I see the word in my mind and then I make my mind pronounce it and...it happens. Like the first time my mind said *akwa* and then I had a glass of water," I explained.

"But why does it know to give you a glass? It could be a splash of water or take you to water."

"Maybe I say a drink of water instead."

"An intuitive leap. You think drink of water and it provides a glass. Is that the same way it worked when you became wind?"

"No, that's not me," I said.

"What do you mean?" But I shook my head. "Inez—tell me."

"Well, there's a voice in my head that sounds like me, but not quite. It repeats a word, something I can't even say or remember later. After a few times, my mind's voice starts to take up the chant and then I say it out loud. That's how it happens. Sound crazy?"

"Lost knowledge spell. Interesting..."

"Interesting? I just thought it presaged my descent into madness. Does hearing voices mean anything to you?"

"It might, but it doesn't help us now. The water trick should. Pick up the peer needle and try using that thought process again," he said and sat in front of me. I put the peer needle up to his chest and waited for it to imbed itself in his heart. The thought was gruesome, even knowing it caused no damage and didn't hurt. Or so he said.

"It's not working," I said, putting the needle down. It was the same story each time.

"Did you use the same technique as you did with the water?"

"I think I see the flaw in your method. I've seen a glass of water before, but I have no idea what your memory looks like. How can I call it up without knowing what to look for?"

He pondered that for a minute or two while I spun the glass on the floor.

"Close your eyes," he said.

"If you're hoping to get me to meditate, I advise against it. I'm not the most patient."

"Miss Garza, close your eyes and concentrate. Please," he said. Surprised by his plea, I closed my eyes and wondered what would come next. "It was a spring day, cool but comfortable enough for strolling..." he said.

"Is this you as a dog or are you thinking about a person because you have a thick coat and don't feel the cold the way we do...?"

"Miss Garza I am not above corporal punishment and if biting your injured arm will better focus you—"

"Okay, okay. Sorry, I just needed to ease the tension."

"As I was saying..."

Chapter 24

The woods were in full bloom with the smell of wildflowers in the air. A bullfrog croaked nearby. Shimmering light brightened the scene from the sun reflecting off a lake. It was a perfect spring day.

A boy dressed in a distinctive cobalt blue blazer and dark gray pants held a brass horn tightly in an unsteady grip. In the other hand was a pair of cotton balls, which he fumbled to secure in his ears.

Two barks and they were off running, one on four legs and the other on two.

Their destination, the other side of the lake toward the bay. It was an odd place to look for a cat, but this cat was different.

There he stood, The Cat, in his boots with a fiddle almost as tall as him at his side. He didn't even look concerned—just amused. Exposing one sharp claw he reached to his side and idly strummed a few strings.

"Oh Rowley, trying to be a hero—you know what they say about those who can't do," he purred. The boy in blue held the horn tighter. He shook his head like someone who heard nails on a chalkboard.

"I have one for you. It's about curiosity and cats," was the reply.

The Cat hissed. Still the boy held firm. The boy in blue, El Niño Amoratado had the same ability as his namesake to block out pain and yet he looked visibly nervous.

"Your blue friend is in over his head. He can't even hold that instrument properly. Should I show you how to correctly hold a musical instrument?" the Cat asked and swept the fiddle into playing position in one graceful sweep. It was almost his size, like a micro-sized double bass. The Arco children were dead and half the town had gone mad—all because of a Cat who played a fiddle.

Pulling the bow from a back harness like an archer prepping to let loose a volley, The Cat shot two notes into the bay. The water churned and bubbled like a cauldron on the boil, creating breakers. Small at first, but then the waves grew larger and denser. They threatened to inundate them all. The Cat stood back to admire his handiwork, purring with delight.

Another two barks and the boy in blue put the horn to his lips and blew. The first note was tremulous, but the next was stronger. Soon he was playing a melody, triumphant and pure and the waves froze in mid-air. The Cat hissed and spat, jumping in the air to swipe at the boy, but was met with teeth and large paws swatting him down.

But the boy had been frightened by The Cat's attack and stopped his song. The waves moved again, blotting out the sun with their immense size. They could hear the screams from the town center.

Two more barks and the boy put the horn back to his lips as the wave crashed down around them. All three went under, thrashing in the undertow. But the boy broke through the surface and blew again, stilling the roiling water. With panic and desperation as an anchor, the boy blew one long, loud note directly at The Cat. The sound was too much for the dog and he swooned at the edge of the shore. That ended the memory.

I SAW IT ALL THROUGH his eyes. I almost felt the moment Rowley was wrenched from the memory. The peer needle shot out from his dark fur into my hand, leaving no trace. He was shaking and whimpering softly. The retreating strains of my magic tickled the tips of my fingers. Even if he had given permission to see his memories, it felt like a violation. Now I knew why peer needles were illegal.

"Did it hurt?"

"Then or now?" he asked hoarsely.

"Both, I guess." I moved closer to him.

"Let's call it an echo of pain. I carry the regret, the guilt, things I should have noticed, didn't do. Then, it must have been painful—it knocked me out for three days. The pain I just felt can't compare to that. It was foolish of me to have trusted Cat... Well, now you know," he said quietly, and I got the feeling that he wanted me to accept some sort of apology.

"It wasn't your fault and you fixed it anyway," I replied.

"Did I? He's back and we still don't know where the horn is. Afterwards, when I woke up, I didn't know if anything had changed. We had taken the precaution of spiking the water supply with tamp root, but it was...a long time before I walked in the woods alone. Mrs. Arco stayed mad as a hatter and...well, it was awhile before the Cup & Board was normal again," he said with regret.

"As to what happened to the horn, we have the KM report of the Arco children's deaths. We know the confrontation at the bay between myself, El Niño and The Cat happened after that, and not that long after, so I'll aim for the day of their death and just hang around."

"And risk being seen? Not a good idea. It was two, maybe three days after their fall—I think. My mind was a little scrambled after the woods. Time before that is a little fuzzy around the edges," Rowley replied.

"We can't risk sending me in too late and missing it. Then I'd have to do it all over again. At least I know the where and the time of day. I'm sure there was some sort of report in the Cups about a tidal wave."

"Not really. Nothing was reported with particular accuracy in those days. Especially during The Cat's reign of terror. I've looked; trust me," he said, his normal tone returning.

"Then I'll have to show up a little early to make sure I don't miss it. It's the only way." I wanted to discuss Mr. Fell's theory that Mythos was behind the first appearance of The Cat, but it wasn't the time. Rowley looked shaken up enough from this short trip to the past. Continuing the journey at this point felt cruel.

"I am aware of our options, Miss Garza. I simply don't like them."

"It's settled. Now teach me time spells."

"There are two things you must know about time spells, Miss Garza. One, it involves mirrors. And two, it's going to hurt—a lot."

DESPITE ROWLEY'S WARNINGS, I knew I had to go through with the time spell. It was not something I looked forward to, but now I knew why so few people messed with this kind of magic. It was also why I found myself sitting on my bed and listening to the oddest argument I'd ever heard.

"If anyone is going to hurt her, it's going to be me. I'm her mother and would be kinder than you," insisted my mother. Clutched in her hand was a sharp knife and she used it to punctuate her words.

"My point exactly. This can't be done kindly. Time spells require sacrifice. Essentially she is ripping through the fabric of time and therefore must be torn as well. If I bite her, we ensure that the sacrifice is made," argued Rowley.

"The spell says nothing about ripping or tearing. It just says a blood sacrifice must be made to the mirror. Next you'll want to throw virgins in volcanoes," countered Mamá.

They were fighting for the chance to cut into the crook of my arm and I wasn't sure who I wanted to win. Mamá would be gentle, but squeamish and the thought of my mother coming at me with a knife was sickening. Rowley would definitely meet this challenge with business-like efficiency, but I'd ribbed him often enough to wonder if he would relish the idea of drawing my blood.

"Can't I do it myself?" I asked. Slitting my own wrists was just as repellent, but at least I could end this argument.

"No, *Nena*. No one should have to do that—ever. Plus, the amount we have to collect is substantial. You'll probably pass out before it's done," she said mournfully. I'd been surprised by how well she had taken the news, but her voice couldn't hide how little she relished it.

"And neither one of you are concerned that I might not wake up?" I said lightly, but I felt a small twinge of ice in my belly.

"Not really. You healed yourself very nicely. If anything, we should be concerned that you'll try to protect yourself and heal too quickly," replied Rowley coolly. Mamá's holding of the knife was looking better and better.

"That's why I should do it. I can honestly say there isn't any part of my daughter that fears me. Can you say the same?" said Mamá with an edge.

Rowley had no response and with grim determination, Mamá opened the door and sent him out. I sat taking deep breaths reminded of the times I had cut myself or needed a bandage removed. Mamá would sit by me and tell me how it would only hurt for a second and that she liked it less than I did. Afterwards there would be a reward and I would forget why I had been so nervous.

Mama couldn't say that now and there would be no reward after. I could only hope I passed out before I had a chance to stop my mother from draining a cup of my blood. Mamá just pursed her lips together and sat next to me on the bed.

"You don't have to do this. We can ask Viktor for more tamp root and take care of the town," she said, looking into the distance.

"That wouldn't get rid of The Cat. This is the only way," I replied. Rolling up my sleeve slowly, I felt my head start to pound from the tension. I looked down at my veins and touched the delicate skin in the crook of my arm. It wouldn't take too deep a cut, but I still felt a tremor of fear and anticipation roll down my body. Putting my arm in Mamá's lap, I closed my eyes and turned my face away.

I knew there was already a collecting basin on the floor. She placed it between us and my arm hovered over the cool metal bowl. "Do it—don't count or hesitate. I might lose my nerve."

I thought of being with Zavier. Of laughing with Toman. Becoming Meiri's friend. Nothing too concrete so my Powers wouldn't try to take me away or attack my mother. The slice of the knife made me bite down on my tongue to keep from crying out. I didn't want this to be any more unpleasant for Mamá than it already was. Warm wetness dripped down my elbow and I felt the knife again sliding across. This time I couldn't help but gasp and try to pull away. But Mamá held my hand firm, keeping me over the bowl.

Bile rose in my throat as the smell of metal filled the room. My vision swam and I couldn't hold my arm on my own. I was slipping away and for a moment I panicked—fearing I was losing too much. Tendrils of ice began in the pit of my stomach wanting to stretch and protect me. I clenched my stomach as best I could, but my strength was fading.

"We're almost done, Nena. Hold on for a few more seconds," she said in a choked voice.

Why had I agreed to this? I was mad if I thought this was a good idea. If this was what it meant to have Powers and protect my family I would happily give up everything to hide in my room and let whatever comes take over. But that was pain talking and I couldn't give in. After seeing Rowley face all he had, watching Zavier recover stoically and with grace, it would be wrong to flinch now.

A tight strip was being tied around my arm, so hard I grit my now-chattering teeth. Mamá was saying something soothing, but I barely heard her. I opened my eyes and saw the now-full basin on the floor and a bandage being put on sensitive skin on the crook of my elbow.

"You have to say it, Inez. Inez? Wake up and..."

"*Bher uper reidh dhghyes yer.*" I whispered the words of Power to give my blood the ability to let me travel in time. It would take a day for the spell to take hold in the cup of blood my mother held. For a panicked moment, I worried I wouldn't be able to complete the spell and we'd have to drain me again. Where the strength came from, I didn't know, but I felt a shock of coldness envelope my arm. Then I let myself fall back and closed my eyes again.

WHEN I WOKE UP, IT was night. Zavier was sitting at my bedside and he smiled when he saw my eyes open. The quilt was tucked under me tightly, yet I still felt cold. His hand brushed my cheek.

"Didn't I say to be careful?" he asked in a soft voice. "Your mom told me you overdid it today and had a bit of a relapse."

"Yea, that's right. I'll be more careful next time," I replied. I was still a little woozy and didn't bother trying to sit up. The room still had a slightly metallic smell to it, but that could just have been my memory imposing that.

"I can only stay a minute. I'm back on patrol again, but I wanted to drop by and see how you're doing. I think I'm getting some time off tomorrow. I can come by—"

"No! I mean, I feel terrible, and you don't want to see me as a patient. I think I just need a few days to get back in order. Take some time to sleep," I said quickly. I could see the dark circles under his eyes and his clothes were rumpled. It was a reasonable request, especially since I wouldn't be here—but he still looked disappointed.

"You're probably right. Promise me you'll spend the time in bed, resting," he said with mock severity. He leaned over and his kiss made my head spin. His departure was a relief and I fell back to sleep knowing tomorrow would be a long day. If all went according to plan, tomorrow I would go back in time.

I WOKE UP TO THE SMELL of eggs and sausage. My mouth watered at the thought, but getting downstairs to eat it wasn't as easy. I was still a little woozy from yesterday, but I knew if I couldn't even get out of my room it would be impossible to convince my mother and Rowley I was up for the challenge ahead. I couldn't look like an invalid.

The bandage on my arm was itchy and uncomfortable. I unrolled it carefully, remembering the pain. As the white gauze fell to the floor, I inspected the damage. A faint line of a scar long healed remained, the skin still sensitive.

Mamá was busily manning the stove when I got to the kitchen. She flipped eggs and turned sausage with efficiency. A glass of orange juice sat next to a huge mug of Lita's fortifying brew, which I gulped down.

"Good morning," she said, still facing the griddle. She sounded tired.

"Morning. Thanks for sending Zavier up yesterday. That did happen, right? I didn't dream it," I said, taking a seat. Mamá shoveled food onto my plate and I could see the puffy circles under her eyes. She gave me a small smile.

"I thought you should see him before you...go. Who knows when you'll come back to the present," she remarked and turned back to the griddle. She sounded so crushed. I had to give her a bone.

"Come with me. That way you won't worry and I can—"

"*Nena*, I know you can do this. I know if I'm there, I'll worry more watching you in danger," she said, taking my hand. She stroked the spot where yesterday she had slashed with a knife. Her eyes remained dry, but I heard a slight catch in her throat. "Besides, Rowley got me some more tamp root. Not enough for everyone, but enough to keep the KM safe."

"Where did he get it? And how are you going to give it to the KM without telling them about The Cat? Some of them don't believe he's behind all this uproar," I said.

"Let me worry about that. You have enough on your plate. Eat up—we have to get you dressed and ready to face the mirror," she said and turned back to the griddle.

As I cleared my plate, she would scoop more on to replace it. We continued that way for an hour.

IN FRONT OF THE WARDROBE, Mamá put the finishing touches on my antiquated outfit. It had belonged to one of my ancestors who had a fondness for ruffles and bows. The bustled skirt was completely impractical, not to mention the elaborate hat. I felt and looked ridiculous, but it couldn't be helped. After the gargantuan breakfast Mamá had fed me, I was surprised the waist fit. As I gave myself a critical look in the mirror, I heard footsteps on the stairs.

"Are we expecting Rowley?" I asked, tugging on the tight sleeves. I turned and saw Meiri and Toman wearing period costumes, as well. Meiri looked quite good in a light pink dress and Toman was jaunty in a red vest and top hat. "No, absolutely not. They can't come."

"We didn't ask you and we're coming," said Toman looking pleased with himself.

"I would feel better if you had company," said Mamá.

"Plus, you're less likely to do something stupid if you have other people along," said Meiri. She had the look in her eye of an executioner—someone whose aversion to the task had been overridden by grim purpose.

"Toman, someone has to watch Dottie," I said, terrified at the prospect of dragging two people into my crazy plan which could trap us in the past.

"PJ will and your mother promised to check in, too," he replied.

"And what did you tell him or Dottie for that matter? 'Don't worry, I'm just taking a little jaunt to the past,'" I asked, momentarily panicked that the circle of this secret just got bigger.

"Who do you think I am?" he asked in mock outrage. "I told him I was taking over for your mother watching over your recovery. I made myself sound very selfless, too," he said, a hand over his heart. I resisted the urge to clap and instead tried his co-conspirator.

"Meiri, I'm going to look for The Cat. You know that, right? And how long until your mother sends a searching party to my door?" I heard the beginnings of hysteria enter my voice.

"You take a lot of risks for us. It's only fair we take some with you. I'll be fine. As for my mother, let me worry about that," Meiri said with a swallow. "Anyway, we can help."

"How? You have no Powers. If I get into trouble, you're both stuck."

"Not necessarily. Time doesn't like disruptions. The problem won't be coming home, it'll be staying there. This time will try and pull you back, but with more people there you'll have an anchor of sorts," said a recently arrived Rowley. He nudged his way into the room, settling between Meiri and Toman. "And I think you'll take fewer risks if you know you are responsible for others."

I was outnumbered and I didn't know if it was a good thing. Toman came to my side and gave me one of his bear hugs.

"We want to help. After that bloodletting you're not at full strength. Lean on us," he said softly. I had to bite the inside of my mouth to keep from tearing up. I was so touched.

"Thank you both," I said thickly. "Let's get going."

STANDING IN THE DARKENED mirror shed with my friends, I felt a little less apprehensive about what I was about to do. In Meiri's hand was a modern clock and in Toman's was yesterday's "sacrifice." I could still smell the metallic sweetness and had to swallow hard to keep it together.

The mirror slowly rippled to life. I was still becoming accustomed to the idea that an entity lived in it. Knowing meant I couldn't callously push it aside and hope it wouldn't hold a grudge.

"Hello, I understand that you have no reason to trust me or any humans for that matter, but I do need your help," I began to the mirror.

"Inez, who are you talking to?" asked Meiri.

"Is this a new spell you've been working on?" asked Toman.

"Inez Garza. And you've brought others. As I've noted, humans tell other humans they are untrustworthy right before asking to be trusted. Is that what you're doing now?" asked the entity. I still didn't know its name, which said something about the trust between us.

"I am hoping you'll trust me because what I need from you will require more trust than I likely deserve," I replied, painfully aware that the mirror hadn't even trusted me with its name.

"Inez, did you lose too much blood. Who are you talking to?" Toman asked. It occurred to me that Toman and Meiri couldn't hear the mirror. Before the glass shard embedded itself in my finger, I could only hear when the mirror came to life, but never a voice.

"I'm talking to the mirror," I said. I had the benefit of standing in front of Meiri and Toman and didn't see the inevitable look that passed between the two of them. "What do you know about time travel magic?"

"I know that kind of magic is foolish for humans. You don't comprehend the intricacies of time. You think it travels in a straight line. Time travels in many directions but it moves like a dance. Interrupting that dance causes chaos," said the mirror.

"It requires a mirror and a lot of blood. I brought the blood and now I'm asking you to help with the rest," I said, ignoring the mirror's comments.

"Does this mean all the mirrors can talk? Are we walking through their bodies when we travel? I think I should stay behind," said Meiri.

"We need you, Meiri. Stop worrying so much about what magic can do and think more about what *we* can do," said Toman. "Besides, do you really want to be left behind when your best defense will be gone?" he asked, cocking his head in my direction. Meiri blanched and bit her lip.

"There was a time when Lady Sabrina and Beval came to me and said you would ask me to do something that went against everything I believed in. I suppose today is that day," said the mirror.

"There is a cat out there, sowing confusion. I don't know where it will lead, but I can stop him. And whenever chaos ensues, the first thing to break is usually glass." I waited in the silence, wondering if I'd gone too far.

"Get on with it," it said and shimmered away.

I sensed the loss of the entity like an empty void, as though the soul had left the mirror. If the others felt it, they didn't say.

Toman brought the bowl forward and put it on the ground before me. With my paintbrush I dipped into the viscous liquid and slathered it over the surface of the mirror. At certain points I had to hold my breath, which was a mistake wearing a new corset. I swayed a little and Meiri held up the bowl while I painted the top. Before

I was done, I started to hear the chanting in my head and began to repeat it out loud.

"*Gwa Reidh...Gwa Reidh...GWA REIDH...*"

I put down the brush and closed my eyes. I felt Meiri's gloved hand slip into mine and Toman's arm hook around my waist. I could hear the mirror shimmer, but the sound was different. Instead of a tinny bell, it was more of an echoing gong. I felt the thrum vibrate through me and with my friends I stepped forward into the mirror toward the unknown.

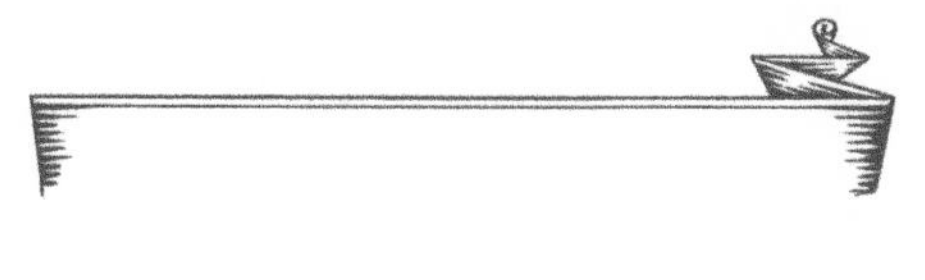

Part Two

Chapter 25

We stepped through into a room and for a moment it felt as though we never left. Small differences signaled we had. The air in the room was warmer. In our own time the mirror shed was made of opaque glass, fashioned by Beval. In this time the shed was still opaque, but ornately painted and made of wood. I knew that within a generation the mirror would be moved into the house while work was done and then back out to the remodeled shed.

In this time there were no other mirrors in this room other than the one we'd traveled through. I sensed no entity in the mirror although the shard in my finger was throbbing. And that wasn't the only discomfort. An echo like the aftereffects of a thrumming gong was now playing inside of me, low and vibrating.

"Did it work? Are we all in one piece?" asked Meiri. She was tugging on her sleeves and smoothing down her hair as though we had been blown by a breeze instead of ripping through time.

"First things first. Make sure we came through with everything," I said, checking my bag. In it was money, a change of clothes and a first aid kit.

"I still have the watch and the money and the *cup*." Toman whispered the last word as if someone might overhear us and know he carried a container of my blood.

"Me too. Money and a sewing kit. I also have the jar of tamp root juice and a thermos of your fortifying tea," said Meiri. She fiercely clutched the jar I knew was filled with Meiri's tonic.

"Good. Give me the...the cup. I have to frost it," I said. Rowley explained more times than was strictly necessary that my blood was the only way to return to our time and unless I wanted another bloodletting, I needed to keep the cup of my blood frozen so it wouldn't lose its potency. Freezing objects was easier than superheating them, but it was still a drain on my Powers and I felt slightly off kilter. I reached for it and almost stumbled, but Meiri caught me.

"Are you okay? You probably need some tea. Sit on the floor and I'll pour you some. Please sit, but carefully. You don't want to mess up the dress."

"Yes, Meiri that's our biggest concern now: Inez keeping her dress tidy. She almost dropped the blood," yelled Toman, but he helped me to a seat where, relieved, I sank down into its cushion.

"I'll drink, but let's go over the rules again," I said, taking a gulp of tea. It did nothing to silence the vibrations in my body.

"You're starting to sound like Rowley. Lighten up," said Toman with a chuckle.

"Sorry. That was—intense," I said, taking another sip. Traveling through time had been smooth, but the arrival was jarring.

"No, Inez is right. Let's go over the rules again," said Meiri, looking on edge, still clutching the root jar.

"Okay. Why are we here?" I began.

"To find out what happened to the horn," said Meiri.

"Obviously, we're going over the story we're telling anyone who questions us, Meiri," said Toman, but he put his arm around her kindly.

"Right, we are visiting from distant Faery for a few days and staying with a friend on the border named...named..."

"Simon Drake. The borders aren't patrolled now, so no one knows anything about the outer reaches. We're going to tail Rowley and when he finally talks to El Niño Amoratado we'll know that the next day is the big event," I said, getting to my feet. "Now let's get to the outbuilding. Rowley said no one goes in there and we can set up camp."

Meiri pulled out a sheet of paper with a detailed map of the Garza estate. My ancestors preferred more grandeur than Mamá and Lita. Most of the outbuildings, which housed retainers and supplies, were gone in our time. At least a few were empty there now.

"Shouldn't we...? The mirror?" asked Toman. I saw his point. Mirrors at rest were still active visually, with swirls and ripples. The mirror looked, for lack of a better term, dead. The surface was dark and two-dimensional.

"It can't be helped. If we call the mirror back it may not agree to a return trip later. We can't call it back until it's time to go," I said.

Rowley had explained that magic mirrors live outside of time, which is why they can be used for time magic. But calling the mirror now would really call the entity from our time and from there it got too confusing to keep up. The bottom line was I had to leave the entity wherever it was until it was time for us to get back to the present—future—whatever.

I took the cup from Toman and concentrated on frosting it.

"Gel," I whispered, holding the cup in both hands. Rowley had stressed precision to avoid freezing Toman, Meiri, the shed and myself. The thrumming within me made it harder to concentrate. I repeated the word of Power louder and my fingers tingled as the glass chilled and turned cloudy. I heard Meiri gasp and Toman patted my shoulder encouragingly. My warm fingers stuck slightly to the surface of the covered cup. I hid it behind the mirror. I hoped it would stay there until we were ready to return to our time.

"That way we can come straight here after seeing where the horn ended up," I reasoned.

"Are you sure we shouldn't take the cup with us?" asked Meiri. She looked reluctant to leave the shed.

"Do you want to carry around Inez's blood? Because I don't," said Toman, who shuddered despite having been the one who'd carried it through the mirror.

"And I don't want to run the risk of forgetting it somewhere or spilling it because we're on the run for some reason," I added. I hoped our time in the past would be uneventful, but that wasn't something I could count on anymore.

We opened the door slowly and checked to see if the coast was clear. Slipping out of the shed, I felt the vibrations in my body get a little lighter, but the gong in my chest was louder.

"Do you guys hear that?" I asked.

"Hear what? I don't hear anything. *Is it music?*" asked Meiri with a tinge of panic in her voice.

This was going to be a long trip!

"No, nothing. Sorry," I said and stumbled again.

"I think you need some food. Let's get over to Horner's for a bite," said Toman and we agreed. Making our way to the city center, I wondered what the older Canto had in store for us.

MY FIRST THOUGHT WAS that buildings I thought of as landmarks were glaringly absent. Where was Froth?

"No Wee Willie Winkie Theater? Tragic," said Toman.

"They're building the library over there," said Meiri, walking sedately. "Inez stop clomping. These dresses require smaller steps."

"They're not practical. What if we need to run after Rowley or run from...something," I said, stopping myself from mentioning The Cat.

"That's why we have Toman," said Meiri. "To chase and carry."

"Thank you, Lady Meiri. Shall I carry you as well or is my touch beneath you?" said Toman with a mock bow.

"Children, stop squabbling. If I need to run, I'm ripping a slit in this ridiculous dress and I don't want to hear about it," I said. They were both a little edgy and with the gong going off in my head my headache didn't need any encouragement from their bickering. We fell into a charged silence while we looked around the town we knew so well, but now had to relearn.

"What's that smell?" asked Meiri.

"Manure. Horse manure," said Toman knowingly. "Rowley said using horses more than mirrors was in fashion for a short while. Just another way for entitled nobles to display their treasures, if you can call horseflesh a treasure. I'm glad it ended. It smells like the stables exploded.

"You know, even with the buildings that are missing, Canto looks basically the same," I said. It was comforting to know where things were, considering we had likely embarked on a wild goose chase.

"There's Horner's. Let's get something to eat inside. I don't think I could eat out here," said Meiri putting a gloved hand to her nose.

HORNER'S SMELLED HEAVENLY in any era. The aromas from freshly baked pies wafted through the air, temporarily erasing the memory of horse manure. There wasn't a counter—anymore...or yet, I suppose—but we were allowed to seat ourselves. Only a few tables were occupied, and we chose one near the window.

"Welcome to Horner's. Today's savory special is fiddlehead fern quiche. I recommend the lemon meringue for dessert," said the waiter, making eyes at Toman. Toman smiled back.

"Three of each, thank you," said Toman. The waiter smiled and walked away with our order.

"No attachments, remember? That includes flirting with strangers who might remember you and change the course of their lives because of it," said Meiri. She was peering out through the window, on alert.

The waiter returned quickly, laden with plates of delicious-smelling food and utensils, lingering a moment or two longer than he needed to as he handed a fork to Toman.

"Thank you," said Meiri tersely. The waiter rolled his eyes and left. "Seriously Toman?" she whispered.

"I'm not even going to say it, but you know what you need," Toman whispered back, making an indecent hand gesture.

"Can you please hold off on your squabbling until later? Let's just eat, okay," I suggested, my headache intensifying. I closed my eyes and rubbed the front of my forehead, hoping the pain would subside. Toman and Meiri ate in silence while I had to make an effort to chew and swallow. With the three of us sitting quietly, I was able to hear a conversation at a nearby table.

"There's another war on the Mundane," said a well-dressed man. The deep tone of his voice carried easily. His profile was handsome with a strong chin and hair that kept threatening to fall into his eyes.

"Aren't there always? It's half the reason my family left. Mind you, with all that's going on, maybe we should relocate," said the other who then took a sip from his cup. His profile was also attractive, but pinched. Or maybe his pursed lips made it seem so. The first man continued eating his slice of pie thoughtfully, before lowering his fork.

"You don't believe all this cat nonsense, do you?" asked the first.

"I don't know who's behind it all, but it's madness out there. And you heard about the Arco children? Terrible business," said his friend.

"They were bound to come to a bad end, but still..."

"Yes. They're talking about double patrols now. This may be our last decent meal for a few days," said the first. It sounded like we were back in our time. The two must be KM and with no Froth yet, this was where they spent their time. I wondered how Zavier was doing. At that moment, the two men at the other table noticed our little party.

"Are you from Canto? I've never seen you before," said the pinched-faced one, turning to our table. His face still held a look of distaste that was oddly familiar. Meiri choked on her pie.

"No, we're visiting from Faery—the other side. It's our holiday," I replied with a forced smile. Toman nodded his head vigorously.

"This isn't the best time to come to Canto. My name is Sebastian," he said with a tip of his hat. His smile was warm and friendly as he took in my appearance. His appraising look gave me pause.

"Or maybe this is exactly why we're having problems now. You know they probably have magic," said the other with a dangerous edge. Rowley told me to expect this. The borders between Canto and Faery were fluid. It was widely known Mythos was more lenient with inherent Fae mages than they were with Canti. It was the reason anyone with magic or carrying magical objects from Faery was prohibited from entering Canto, but it didn't keep speculation about who crossed the border any less critical in certain circles.

"Excuse my companion, but we've had some difficulties of late and there are some who think it's magical in nature. Podkin, don't be so suspicious," said Sebastian. There was a resemblance to our Podkin although this one wasn't as muscular. His attention subsided a little, but he still gave us occasional cutting looks. "Perhaps we can walk you back to your lodgings?" he offered.

"We don't have time—patrol's starting soon," Podkin reminded him and stood up abruptly, making for the door. Sebastian shrugged apologetically and took my hand. Lifting it to his lips he lingered a moment and looked into my eyes as he kissed it.

"I hope we'll see each other again. And if you have any problems at all, just give my name. Enjoy our town—but be careful," he said, and with an incline of his head, and left with his impatient friend.

"Another conquest for Inez. Should Zavier be worried?" asked Toman good-naturedly.

"I could say the same for you," I replied, looking at the waiter giving Toman an extra smile. "I won't tell PJ if you don't tell Zavier," I said, finally starting to feel at ease. Our story had worked on someone, and my headache was receding.

"If the two of you are done comparing spoils, can we focus on what they said?" pressed Meiri. Her tone was becoming more strident and her hands fidgeted with the napkin by her plate.

"They said to be careful, but we already knew that," said Toman.

"Yes, but they also said they have thirty-six-hour patrols, which means the woods are going to be watched. And now, with Inez having an admirer, how long do you think it'll be before they know we're not on a vacation?" whispered Meiri. "This doesn't bode well."

"We'll think of something," I said dismissively, but now I was worried, too.

Chapter 26

It was inevitable that not all of Rowley's information would be accurate. The knowledge of the KM patrols made our work more precarious, but we couldn't waste the trip.

One thing felt the same, regardless of the earlier time we were in. The woods were still a haven for me. I recognized the smells, the sounds and even the tell-tale signs of smuggler activity. Lloras were murmuring low and tracks to their secret nests were there for those who knew what to look for. The low chime was still thrumming, but it felt lessened here.

I'd sent Toman and Meiri off to the Cup & Board to read through the cups and catch a glimpse of Rowley. I took a moment to breathe deep—there were precious few such moments lately.

Before I'd left for the past, I was honest with myself: Finding the horn might not work. It could have disintegrated after being used. It could have been stolen by someone we couldn't trace. So many possibilities and no room for error. That's when it occurred to me that we should have a contingency plan.

There was rustling coming from a bush. I froze, hoping it wasn't something I would have to confront. Even without proof of danger, my body went into protection mode. With my head still throbbing from the echoing gong, the cold shooting through my core was sharper. It dried my throat and made coughing painful.

A squirrel emerged from the bush, its cheeks full of acorns as it skidded past me. I couldn't say if it was running from anything other than me, but my smuggler instincts remained on alert.

This was the very reason I had sent the others to town. I couldn't risk having to protect them and myself while I made my search. Meiri was on edge, snapping at us and jumping at her own shadow. I hoped a little of the familiar would soothe her and I made Toman promise to behave himself. In a show of good faith, he offered to take her by Green Gardens before we met back at the shed.

Bringing them along was a double-edged sword. On the one hand, it was nice to have support. But the support had been minimal so far. On the other hand, I had to admit I liked knowing I wasn't alone in this strange time.

I finally came to a clearing. Growing in profusion was tamp root. In my time, the root had practically disappeared. On one of the few occasions the hidden market and Birthright had worked together to mutual effect, they eradicated the tamp root, the only known naturally occurring antidote for magical influence. But I knew the Jabberwocky's ancestor had kept a healthy supply to cultivate for private and profitable use. That was how Viktor had a supply now.

And yet I was surprised at the abundance of it in this time and dismayed that I couldn't take as much as I wanted.

Unless my plan worked.

I'd taught myself a compound spell to quickly grow more tamp root and that meant I needed to take only the extra, hopefully ensuring I wouldn't affect the supply in the past. I intended to collect enough to take care of Canto.

I quietly reminded myself of the words—*aug wrad*, increase root—and then bent to one of the patches of root. My protection spell was faint now and I realized happily that it no longer left me woozy and nauseous. I reveled in my growing magical strength and wondered whether I could attribute it to becoming accustomed to it or to the fortifying tea from Beval's journals.

With a pang of regret, I knew I wanted to share my success at finding some measure of control for my Powers and remembered that no one in this time would understand. *Stop feeling sorry for yourself, Inez.* I shrugged and bent to my work.

I dug my fingers deep into the soft earth and whispered, "*Aug wrad.*" The Power rushed to my fingers in an unexpected surge. As the sensation dissipated from my hands, I felt it pulse in the surrounding soil. I watched with rapt attention as each tamp root gave rise to a twin. At least it worked on seven of them. I moved to the next patch invigorated by my achievement and exhausted at the prospect of how many times I'd have to repeat the process.

It was after an hour's worth of tugging roots from the dirt that I felt eyes on me. Someone was watching my actions, but not approaching. My protection spell sparked at the intrusion, making me cough again. My hands itched with the tingle of magic.

"Hello? Is someone there?" I called, putting down my sack of roots. Nothing stirred, but I could still feel the eyes on me. I looked down at my dirty hands, my fingernails caked with earth. The thrum of power flooding them made no visible sign, but was just as real as the filth.

"Hello?" I asked again.

"Whatcha doing?" asked a little voice.

She emerged from the other side of the clearing. From the looks of her she was about eight or ten, but her eyes took everything in. Something in the way she looked around reminded me of someone.

"What are you doing in the woods alone?" I asked, standing in front of the sack.

"Trying to catch a cat," she said with a satisfied grin. That smile was so familiar that I had to stop myself staring.

"A cat? Do you mean The Cat?"

"I suppose. He walks around the woods sometimes wearing boots and carrying a violin," she said. "I want to take him home."

"Have you heard him play?" I asked, looking around.

"No. Do you think he can play it? That would be amazing. Anyway, following him was something to do until I started following you and your friends," she said, stepping forward. She was wearing only a shift and oversized boots, but the way she spoke told me not to be deceived by her appearance.

"Following me?"

"Yes. I saw the three of you leaving the Garza's fishing shed," she said, poking around the sack. "What's this for?"

"I'm gardening... You saw us?" I asked in despair. My use of magic had been liberal.

"Yes. No one uses the shed except me so when I saw you come out I wondered who you were. Are you an escaped princess running from the clutches of an evil king?" she asked with relish. "Are the plants to break a curse?" I was tempted to tell her she wasn't completely wrong. Instead I put down my sack and looked at her intently.

"How old are you?" I asked.

"I am nearly ten."

"Won't your mother get worried with you wandering the woods alone?" I asked, worrying about the same thing.

"Not if she never finds out. She's busy lately arranging my betrothal," she said and stuck her tongue out comically. "My tutors say I should use my time to prepare for marriage, but that's all I get to do. Whenever I can, I run off for the afternoon. Won't your mommy get angry that you ruined your dress?" she asked.

"Actually, my friends might," I replied. Imagining Meiri's face when she saw the mess I had made me laugh. "Where's your dress?" I asked her, wondering why she was wandering the woods in underclothes.

"I put it in my hiding place, so no one knows I'm getting muddy in the woods," she said conspiratorially. She leaned in close and whispered, "Were those your attendants, sworn to protect your honor?"

"I think you read too many novels. We're just visiting from Faery and took a wrong turn— That's all," I blurted out. She gave me a long penetrating look, sizing up my lie and finding it wanting.

"When I'm older, I'm going to travel a lot. And learn about everything. Nobles can't have professions, but if I have a daughter, I'm making sure she can do more than curtsey—and no arranged betrothals. That's really why you're here, right?"

"What's your name?"

"I'm Alda. What are you going to use those roots for?" she asked, picking one up and sniffing it gingerly.

"Take them back with me. We don't have it where I come from. Alda, why were you at the fishing shed?"

"I started going there after I found out about my betrothal. He lives on the estate...Gabriel. That's when I found the hiding spot," she said.

"Gabriel? Do you mean Gabriel Garza?" I asked, finally putting the pieces together. "Is your name Esmeralda?"

"Yes, but I like Alda. Can I stay with you if I promise not to tell anyone about you running from an evil prince?"

I was struck dumb for a minute. She looked familiar because she was—almost. I was looking into the face of my great-grandmother and she talked like Lita.

What if I hadn't come here? There was no mention of her encountering The Cat, but what if by looking for us, Alda accidentally stumbled upon The Cat? She could have been hurt or worse and maybe her future would change and mine as well. Rowley was right about having to be so delicate with my actions, anything could change the smallest elements of the past. It had been an errant thought as I plucked up roots, wondering if the roots I picked this day in this place meant there wouldn't be any in the future when Meiri goes mad after her encounter with The Cat. I couldn't risk changing everything—and perhaps cause a future where Lita wouldn't exist.

"First, I want you to promise me you won't wander in the woods by yourself. That cat is dangerous. Second, can you show me *your* hiding spot?"

"Sure. Are you an escaped princess?"

"No, but I am on a mission. I'll fill you in if you let me stash these roots in your hiding place."

"A real adventure? I think you'll be more fun than that dumb old cat."

The streets away from Canto's city center were mostly deserted. An eerie calm had settled over the place that was usually so full of life and bustle. A few awnings were off kilter and a wall or two had scribbled warnings on them about madness and cat fever. Businesses were barred shut and the people we did encounter kept their eyes averted, looking to the ground. Only the main avenue with the heightened KM presence was populated.

"How long has it been like this?" I asked Alda.

Since leaving the woods she'd taken on a more composed air, but I attributed that to her putting her dress back on. It settled on her like a mantle of maturity, but her eyes still darted to and fro, betraying her age—or something else. The unease in the air was palpable.

"People have been running home for weeks now, but it's only gotten this bad over the past few days. The Arco twins were found dead yesterday, and everyone is talking about it," she replied evenly.

I was glad I had insisted on walking her home. As is turned out she lived in the palace because her mother was lady-in-waiting to the

Queen. It was a relief to know that my ancestor had royal protection during this craziness.

"Aren't those your attendants?" she asked, pointing up ahead. I was startled to see Meiri and Toman walking toward us. We were supposed to meet at the shed. When they saw me they practically ran.

"What are you two doing here?" I asked. Meiri's eyes were wide and Toman was perspiring.

"We were looking for you," replied Toman. "We found... Who's your friend? She looks like..." Toman's eyes darted between Alda and me. He covered his open mouth as though trying to hold back a comment. Meiri continued to look startled.

"My name is Alda. I saw you come out of the Garza's shed and Raquel said I could join your adventure," she said with a big smile. Toman's eyebrows shot up and mouthed, *Raquel*?

"Did you, *Raquel*?" Toman asked me, pointedly.

"Who's Ra...?" Meiri began.

"Alda thinks I'm an escaped princess from Faery, but I had to tell her the truth," I said quickly. "That we're here on a mission from Faery to lift a curse from our kingdom and I need tamp root to make a potion." Toman tilted his head and nodded while Meiri remained blank. I was becoming concerned.

"Well, *Raquel* how did it go?" asked Toman.

"Good, but I promised Alda that she could help me tomorrow if she let me walk her home," I replied. "But it's getting late so I should make sure she gets there. Why not come along?"

"And where does she live?" asked Toman, incredulity warring with amusement on his face.

"I live in the palace. I'll show you how to get there," she replied. I kept stealing glances at Meiri, hoping she would keep it together until after we dropped Alda off. The palace looked the same and after waving goodbye, Alda found a guard to escort her inside. We waited until we'd left the stables to talk.

"Explain," said Toman, pulling into a deserted alcove. Meiri made no sign that she'd even heard him.

"You first. What's with Meiri?" I asked.

"We saw The Cat. He was strolling around Green Gardens. He didn't play or anything, but seeing him really spooked her. She's barely said two words since we left," he said in a hush.

Meiri pulled out a flask of what I knew was tamp root tonic and threw it back like a shot. That was when I realized we should have left her at home.

"Now it's your turn. Tell us why we now have a tail named Alda."

"She found me in the clearing. She was looking for me—for us—and that's why she entered the woods. If we hadn't come she never would have been in danger," I said, still keeping an eye on Meiri. I gestured for the two of them to follow, and thankfully they both did. We walked down one of the empty streets in the direction of the shed.

"It's not your fault. But we can't have a child following us," Toman replied.

"It's my fault she was in the woods. She wanted to find us and The Cat. What if she had? Do you know, she's already betrothed to Gabriel Garza? If anything had happened, Lita wouldn't happen, or my mother or me! What was I supposed to do?" I felt myself getting agitated. The empty streets were welcome, considering my outburst.

"Okay, okay. I guess it makes sense. Wow, this is really getting complicated. So, what's your plan now?" he asked, placing a reassuring hand on my arm.

"Well, she can come with me tomorrow to get more of the root. She has a hiding place near the mirror where we can store it, which should make things easier when we finally leave. Maybe if she thinks all we're doing is grubby work she'll lose interest in us before I go looking for Rowley and The Cat. You and Meiri can keep tabs on Rowley..."

"No. I...I can't," said Meiri finally roused from her stupor. "I'll come with you tomorrow. I'm better with plants than surveillance and if anything happens, you can do something. Really shouldn't we just stick together? Toman shouldn't be..."

"Toman's immune," I replied.

"What? How do you know that?" asked Meiri.

Toman gave me a look of warning and I knew I'd have to betray a trust he'd placed in me if I shared his secret. I stayed silent under Toman's scrutiny and Meiri's eyes ricocheted between me and him. Toman finally shrugged.

"After conservatory, I was set to be a court musician, but I had an accident. For a short time, I lost my hearing. But I was able to procure a remedy that was frowned on by the healers."

"You used magic?" Meiri asked.

"I had a hidden market connection who found me a magical cure. So, the upside is I can hear, but I can't hear music without external assistance," he said, casually. I knew how hard that admission had been for Toman. He was a performer known for his musical abilities and he just admitted it was all fake.

"More magic," said Meiri, who then looked at me.

"I was able to procure carillon weed," I said and Meiri's eyes grew wide.

"But that's—"

"Illegal. Meiri, you seem to keep forgetting my profession," I said.

"I was going to say dangerous. Consuming anything enchanted always has consequences. Especially long-term use."

"We were both aware of the risks. In my case, it's very small," said Toman. We had been lucky. Toman only tasted sweet things now. All other flavors were as bland as water. Carillon weed was fully capable of stealing all of another sense to bolster the sense being enchanted. The user consumed it according to need. For Toman it meant concentrated drops in his ear before performing.

"Toman, I think we're past secrets here. Your tone deafness is nothing to be ashamed of and it might actually save your life now," I replied. Meiri was thinking quietly.

"Well, it's only a theory, but I see your point. Maybe Meiri should come with you. I can follow Rowley around faster than either of you with those dresses."

"If you can call what Inez is wearing a dress anymore. Did you roll around in mud?" asked Meiri, looking a little more herself while scrunching up her nose at my appearance. "You can't walk around like that and expect people to ignore you. After breakfast tomorrow, we'll have to buy you a new dress," she said decisively. Meiri was never more at home then when she told other people what to do.

"She's right. We'll split up after breakfast and meet back at the shed before it gets dark," replied Toman, looking at my dirt-crusted dress. The ruffles, which had been a cream color, were now a crumpled gray. My gloves were covering my grimy nails and the satin shoes were beyond salvation.

"We didn't bring enough money to buy a new dress," I replied. "Do you want to starve?"

"We just might tonight. Nothing's open now anyway, so we can't get anything to eat tonight," said Toman. My stomach growled in protest. After an hour of hard labor followed by a long walk, the thought of skipping a meal was almost torture. "We should get off the street before the patrols ride through."

"Agreed. Let's get back to the shed and get some sleep. Maybe sleep will take my mind off being hungry," I said. We trudged back toward the Garza estate listening to the symphony of our hungry bellies. I regretted leaving most of my meal behind at Horner's.

The hinges on the door of the shed were stiff and squeaky but opened with a bit of effort. Inside it was dark and musty, but the floors were clean. A few old straw mattresses were in a heap, which we laid flat and fluffed the best we could. Meiri slept furthest away from the door and fell asleep the fastest. Toman tossed for a bit, but soon joined her in dreamland, breathing evenly.

I lay awake, hearing what was now the soft echo of the gong. I was glad Meiri was coming with me and Alda the next day. I didn't want to worry them but when I'd walked by the mirror shed with my burden of roots I had felt a gentle tug on my back. It reminded me of the feeling I had when I had my dream with Lita and Beval. It was pulling me back, light yet persistent, wanting me to return to my own time. It frightened me how hypnotic the gong was and how persistent the pull from the mirror was.

I felt like time's prey. It tempted me to drop my own pursuit and ignore everything. This was the lure of magic—to have Power and to wish for the freedom to do as I pleased. But I knew that was an illusion. Too easily could I be overpowered and fall under.

Hearing the gentle sighs and exhales from my friends reminded me I had a responsibility to keep them safe and return them home. Maybe Rowley knew this very thing would happen and that having Meiri and Toman would make it harder for me to turn my back on my real life.

I should have been affronted that he had so little faith in me, but I was relieved that he had understood what I would be going through. It was probably what he had experienced, having been friends with The Cat. This trip was making me understand Rowley better. How many years had Rowley dutifully waited for my arrival? Was it any wonder The Cat and his remorseless use of magic had been tempting? There were times I had thought it would be easier to use my magic to get something done...if I didn't care about the consequences or my responsibilities to others.

Thoughts like these swirled in my head like a melody with no fixed end. It wrapped itself around me, entrancing me to a semi-sleep that made me aware of everything—but conscious of nothing. I must have fallen asleep briefly, because as the morning light crept toward me, I finally stirred. The chilly damp smell spread, pervaded my senses, reminding me that a new day had begun.

Chapter 27

I woke up pinned to the ground. I couldn't thrash or flail—I was just stuck. The warmth of the sun let me know that I was no longer in the shed. I was rooted, unable to move, yet oddly calm.

What brought me here? Who brought me here? Was it The Cat or did the Rowley of the past do this? He said they played pranks on people. I was searching my brain for answers that seemed unimportant somehow. I was safe. I knew that and felt it in my....

Branches?

The thoughts came flooding back. Waking up, longing for stability and a sense of place. The sun creeping under the door. My overwhelming need to escape the confines of the stuffy, darkened shed. Wanting to run and find my way home. Rowley had warned me about this.

"Your moods affect your magic and your magic can affect your moods. While you're in this growing phase—learning your craft—either your magic or your moods can overtake you. That's what you experienced with your wind spell. It's a danger unless you can learn to control both your Power and your feelings. Powers this strong shouldn't have waited this long to be trained," he'd concluded, and I proved his point by igniting sparks in the ground. For his part, he didn't even flinch...just swished his tail and walked away.

Now I was fully aware that where I was, what I was, was a tree. Or part of one. I had thought of home and felt the ache of wanting to return to my roots, to be grounded. The great oak I found not far from the shed reminded me of the trees back home. I felt the distant touch of the Remembrance Tree. I had lain against it and that voice in my head chanted.

Syu....Syu...SYU

I'd studied enough to know it meant to bind, but the gong vibrating through me, the lack of sleep and the longing in my heart didn't care what binding myself to a tree would mean. But now I heard another voice.

Coward!

I couldn't tell if it came from me, or the voice in my head that Rowley said was an echo of lost knowledge, or maybe it was the tree to which I was grafted. It didn't matter. What mattered was that what the voice said was true. This hiding in a tree was cowardly and Meiri and Toman must be frantic trying to find me. I had to move.

I'm no coward. Concentrate... Get free... I'm a person, not a tree...

The voice was then quiet. Still. Silent. It wasn't letting me off the hook so easily. I knew why. In my heart of hearts a part of me wanted to remain. If so, I would hold fast—as a tree gripping the earth no matter what hurricane blew by. Let the world do its worst, but I would still stand. I would still stand. I would...

Bheid...Bheid...BHEID

It was the answer. I'd survived so much already. I couldn't let the people I love complete our task without me. It was time to move. BHEID.

The sensation of pins and needles coursed through me. I heard the rush of blood circulating again, pulsing in my head. My toes wiggled free from the ground, loosening my grip on the oak. Rough bark scraped my palms as I pulled them across the trunk. My hair fell in cascades down my back, tickling the back of my neck. The deep, rich voice of the tree said in a whisper, "Farewell, little one."

"I'm not a tree. I'm not a tree!" I shouted with a bittersweet laugh, hugging myself.

"No you're not. You're a witch," said a voice too close for comfort. His hand darted out and grabbed my wrist.

Looking into the eyes of Podkin, I knew I was in trouble.

Podkin's eyes were bright and hard, sneering at me and holding fast. But they weren't the eyes of the Podkin I knew from my time. The hostility was the same and he had the same iron grip. I knew I couldn't let my body react or I'd prove his point for sure. Breathing steadily was becoming an effort.

"What are you talking about? Let me go," I said, trying to sound meek. He gripped harder.

"I saw you, you witch. You stepped out of that tree. I knew you and your friends were trouble. Sebastian didn't believe me when I said you were magical. Maybe not the man—he looks common enough—but the other one. The nervous one with her nose in the air. You're renegade royals aren't you? Trying to hide your Powers," he said, gripping my other wrist. Mamá had warned me the time we were returning to had growing suspicions that people coming from Faery were likely gifted with magic.

His face was almost touching mine, spitting and spewing his contempt. I felt the icy tendrils inside me, willing themselves free, but I held them back.

What is it about people here and runaway nobles?

"I don't have any Powers. I...I got pulled in. I don't...know what happened. Please let me go," I pleaded. He yanked my arms above my head and pushed me against the tree. If he kept this up, soon the protection spell would win.

"Show me then. Or do you think I'm stupid enough to let you go so you can turn me into a toad or maybe a tree? Is *that* someone I know?" he asked gesturing toward the oak. His eyes were shining with hatred and I shrank away from him.

"You're crazy and you're hurting me," I replied calmly. My control was ebbing. Then I heard it. A rustling sound coming from the left of me. Out of the bushes walked Sebastian.

"Podkin, what are you doing?" asked an advancing Sebastian. His eyes darted between my face and Podkin's as he took in the scene.

"Don't be fooled by the pretty face. This girl is a monster. I saw her turn into a tree, or she was a tree and she became human again—if you can even call her human," he responded, gripping my wrists even tighter. "Magical beings aren't allowed to be here without notification and an escort. We have to send her back."

"I don't know what he's talking about. I'm not magical. I'm on vacation. The trees...in Faery look different than...here and I wanted a closer look. That's all," I said through gritted teeth. Sebastian looked appalled and pulled Podkin off me.

"Thank you," I said, rubbing my wrists.

"You can't go looking for monsters everywhere, Podkin. She's just a visitor. And look, you probably thought you saw her as part of the tree because of her dress. It's...remarkable."

I looked down at my ruined gown, but instead found a new one in a rich brown that mimicked the tree. The silk was matte instead of glossy, giving the impression that I was wearing bark. Flattering bark. I suspected it was the tree's doing. I smiled and felt my eyes start to sting.

"And look what you've done. You've made the girl cry. Inez, is it?" he asked, taking my hand gently in his. I blushed more for getting teary in front of strangers than because of the gesture. He smiled broadly. "Have you had breakfast? Come with me."

He tucked my hand into the crook of his arm before shooting a disdainful look at Podkin.

Podkin was fuming and the look he gave me was full of malice. If I thought Chief Podkin was bad, his ancestor was ten times worse.

As we left the field I heard the voice of the tree whisper, "Be careful, little one."

WALKING ALONG THE LANE, held close by Sebastian, I had the same feeling I experienced when I spent time with Arch. Not that Sebastian was anything like Arch, but he was handsome, charming and uncomplicated. I would never do anything to jeopardize what I have with Zavier, but Sebastian's attention still made me smile.

Not far from the town center, we ran into Meiri, Toman, and Alda. Alda waved wildly at the both of us.

"I see you've met Alda." Sebastian chuckled.

"She's like a one-girl welcome wagon."

Toman rushed up and gave me a bone-crushing hug, while Meiri hung back, looking drawn.

"Where were you? What happened?" he asked.

"Where did you find that dress?" asked Meiri.

"I just needed a little fresh air and...well, Sebastian invited me to breakfast when he...he found me," I said, unwilling to discuss the encounter in the woods. Sebastian looked at me curiously, but didn't add anything to my explanation.

"And the dress?"

"It's one I packed. No big deal," I replied, touching it compulsively. I wasn't one for frills and bows, but even I was awed by it.

"So, are we going to the...?" began Alda, but Meiri spoke over her.

"Breakfast sounds wonderful, but we do have plans this morning. Don't we, Inez?" said Meiri, pointedly.

"I thought your name was Raquel," said Alda, but Toman shook his head at her and she quieted.

"Yes, we do. I'm sorry if I forgot our schedule. Thank you for the invitation, Sebastian," I replied. I was hungry and it was hard to say no, but we were attracting too much attention already. Podkin and Alda were proof that we hadn't gone unobserved. Sebastian released my hand from his arm only to capture it and kiss it, looking into my eyes as he did. I felt my face flush in response.

"Some other time. Do be careful in the woods. You never know who or what you might run into," he said with a tilt of his head as he turned to leave.

"I'm telling Zavier," Toman said with mock horror.

"Not now. Inez, what happened?" asked Meiri.

"Nothing too important. Let's get food—I'm starving. And Alda, I need you to tell me anything you know about KM Podkin."

BREAKFAST WOULD HAVE been silent if not for Alda. She didn't have anything useful to tell us about Theodore Podkin other than what I suspected. He was a member of the Academy and against magical use, but that in itself wasn't criminal. Still, I couldn't resist a small thrill of fear knowing he knew what I was—or at least suspected.

What if he convinced Sebastian I was magical?

I was puzzled by how much that bothered me—that he would feel betrayed or think less of me for lying. It's not as though I would ever see Sebastian again.

I let Alda's suspicions of abused princesses, evil lords, and secret plots spin itself on and on to avoid looking up. I could feel Meiri's eyes on my gown and Toman's eyes on my face, willing me to talk.

If they were looking for a confession, they would wait a long time. I had no desire to tell them about the tree. Something about the encounter had felt sacred and personal. Explaining it would have taken away from the experience. Anyway, I could barely explain it to myself but for the first time since we arrived the gong inside me wasn't oppressive in its tolling.

"Are you with us?" asked Meiri peevishly. I looked down at my plate and saw I had been making swirls in my syrup. It resembled the grooves in a tree trunk.

"Yes. Sorry. Here's the plan for today: Meiri, Alda, and I will go harvest some more roots and take them to the hiding spot by the mirror. Toman, you can... You..."

"I'll go over to the Cup & Board to see if anything *interesting* is going on tonight," he said with a smirk. I smiled at his cleverness. Alda couldn't know we were hunting The Cat ourselves or she'd want to tag along. Toman still looked concerned about me, but the smile he returned was genuine.

"I can tell you about all sorts of things going on. Especially at the palace. Maybe you can come to one of the concerts tonight," Alda said hopefully.

I had to sever this connection—for her sake—but I was also tempted to see where she lived and meet more of my family.

"We'll see. Let's meet back here around lunchtime and then we can walk Alda back home," I replied.

"Home? That's so dull. Can't I come with—?"

"No, we had a deal. I said we could spend the morning together, but you promised to stay safe when you're not with us. What if the evil lord finds you and tortures you for my whereabouts?" I added for dramatic effect. Meiri snorted while Toman held back a laugh, but Alda's eyes grew so wide and earnest I knew she believed me.

"I won't fail you," she said gravely, and I had to hold back my own laugh at this child who was my great-grandmother and who, in this moment, suddenly sounded like Lita.

Alda skipped ahead while Meiri and I trailed behind. I could feel Meiri's body tense. She was taking deep breaths and small sips of the tonic.

"That stuff will dry you out," I said.

"And how do you know that?" Meiri asked, taking another discreet gulp.

"I just do. Plus what if we need it later? My theory about Toman being immune is only that. He may not hear music, but maybe he feels it or something," I replied, taking the flask from her. She looked ready to rebel with flashing eyes and her drinking hand closing into a fist, but another deep breath and she trudged on.

"Not much further," said Alda, as she started to unlace her bodice while still in motion. She shed her clothes neatly, folding them in a perfect square. At near ten she was neater than I was as a grown woman. *Are we really related?*

"Inez, I know you don't want to talk about it, but I'm not as fragile as you and Toman think. You can tell me what happened this morning," Meiri said, pulling me aside. I looked up and saw Alda placing her dress in a tree hollow and watching a bird construct a nest. She was still within running distance if anything happened.

"Look, there's not much to say. I needed some air and...I can't explain it all, but I used some magic and Podkin showed up there," I said, crossing my arms.

"He saw you?" Meiri asked.

"I don't know what Podkin saw, but he thinks he saw me use magic. He called me a witch and...anyway Sebastian turned up and saved me from turning Podkin into a toad," I said with a nervous giggle.

"Don't joke. He's part of the Academy and a KM... Podkin could turn you in," she said.

"For what? What he thinks he saw? And as far as he knows I'm from Faery. We all are," I said, dropping my arms. I made for Alda and the clearing, but Meiri grabbed my arm.

"What about the dress?" she asked.

"It was a gift, okay?"

"From Sebastian?" she asked as I twisted out of her grasp. Her hold on me felt eerily like Podkin's. As much as Meiri cared for me, she wasn't thrilled about my magic. Her recent run-in with The Cat had only made her disapproval more pronounced.

"No. From...from a friend. Now can we get to work? I don't like the idea of being in these woods any more than you do."

Alda was already pulling up roots with gusto when I got to the tree. Reluctantly, I unlaced my gown as though I was shedding my armor or a comforting blanket. I stood in only my long shift. It had enough fabric to be considered a full dress in our own time. I laid the gown reverently on the stump and whispered to the tree, "Keep it safe."

I wasn't certain, but I thought I felt a warm breeze embrace me, dispelling the sudden chill that had been tickling my exposed flesh. I moved to another section of roots and quietly whispered my spell, making sure to keep my back to Meiri and Alda. When I finished, more roots sprang up and Alda seemed not to notice.

Meiri removed her dress with the efficiency of someone who was used to complicated clothing, and stood there in her shift. Already she was in her element, telling Alda how to better pull the roots without hurting the surrounding plants.

Without intending to, I let them do all the pulling as I unobtrusively patrolled the perimeter. While the trees afforded comfort, they also provided excellent hiding places for a cat-sized body. I didn't think we were being followed, but The Cat had snuck up on me before. And now I had Podkin to worry about, too. I kept myself on alert as Meiri and Alda toiled in the earth. Alda made a comment about my lack of participation, but Meiri, looking more relaxed than she had in a while, said I was participating in my own way.

She smiled up at me and I knew that, at least for now, Meiri wasn't afraid. I was happy to give her that time, just as the tree had done for me.

Unfortunately, we hadn't thought about who was taking care of Toman.

Chapter 28

Meiri and Alda chatted animatedly about plants as fully clothed yet again we walked back to the mirror with the roots. It was unlikely we'd use Alda's hiding spot again and I hoped we'd return to our time soon. Allowing Alda any more involvement with our visit was too risky—she might learn more about the future.

I watched her with Meiri and smiled. I now realized who had instilled a love of herb lore in my grandmother and was amazed by how much Alda already knew. I supposed spending her free time in the woods had given her an education. Meiri was happy to talk about one of her loves with someone who understood. It was good to see Meiri so calm.

I could tell when we were approaching the mirror. I felt that invisible tug again, tethering me to the building. Meiri and Alda had to go into the shed while I stood fixed in place. A moment of panic engulfed me when I realized that Meiri might have the same problem I'd had getting out of the shed, but my worries were unfounded.

"Inez? Are you all right?" asked Meiri, taking my hand in hers. The contact unfroze me enough that I could put one foot in front of the other, straining against the invisible string pulling me back to the shed and the mirror. I continued to hold Meiri's hand until we were well clear of the structure and had almost reached town.

"What wrong?" she asked when I dropped her hand.

"I'm not sure. You didn't feel anything?" I asked, the numbness of my legs giving way to oversensitivity. The fabric of my gown now rubbed me uncomfortably.

"Feel what? I know something's going on and you're not telling us what exactly. Let us—"

Whatever Meiri was going to say died on her lips. Sebastian was running toward us at full tilt. *Had Podkin convinced him that I was a danger? Was he coming to arrest me?* The only thing that kept me from taking off was the look on his face. It wasn't hell-bent or angry—it was afraid and concerned. When he reached us my mouth was already dry with fear, as though I already knew what he was about to say.

"Your friend has met with a terrible accident. You must come with me to the healers—they do not know if he will survive."

WE ARRIVED AT THE HEALERS' home out of breath and disheveled. The long building with its large windows and attached greenhouse looked the same as it did in my own time. The chalky whitewashed exterior made me think of Lita and the years she'd devoted to her patients. All of them appreciated her skill, but they loved her for her steady capability. I needed a little of that.

Only Sebastian's authority got us in as the attending nurse thought Meiri, Alda and I looked disreputable, with dirt under our fingernails. She was lucky he did get us in because I could feel my Powers rising at the thought of anyone preventing me from seeing Toman.

Meiri stayed in the lounge with Alda as Sebastian escorted me upstairs to the ward. In a large room with many beds, my eyes were drawn to one. I walked over as if in a dream. My movements were not my own and all I thought of was how I would explain it to

Dottie. The loss of her son would surely kill her, and then I would be responsible for two deaths.

He'd never looked more vulnerable. Toman's face was a pale gray and his eyes were closed. The slow rise and fall of his chest was my only reassurance that he hadn't already died. A thin blue sheet was pulled up to his chin, but his right arm bulged underneath. I sat down heavily on the chair next to the bed and brushed a stray hair away from his face.

I thought to myself that he wouldn't approve of himself, looking so scruffy. Sweat beaded out on his forehead and I wondered if he was in pain. I wanted to hold his hand, to let him know I was there because I still hadn't found my voice. I reached for the edge of the sheet gently but was stopped.

"I don't recommend you look under there, miss," said a thready voice. "It's not for a lady's eyes."

The man looking down at me looked kind but was firm in his belief. I felt Sebastian grip my shoulder, reassuringly before pulling the healer aside. I knew they were discussing Toman and whether it was better if I left, but I didn't respond. I was watching my best friend slip from me.

Then I was angry. *Who are they to Toman?* I was his best friend and they should be discussing his options with me. I wouldn't let Toman die. And I couldn't and wouldn't be responsible for what happened to anyone who tried to stop me. I reached for the blanket this time with purpose. I would see the damage and correct it, no matter what.

"Miss, please come away—"

"Miss is staying right here. His name is Toman, and he is my responsibility," I said, my voice unexpectedly breaking with emotion. Tears pricked the back of my eyes, but I held them back defiantly. "You tell me what happened and what you intend to do to fix it because I won't leave without him!"

Both Sebastian and the doctor looked perplexed—as though they never counted on someone talking back. It would have been funny if the situation weren't so serious. I pulled back the sheet and saw Toman's face twitch in response. His right arm was enveloped in gauze from his fingers to his shoulder. It smelled sickeningly sweet and was caked in a rainbow of blood and horror.

"What happened?" I asked, but already knew the answer.

"I...I found him near the Cup & Board with a gash from his wrist to his upper arm. He was muttering incoherently. It was bleeding profusely and...and I got him here as quickly as I could. It was a jarring ride on my horse, and he passed out from the pain," said Sebastian reluctantly. The older healer reached for the sheet still gripped in my hand, but my quelling look stopped his hand.

"Have you tried fortified honey?" I asked. When I'd treated Meiri's arm, her wound was jagged, but clean as was my own when Zavier bandaged it. Toman's looked and smelled as though he'd sustained his injury days ago. I knew that fortified honey was a controlled substance from Mythos with healing and enchanted qualities and that it was always available at the Healers' Homes, but its use wasn't well known. My question was more than the healer expected. He grimaced and crossed his arms forcefully.

"Fortified honey? Young lady, do not presume to know more than me. Fortified honey is for minor cuts and scrapes and produces dubious results at best. There is powerful magic at play. You should prepare yourself for the worst," he said with a tone that brooked no argument. He looked affronted that he had to explain himself to me, but I wasn't interested in his ego. I needed to get my friend away from there.

"Well, since you decided that he is beyond your care," I said, my voice rising, "I'll take him back home. Sebastian will you help me carry Toman out?" I asked without waiting for a response. I pulled away the sheet completely and tried fashioning a sling for his arm.

"This is highly irregular. I don't think you understand—" began the healer.

"No, you're the one who doesn't understand. I'm taking him away. Now. Give him something for the pain and get out of my way," I said through gritted teeth. I understood the healer was doing what he thought was necessary, but my Powers were itching to throw him against a wall. Something in my eyes must have told him I wasn't kidding because he turned on his heal, muttering about uppity women.

"I don't know if I can help you," said Sebastian.

"Fine, then you can get out of the way, too. Just send Meiri upstairs," I said curtly. Toman's breathing was growing shallower, and Sebastian wanted to argue? I didn't have the time. I had a wave of homesickness, and found myself comparing the two men, knowing that Zavier wouldn't have asked questions.

I still didn't know how I was going to get Toman out of there. He was lithe, but he wasn't light. I would have to transport him out using magic and then I would be arrested or deported and Toman would die. I had to think of something else. Then the voice came.

Gel...Gel...GEL

To freeze? How did that make sense? I couldn't imagine how freezing Toman would improve his condition and I would be stopped if I tried carrying out a Toman-sickle. My hands were tingling and my level of frustration was threatening to spill over with tears or a burst of magic. I couldn't lose Toman like this but moving him would likely be the end of him.

Time slowed and the voice in my head that occasionally supplied words of Power said clearly, "*Gel kerd*."

Suddenly, it all made sense. Not freeze as in cold... Rather freeze as in stop because I remembered *kerd* meant heart. I knew in that instant I had to stop Toman's time, or at least hold it back. If I did, would it look like he died? That might be okay because then that doctor could congratulate himself on being right and leave me the hell alone.

I closed my eyes and stroked his cheek, feeling the feverish heat subside. In my mind I chanted *gel kerd* and saw him go still—suspended in time. My hand went cold; the tips of my fingers grew stiff and blue-tinged. I pulled it back, biting back a gasp of pain. Toman looked dead and it was easy to let a tear roll down my cheek. I laid the sheet over him again, covering his face. The fabric didn't stir.

"I'm so...so sorry. I can make any arrangements you need—"

"All I need is for you to help me get him out of here. He wouldn't want to be left behind," I said with real anger. Sebastian lifted Toman as though he were a rag doll as I clung to Toman's good arm with my good one and left the hospital.

SEBASTIAN TOOK US TO his rooms in a boarding house. We were lucky that the matron was out because she probably would have objected to having a dead body on the premises. I'd refused to let go of Toman's hand for fear that breaking our connection would destroy the spell. I also refused to even look at Sebastian.

He withdrew with Alda after depositing Toman's body gently on the floor. I left Meiri to give our thanks because I had none to give him. I was too busy trying to formulate a plan to save Toman.

"What is your plan, Inez?" asked Meiri. She took short, shaky breaths.

"I'm going to save him. Can you find my first aid kit?"

Meiri rummaged around her bag and pulled it out with clumsy fingers. It fell with no harm done, but my nerves were already raw. "Be more careful!" I snapped and I saw Meiri biting her tongue instead of lashing back.

Unwrapping the arm was a two-person job we did in utter silence. The hand I'd used to cast the spell had thawed and I wondered if I was too late. But I kept on unwrapping with Meiri, hoping against hope.

His arm was a purple, putrid mess. The smell alone would alert the other boarders. A boarding house full of KM.

I moved his arm gingerly, but he didn't react to my touch at all. I needed to find the edge of his gash. The doctor was right, this wasn't a simple matter. I refused to give way to despair and smeared the small jar of salve on his wrist. I felt the enchantment in the fortified honey, thin as a whisper—not enough. I'd taken Lita's entire supply with me, not knowing what would greet us when we stepped through the mirror.

Nothing happened. I rubbed deeper and deeper into the gash. I didn't know how much time passed before Meiri braved my wrath.

"It's not working, Inez. We have to—"

"We have to *what*? Leave him here and go back home to tell his mother that he died? Or should we continue our search and hope for the best, huh? I know this is all too unpleasant for you..."

"Inez, don't. I know he's your best friend and you don't think I have the right to an opinion, but if we get caught, what then? Damn Canto?" In any other instance I would have been shocked by Meiri's language, but this wasn't the time for shock—I was angry.

"Damn you."

"Well, you're half right because if you're going to stay here with Toman then we're all damned. Listen to me. We have to deal with this," she implored.

But I wasn't listening. I could feel the tingle coming back. The voice was whispering urgently now.

Sreu...Sreu...SREU

I recognized the word. To flow...I had to bring Toman back before I could save him. I closed my eyes and shut out Meiri's naysaying and my anger toward Sebastian. I chanted, "*Sreu, Sreu, SREU.*"

Little by little I felt the heat return to Toman. His arm was on fire, and I could feel his pain. He was dying and I had to save him.

My hands were still tingling from their efforts; I gave myself no time to think or consider. I placed my hands on his ruined arm and chanted "*gwei*"—to live. Another healing spell.

My fingers felt cool but slowly they began to warm, as though pulling the sickness out of Toman's arm. My chest tightened and my breathing became labored. The room began to sway, or maybe that was me.

By then my hands were on fire and I had to grit my teeth to keep from screaming out in agony. In that moment I sensed how close to the brink Toman had been, and now I was too. I heard Meiri's muffled voice shouting at me, but I didn't understand what she was saying.

I opened my eyes and saw Toman looking back at me. He was mouthing something over and over again, but with my head spinning it was too hard to concentrate.

Then he grabbed my hands with his good arm and said very slowly, "Let go."

I did and everything went dark.

Chapter 29

I woke up and my head was sore. So was my cheek. Another smack made me exhale audibly.

"Oh thank goodness. Inez, we have to get out of here," said Meiri. Toman was sitting over me poised to slap me again.

"Toman? You're okay?" My voice sounded so weak.

"We can talk about it later. We have to leave or that KM will wonder how a corpse came back to life," urged Meiri. They both helped me up and I heard the gong twice as loud.

"What's that sound?" asked Toman. His eyes scanned the room before coming to rest on me. "Is that coming from you?" he asked, peering at me intently.

"You can hear it? The gong?" I asked.

"Has that been happening all this time?" He looked at me sadly. I knew he would ask more, but he was thankfully interrupted.

"Can we talk about it later? Inez I know you're weak, but we need to get to the shed without being seen," said Meiri. I knew what she was asking and the idea frightened me. Toman had to help me up and despite having his support I felt wobbly. Just thinking the word of Power redoubled the pain in my head and the incessant peel of the gong.

Toman and Meiri caught me as my knees gave way. I didn't have the strength to move us using magic. We needed another plan. I looked around the room, frantically wishing for a secret door or something that could give us a discreet exit from a boardinghouse full of KM. A boarding house full of KM? My eyes alit on a partially open closet door.

"Toman put on one of Sebastian's uniforms. We can slip out with you if they think you're one of them," I said, still foggy but scared enough to work through it.

"His clothes won't suit me," argued Toman.

"Are you really arguing for fashion's sake?" I asked, but I saw his point. Sebastian was at least three inches taller and a handspan broader than Toman.

"No...just... All right. Let's do this quickly," he said and started getting undressed. The uniform was big on him, but not enough to attract notice—I hoped. Meiri looked out into the hallway and found it empty. With both of them supporting me, we moved down the stairs as quickly as my shaky legs would allow...only to run into the house matron.

"And just who might you be?" she asked Toman. I watched with dread as she took in his appearance. His oversized uniform couldn't bare this much scrutiny. She also gave Meiri and me the once-over and pursed her lips at my clear unsteadiness. To her I must have appeared drunk.

"I'm a...new recruit. I was taking a look around the rooms hoping to...find lodging," he said, still looking a little worse for wear. She looked at him intently as though she could tell he was up to no good.

"Well, I run a respectable boarding house. We don't allow women of loose morals here," she said indicating Meiri and me.

"Understood," he said, with an almost straight face. Meiri looked apoplectic at being thought to be a whore. I just draped myself on Toman's arm and pushed us out.

"What did you say your name was?" she asked, but Meiri pulled me along faster than I thought possible. The blast of fresh air, even tinged with manure, revived me enough to walk briskly under my own power. Meiri was setting a pace she'd never shown before and Toman was breathing hard.

I found it difficult to keep up, but I didn't dare slow down. We ducked into a cramped alley when Meiri pointed out Sebastian heading back toward the boarding house. The alley stank of horses and manure and Toman groaned in disgust as he extracted his boot from an offensive pile.

We watched as the matron met him at the door and began to gesticulate wildly. Sebastian spun on his heels, craning his neck left and right as though searching for someone. When he saw nothing, he ran inside, the matron following. The door slammed shut.

We waited a few minutes before leaving the alley and then hastily headed to our hiding place.

"SO WHAT HAPPENED? HOW did you get injured?" I asked Toman once we reached the shed. He had barred it and sat against the door for good measure in case someone tried to push their way in.

"I saw Rowley meet with the horn player. It's going to happen tomorrow. Thank goodness because I don't think we can afford any more close calls. Rowley and the horn player met in the Cup & Board and I was going to follow the horn player, but I ran into The Cat instead," he said with a shiver. He and Meiri shared a look as though now they understood each other.

"Also, I found out you were right about the music not working on me. Knowing that just made The Cat angry, so he lunged at me. All I remember was a burning in my arm. Then I woke up in the boarding house and you were passed out. You've got to stop doing that," he added with a shake of the head.

"I'll work on it. But why can you hear the gong now while Meiri can't?"

"I have a theory. Listen to this," he said and then began to sing. Not beautifully, but definitely on pitch and without the carillon weed. "I think The Cat infused me with music somehow so now I'm not tone deaf. At least that's one good thing that came from all that."

"So that means you can't come with me when Rowley and Blue confront The Cat," I said with a sigh. I was surprised how much I had been counting on his support since Meiri couldn't come.

"Inez, I don't think we should keep this up. We should go home with the root and make the best of it," he said. Meiri quickly nodded in agreement, but I knew it wouldn't end with just the root.

"I have to know what happened to the horn and El Niño. Someone recently reminded me that there is more at stake than just one person," I said, looking at Meiri.

"Inez, I'm sorry—" she began.

"Don't be. You were right and I do have a responsibility to Canto to find a way to get rid of The Cat.

"Tomorrow the two of you will hide in the shed until I come back armed with the knowledge of the horn's location, the only thing that's stopped The Cat in the past. Toman you should get some rest. You still don't look well," I said.

"I could say the same to you, but I'm too tired to argue. A nap would be nice," he said and pulled the mattress over to the door and fell asleep.

"Does the gong hurt?" asked Meiri.

"Not really, more of an irritation," I lied. "Get some sleep."

"Is that what was happening at the mirror shed? Was the gong keeping you there?" asked Meiri

"I don't know. I just feel this...pull back to the mirror when I'm there, like it wants me to return to our own time. Lucky for us, we go back tomorrow."

WE WERE ALL LAYING down in the shed. Meiri was breathing evenly. She slept in complete stillness, but I heard Toman tossing and turning. He finally stilled, but I knew he wasn't asleep.

"Have you ever thought about death...about dying?" asked Toman in a whisper.

"Lately, a lot," I replied. I thought about all the near misses recently: when I thought Toman was dead; when Zavier almost died; and my own many brushes with mortality. It was an odd conversation to have in the dark. In a time that wasn't my own and populated by people long dead, but somehow it felt appropriate.

"I mean, have you thought about your last days? Rowley explained how this whole time spell thing works. He explained that, by doing this, you'll lose time from the end of your life. What if those last days were going to be amazing? It could be my last big bow on stage, or just a beautiful day I'll miss, or even—even the day they find a cure for a mysterious disease," Toman said wistfully.

I knew Toman was thinking about his mother and how her days were slowly slipping away. I couldn't imagine that. I was worried too that by being with me, they might risk their own final days.

"We'll think of something, Toman. I cured myself and you—maybe I can do the same for Dottie," I replied and we lapsed into a thoughtful silence. This conversation was stirring up memories of another conversation.

"Healing is a type of time magic Inez," Mr. Fell had said. "If you didn't have Powers, you would have died from this infection. You should have died. I'm not saying I wanted that—I'm quite fond of you—but it's the way the world works. Time is jealous of his gift and when you rob him of it, he stalks you, waiting for the perfect time to exact his revenge. Healing magic should only be used in dire emergencies because just like a time spell, it takes some of your time away."

I couldn't tell Toman that saving Dottie would cost me more life. Dottie was all the family he had. It would be like me losing Mamá. I couldn't conceive of a time when she wasn't around. I would be lost. And so would Toman be lost without his mother. However, if time was already stalking me, I might as well make the most of it.

We both grew quiet for a time and as the minutes ticked by, I closed my eyes and hoped sleep would come.

"Are you still awake?" whispered Toman. I considered pretending to be asleep, but that would have been cowardly.

"Yeah."

"If anything happens tomorrow, take care of Dottie for me," he said casually, but I knew he was thinking about this because he'd almost died.

"Toman, you're going to be fine. We're going back soon, and I'll cure Dottie," I replied, lifting myself up on an elbow.

"Okay. But if anything does happen, bury me in this outfit. I look too good in it not to wear it again," he said with a smile.

"Deal, so long as you don't bury me in anything like this. I think I deserve a comfortable afterlife," I replied, and we laughed genuinely and loudly.

"What? Is it morning?" yawned Meiri.

"No, go back to sleep," I said then rolled over and closed my eyes to contemplate the day ahead.

Chapter 30

I must have slept because I woke up to Toman nudging me.

"It can't be morning already," I complained, even as I saw the sun creeping under the door.

"Tell me about it. Sunshine over there almost tore my head off for interrupting her beauty rest. I think I heard her saying a name in her sleep. 'Jacque,' was it?" he teased.

Meiri sat up. "I wish. I mean, no. I was dreaming about that horrible hospital. I thought the manure smell was bad. And sweetie, were I you, when we get back I would take three showers—you reek," said Meiri, wrinkling her nose at Toman.

"Sorry. Dying is a smelly business. I'll try to decompose more florally next time," he quipped.

"Don't worry Toman. If we're keeping track, next time it's Meiri's turn to nearly die. Then you can complain about her odor." I laughed.

"Inez, only you would make jokes about people dying." Meiri sniffed.

"I think I've earned it. Okay here's the plan for today and no one is allowed to get themselves in trouble, almost die, or do anything else that will keep us here any longer," I said.

"Damn right," agreed Toman.

"So, I'm going to get you two to the mirror shed while I stake out the bay. Rowley's memory looked pretty early in the day, so I don't think we'll have to wait long..."

"What do you mean 'get you two in the shed'?"

"I mean we'll meet at the shed and go straight home after I find out where the horn ended up," I said, smoothing the hair back from my face. I didn't need a mirror to know I looked a mess. If Meiri and Toman were any indication, we could all use a good scrubbing.

"Excuse me. Explain the shed, please," said Toman.

"I feel strong enough to send you to the shed with my magic. Now before you say no, think about it. Toman, I can't have you walking around town when everyone knows you're dead. And there's a pretty good chance Sebastian saw the *three* of us running from his rooms. Not to mention that landlady of his being able to identify us. She probably filed a report. My solution makes sense. I worked it all out last night," I said. I stood up and offered Meiri a hand to do the same.

"Last night? You mean the night you barely slept? Of course it sounded like a good idea in that state of mind," chimed in Toman.

"You have a better one?"

"Well at least one that doesn't involve you using magic on us without being around to see the results. We can just sneak around the edge of town..."

"No, no, no. I won't walk around town waiting for *that cat* to find us or some KM on patrol to identify us. I don't like Inez's plan, but it's the best option. You should have more faith, Toman. Inez brought you back from the dead," smirked Meiri. I was oddly buoyed by her faith in me. And to be honest, I had the same reservations as Toman, but someone among us had to be brave. Or at least fake it.

"He wasn't dead," I replied hearing my stomach growl. Another morning without breakfast. "When we get back I'm going to plant myself in a booth at Froth and eat until I'm sick."

"Ditto," replied Toman.

"My treat," said Meiri. "Now, let's get this over with. I can already taste the pancakes waiting for us in the future."

MOVING TOMAN AND MEIRI from one shed to another with my magic had been oddly simple. I'd gone with them, taking Toman's concerns to heart—that I might accidently leave them somewhere else. The gong thrummed louder from inside the mirror shed, but now that Toman and Meiri were aware of it, they pushed me out. Toman no longer heard it, which was a relief, considering I had to leave him in the shed for an unknown amount of time.

I headed out in search of Rowley and The Cat, still heartened by my easy use of Power.

I'd chanted my words out loud and it seemed to make the difference. My use of magic at the Healers' Home had been what Rowley had called astral magic, and abstract Power. Abstract mages could cast spells with their minds, though Rowley cautioned that using abstract Power was draining. But I had done it. If I could get the hang of my magic, it should be easy to thwart The Cat.

The early morning sun was warm, and I longed to strip off all my layers and enjoy the heat on my body. It was one of those spring days that was a preface to summer. No matter how much I wanted to get back to the present, I would miss this. Winter was not my favorite season.

The forest was quiet and empty. There wasn't even the sounds of nearby animals. That was odd and put me on my guard. Was The Cat taking this route to the bay, too? I needed to make sure I wouldn't be involved in the confrontation, just a witness. Bumping into The Cat or Rowley and Blue for that matter would make a mess of things.

My skirts kept getting caught on bushes and fallen branches. I knew I couldn't walk around the woods in my underwear, but I gathered up the skirt fabric and tied it up above my knees. Anyone who saw me would be scandalized, but not offended. As I fought with the knot I didn't realize that someone was sneaking up behind me. But my protection spell did.

"Ouch! What was that?" asked Sebastian. I jumped back from his touch, my heart racing. He looked me up and down, from my sleep-matted hair to my disheveled and grimy dress all tied up. He advanced on me with hands outstretched, then fell back with a considering look on his face. He settled for standing directly in my path, but didn't touch me.

"What are you doing out here?" I asked.

"My job. What are you up to?" he asked, his suspicion obvious.

"Nothing. Just walking. And I should get going..." I began and he mirrored my steps.

"Oh no you don't. What happened yesterday? I saw you running from the boarding house and I'm pretty sure I saw your dead friend running, too," he said, blocking my path. He raised his hands though still made no move to grab me.

"You were seeing things. I just had to go and—"

"I'm not an idiot. What is going on?" he asked. "Is Podkin right about you? Because based on what I've seen I'm starting to believe him."

"Believe what you want. I have to go," I said, stepping around him. He moved again, blocking my escape from his questions.

"You're not going until you talk. Or should I haul you in on charges?"

"Who's stopping you? You want to arrest me?" The look on his face reminded me of Zavier when I snapped at him. He paced in front of me, pinching the bridge of his nose. I knew I should run, but I was genuinely torn. It didn't help when he stopped his back and forth and stood before me, his eyes pleading.

"No. I want to help," he said gently. I had begun to concoct a lie in my head, but it fizzled out. He was so earnest, and I knew his fear was *for* me, not of me. Maybe it was my desire to finally share the truth with Zavier, but I decided this would have to do for now.

"I'm not from Faery. I'm from Canto, just not a Canto you know," I began.

"What does that mean?"

"It means...I came from Canto...from the future," I answered, grudgingly.

"The future?" he asked.

"About a hundred years in the future," I said and then told him the whole cat story. He listened quietly with a blank expression. I couldn't tell if he thought I was crazy or lying, but he didn't make a comment until the end.

"So why can't you stop The Cat here?" he asked. I wasn't prepared for a sensible question.

"Oh...I can't change the past. It might do something to my present. You'll be happy to know that the reign of cat terror all ends today and I'll get the information I came for. And tamp root is good for curing madness," I added. He looked at me with new eyes, trying to understand what I was throwing at him in a ridiculously short amount of time.

"You used time magic? Does that mean Canto gets back its magic in your time?"

"Not all of us. Well, only me really," I replied. Then I realized what he was asking. "Are you a part of the Society?"

"Yes. I guess that means you're the one from the prophesy? The Ternion. You should have told me. I could have helped you," he said.

"Like you helped me at the infirmary?" I thought about him and the healer trying to steer me away. He remembered too.

"I'm sorry about that. I just—"

"Now you know, so if you want to help, go check on my friends at the Garza mirror shed. I need to finish this so we can get home," I said, turning away.

"I could help—"

"No, you can't." I turned back and told him more gently, "It's something I have to do alone. Please stay away from this. Otherwise, it could change your future." And I ran further into the woods.

I sat on a rise above the short stretch of shore where the drama of Cat, Rowley and the Niño Amoratado played out. I watched, transfixed and recognizing the scene from Rowley's vision with the peer needle. I was too far away to hear any of the interplay. It was all body language. The Cat on two legs was leaning carelessly against his fiddle, its slightly taller frame somehow anchored to the beach. El Niño stood with the horn tightly in his grip, obvious even from my vantage point. Rowley stood on four legs between the two musicians, his posture tense. I'd seen that particular pose before—it was the one he used when he told me how much of a disappointment I was. I felt a pang of pity for The Cat, but it was small.

The Cat's paw extended, and I saw the glint of his nails as they idly strummed the delicate strings of the fiddle. A soft strain of music reached my ears, but my attention was on the bay where the waters moved unnaturally. Rowley barked in the direction of El Niño, who raised the horn to his lips.

I knew from Rowley's vision it was only a matter of time before the real battle began. Although I knew this event was already a part of Canti history, I couldn't stay on that safe bluff watching Rowley. Despite my common sense telling me to stay away, I ran toward the beach.

By the time I reached the bay, the battle between Rowley, the horn player and The Cat had already begun. The wave, which started The Cat's legend, was already at its peak and ready to inundate all of Canto. Rowley and El Niño were losing ground and The Cat was reaching for his fiddle.

My protection spell sensed the danger and tightened around me. Seeing Rowley struggle made my Powers surge; I wanted to help. My fingers tingled painfully with unused magic, longing to be unleashed. Clenching my jaw and curling my rebellious fingers into fists, I pushed back the urge. I knew that doing anything in this moment could alter the past. From my vantage point, up on a hill, I heard the screams coming from town as they saw the gargantuan wave blot out the sun. It was almost over.

I saw The Cat, Rowley and El Niño Amoratado go under one last time and I heard the sound of the horn come from the waterlogged trumpeter, a clarion call, sweet and strong, stilling the water.

The Cat disappeared with a look of surprise on his face. Rowley was unconscious on shore, and I wanted to run to him. Though I knew he was alive, I wanted to be reassured. El Niño sank beneath the surface, clutching the horn, and he didn't resurface with it.

I was torn. I could swim out and rescue him and the horn, but Rowley's warning had been definite. I could not change the past and I had no idea how much damage I'd done already. But I couldn't let him drown. How would I look at myself in the mirror knowing I could have saved his life but done nothing? I stripped off my gown, ready to dive into the deep.

Then a hand clamped over my mouth and dragged me back to the woods.

The more I fought, the stronger my captor's grip on my arms. My muffled yells fell on deaf ears as I was lifted into the air by strong arms and dropped forcibly to the ground. The pain that shot up my back knocked the wind out of me.

As I gasped for breath, I looked up into the red face of Theodore Podkin. His eyes shone with unspoken malice and in one hand he held a rope. In the other a knife. I took gulping breaths as he crouched down next to me, his knife dangerously close to my throat.

"So witch, did you do that to scare us? Were you going to flood the town? I knew Sebastian shouldn't trust you," he sneered. The edge of the blade hovered and then skimmed an invisible trail down my chest. At that moment I didn't care about my safety.

"There's a...boy in the bay...and he's drowning—"

"You did that! Did he come upon you practically nude and so you punished him? Having second thoughts about taking his life, are you? I will have no such problem with you," he said, his blade stopping at my stomach. I was still more concerned with saving the horn player. My Powers in water were limp and would be unable to find him. I needed to help him.

"Please, I won't go anywhere. Just let me get to him before—"

"Why should I trust you?"

"Because she's telling the truth," said Sebastian. He was standing behind Podkin with his own knife. His face was flushed as though he'd been running and the sweat running down his temples confirmed that.

"Are you bewitched? How do you know she's telling the truth?" asked Podkin, his grip on the hilt of his knife tightening.

"I just do," he replied, inching closer.

"Fool. I'll tell them how you helped a witch. Now come here and help me tie her up," he replied savagely. Sebastian looked from me to Podkin, caught in an impossible situation. He sheathed his knife and knelt by Podkin.

"I'm sorry," said Sebastian.

"Don't bother," I replied, disgusted. But then Sebastian picked up a thick branch and clouted Podkin over the head. He fell back, unconscious as I looked on in shock.

"I wasn't talking to you," he said, grabbing the rope and tying the feet and hands of Podkin. "Are you okay?"

"Forget about me. There's a boy drowning in the lake and—"

"No he's not. He ran past me on my way to find you. He was heading for the border," Sebastian replied, tying another knot in the rope. He pulled Podkin to a sitting position and leaned him up against a tree.

"Was there anything in his hand?" I asked.

"No. He was sopping wet, running in his undergarments. There really wasn't anywhere to hide...anything. Unless it was small," he replied.

I couldn't resist the reply that escaped my lips.

"That was a decidedly unladylike thing to say," he joked.

"I keep telling you that I'm not a lady," I replied.

"Somehow I doubt that," he replied, looking deep into my eyes. He took off his coat and draped it over my bare shoulders, my dress still discarded by the bay after Podkin prevented me from jumping in to save Rowley. "We should collect your things and move before Podkin wakes."

We moved back down to the shore, and I found, then put on my gown with numb fingers. The warmth of the day was lost on me as I realized that I had failed in my attempts. Now the horn lay at the bottom of the bay, possibly lost forever. My magic in water was spotty at best. It was small consolation that I knew where it was, but it was little better than what we knew before.

After a third attempt to lace my bodice, Sebastian took hold of the strings with sure fingers. He stood close behind me and could feel his breath on the back of my neck, a complete contrast to Podkin's rough treatment.

"Your friend...the one who died... Is he your intended?" he asked, finishing up the last lacing.

"Toman? No. He's my best friend, but only a friend," I said, feeling my traitorous pulse quicken at his proximity. *It's just a reaction to his gallantry.* One of his hands rested lightly on my waist.

"But in your time you must have...someone," he said more as a question than a statement. I turned in his grasp and barely trusted my voice to respond to his soulful eyes. I swallowed and nodded instead.

"I see," he replied softly.

We walked along quietly for a few minutes, careful to skirt in a wide circle away from any route Podkin would take. Passing back from the shore, we'd untied him, so he wouldn't have proof of his captivity. I worried about what would happen to Sebastian after I left and Podkin turned him in. Sebastian brushed it off.

"Podkin turns someone in once a month. He's a zealot and his connection to the Academy makes him less credible. I wouldn't worry," he replied.

"Did you check on my friends?" I asked, suddenly remembering them.

"Yes, I even posted a guard," he chuckled.

"A guard. Won't that raise suspicions?" I asked, picking up my pace.

"Not this guard," he said with another smile.

"Alda? You put Alda there, didn't you?" I smiled back.

"It was more that she put herself there and refused to move. She has some fantastical ideas about what you're doing here. Honestly, I think she wanted to make sure you didn't leave without saying goodbye," he said, grabbing my hand. And I was saying goodbye to people I'd never been meant to meet and who were already long dead in my time. I considered myself lucky to have been given this opportunity, despite all the danger. A complex jumble of emotions swirled within me.

"She's my great-grandmother, you know. Do me a favor and watch out for her after I leave? If anything happens to Alda, I might not happen," I said with a smirk.

"And that would be a great loss indeed," he replied, still stroking my hand. He leaned forward and gave me a gentle kiss on the cheek.

It was something Zavier would have done, and I felt my face redden slightly.

"Have a safe trip back." With a slight incline of his head, he left me by the shed and continued his patrol.

"DO YOU HAVE TO GO BACK?" asked Alda, her words muffled as she hugged my waist. My concerns for her safety had lessened since the Cat had repeated history and disappeared, but my staying was just as dangerous to Alda. Every decision I made had the potential to change her future and my own. I unpeeled her arms from around me and crouched down to her level. Her face was so familiar that I felt myself start to tear up.

"You know I do. We can't have an evil lord win, now can we?" I said and stifled a laugh at her earnest look.

"Will you come back?" she asked.

"I don't think so. But who knows? Maybe you'll see me again when you least expect it," I said and wrapped her in an embrace. "And give the Garza boy a chance. Maybe he'll be the prince in your story." Her response was a gagging sound, followed by sticking her tongue out. I had to laugh. "Just try, okay?"

"Okay. I hope you defeat the evil lord," she replied, pulling away.

"Me too. Bye."

"Bye," she said and waved as she raced down the road toward the palace. At least I knew she wouldn't be hurt by The Cat. He was now in our time and my responsibility to stop for good this time. I opened the door to the shed and found Toman and Meiri snacking on fresh bread.

"I'm out risking my life while the two of you munch on food? Is there any more?" I asked, salivating at the smell of fresh bread and melted butter.

"Don't be so melodramatic. I saved you two slices so we can fatten you up and leave this place," said Toman, handing me the warm bread. I took a bite and sighed at the warm heaven melting on my tongue. "Success?" he asked.

"Well," I said between bites, "I know where it is... At the bottom of the bay."

"Oh no. How are you ever going to find it?" asked Meiri, licking her fingers without a care.

"She'll figure that out, but I was talking about success with KM Gorgeous. Did you at least give him a kiss for helping out?" asked Toman and I felt the blush rising to my cheek. "You did!" he accused.

"No, he gave me a peck on the cheek, that's all. I'll admit he's good looking, but he's no Zavier."

"Plus, he's already dead, Toman. What sense would it make?" asked Meiri, brushing crumbs from her dress.

"I know. I know but it's pretty romantic," he said, faking a swoon.

"All right. Did you find the cup?" I asked, popping the last bites of bread in my mouth.

"No, because I'm loving this place and want to stay here... Of course I found it," said Toman rolling his eyes.

"Then let's go home," I replied.

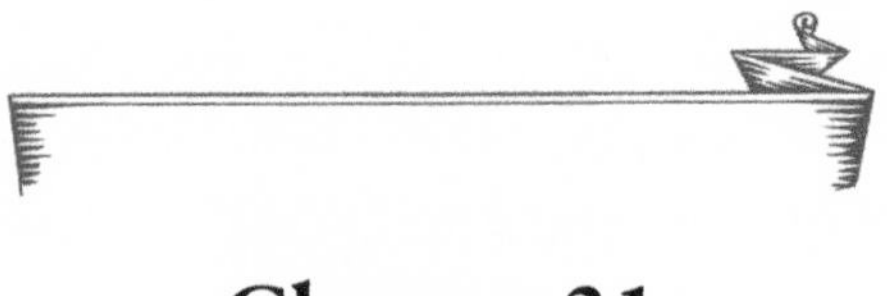

Chapter 31

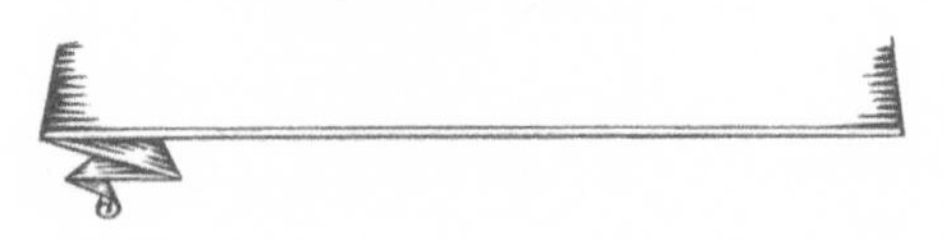

The shed was a dark box of frigid wind. It's how we knew we had returned. Gone was the light spring breeze and in its place was a harsh winter chill.

"That was anti-climactic," said Toman.

"Were you expecting a parade?" asked Meiri, picking up a bag of roots.

"Not exactly, but after everything..."

"After everything let's be glad that we came back whole and alive. Why don't the two of you go in the house and change while I call the mirror back? Don't forget the bags," I said, brusquely.

"Aye, aye sir," said Toman with a mock salute. Meiri muttered something and Toman giggled, but they left with the bags of tamp root while I stayed in the shed without argument.

I hadn't meant to be bossy, but I didn't want them here to watch me flounder through a return spell. After all the magic I'd done, my limbs were wobbly and my mind flitting from thought to thought. It was probably a need for fuel and my stomach grumbled in agreement. At least the gong had stopped. The echoing silence was welcome.

There were an inordinate number of words relating to home in magic. Standing in my own time, on my own land, I understood why home was so important to a mage. My Powers felt steadier than they had in the past. I'd performed extraordinary magic, but I'd also been unmoored by the time travel, like a ship that lost its anchor. Any sharp wind would have sent me adrift to who knows where. Here, I sensed the solidity of place. And yet, all those words related to home didn't give me a notion of how to call the mirror entity back.

I laid a hand on the mirror and closed my eyes, willing myself to concentrate. Now that I knew an entity lived in our mirror, an entity that was hostile toward me, my urgency was lacking. But despite my lack of desire, I'd made a promise. A smudge of dried blood in the bottom corner was evidence that I could do this. I just needed the right words. This couldn't be another accidental bonfire in the kitchen.

It was the one part of my plan I hadn't thought through. Sending the mirror away had been a gamble, but it worked because the mirror had agreed. There wasn't a messenger service to find mirror entities once they had retreated. The spell had to be simple, and I feared using too much magic would kill the entity as it had on Piar Farm. I thought of Beval, quietly working on his mirrors almost with affection. He cared about his work because he cared about the entities. Were they like his children or his partners? I had no such pull, but I did care if I'd made a promise and broken it out of fear.

"*Ag gwa tkei dem*," I said into the dim room. Like a distant bell, I heard the mirror arrive before I really felt it. It shimmered slowly as though it had been awoken from a deep sleep.

I waited for it to speak, but it continued to ripple and shimmer.

"I'm glad you're back. Is everything okay?" I asked and waited for a response.

Have I lost my connection to the mirrors?

"Thank you for keeping your promise. Perhaps some humans are worth trusting but take care Inez Garza. Mirrors are rarely their own masters." Then it abruptly stilled. I sensed it was still present, but the silence was either a rebuke, or a dismissal. I chose to believe the latter and left.

THE FRONT HALLWAY HAD a puddle of melting snow to which I added another measure. The footprints led up the stairs, but I was too drained to follow. Mamá walked in from the kitchen with a mop and made quick work of cleaning the tiny pools.

"There you are. Is the mirror working again?" she asked. I nodded, not wanting to talk about its odd behavior.

"That's good. Did everything go all right? I couldn't get anything out of Toman or Meiri, but they looked...grim," she said thoughtfully. "I sent them upstairs to change."

"We haven't eaten in a bit. Only bread and butter. That's all. I should—"

"You should tell me how it went. I saw all the roots," she said, steering me to a seat so the mop could do its work. "I already have the first batch steeping."

"It went fine. Is there enough, do you think?" I asked, still preoccupied.

"Maybe. What happened?"

"Nothing. I saw where the horn is...was...whatever. It fell into the bay," I replied.

"Did you tell her about Sebastian and Alda yet?" asked Toman from the top of the stairs. He rushed down, now comfortably clad in his own clothes.

"Who are Sebastian and Alda?" asked Mamá.

"Some of the people we met when we were in the past. It's not important," I said, giving Toman my severest look. He just shrugged. "I was telling her about the horn—you know, the reason we were there?"

"Such a mood. She needs food, I think," said Toman. "And I remember being promised enough to make me sick."

"Did someone say food? I'm starving," said Meiri, walking sedately down the stairs. All traces of our escapade had vanished and she looked like a fashion plate again.

"Inez, why don't you change while I get some food together?" suggested Mamá. But I knew her plan. She would ask all the questions she could while I wasn't there to censor what my friends shared.

"Better still, I'll come and eat now. I don't think I have the energy to get cleaned up without a little fuel," I replied, eyeing Toman and Meiri. Toman looked all wide-eyed and innocent while Meiri looked between the two of us, wondering what she'd missed. Mamá was undaunted.

"I think I have some leftover pie. You can eat that while I cook something," she said, walking toward the kitchen. She winked at Toman and I knew they would find a way to gossip about our trip, but I found it hard to care after I heard the word pie.

THE MEAL—WITH DESSERT eaten first—was fairly quiet. The three of us tore into our food as though we'd never seen a meal. Mamá looked alarmed at how much we packed away, but she kept her comments to herself. After a fourth helping, I finally felt settled and sated enough to ask my own questions.

"How has it been around here?" I asked.

"Quiet. Eerily so," replied Mamá. She worried her hands, as she thought.

"And?"

"Just that. There haven't been any riots or anything, but no one is venturing out. It could be the weather, but I don't know. The KM have been patrolling non-stop."

"What about the KM? Is he...is everyone all right?" I asked, clumsily.

"If you're asking about Zavier, I haven't seen him since the day you left. But since he's the crown prince I think we would have been told if something had happened. He's been really busy," she said, putting her hand on mine.

I felt myself loosen a little and realized how tense I'd been, wondering if he was safe. I knew I couldn't put off a confrontation with The Cat much longer. I said as much out loud.

"Then I hope you have a way to float the horn out of the bay because the bay is frozen solid," said Mamá, clearing the plates. Her hands were a little unsteady and I knew it was from mentioning magic. It was to her credit that she didn't want to show her anxiety to me.

"It never freezes," I said. My Power was already shaky in the water, so how would I overcome a frozen barrier? I'd used vast amounts of magic in the past, the strongest being my healing spell on Toman. It had been taxing and Toman was one person. How would I overcome an expanse of water?

I needed more Power. I needed a way to amplify my magic. A crazy idea rushed to the front of my thoughts—the augmenting lens. I knew telling Mamá or Rowley would cause another argument, so I kept the thought to myself. Out loud I said, "Maybe I can find a way to melt it."

"*Nena*, what are you thinking about?" asked Mamá.

"Nothing," I replied, but I was already thinking of a way to break into Viktor's house.

Chapter 32

The next few days were a monotonous blur. Helping Mamá steep the tamp roots and extract the juice broke up the time. It was a nice surprise to find that the recipe we used was written by Alda Garza. The notebook was old and had quite a few dirt smudges. I pictured her writing out the steps in an elegant hand while covered in dirt from another adventure in the woods.

I didn't tell Mamá about Alda or Sebastian or Podkin, for that matter, at least not much. My time with all of them felt like a secret that I wanted to tuck away, although I couldn't explain why to her or myself. It became part of all my other secrets and lies and remained as they did, reluctantly at first, but then staying locked away with increasing ease as the days progressed.

For her part, Mamá didn't pry. I didn't know if that was her way of giving me space or if she really didn't want to know about all the trouble we got into while in the past. The only difference I could detect was her constant calling out to me if I left the room to know where I had gone. I didn't mind too much, but if that continued it would make my plans all the harder to execute.

And the plan *was* brewing. At first I thought I would wait out the frost, hoping that the bay would unfreeze in a surprise heat snap. But the snap never came, and winter reasserted its icy grip with three days of continuous snow. Ice ball had been cancelled indefinitely with the KM working around the clock.

It made me antsy and impatient because I knew one more day of waiting was another day that Zavier was out patrolling within reach of The Cat. I still hadn't seen him since returning to the present and our only contact was through messengers. I couldn't bear the thought of something happening to him, despite all the tamp root I had collected. Toman's brush with The Cat had been vicious and uncontrolled compared to Meiri's or my injuries. Time had made The Cat calculating and his continued silence meant he was likely planning something big.

On the fourth day, when I thought I would jump out of my skin, there was a knock at the door. Mamá got there before I could and standing framed in the doorway with swirling snowflakes dancing around his feet, was Zavier. He was saying his hellos to Mamá and unable to resist the urge, I ran at him and hugged him tightly. He felt so warm and real and it wasn't until that moment I realized how much I had missed him.

"Hello to you too," he said, hugging me back. The door was still open and small ice crystals of snow landed on my cheeks. I didn't even mind. "How are you feeling?"

"Are you all right? Has anything happened? Is there—?" I asked.

"Slow down. I can barely keep my eyes open and you want a report? I thought I was avoiding Podkin." He chuckled. At the sound of Podkin's name, I flashed on the memory of a different face with menace in his eyes and cruel intentions in his heart. And that made me think of another face and I blushed.

"Sorry. How long have you been patrolling?" I asked, letting him in. He caught my hand and turned over my arm, now fully healed. He nodded with satisfaction and removed his coat.

"For two days straight with only twenty-minute naps here and there. I was hoping I could crash here for a bit. If I go home, Hortensia will just ask a bunch of questions, as will the council," he said, stifling a yawn.

I took a closer look at him and although he was smiling, I saw the dark circles under his eyes and the beginnings of stubble on his jaw. His coat was soaked through from walking around in this weather and his boots were a muddy mess.

"Stay as long as you need to, Zavier," replied my mother, taking his coat and pushing a seat under him. She hung it by the hearth to dry it out. He removed his boots and slumped down in the chair. I thought he would keel over any minute.

"Why don't you lay down in my room? I can wake you in a bit for some lunch," I said, helping him back up. Mamá looked back sharply, and Zavier looked decidedly uncomfortable.

"I can just take the couch in the sitting room," he replied, moving the chair back.

"No need. You've been walking for days. You deserve a comfortable bed. I'll take you up myself," replied Mamá firmly.

"I can take him up. And then I'll come right back down. I have work to get done in the herbals room anyway," I said, taking his hand in mine. I didn't give either one of them a chance to argue as I dragged Zavier by the hand up the stairs. His lack of resistance was proof of his exhaustion.

My room was neater than usual since I'd been working with Mamá for the past few days. The bed was completely clear and nothing too shocking had been left about. Cochi was sleeping peacefully and unlikely to wake Zavier with her squeaky wheel.

"Get comfortable and I'll wake you in a few hours," I said, turning down the bed.

"I'm tired, not dead. You don't have to do that," he said, taking my hand. The crooked smile on his face and the fatigue in his eyes were surprisingly sexy. I couldn't help but kiss him and he responded with more alertness than I had given him credit for. The unmade bed was suddenly and glaringly present. I knew Mamá would do one of her "check-ins" at any time. Still, his body pressed to mine and his hands holding my waist were a delicious torture. Footsteps on the stairs, broke the spell.

"Some other time," I replied, breathlessly. "Now get some rest. I'll be back in a bit."

"Good idea. If you'll excuse me, I could use a little privacy," he replied, his own voice a little breathy. He didn't need to explain, so I just nodded and headed to the hallway. Mamá had just reached the landing.

"Is he all tucked in?" she asked with a suspicious gaze.

"He's so tired. Let's give him a few hours," I replied with as much innocence as I could muster, but I knew my face told a different story. I made my way back downstairs, away from Mamá's prying eyes.

STRONG HANDS HELD ME closely while persistent lips kissed mine. Stray caresses made my breath catch and I yearned for more. The heady feeling made it impossible to know if we were standing up or laying down, but it didn't matter. Skin touched skin, raising temperatures to an unbearable high. I heard panting and the situation was quickly becoming frenzied.

I needed to move, to look into the face so near my own. I gasped, seeing Sebastian smiling down at me, but his eyes were wrong...sinister and threatening. I looked down to see myself wearing only my undergarments and the ground was rough and uncomfortable. I was in the woods and though the face that hovered over me was Sebastian's, the eyes belonged to Theodore Podkin.

I tried to scream, but the sound was muffled by another breath-stealing kiss. My limbs were leaden and I couldn't move. Passion gave way to panic as I fought back, but only in my mind. A whooshing sound filled my ears as I saw the giant wave from the bay crest overhead, blotting out the sun before crashing over us.

I woke up with a start. Disorientation gave me a moment of alarm, when I wasn't where I expected to be—in the darkened shed in the past. My heart thudded quickly and unevenly as I took big, gulping breaths to calm it. *Where am I?*

Dusk had fallen and it took a few more breaths for my eyes to adjust to the new light. There was a desk and a closed door I saw by just turning my head. The spicy scent of drying herbs reminded me I was back in the present. I was in the herbals room and that realization brought a wave of relief to my skittish nerves.

I sat up, slowly rolling down the woolen throw. *How had that gotten there?* A piece of paper fluttered to the ground. Reaching down, my hazy mind cast about for something to grasp onto. The note was from Zavier. He had been here... Not here, in my room. I was here in Lita's herbals room.

Further clouding my thoughts were the delicious smells wafting in from the kitchen. I remembered I'd come down to give Zavier a chance to get some sleep.

Mamá must be making dinner early, I thought. I opened the folded note and read it with deliberate concentration:

> *I didn't want to wake you, but I had to go. I'll swing by tomorrow. Love, Zavier.*

I wish he had woken me. I could have done without that dream. I felt oddly guilty for my initial enjoyment and wondered if Zavier had noticed I was dreaming when he left the note. Had I called out or moaned? Even remembering the dream flushed my body in guilt-ridden heat. Absently, I brushed my lips with my fingers, still feeling the ghost of the passionate kisses.

Was this disloyal to Zavier, dreaming of a man long dead? It had been a harmless flirtation, but keeping it a secret made it seem shameful. Another confidence I kept from Zavier. The list was growing longer, and I had to wonder what would finally unsettle it and drown us both with its weight.

The smell of food began to nauseate me and with a cowardice I rarely gave into, I pulled the throw over my head and fell back into a blessedly dreamless sleep.

THE DARKNESS THAT GREETED me told me I'd slept longer than expected. The remnant smells of dinner still lingered in the air, but instead of turning my stomach, they elicited a growl of hunger. I had no idea how much time had passed since my last nap.

Zavier's note was still clutched in one hand while I rubbed my face to alertness with the other.

I entered the kitchen, surprised to see my mother leaning over the sink with a mug in her hands. One sniff told me it was one of Lita's alert brews, a rare thing for her to take in the evening.

"What time is it?" I asked sifting through containers of tonight's dinner. Mamá handed me a plate and fork.

"A little after nine. You haven't slept well since you...came back. I didn't want to disturb you," she replied, taking another sip.

"You should have. Now I won't sleep tonight," I replied, heaping food on my plate. I watched her finish her cup of strong tea and serve herself another. Lines of worry creased her forehead.

"What's wrong?" I asked.

"Does the mirror seem different to you? I even noticed a crack in one of its corners," she replied. "Did you do that with your spell?"

"I thought it had happened while I was away. I don't know." I considered telling her everything but settled for telling her about the being in the mirror instead. She listened attentively and seemed unsurprised by my revelation.

"Beval used to call the mirrors his other children. He even used names for them though he insisted he hadn't named them. I thought it was just him being fanciful," she said with a far-away look. A smile softened the lines of worry on her face.

"What did he call our mirror?" I asked. Mamá thought about it for a moment and slowly her smile grew wider.

"Izar. It means star," she replied.

"Isn't that what he called you?" I asked and Mamá nodded. "Why did you ask about the mirror?"

"While you were sleeping Zavier had to leave. He overslept and asked to use the mirror. It refused to give Zavier passage—it flashed a notice for the public mirror," Mamá replied.

"That's odd," I said thoughtfully. I thought Izar's anger was directed at me, but it never occurred to me that the mirror would take it out on Zavier. Maybe more had happened while I was away than I thought. Sadly, there was only one who could answer that question. "I'll go check on it."

ONLY A LONE CANDLE lit the dark shed. Its flame wavered in my hands with the howl of wind seeping through the cracks and crevasses of the old structure. I heard the light tinkling of Izar's liquid shimmer, as though it was trying to hide the fact that it was watching me. I set the candle down on the floor near the hairline crack, making sure it wasn't a stray hair or a scratch. Running my finger over it, I felt the sharp bite of jagged glass graze the tip. My finger throbbed, dully. The liquid shimmer thrummed a little louder.

"You can give up the pretense. I know you're awake," I said, still inspecting the crack. "Please talk to me. I truly am sorry for having had to send you away, but that's no reason to be snippy."

"No one here is snippy. I am well aware of my role here," it replied with a touch of bitterness.

"What does that mean? You're a mirror and"—I paused not wanting to further antagonize the entity but I knew something was wrong—"I know I sent you away, but it was necessary."

The mirror made a sound that resembled a grumble.

"Even if that were a capital offence, does that give you any reason to refuse service to royalty?" I said, straightening up. The ripples in the surface bristled.

"I let him go through."

"Eventually, but you wanted him to use a public mirror. I've never known you to refuse service," I said. When an answer wasn't forthcoming, I sat down in the chair and waited. I could be just as stubborn as Izar.

"Wherever you sent me—and I don't want to talk about that horrid place—I heard things...things that I don't want to repeat. But I guess I'll have to say them because it concerns your family," it said in a whisper. I leaned in to hear clearly. The hair on my arms stood up with something other than cold.

"There were voices...too many to count, and some asked where I was from—where I'd come from and I told them I served the Garza family. Well, some of the voices became agitated and one in particular became louder and...pitiable I suppose.

One of the mirrors wanted to apologize for what he had done to Lady Sabrina and said it was why he was stuck in the fragment lands, where broken mirrors go. 'I didn't want to do it,' he kept saying over and over again. When he calmed down a little he told me that Lady Sabrina—I believe you call her Lita—

had to die because of a dark secret she was keeping. If she told even a soul it would upend the royal family and bring unspeakable suffering to Canto. He started blubbering about the Feud Wars and treaties and who knows what else, but the broken mirror just kept saying he hadn't wanted to do it," ended Izar in a tense whisper.

I was stunned, shocked. Remembering back to that day in the mirror transport and a voice taunting me with threats about doing to me what had been done to Lita came rushing back. My teeth started to chatter and I felt a tingle in my hands, feeding a fury that clouded my eyes. *How could a mirror kill Lita and why did it matter to the royal family? Was the royal family behind her death?*

"Inez? I'm sorry to tell you like this, but I felt you should know. This is why mirrors wish to remain separate from human affairs and why we should have rights of our own," it said, the voice somehow remote.

"I don't believe you. You're thinking about mirror rights after telling me that Lita was murdered? What does that—?"

"Inez, someone thought it was for a greater good that your grandmother should die and used a mirror to do it because the mirror couldn't say no. What if you had come in here when you did, to send me away, but really wanted me to hurt someone, to kill someone? I would be powerless to stop you. And for his trouble, after carrying out their dirty work, he was smashed. That could be any of us," it replied with vehemence.

I finally sat up and felt the tingling in my hands recede. I couldn't argue because Izar was right. But I didn't feel like listening to logic. Lita had been murdered and the culprit was supposedly protecting a secret for the royal house—Zavier's family. While I knew it could easily be someone looking out for royal interests, it could just as easily be one of them. How could I marry into that family? I knew Zavier couldn't be involved, but I had to assume the King and Queen were. At that moment, as far as I was concerned, Zavier was guilty by association. As if the mirror could read my mind, Izar startled me with its next comment.

"This has nothing to do with your young man. He was a child when all this happened. He may not even know. But you do have to be careful around his brother and the Queen. Who knows what secret Lady Sabrina was keeping, but what's to keep them from assuming you or Lady Filomena know it? You should tell Prince Zavier," Izar said gently.

I'd considered telling Zavier that my grandmother had been killed to keep a secret in his family safe, but to what end? Zavier loved me, but he was duty-bound to his family and beholden to Mythos. How did I know Mythos hadn't ordered the death of Lita? And what proof did I have that she had been murdered? The ravings of a broken mirror who confessed to my mirror, who learned of it because I'd sent it away with magic. My secrets now had secrets and I couldn't tell one without unraveling them all.

And yet I'd always wondered about the nature of Lita's death. There had never been a mirror accident like hers before or since. If it wasn't an accident who could have made it happen? More importantly, what had Lita known?

"Inez?" coaxed Izar. "I didn't tell you my name before, but you should know. It's Izar." I appreciated the gesture and nodded my thanks, but the other revelations weighed heavily on my mind.

"I...I have to go back inside. It's getting cold. Don't repeat this to anyone...any mirror... I need time to think," I replied and grabbed the candle before heading back into the night. As a thousand scenarios swirled in my head only one became clear.

If the secret Lita was hiding was my magic then I was the reason she died.

Chapter 33

I tossed and turned, each time waking up to a new reality.

Could Izar be right? Was Lita's death the result of some royal conspiracy? And could I be the reason she had to die? Was it the king's magic and instability she had to die to protect? Was it something worse?

I reasoned with myself between disjointed dreams of dark forests and breaking glass. It was possible that Izar had overheard something and then filled in the blanks with its own wild imaginings.

Maybe there was a mirror that hurt someone that could have looked like Lita and the guilt made that mirror confess to murder. Who knows where Izar really went?

But a persistent memory of my own kept me questioning my rationalizations. The mirror that threatened me with "the same as my grandmother" had been ominous and ugly. The voice had been taunting and cruel and for an instant I believed what Izar was saying.

I lived in that instant for a little too long. Izar couldn't be right. If it was, why were Mamá and I spared? Unless Lita's death had nothing to do with my magic.

It didn't make sense. Mamá and Lita told each other everything and other than not telling me the biggest secret of my life, they told me everything, too. But something as monumental as Lita's death being a murder would be something Mamá would pursue. No, Izar was wrong and confused and I would forgive the mirror's ramblings because I sent it someplace that was truly frightening.

I believed that enough to finally get some sleep.

THE NEXT MORNING LOOKED like dusk outside my window. A slushy snow fell in heavy swirling flakes. I could smell breakfast warring with the semi-permanent smell of tamp root being steeped. Mamá had taken to sleeping in shifts in order to keep an eye on the process. Her determination was impressive, but I think she secretly hoped that if she brewed enough I wouldn't have to face The Cat. We both knew she was more hopeful than certain, but we also didn't discuss it openly.

I came downstairs fully dressed to ward off the cold trying to permeate Árbol Real. The heated floors kept my feet toasty, but my nose held on to the chill. Mamá was stirring a new batch of roots on the stove. Large glass jugs full of the finished product sat in a line on the floor next to two more sacks of whole root. Thinking of the thousands of people who lived in Canto, it didn't inspire much confidence.

"Good morning. How did you sleep?" asked Mamá pausing in her attentions to the pot.

"Okay, I guess. How goes the struggle?" I asked.

"It goes. Were you dreaming about Lita last night?" she asked lowering the flame. She covered the stock pot and turned her attention to me. I narrowly missed the stool.

"Why do you ask?"

"You were calling out her name. Did you forget your tea again?" she asked with concern. Without being prompted she quickly set a bowl and spoon in front of me along with a small pot of oatmeal. I served myself carefully, being sure to look directly at the bowl instead of into my mother's questioning eyes.

"Maybe. I...I don't remember," I replied still spooning oatmeal into my bowl. I heard Mamá take a deep breath.

"Well, did you at least get to speak with Izar last night?" she asked pointedly. *Had I told her I could speak to the mirror?*

"I did. The mirror's fine. I just think the mirror was shaken up by the experience," I said. I quickly spooned some oatmeal into my mouth to avoid any more lying. Even though it was second nature, it didn't make it any easier on my conscience.

We lapsed into an uneasy silence with Mamá peeling more roots and me eating oatmeal with uncommon precision. I think I was counting bites in my head at one point. I didn't want to share Izar's revelation with her because doing so would make it closer to truth. With everything else that was going on I didn't think I could handle another murder mystery. I knew Mamá wouldn't want me to, but curiosity about Lita's death began to gnaw at me with each carefully chewed bite.

"Do you remember when Lita died?" I asked as casually as I could. Mamá didn't react except to pause momentarily in her peeling. She continued to peel as she spoke.

"Of course I do. She was my mother," she said calmly. "Why do you ask?"

"No reason...but did anything seem strange. You must have written the chronicle for the historical society," I said. Mamá's position as head of the library and the archives meant she had to keep a record of all births and deaths in Canto. She often said it was her favorite part of the job.

"I didn't write that chronicle," she said still peeling. "It was given to one of my assistants." Something in the way she said it gave me a funny feeling, like I was approaching an empty road that looked harmless, but I still didn't want to risk the walk. But the road was open, and I couldn't go around.

"Really? You didn't write Lita's...?

"To be honest, it was a relief to be allowed to grieve like a normal person instead of collecting information on my mother. Anyway, the council thought it would be a conflict of interest if I wrote it. The chronicle has to be fair and honest, flaws and all, and they thought I would unduly inflate her contribution to Canto," she replied with a touch of bitterness.

"Was it a nice one?" I asked, trying to avoid any hurt feelings.

"I...I don't know. I was—upset that I couldn't write the chronicle so I didn't look for a while. Then when I finally realized I was being childish about the whole thing I couldn't find it," she replied with a sigh.

"Couldn't find it?"

"Well, my assistant at that time wasn't as efficient as Betlindis. She was new and a little scattered. As a matter of fact she didn't last much longer than the chronicle being written and maybe a few weeks after that. Then she was gone—said she didn't like living in the capitol and moved to another section of Canto or Faery maybe. Anyway, after she left and I'd had time to stew I decided to read the chronicle and it was gone," she said, and resumed her peeling.

"Gone?"

"It wasn't as strange as all that. There are a few chronicles that have gone missing. They were started even before the Wars, so losing some amongst thousands isn't so odd. Actually, it's quite a feat."

"But to have one missing during your tenure and about your mother...?"

"Remember the chronicle is about the happenings of the year. An entire year is missing, not just your grandmother's life story. But I don't need to see it. I live with her every day. Sometimes looking at you makes me remember or reading her recipes and using her sayings. Even now, with all this steeping and brewing...it's like she's here. And you know what I say..."

"Yes. Gone but never forgotten," I replied absently. Was it a coincidence that my grandmother's chronicle was missing? I wondered what other chronicles had disappeared. Little pieces tantalized, didn't fit and made me more and more curious about the mirror's alleged discovery.

"Now, I know you're not going to tell me what all this is about, so I won't bother asking. I will ask you for some help with the rest of the steeping today unless..."

"Unless what?"

"Oh, I thought maybe you had plans with Zavier," she said with a sly smile. I wanted to join her in the smile, but only my lips obeyed. The chill I'd felt earlier had deepened somehow.

"No, no plans and..." I would have finished the sentence, but there was a knock at the door.

"Speak of the devil?"

"I hope not... I'll go see," I said and was unsure how I would react if it was Zavier on the other side. Luckily I was spared the question because it was Mrs. Haro. A thick layer of snow coated the walk behind her. The wind pelted large flakes, resembling goose feathers, against the house. Her face was red and wind scoured with lines of worry carved into her face.

"Inez dear, I'm sorry to come by so early but I was wondering if you'd seen my Rowley. He's not come home in days and with the weather and all I'm worried. Is he here?" she asked, snow dripping from her coat. It was with a start that I realized I hadn't seen him since I gave him a condensed version of our time in the past. He hadn't even insisted on magic practice.

"No, he's not here. You should come inside," I said, taking her gloved hand.

"Thank...you sweetie, but I—I have to keep looking for him," she replied, teeth chattering. Stray strands of red hair clung to her forehead and her boots were practically encased in ice.

"Mrs. Haro, you stay here with Mamá. I'll go look for him," I said, pulling her in.

"I couldn't possibly—"

"Of course you can," said my mother, appearing from the kitchen. She brought a towel and a cup of steaming tea. "Inez is good at finding things. Let her help you while we both drink some tea." I was proud of my mother for not letting her fears for me get in the way of what had to be done, in this case finding a lost dog. It gave me hope that she wouldn't stand in the way of my getting rid of the Cat. I knew in the end, she would understand what was needed even if she didn't like the idea of me being the one to do it.

"I'll try and make it quick," I said, already pulling on my boots. My coat wasn't as warm as I would have liked, but Rowley's instructions on how to stay warm were still fresh in my memory. I hoped it worked for him, too. "Don't worry about Rowley. He's stronger than all of us."

I set out before Mrs. Haro could object. The snow assailed my face as I waded through drifts that were now shin deep. It didn't take much concentration to want to be warm and the spell worked beautifully. Keeping it up was helping me block the sick feeling that had started when Mrs. Haro arrived. I couldn't help worrying that the cold was not the cause of Rowley's disappearance. With my confrontation with The Cat seeming inevitable, I had to wonder if Rowley had decided to take him on alone. If he had and lost, would we ever see Rowley again?

Chapter 34

I had no idea where to start. My feet made crunching noises in the snow as the wind desperately tried to blow my hood down. All the while, I kept heading toward the forest, knowing Mrs. Haro would have already looked in town. The lift, *crunch,* lift of my steps became mechanical, allowing my thoughts to wander.

What would I do without Rowley? A few months ago, I would have said whatever I damn well pleased, but now I was smart enough to know that he was the only teacher I had that wanted me to be what I hoped to become. He knew I had to be a warrior, a hero, to succeed.

With Mamá, I knew she was proud, but she would have been more comfortable with my joining her in the library. She still saw me as her baby, but Rowley saw me as their only hope—whether he admitted it or not. He didn't coddle or cajole and he wasn't like Viktor who told me what I wanted to hear. He was real and honest and right now I needed him to be okay.

I kept trudging. The footsteps I had made were now a memory and this was quickly becoming a full-blown storm. Even if The Cat hadn't caused Rowley's disappearance, I didn't know how long he could be out in this. My warmth spell was beginning to wane with pockets of cold blossoming in my feet and hands. Flakes of wet snow clung to my eyelashes. I turned in a circle, looking for a clue as to where I'd already been and where I was now. The wind seemed to gather whole drifts of snow and create swirls of impenetrable white and gray.

Where is Rowley? Just then a figure started trudging toward me. It was too big to be a cat, but I was still on my guard.

"Hello? Who is that?" called the figure. Despite wind roaring in my ears, I recognized the voice and relaxed.

"Arch? What are you doing out here?" I asked trudging toward the sound of his voice.

"I could ask you the same thing. Anyway, doesn't the uniform give it away?" He lowered his coat collar, allowing a peek at his KM uniform. "Now it's your turn."

"I'm out looking for..."

"Inez? Is that you?" Another voice called from my left. My heart flip-flopped and I took a startled breath. No amount of rationalization would keep me from reacting to Zavier's voice. After what Izar had told me I knew I didn't see Zavier as just a man I loved with a family I didn't get along with. He was a member of a family that may have killed my grandmother. Did that make him guilty too? Sadly, I probably would have shared my doubts with Rowley were he there. Zavier wrapped me in an embrace and I involuntarily stiffened.

"I was asking her the same thing. Why would anyone want to be out in this hell?" joked Arch.

"And why are you here then?" Zavier asked, but he directed his question to Arch.

"Oh, dear prince—following orders. After your last close call I am to be your personal bodyguard. Trust me I wouldn't be here otherwise," he replied flippantly, but even with the whipping wind and the clumps of falling snow I could see the anxiousness in his eyes. The scare had made the possibility of being the heir apparent too real for Arch. "Now, your reasons, gorgeous?"

"Rowley is missing, and Mrs. Haro came to our house looking for him. With the storm and all I couldn't let her go out and keep looking. So...so that's what I'm doing," I replied, sidling away from Zavier. He noticed, but worst of all so did Arch. A wicked smile crept over his face.

"A-ha. Why not just go home and tell her you couldn't find him? Or better yet—let's get out of here together. I know Zavier has a council meeting to get to so I would happily bring you back to my house to warm up," he said. I saw Zavier clench his jaw.

"Or, Inez could go home and we could look for Rowley. I know how much he means to old Mrs. Haro," replied Zavier.

"I can't leave this to the two of you. I appreciate the offer," I said pointedly to Zavier and ignoring Arch, "but I have to look, and you have other responsibilities at the...palace."

"They can wait. I'm helping, but Arch is free to leave," said Zavier.

"And let you get all the glory, no thank you. If you're both crazy enough to look in this mess, I'll help too. But if any of my body parts freeze and fall off I'll blame the pair of you," he said, and started trudging deeper into the woods. Zavier reached for my hand and I hesitated.

"What's wrong? Are you angry because I left without waking you?"

"No...no, I'm just...worried about Rowley. We should catch up," I said. I felt miserable and conflicted, but I couldn't shake my reaction to Zavier because of his association with the Royal Family. It was ridiculous because he had been fourteen when Lita died, but I couldn't help it. I walked ahead, walking a fine line between getting caught by Zavier and encouraging Arch.

We called out to Rowley, fanned out to cover more ground, and fought back the elements. The storm was getting stronger and calling became futile. At least an hour passed before I started to give way to despair. How would we ever find him in this maelstrom? My hands were like bricks of ice and if it weren't for the fact that it was running,

I would have thought my nose had fallen off. The cold was seeping into my pants, and I wasn't entirely sure that my socks weren't frozen solid. Wiggling my toes hurt.

"Inez? Inez! I think we're going to have to call the search off. It's getting too thick out here and I almost fell into a snowbank," yelled Arch. He was coated in snow and looked like a disgruntled snow beast.

"I hate to agree with Arch, but we're going to have to turn back unless we can figure out where he would have gone. The forest is too big for three people to search. I can make a report with the KM and hope..."

"And hope they give a damn about a lost dog. No thank you. I have to find him now or..." The sentence hung in the icy air and I was unwilling to finish it. A look crossed between Zavier and Arch. We all knew what I was thinking, but they were kind enough not to say it. I couldn't imagine leaving Rowley out here to die after he'd survived so much just to help me. How could I abandon him? He would never shirk his responsibility to me no matter how difficult...

"The bay! Rowley's at the bay," I said with more certainty than I felt. He knew where the horn was and was probably as impatient as I was to find it. Arch and Zavier looked at me as though I were nuts, but Zavier just nodded, took my hand, and led the way. This time I didn't pull away. His faith in me deserved the same of me in him. If Zavier had known about something as appalling as his family killing my grandmother, he would have told me. Zavier was too open and honest not to. It was one of the reasons I loved him, and one of the reasons I couldn't tell him about my magic.

The blizzard intensified by the bay. Large flakes fell at alarming speeds, coating my already-sodden coat. The wind howled like a living thing desperate for attention. We leaned into the gale, moving closer to the shore.

My hunch had been right, and we found Rowley half buried in snow and barely moving. I could see the spots where he had started to dig, now filling with fast-falling snow. He looked so small and helpless that it broke my heart.

"He's still breathing, but he's so cold. We need to get him warm and inside quickly," said Zavier, digging Rowley out. A tiny whimper escaped from Rowley as his paws flexed ineffectively. Without further thought Zavier took off his coat and wrapped Rowley's body in it.

"You'll freeze out here without your coat," yelled Arch, the wind stealing a muttered oath.

"Well, he's already frozen and we can't take the chance. Árbol Real is the closest, but it's still a hike. I don't know if he'll make it." I looked out into the distance in frustration but saw a welcome sight. Swirling bits of pink and purple shimmered invitingly.

"Wait, I can see the Mist House. We can stop there and at least warm up before heading out again," I said. I couldn't worry about the risks of being at Viktor's right now. Rowley's breath was shallow and uneven.

"Great. Lead the way," said Zavier, holding the Rowley bundle with a tenderness that truly touched me. At that moment I knew that I had to let go of whatever feelings I had about his family. Zavier was so earnest and good. I knew he was there because of me, but he cared about all life and would never have agreed to anything that would have harmed my grandmother. I put my hand against his cheek and gave him a light kiss.

"You feel warm," he replied with a smile.

"I am."

WE ARRIVED COLD AND wet at the Mist House, Viktor Lake's home and prison. Or at least the prison of her magic. Her Powers only worked in this space by order of Mythos. How she had escaped being truly imprisoned in a dungeon or rended from her magic was a secret she never shared. There were many things about Viktor I didn't know and even her brother, Mr. Fell, wouldn't share. I pushed all those quiet doubts aside when I called into the swirling mist that was her home and putting myself and Rowley in her hands to ask for help. Rowley whimpered softly.

After what felt like an eternity the door swung open.

"Come in and shut the door quickly behind you," said Viktor, her hood covering her face and hair. The magic disguising her voice rippled through the space. It felt heavier than usual. As far as I knew, I was the only one privy to her true face and sex. It was a surprise when she took the hood down, revealing her high, feminine cheekbones and long white hair. I looked at both Zavier and Arch, but neither reacted. Viktor noticed the bundle Zavier cradled in his arms and she raised her eyebrows in question.

"It's Rowley. He got caught in this storm and we have to warm him up quickly. Can we sit by your fire?" I asked, rubbing the coat covering Rowley. I noticed a look pass between Arch and Viktor that I couldn't quite read. It only lasted a moment, so there wasn't much time to analyze it.

"Get him to the back room—it's the warmest," offered Viktor, still disguising her voice. "Lord Verdant, you know the way." This time the look Viktor shared with Arch lasted long enough to read. Lake looked amused and if I hadn't seen it with my own eyes I would barely believe that I saw shame cross Arch's face.

"Thank you. Arch can you...?" asked Zavier, handing Rowley and his coat over to Arch.

"This way," mumbled Arch and led me to one of the many doors in Viktor's home. Viktor ushered Zavier to another door, bowing him through. I looked back at Zavier and tried to quiet the anxiousness I felt, seeing him disappear from view in the Mist House.

"The room is in perpetual summer. Viktor created it some time ago," Arch said oddly subdued. He placed Rowley on a grassy mound and removed the wet coat. I took my coat off, too. The heat was making me woozy. It really did feel like summer, and I wondered how the house could contain a season in one room. There were flowers and shrubs growing out of the ground and the sun—it was the sun—warmed every inch of me.

It was wonderful, but difficult to fully appreciate, with Rowley lying still on the ground and Arch acting cagey.

"I take it you have a history with Viktor?" I asked, sitting beside Rowley, watching the slow rise and fall of his chest.

"I don't know what you're talking about," he replied.

"Don't be an ass. I know something's going on. What is it?" I whispered. He turned away from me. His shoulders rose and released on a sigh.

"Lake helped me out of a compromising situation, using his particular talents," he said with a sad chuckle.

"Viktor helped you, using magic?" I said and noted he still referred to Viktor as *he*. Normally when people came to call on Viktor, she left her cloak up with a hood large enough to hide her feminine face and flowing white hair. I realized that my wooziness had nothing to do with the heat of her summer room. The amount of magic being used was stifling. It was likely a very powerful glamour that allowed her to continue the ruse of her identity.

"After I joined the KM," he continued ignoring my comment, "VIktor came to me and said that he would keep my little secret if I would procure items for him that I had access to, in my position as a KM and a relation to the royal family."

"He blackmailed you for illegal goods?" I asked, being careful to call Viktor "he" as well.

"Has anyone ever told you you're rather blunt? It's an unattractive quality," he said, finally facing me.

"Zavier likes it," I replied.

"Speaking of Zavier, I noticed the cold shoulder you gave him before and now all's forgiven. Why? Was it the sight of him cradling the canine?"

"Maybe. Why do you care?" I asked a little more sharply than I'd intended. Viktor's glamour was agitating my own magic as it teased the corners of my perception.

"You always want to seem so fierce, but you're like all the other girls. Puppy dogs and rainbows, right?" he teased.

"I don't know about the rainbows, but the puppy did help. Arch, you know that—"

"I know that you're with Zavier and I'm sure the thought of becoming a princess turns your head as much as the next girl. I'm sure you'll rule over us benevolently," he quipped. He wandered the edges of the room like a caged animal.

"I'm more interested in Zavier than a crown," I replied.

"That's depressing," he said and finally came to a stop. I watched as his shoulders rose and fell twice before he returned to Rowley's side. Rowley's breathing had improved, but he was sleeping fitfully. Arch petted Rowley's side pensively.

"Why? Shouldn't you be happy that I care for your cousin?" I asked.

"I would prefer to think that you care more about being a queen, having thrown me over for him," he said and took my hand. "The circles I travel in have a thing for titles."

"Maybe you should look for a girl outside that circle," I said.

"I tried," he said and looked at me in a stomach-flipping sort of way. I pulled my hand back. Archie was so soaked he dripped. "Well, let me see if Viktor has any clothes in my size. I've brought him enough things over the years," he said, clearing his throat. I wondered if I should stop him from snooping around for men's clothes in a woman's house, but a paw reached out and caught my attention. Arch left the summer room before I could call him back.

"I thought he would never leave. Never let him pet me again," growled Rowley faintly. His eyes fluttered open. I couldn't help myself; I laughed and hugged his head.

"Miss Garza, if you wouldn't mind..."

I loosened my grip and Rowley scrambled out of my embrace. He teetered for a moment before gaining his balance.

"What were you doing? Are you completely insane? Do you have any idea what could have happened if we hadn't found you?" I said, unable to keep my voice from rising. Rowley made a shushing noise and lay back down.

"The Cat... He's been prowling around the bay, and I knew he was searching for the horn. Lucky for us, cats hate water, but soon he'll lose patience and try and get to it before we do." His voice was still faint, but it held the ornery edge I was familiar with.

"Then why didn't you use the heat spell that you taught me?" I whispered, fearing the walls had ears.

"It's fading," he replied.

"What's fading?" I asked.

"My magic. My purpose was to find you and train you for the battle ahead. Now that I'm doing that, my magic is starting to fade away. It means I can't call the horn up from the depths of the bay. Your magic is strong enough, but you lack sufficient concentration. It's not a criticism—it's just an observation. Given time, you will be able to, but water dilutes your spells, and we can't amplify it," he said. His eyes fluttered closed for longer than a blink.

"The magic that you say is fading—isn't that the same magic that's keeping you alive?" I said, shaking him awake.

"Yes," he said, coming back around.

"Well, you're not done teaching me so don't use this as an excuse to give up," I said lightly, but I couldn't swallow. I never considered that Rowley might not be around forever.

Today had brought me face to face with that possibility but finding him had quieted my fears. Now I was confronted with the idea again.

"I have no intention of leaving any time soon. You're clearly not ready yet and as soon as I thaw we will work out a schedule to work on your—"

"A schedule. We're running out of time. You said I had the strength but not the concentration. What if I could just boost my Power to overcome that? Would that work?"

His mention of amplifying my Powers had made me think of the stifling magic Viktor was using. Magic that Viktor had never employed at this level before.

"Perhaps if you were willing to use the other three shells—"

"The two gentlemen are getting dressed, but they could come back at any time," said Viktor from the doorway. I looked from her to Rowley and back again. He didn't seem surprised by her appearance either. She was definitely using something like Lita's augmenting lens if even Rowley didn't notice her female form. I took it as confirmation that she had an augmenting lens.

"A quilt would be nice if you can manage," I said tightly. I stood and followed Viktor down the hallway. I caught up to her in two strides. "What are you doing?"

"Getting a blanket for that dog," she said with a smile.

"You know what I mean. Why are you walking around without your hood? Why isn't anyone reacting to your appearance?" I demanded.

"Oh. I recently acquired an *objet magique* that helps with my current glamour enchantment. A magnifier. Now I can disguise my voice and appearance if only in the confines of my home," she said in a satisfied whisper.

"You look the same to me," I said. I looked at her again, intently. Other than sensing the magic on her, which was heavier than usual, she looked no different.

"You can see through my enchantment. It must be abstract magic," she mused. "I'll get that quilt now."

After she left I started to formulate a plan. Somewhere in this house was a magnifier or augmenting lens, maybe Lita's, probably gotten for her by Arch. If I could get my hands on it I could amplify my Power and get the horn out of the bay. I returned to the summer room.

"I know what we can do to get the horn," I whispered to Rowley.

"I'm sure I won't like it," he replied.

"Let me worry about the horn, and you concentrate on getting better. I'll be right back," I said and put my now-dry coat on Rowley. With trepidation, I began my search of the Mist House, hoping to find the answer to our problem.

Chapter 35

Despite all my visits to the Mist House, I'd never made it further than the front room. The corridors glowed with swirling colors, reminiscent of my cowry shells. Some coalesced to form doorways that faded as I walked on. Others remained and strange music played behind one particularly small door. Plenty of marketeers would give their right arm to have access to all this magic and I marveled at that as I walked through it casually now.

Not for the first time I wondered what had happened to Viktor to end up here, enveloped in so much magic—but magic she could only use within her home. Mythos had devised this rather elaborate prison for Viktor instead of rending her of her Powers or throwing her in the darkest dungeon available. Was this what awaited me if I were discovered?

There's discovery—and the consequences of that discovery. I couldn't help wondering, walking down that dark passage of infinity, whether it wouldn't be better to let everyone know that I did have magic. And it was that very magic that could and would save us all from The Cat and anything else that threatened Canto.

But this house was what had happened to Viktor. A house she couldn't control and she was beholden to Mythos. *And why is she helping me? Isn't she bound to tell the Mythosian envoy about my magic?*

All this brooding was useless, and the magnifier wouldn't be found by my hemming and hawing. Any minute Zavier, Arch, or

Viktor could emerge and catch me snooping. I pulled out my Pandora Key and held it tightly in my hand.

Stealing was nothing new to me, but avoiding magical detection from another mage was.

Some of the doors I passed had light spilling out from underneath their frames. Others had exotic smells or echoing sounds reaching the hall. It was unlikely that she would keep her new toy in one of these rooms—I'd want to keep something that enhanced my magic, near where I spent most of my time—so that pointed to the great room, right at the front of the house. *How will I explain my perusal there if I'm caught? And where can I hide the lens if I find it*?

The problem was she would sense magic on me the same way I sense it on her. I would have to improvise something, but those considerations were all moot if I couldn't find it.

WARM LIGHT ILLUMINATED the front hall, casting shadows in some places and highlighting others. Viktor wasn't back yet. I turned slowly in that round room, aware that I hadn't paid enough attention to its contents to notice if something new was present there now. Here, on shelves and tabletops were not just books but treasures—harmless and illicit. I hadn't taken much time to notice the figurines or random ornamental boxes that stood guard around the books, but now I wondered which had been found and which had been "gifted" by Arch.

At the same time, I was discouraged by the sheer volume of goods shoved into this room. The item I sought could be anywhere... Perhaps Viktor even kept it on her person? There was no way around it—I just had to rummage.

I decided to be methodical and start with the shelf closest to the entrance. It couldn't hurt. My back was to the door, but there was no helping that. I began with a small yellow box, smooth with a matte finish. I opened it and closed it immediately, trying to trap the smell before it pervaded the room. The odor of bad breath invaded my little space and made me scrunch up my nose, but it dissipated quickly.

I was reluctant to open the next container after that mishap, but the shiny black box held no smells. It did have a long, skinny tongue rolled up in a loop. I think it was a snake's tongue, but I couldn't be sure.

What is Viktor doing? Then again, turning this on herself, Inez wondered what anyone going through Lita's herbal room would think of her? At least I knew Lita was using her strange ingredients to help others, while Lake's hoard felt sinister. I continued checking boxes, moving from shelf to shelf quickly.

"Looking for something?"

Startled I dropped the striped box I held, which knocked over a few others. At the same time, I felt my protection spell perk up. Then just as suddenly it vanished with only the barest desire from me to dissipate it, magic I struggled with on more than one occasion. Why?

One of these boxes is the amplifier!

"Just a book," I stammered. "Something to read to Rowley while we're here."

"Nice save. Never try and keep a secret—you're lousy at it," quipped Arch.

The stories I could tell him...

I almost laughed, feeling a thrill of hysteria bubble up. He looked at the mess of boxes on the floor and arched his brow in question. "If you're looking for Lake's goodies, you came to the right room. I recognize most of this stuff."

"Well, now that you mention it, I was looking for something that went missing from home and I wondered...?" How much could I tell Arch? He was already suspicious.

"Wait; I may be a lot of things, but I wouldn't steal from you. Even if Viktor asked, I'd turn myself in before I'd do that," he replied emphatically. He looked so earnest and devastated by the thought I was suspicious of him, I wanted to soften the blow.

"I never thought you would, Arch. But maybe you did it, inadvertently? It was stolen from the house, and we can assume by someone up to no good. You could have taken it from someone you arrested who actually stole it from me," I pointed out. I took quick glances at the boxes in front of me, trying to remember what the augmenting lens looked like. I'd found a diagram of it in Lita's things.

If it's here, how can I get it out of here with Arch watching so closely?

"I'll work that one out later. What are you looking for?"

I hesitated, but he looked determined. "An augmenting lens," I responded. Arch whistled in response.

"Where'd you get one of those? I've only ever seen them at the palace for parties," he replied.

"It was my grandmother's. She was a healer."

"How'd she get one of those? Did she steal it?" he asked with a smile.

"No, at least I don't think so. She was lady-in-waiting to the old queen for a long time. Maybe it was a gift or something," I said with a shrug.

"Okay. Well how do you know this one is your grandmother's?" he asked.

"Stealing from my grandmother is considerably easier than trying to smuggle something out of the palace," I answered.

"Good point. Well, I know what they look like so let's see here," he replied, kneeling on the floor. Side-by-side we sorted through the boxes for the right one. I could feel the heat from Arch's body radiating off him and his hands brushed mine more than once. I used my hand to check underneath the shelf, hoping it had rolled out of sight. Arch did the same.

His hand curled around my fingers, and he looked over at me while waves of guilty queasiness rolled through my stomach. I was using his attraction to me against him. It was a kind of deceit I wasn't used to engaging.

"I think I found it," he said softly, and he deposited a small cube in my hand, withdrawing his. I opened it and inside was a glass lens as large as my palm. It was warm to the touch and flashed a warm green color. My magic almost immediately responded with a flush of warmth. I looked up feeling Arch's breath on my cheek. Our eyes locked for a brief moment and I was certain he meant to kiss me.

"And I have found you. What are you doing in here?" asked Viktor from the hallway. Years of smuggling priceless magical objects had taught me slight of hand. I shifted my body casually, effectively hiding the lens, but leaving the box.

"We were looking for a book. One of the countless you keep recommending to me, Viktor," said Arch casually. He lied as well as any smuggler, but then again I supposed he was a smuggler.

"*Now* you're interested in books?" replied Viktor, her eyes looking about the room. They lit upon the spot where we'd found the box with the magnifier. The lid was closed, but she gave me a pointed look.

"He's right. He was helping me find one to pass the time," I said, pushing the other boxes under the shelf with my foot. "But you startled us and now there's a mess on the floor." I bent to pick it up and covertly put the box back. Arch hadn't reacted to Viktor's appearance so apparently the lens could be used without its box. Viktor nodded knowingly.

"You're showing her my collections. Does she know who got them for me?" she said pointedly. "I'd hate to compare secrets and I think you would too," threatened Viktor.

"Tell them and see what happens to your little collection. I may have some explaining to do, but we both know that I am more important in Canto than you are. Let's go Inez," he said, taking my hand and walking to the door. With my other hand I pushed the delicate glass beneath my shirt to lay against my back. The rounded edges cooled against my skin and another wave of warmth washed over me. Viktor stood in front of the doorway, barring our way.

"Not so fast," said Viktor. Arch pushed forward while Viktor pushed back. Even if I wanted to make a show of my Power, the augmenting lens was leeching energy from me as though it was feeding. Viktor's magic grew heavier.

I glimpsed the glamour she was projecting to hide her identity and both her false face and her real one looked ready to fight Arch. Arch clenched his hands.

"Is there a problem here? Arch, you okay?" asked a newly arrived Zavier. He was of a height with Arch and Viktor, but something in his stance made him more imposing than the other two. Walking by his side and a bit wobbly was Rowley.

"Victor thinks that Inez and I were doing something naughty in his great room. Of course, it isn't true, cousin," said Arch with a taunting hint that maybe naughty wasn't the right word. Zavier refused to be baited and looked at me instead.

"He's blocking us because he thinks we stole something," I said, keeping my eyes on Viktor. The lens was hidden deep in the folds of my clothes and I knew Zavier wouldn't conduct a thorough search of my body in such company.

"I can assure your Majesty—" began Lake. She knew she couldn't say she believed I had her augmenting lens.

"Thank you for your hospitality, Viktor, but we should probably get going. The snow has finally stopped, and Rowley is strong enough to get back home. I will make sure your blanket is returned and ask that you please steer us to your mirror room," said Zavier with cold cordiality.

"I don't have a mirror room," replied Viktor. "That privilege was taken from me." If Viktor or Zavier were about to say anything, both of them quickly gave me their full attention as I listed toward the ground. Arch caught me, but I pulled away as I felt the protection spell spread. Just as quickly the spell dissipated and I saw Viktor's eyes go wide.

"I think I just need some cool air. That summer room is stifling, and this room isn't any better. Can we walk, please?" I asked, looking at Zavier. He was looking at Arch's hand, again supporting my arm, but his face remained impassive. I wanted to pull away, but my knees threatened to buckle.

"Are you sure?" he asked with the same cool voice, but I read the concern on his face.

"Positive. Thank you again, Viktor," I said, reaching for Zavier to let him take my arm instead of Arch. "Thank you, too Arch." I hoped he understood that I was thanking him for more than holding my arm. He nodded his understanding and walked ahead of us.

Clutching Zavier's arm, I left Viktor's house in pain. The lens was warring with my magic, and it took all my efforts to keep it from having free reign. I looked back at Viktor's only to see her pull up her hood. She didn't call out as I had expected, and I silently thanked the Goddess for my two escorts. Rowley growled low before setting out in the deep snow and I couldn't be sure it was meant for our inhospitable host or if he could smell the lens I concealed.

Chapter 36

I managed to reach for the lens when Zavier stopped to adjust Rowley's makeshift quilt coat. Sliding it into my coat pocket, with a few layers of clothing between my skin and the lens immediately corrected my unsteadiness. It was like I could breathe again after having a heavy bolder perched on my chest.

Arch was walking double time, trying to move ahead. I couldn't be sure if he was trying to escape Viktor, Zavier, or me, but he definitely had the air of someone who wanted to get away. Keeping up was proving difficult, but I managed to close the gap with Rowley and Zavier not far behind.

"Arch, wait up," I called, but his speed didn't abate. I stopped to take a breath; Zavier and Rowley stopped, too.

"You know I hate to ask this," said Zavier.

"Then don't, please," I said.

"Oh, he doesn't mean you. His Highness wants to ask if I did indeed steal something from The Crooked Man back there, don't you?" said Arch, spinning back around. He crossed his arms, waiting while I looked between the two of them, their faces as glacial as our surroundings.

"Did you?" asked Zavier in a monotone.

"What if I did? What if I did take something to help your girlfriend? Would you care then? No, you don't want to know—you just want to make me look bad in front of Inez. Well, I won't help you."

"Arch, he didn't mean—" I began.

"Don't. Just don't. It's bad enough you're with him. Don't fight his battles, too." Arch crossed his arms in defiance.

"She's not fighting anything for me. I just wanted to know what happened back there," Zavier said and reached for Arch's retreating figure. His tight grip on Arch's wrist made me nervous and Arch's violent shaking it off made me doubly so. They faced each other, their breath visible in the icy air. It reminded me of two bulls about to charge each other.

"Both of you calm down! Did you forget about Rowley? You know, the one who almost died in this cold? Let's get home and then you can continue being jackasses without me," I said, standing between them. Rowley added his opinion in the form of a low growl which shook Zavier out of his standoff.

"She's right. Let's get moving," said Zavier, loosening his posture, but with the same steel in his eyes.

"Of course she is, but I think I can do one better. I'll leave the two of you to walk the dog. I have places to go. I'm sure your Highness will make it to the palace safely," Archie said with a mock bow and trudged off at a determined pace. We watched as he was swallowed up by the winter forest.

"You just had to ask, didn't you?" I accused.

"Should I have asked you instead?" he countered. His eyes were full of questions and I almost broke. I wanted to shout "Yes we did steal something, and I had to because I'm magical and have to save us all." I wish you could help me, but in the end I'm all alone in this and all my lies make me understand Arch a little more."

But all I did say was, "Let's go. I'm cold."

His eyes still held a question, but he kept it to himself either from fear of another argument or because he already knew the answer. I was spared telling another lie, but I still felt the weight of it as I trudged through the forest with Zavier and Rowley.

ZAVIER HADN'T STUCK around after dropping me off and reuniting Rowley with Mrs. Haro. He gallantly offered to walk them both back to the Cup & Board, but that meant we didn't discuss our time at the Mist House. I considered finding Arch to apologize for using him, but I thought I'd done enough damage with him.

It had been so much easier thinking of him as the shallow pretty boy. Continuing to see him that way would make my guilt a lot easier to deal with. If he changed it would make Zavier a lot nicer to him. *Or would it?* He saw all of Arch's faults—his carousing with women, his laxness with the King's Men, among other things—and I did too, but they seemed less intolerable of a sudden. My guilt at further straining Zavier and Arch's relationship was nearly as smothering as the magical object in my possession.

Its insistent presence shook me from my morose mood.

I went straight to my room and removed the lens from my pocket. I sat on my bed with the augmenting lens inches from my fingers. I could blame it for so much. My moment with Arch. My strained goodbye with Zavier. But it was also my salvation—if I could figure out how to make it work.

Involving Rowley or Mamá was out of the question. They would reject my idea out of hand, and I didn't have the luxury of time to argue with them. Didn't the saying go "It's better to seek forgiveness than ask permission?"

Maybe Meiri could help me. She'd seen it used in the palace, right? I hadn't spoken to her since we came back from the past. I think Meiri was securely under lock and key, but she could always be persuaded to jump out her window. A mental picture of Meiri dressed all in black, avoiding patrols and jumping over the Green Gardens hedge made me giggle.

I was still laughing when I looked over at Cochi's cage. She wasn't running in her wheel the way she normally did at this time of night. She was in her cubby, one eye staring through the spy hole and her whiskers frantically twitching.

"What's wrong girl?" I asked, sticking my finger between the bars.

"I think I may have scared her. She doesn't understand freedom," was the reply from the shadows. It was then that I noticed my open window. The outline of a tail swayed back and forth, and I watched, transfixed, as The Cat emerged.

"We should talk. We have so many friends in common."

He was smaller than I remembered. Then again, I'd only seen him in snatched moments with pressing matters taking precedent over investigation. In the relative calm of my room, he looked like an ordinary cat.

I knew panicking was what he thrived on so I fought against the urge to keep my protection spell at bay and let it spread throughout my body. The Cat frowned. *Does he detect my magic?*

"I don't remember inviting you into my room, so see yourself out," I said, and deliberately pulled a chair up to Cochi's cage and focused only on her. I also slipped the lens under the bedding in her cage. Out of the corner of my eye I saw him look perplexed by my reaction, but he quickly recovered.

"I think we can move on from this cat and mouse game. Although I am partial to catching the odd mouse or two." He chuckled. "I know that mongrel mentor of yours told you all about me—heaven knows he told me all about you: what you are; what you can do; what you're protecting," he hissed.

I looked around my room with a keener eye and noticed how everything was out of place. At that moment I was grateful I'd decided to hide the cowry shells behind the wall in the herbals room.

"I've never known Rowley to be chatty. Care to swap stories?" I asked, affecting the nonchalance I used with Áliz.

"Aren't you delightful? And so clever to get all better all by yourself. Did Rowley tell you he taught me to imbue my claws with magic? I suppose we're both his students," he purred. I kept my face impassive, but my mind reeled with the information. *Rowley, careful cautious Rowley, taught The Cat how to harm others with magic?*

"I'm giving you until the full moon to bring your shells and Rowley to me," he continued, passing a claw across the bars of Cochi's cage. My chinchilla stilled, watching The Cat. "I have no intention of remaining here—Canto has lost its appeal. But if you don't agree there's a certain someone I know who isn't immune to my...persuasion. So dutiful, so princely. Do we have a deal?" He fanned out his claws to emphasize the point.

Could I stall? He was giving me a week—would that be enough time to get the horn? I'd already seen Zavier defenseless against magic and I couldn't leave him at the mercy of his brother, let alone a malevolent cat.

"Tick tock goes the metronome. Shall I start with a dance?" It was then I saw the fiddle. He reached for it and poised himself by the window, ready to leap.

"Deal, but no music in the meantime—anywhere," I said, my voice sounding strangled to my ears.

"Oh, I guess I can keep myself busy elsewhere. Done. Find me at the lake." He did jump then, and I raced to the window. I looked down and by then there was no sign of The Cat or his fiddle.

THE DECISION TO SEEK help had been harder than the magic required to get me there. I'd locked the door after telling Mamá that I was researching and going to bed. The precaution was more of an early warning because I had yet to find a lock that Mamá couldn't open. It must be a parent thing, but I used a little magical assistance for that too.

After traveling back in time, moving through Canto was easy. It hadn't been as transformative as becoming air again, but I had only been off my destination by twenty or thirty yards. The words came to me easily after bringing the mirror being back. *Ag bher tkei Mist House.*

So why are the last few steps to the Mist House so hard?

At this point Viktor probably already knew I was there, but opening the door was somehow beyond me. It wasn't a magical thing—it was a mental thing. I didn't trust Viktor, and she already knew too much about me, about my family, about my magic. And it was her fault we were in this mess in the first place. The more I turned the problem of The Cat over in my head, it made sense that Viktor was somehow involved. When I'd overheard Hortensia and the Mythosian envoy discussing The Cat and the envoy's "agent" I couldn't ignore the possibility that the "agent" referenced, was Viktor.

I wasn't scared... I was angry. Livid, that by association Zavier, Meiri, and everyone had been threatened. I didn't even know why, but that was beside the point. Viktor could help, but I hated needing her. Especially after what I'd done.

The door creaked open, revealing a room overly brightened with candles. The smell of spent matches was thick, as well as another smell I couldn't place, but it was familiar. Viktor spun around instantly, her eyes as big as saucers. Her magic, which with the augmenting lens had been oppressive, was now light and insubstantial.

"Oh, it's the thief! Come to take something else—maybe the clothes I'm wearing?"

"I didn't steal—"

"Don't insult me. We both know you took my augmenting lens. Why are you here?"

"I came to ask for help," I asked through gritted teeth. I couldn't manage contrite, but I could try humble. Clasping my hands in front of me, I looked down at the floor.

"My help? Interesting. Why should I help you? It's your fault I'm in this mess now." Her indignation robbed me of my ability to remain cool.

"Wait, you're blaming me? I know you called The Cat back so don't you dare blame me for this," I yelled. My hands tingled painfully, wanting to be given free reign. It was tempting and the awareness that I could do it—blast her and her little hut to smithereens—was intoxicating.

One slip of the finger and I could turn it all to dust, vent my frustrations and be done with it. But the look on her face caught me. Her usual warm complexion was sallow and heavy; dark rings circled her eyes. Even her clothes were askew, and the firm set of her mouth read less as determination and more like fear. *Did I do that? Or was it...?*

"He turned on you, didn't he?" I asked more gently. Her drooping shoulders was confirmation enough. "Did you really think you could control him? The Cat's been using magic since before you were born." Time for Viktor to feed The Cat's bitterness with tales of hate and to revel in the idea of revenge. The Cat had been wronged and as much as I knew his way was wrong, I understood his motives. He was treated badly by the humans who kept him and then was banished for using his Powers. How might I have behaved if I hadn't been lucky enough to have a loving family and inherent magic?

There were times I wanted to use my magic on Hortensia or Eugenia, but I knew better. Viktor on the other hand... Her motives were more of a mystery.

"Why did you do it?" I asked.

"Have you so little faith in me? In what we can achieve together?" she said, then slumped into a chair. This moment felt familiar. I'd accused her of helping Rex and Yvette when they tried to steal my shells. And yet something was different this time.

"I didn't call The Cat on my own, but I won't say I'm blameless." She rose and crossed to a cabinet I'd overlooked. On top was a picture of her, much younger, with a man. It looked like Mr. Fell.

"Inez, don't you ever wish you could tell everyone who you are—really? Imagine a world where we all have our magic back. People with knowledge would be revered instead of hunted and harassed. But this world begins to look more and more like the one our ancestors escaped. If we could change the minds of those who are against magic, we could be ourselves," she said in an angry whisper. "The Cat, with his magic fiddle, could make all that possible."

"And how is that supposed to work?" I asked, genuinely curious. She sat down heavily; her eyes never left the floor. The silence stretched on and I wondered if she would answer the question.

"The Mythosian envoy approached me with a request from Mythos, but we both knew it wasn't a request. Their magic couldn't be linked to the return of The Cat. I wasn't given any reason as to why he had to return, but I can guess.

"It didn't matter. I knew that if I brought him back, he would be beholden to me. But I was wrong," she said on a sigh.

"What would that do for you if he had been?" I asked.

"Don't you see? The Cat could be let loose on Mythos and then we'd demand our magic back and they would need us. And I would protect you," she added.

"What?"

"I didn't think that last part would be necessary. I know you understand that this is the way to fix Canto. I knew I could convince you to be on our side..."

"You mean control me so you could control my magic? I'm guessing The Cat had other plans?" I asked, oddly distanced by her words.

"He wanted to enchant you and when he found out that his fiddle wouldn't control you he went a little mad," she said, her eyes downcast. "Then I realized he knew about the shells and that he never intended to follow anyone's plan. All he wanted was to pick up where he left off before he'd been banished by the horn and get his revenge on humans."

Idly, I wondered if Hortensia felt any remorse for her part in our predicament. Hortensia was the one who'd contacted the Mythosian envoy to release The Cat on Canto. In a way she had gotten exactly what she wanted. If The Cat got any more out of hand, she'd be forced to call on Mythos for help and Canto would be under even stricter scrutiny. *And Zavier would have a new fiancée.*

"Well, lucky for us, I have a plan... But I need your help," I said. I pulled out a small sack which contained the augmenting lens safely nestled in its folds. This woman had just admitted to betraying not only me but all of Canto. She had endangered the Enchanted Isles and a small part of me understood. Worse yet, that small part wasn't even angry. I sympathized with her. Had often wished to get rid of secrets. Just to be me.

I longed to step out into the light and tell everyone who I really was. She wasn't wrong about my feelings. Maybe I would have gone along with it if I hadn't met Rowley or if I'd been forced into the life Viktor led. But then I thought of her brother, Mr. Fell, who managed to know all his sister did and still smile. He was a respected member of the Royal household and spent his life helping. How did their paths come to diverge?

Should I have gone to him for help?

I'd considered that, but I knew he was more aligned with my mother and Rowley. As much as I hated to admit it, some things required someone who's morality was more malleable. I lifted the lens out gingerly and showed it to her.

My choices were few and time was running out. Her hand closed over mine and the lens, her eyes lit up with new purpose.

"Show me how to use this and I can take care of The Cat," I said, feeling the lens flicker to life. Viktor, with renewed vigor, smiled in a way I'd come to dread.

"I will show you for a price. When this is over, I want the lens back." I nodded mutely, knowing I'd made another devil's bargain with her.

"Let's begin."

Chapter 37

For one day and two grueling nights Viktor taught me about the lens. We ran through drills with equable earth, playful air, and even consuming fire. But water remained elusive, remote. It required all of me. Not just my determination, but my desire, my humanity. When I focused my want, the lens laughed like a rushing brook. It met my will with the force of a raging river. When I confronted it with my humanity, it stayed cool and unreadable, unmoved by my magic.

"Even after all your practice at the bay? I would have thought—"

"Yes, I know," I said testily. A glass of water just out of my grasp, mocking. I remembered the ease with which I'd called water to me after awaking from my injuries. Why couldn't I do it now?

"That's why I thought the lens would help." I pointed dismissively at the box that housed the lens. Something in Viktor's face changed and she picked it up, almost reverently.

"Your problem is you see it as a tool. It's not just a tool. It's people. Literarily people!" She snorted at my blank expression. She held it in the palm of her hand, inspecting it like some specimen.

"Not all those who were stripped of their magic were left Powerless. Workers of great magic weren't always rended. For a time, they became magic surrogates to people in Mythos, but neither side liked the arrangement. No one likes to be contained—no one," she whispered more to the box than to me. "So, they fought—the magical surrogates and the Mythosians ungifted in inherent magic—each group trying to gain the upper hand.

"One truly diabolical Mythosian mage figured out a way to pluck the soul out of each augmenting lens—as they were called—and contained each one in a box." Her smile was a brittle thing, but even after it came the smile never reached her eyes.

"This mage presented her achievement to the Mythosian assembly and even to the Arbiter herself, and for her trouble she was vilified and told she wasn't fit to be around people. She was banished to the Outer Isles, but her knowledge was still used. That, my dear, was my ancestor. No one liked to talk about it and slowly the truth was lost, but my family remembers the story. As does Mythos.

"It gifted me with this gilded cage. Sadly, I can't even blame Queen Hortensia or King Xander— They don't even know what they have in these...things. But you do," she said, slamming the cube onto the table in front of me. Her face came within inches of my own and it took more nerve than I wanted to admit to keep from flinching. "One thing an augmenting lens knows is symbiosis. It expects your respect and your allegiance. Weakness is something to scorn. Water is no different. Now try again."

"You're Mythosian?" I asked, shocked and yet somehow unsurprised by the revelation. Was that the reason she'd been able keep her magic, albeit contained in the Mist House? Viktor pursed her lips and snorted.

"My family hasn't been Mythosian for centuries, but every so often one of us displays the inherent magic all Mythosians can claim. You and I share the same blessing and curse. And now I share with you my ancestor's legacy; or I should say my ancestor. Hers is the soul trapped in that box," she said, caressing the intricate patterns along its side. She lifted the small latch and tipped the lens onto the table.

My mouth had gone dry. I now understood why she had been so reluctant to part with it. Looking down at the miniature casket I was repulsed by the idea of someone's soul being contained in a box. And the realization dawned: That could have been me.

Tentatively, I reached out a finger and grazed the top of it. Ridges and whorls covered it on all sides, making it more like a decorative ring box. Did it reflect the mage within or did Viktor's ancestor want to make the present more pleasing to the eye?

I put the lens in the palm of my hand. It was still warm to the touch, but inactive. Viktor had taught me the words of Power that made it work. I didn't tell her I had a long list of words because I still didn't trust her. Tonight's revelations hadn't changed that. But inactive wasn't the right word. It was poised, waiting.

The warmth hadn't changed, but I sensed it sensing my magic.

I stared at it, the lights from the candles dancing in its confines. How did one respect a lens? Knowing it was or had been a person made it easier to contemplate, but no less difficult to execute. Agreement? Command? I couldn't tell what would work. I knew I had to consciously will it.

I slowly closed my fingers around the lens, its edges rougher than expected. "*Gwei*," I whispered and a dim violet light shone from its center. It shimmied to life, expanding ever so slightly in my palm. The sensation was of being pulled in, yet pushed out, like gasping for breath while running a marathon. I could visualize it as a continual osmosis with me taking in what it let out then that changing directions.

It was more elegant than mere inhale and exhale—it was a dance of wills. It never spoke, but I clearly understood that it could have so easily been me and mine trapped in a box. A genie to someone else's whims. I had to acknowledge that, acknowledge the fear that I was just as trapped as the soul in this box.

"*Magh*," I said, my voice hushed but firm. It was then I heard Viktor's sharp intake of breath.

The glass of water was no more. In its place was a sculpture, made entirely of water moving and flowing with a miniature image. A transparent woman with a face of resignation stared back at me. She inclined her head in acceptance before sparing a glance for Viktor. The resemblance was obvious and then the moment was gone and the water moved back into its glass prison, without spilling a drop.

Shimmering spots clouded my sight and I realized I'd been holding my breath. Putting the lens down, I reached for the cup, unable to believe what I'd just seen.

"You're ready," Viktor whispered and took the glass from me. She whispered the final word, "*Swep*," with reverence and placed the lens in its box before handing it to me.

I RETURNED HOME IN a kind of trance. Everything had speeded up, but I was still moving in slow motion. Unlocking my door had taken a deliberate effort, just as putting the augmenting lens and case back in its cloth sack had been. My mind made decisive commands... *Left foot, right foot, left foot, right foot. Careful of the stairs.* I was Powerful and weak all at the same time. I descended to the kitchen under my own power, but unaware of how I'd done it.

"Hungry? You've been up there awhile. I'm not surprised. Find anything interesting? Inez?"

I heard her speaking and the next logical step was eluding me. I managed to blink in her general direction, making her eyebrows furrow and squint. Deftly she took hold of my arm, and pulling me by the elbow, sat me down.

"Inez? What were you doing up there? Did you find anything? Inez? Inez!" she yelled shaking me. Finally, I shook myself, feeling the vestiges of frozen comprehension start to thaw.

"I know how to get the horn back. I know where it is and how to get it back. I was just...just..."

"You're just going to have a bite to eat and then we'll talk about what you've been up to," she said, fixing me a plate. I started to protest, but she waved that away. "*La cáscara guarda el palo.*"

I ate silently, still having a hard time making my mouth work. By the last bite, I felt myself again relishing the flavors, but Mamá was looking at me like I was fragile glass, liable to break if handled indelicately.

"I'm fine. I'm fine. Sorry if I scared you, but I've been at it for so long I think..." I didn't want to lie. It was enough effort to feel normal again. "I've been working with an augmenting lens and I think it took more out of me than I realized." I didn't mention Viktor.

"Those things are dangerous and—"

"Everything I do is dangerous, Mamá. It can't be helped," I said, serving myself some more.

"It can be helped. We can help you," she said, grabbing my wrist. I could see the war going on in her mind. She knew this was something I couldn't avoid, but her job as a mother was to protect. Where had that thought been when there had been opportunities to tell me about my gifts earlier?

"Thanks, but I'll manage," I said a little more sharply than I intended. "I know you want to help—everyone wants to help, but I can't risk exposing all of you to that cat," I said more gently.

After his visit and the threats he made to Zavier and Rowley, I was more determined than ever to keep everyone away from this. I could still see Toman's ruined arm and the look of insane panic on Meiri's face after their run-ins with The Cat. How long before he threatened Mamá if he saw her involvement?

"I should be back soon. Thank you for...this," I said, pointing to the food, but I meant so much more. I didn't know how to say it, so I hugged her fiercely and went upstairs. The box in my room was waiting.

Chapter 38

Before I left on my errand I had another box to retrieve. The herbals room was now a tamp root containment room, but the smells of lavender, calendula and a myriad other herbs mingled happily with the new addition. There were crates full of tamp root tonic and Mamá had yet to confide in me how she intended to distribute it to anyone exhibiting the same madness Meiri had experienced. I didn't press her because I knew she was happy to have something to do that lightened my burden.

I pulled back the heavy wooden table from the wall, rubbing out the scuff marks it left with my shoes. As a thief I'd learned long ago that people who thought they were being clever hiding valuables in walls or under floors invariably forgot to erase the evidence of opening and closing their hiding places.

The stone that comprised the wall had enough irregular shapes that one wouldn't know if there were hiding places behind any of them or all. The rock I had chosen was neither one of the larger ones nor a small one. I took care to keep a bucket of dirt handy to reseal it and splashed water across the entire wall to mask any appearance of tampering. My box of magical cowry shells practically hummed when I opened the latch.

Three of the four swirled as the Mist House did and the other remained inert. I held the latter, wondering if Rex was really trapped inside it. Was his imprisonment like that of Viktor's ancestor?

I banished those thoughts and placed the shells on the ground. Transporting them along with the augmenting lens seemed dangerous to me, but even more dangerous was trying to use both inside the house. That was why I'd decided to use them first at the secluded section of the bay where I'd practiced water magic. There was no time to lose. I had been given a deadline.

I heard Mamá's footfalls in the hallway.

"Inez why don't you— What are you doing with *those*," asked Mamá. She pointed at the box of cowry shells but remained in the doorway of the room rather than coming in. Her jaw tightened and a grimace puckered her face.

"I need to use them," I said, rising. I moved the table back, toeing the ground and removing the marks. As I placed the box of shells on the table, Mamá winced as though she expected them to explode from mishandling or some such.

"I thought you decided not to take in the rest of their magic. Is Rowley pressuring you again?" she asked.

"The only pressure I have is the thought of one of you being caught by The Cat. And I'm not taking in the magic, or at least not really. I'm going to borrow a little magic to pull the horn out of the bay," I replied.

I'd worked it all out in my head. If the purpose of the augmenting lens is not just to amplify one's magic, but to act as a surrogate to other magic, it stood to reason that I could use the lens to tap into the shells without retaining any of the magic.

The only flaw I saw in my plan were the shells. How would they react to being tampered with? I hoped my connection to them was enough for them to consent to being used in this way. My line of questioning didn't seem so far-fetched to me after learning about the mages trapped in the augmenting lenses or the entity of the voice in the mirror. In my mind, the shells were now entities as well.

"*Nena*, this sounds too risky. I have all that tamp root tonic and I found a masking agent that will keep the tonic from being too diluted in the water supply. The rest I'll keep on hand for Mr. Fell to give the healers. If The Cat finds us immune to his fiddle, he'll lose interest in Canto," she said, her eyes beseeching.

"And then terrorize Faery or move on to the Outer Isles. I can't take that chance. He needs to be stopped and for good this time. We can't all hide," I said, grabbing the box to my chest. The hum reminded me of the gong I'd felt when I time traveled, but this time it was soothing.

"What do you mean by hide?" Mamá asked.

"Mamá, you kept my magic a secret for so long that I think it's become a habit for you to try and hide everything from me. Mr. Fell talks about the Society and all the plans you made. Lita and Beval left me the words of Power. Rowley's lived for centuries waiting to teach me, and even Viktor defies Mythos to help me. What are *you* doing?" I challenged and with those words knew I'd gone too far.

Mamá pulled back from the door, her mouth agape and her pallor ashen. And yet she straightened and fixed me with a stare reserved for the worst of transgressions.

"None of those people are your mother. They have no idea what it is to be mother to the Ternion. All they see is what you can do for them, for Canto, but I see my daughter. Someone who, through my recklessness and pride, now has to worry about everyone else. I worry about you and that's it. You call it hiding... I call it my responsibility," she said, her voice a dangerous whisper.

"And what about my responsibility?" I countered.

Reasoning with Mamá when she was in this state was futile, but I couldn't back down. The box of shells hummed a half pitch higher.

"He already got Meiri and Toman and he threatened Zavier. I will not—" I never finished my sentence. In my mind the word *skeud* echoed and Mamá was tossed into the hallway. I dropped the box and ran to her. My neck swiveled left and right, searching for the source of her sudden flight. And then I felt it—the telltale pinpricks in my fingertips, the warmth of the augmenting lens box.

Mamá shook her head and slowly sat up.

"Don't move. Are you hurt? What did I...?" I babbled, supporting her back. She grabbed my hand and squeezed.

"I'm fine, *nena*. It was nothing," she said. "It was just an accident."

I dropped her hand and ran as quickly as I could. The door slammed in my wake, cutting off Mamá's calls.

WITH AMPLIFIER IN HAND, I made my way down to the bay. At least I knew I couldn't hurt anyone there. I needed to make this right. It would never stop—constantly trying to help and by doing so, hurting people I loved.

It all started with those damned shells. Last time it was a crazy man I'd had to imprison in one of the eggs and by that action, a woman was made an orphan. Now it was a cat. What would come next? I'd thrown my mother against a wall. The weight of that crushed me. I wanted to go back to my old life of smuggling and being a small part of bringing back magic. It would cause far less trouble than almost blowing up my friends, family or whole neighborhoods.

I reached the edge of the water and closed my eyes. I concentrated on summoning the cowry shells and with little effort they appeared before me on the bank, the lid of their box already open. The augmenting lens was working already. I couldn't believe how well it worked.

Kneeling before the shells, I searched my mind for the appropriate spell to destroy them. Their existence had caused too many problems—close calls with my magic being exposed, Mamá being kidnapped as leverage for them, the royal family almost being overthrown—and now I'd hurt my own mother with the magic I already had. What would more do? The shells weren't safe and neither was I. If I wasn't ready to take in their Power, I had no business keeping them. I had a twinge of regret that I wouldn't be able to remove Rex before I did. Betlindis had taken the loss of her father better than I thought she would, but she still looked lost without him.

"*Bheid gwhen*," I chanted, the words coming from memory. I felt resistance from the cowry shells, a shield blocking my command. Pushing against it was useless, so my magic searched for a point of weakness, a way around instead of through. Then I felt it. A small sliver, a crack in its defenses and I somehow knew it was Rex.

It made the shells vulnerable to have something inside them—wanting to be free—which had nothing to do with their purpose. I wedged my will into that flaw, trying to open it more. But there was something on the periphery, distracting my attention.

The fissure was closing, and I needed to push the diversion away. The lens almost hummed in harmony with the shells, so content was it to carry out my command. The crack opened the width of a hair and then I heard the familiar voice.

"*Nena*, are you okay? You can't blame yourself. You need to know—" I never heard the rest of my mother's sentence. I felt her resistance and suddenly it was gone along with the gap in the shells' defenses.

"Mamá? Where did you go? Mamá! What did I do? Oh no, what did I...?

"You pushed her into the shell," replied Viktor. I was so startled that I knocked her off her feet.

I couldn't breathe or think. I kept shaking the only magically inert shell in a vain hope to release my mother and whatever else was inside it. I didn't care. Magical backlash be damned. *My mother can't be gone.*

"Inez, you have to stop. It won't help and if you did open it what would that do?" said Viktor, scrambling toward me. I couldn't stop shaking and she wrapped herself around me like a blanket, trying to steady me. She saw the lens on the ground, picked it up and tossed it in the bay.

Magic hung thickly in the air. The last vestiges of my disastrous spell were as tangible as the shell still clasped in my hand. Tears spilled over onto my already wet cheeks as I felt the magic meant to strengthen my own, descend. In an instant the pain and loss I had been feeling faded away.

I wanted to scream, to rant, to wail, but nothing came. I was in a state of detachment, and I welcomed the relief. Words were being said to me, but they didn't register. The bay looked the same, cool and remote—without a bit of pity. The sky was still blue. It was still cold outside, but now it was cold inside, too. I was shaking, but not of my own accord. It took a few minutes to realize Viktor was shaking me.

"Inez, do you hear me? You can't tell anyone what happened," she said, her voice modulated as though speaking to a child.

"What? What are you talking about? I have to get her back. Maybe the King's Men or the Queen?" I reasoned.

"Inez, they will see you destroyed. They will imprison you if you're lucky. More likely they'll send you away and erase your memory of any of it," she said.

"But I can't...I have to—"

"You put her in the shell and only you can get her out. If you're sent away she's gone for good," Viktor said and when I didn't respond, she slapped me. The stinging heat woke me from my stupor. My ear rang flatly. My teeth were rattled with the force of it. I looked at her without knowing what to say.

"We will say there was an accident. That your mother fell in the bay. We'll have to get you soaked so they think you went in after her.

A search will be mounted and she won't be found," she said slowly, spinning the lies I would have to tell to save myself.

"After a few days the search will end and then you'll have to plan a funeral," she said with such frankness that I could only respond with a nod. *Did she do this before?*

She led me into the water and for once I was glad of the cold and numbness as I sank into its murky depths. Viktor pulled me out, perhaps fearing I would consider remaining there. I walked toward town, leaving Viktor and the shells behind.

IT WAS TWO DAYS BEFORE the search ended. In the meantime, I locked myself away in the herbals room trying to find a solution to the problem of my mother being trapped in the shell. I barricaded the door, so no one could come in. There was plenty of banging and yelling through the wood, but I ignored it all. A note was pushed under with Toman's handwriting, but I didn't bother to read it. None of them understood—she wasn't dead and when I figured out how, I could fix everything.

I redoubled my efforts even as I wondered how unconcerned I felt. When Lita died, I'd cried for weeks and now that Mamá was gone I was indifferent. Something was wrong, but my puzzle about how to save my mother would distract me from looking too deeply into my lack of emotion.

Zavier's handwriting on official King's Men stationary arrived under my door, telling me the search was over and my mother was still lost. I read that one in the hopes that it had all been a mistake, a bad dream, and she was found. I appreciated that Zavier said lost and not presumed dead, but it was all euphemisms at this point anyway.

At the end of the third day, Mrs. Haro became desperate and got past my door, I assumed with Rowley's help although he didn't stay long. She came armed with food, a pile of mail, and a lecture that went on for an hour. She cried at times, but held me throughout. I couldn't cry, but the chill I felt dissipated a little in her presence.

"You need a bath and some food," she said.

"I won't go upstairs," I replied peevishly. I didn't want her pity or sympathy. I knew I didn't deserve either. It was my fault this had happened.

"Isn't there a bath down here? I'll find your clothes. The...the funeral is tomorrow," she said with a sniff.

"What funeral? She's lost," I said and surprised even myself with how coolly I delivered the verdict.

"Inez, everything's already been arranged. Your young man did most of it," she replied. For some reason I felt nothing, knowing Zavier had planned my mother's funeral. I processed the information with detached calculation.

What would they put in the coffin? Did it matter if I went or not? My mind grabbed onto minutiae, dissecting each bit of news as though I was looking at someone else's life. Mrs. Haro had continued talking, but I heard none of it. I walked to the kitchen, leaving her befuddled by my abruptness.

WATER DRIPPED DOWN my face, washing away the tears that never came. I just stood under the shower letting its steamy heat scald me. Turning my face into the stream I held my breath and opened my mouth. I used to pretend that I could breathe underwater like a fish, opening and closing my mouth to let the accumulating water run off. Now I knew what real drowning felt like with the burden of everything crashing down on me, overwhelming my senses to the point of shutting down. And yet I couldn't identify any emotions.

Am I angry? Guilty? Sad?

The more I wondered, the emptier I felt. Suddenly the water was too hot, the pain too much and the water stopped. I looked up to see the jets of water suspended in the air overhead as though a sheet of glass kept it from pelting down on my head...

Now I learn control.

My first thought was to run and tell Mamá. The pain of realization crested suddenly and then receded just as abruptly.

I heard myself laughing, a giggle at first and then a hysterical cackle at the absurdity of it all. The water continued to hang poised, liquid still frozen in place. Why couldn't I have done that a week ago? My cheeks began to hurt and my eyes glazed with unshed tears, but the laughter didn't abate.

"Inez dear, are you all right in there?" I heard the muffled voice of Mrs. Haro call. I couldn't breathe and respond, so I chose the former.

The deep breath brought back an odd sense of calm and the water resumed. Mrs. Haro's question hung in the air now. What a thing to ask. Would I ever be all right again? I didn't know, but I couldn't share my concerns about my sanity with Mrs. Haro.

"I'm fine. I'll be out in a minute." It was a comfortable lie. One to set Mrs. Haro's mind at ease that I hadn't gone mad. Nevertheless, I was mad, in every sense of the word. After seeing what magic had done to Austra and Xander I knew the truth. Eventually magic drives everyone mad...if you used it.

After assuring herself that I wasn't going to do anything crazy, Mrs. Haro left with the promise she'd see me at the funeral. I promised I wouldn't walk over alone, but at this point lying to Mrs. Haro was getting easy.

Chapter 39

The next morning was a dismal one, befitting the occasion.

Rowley was waiting for me after I dressed. I vaguely noticed the dress was the same as the one Mamá had worn to Lita's funeral. I didn't bother to ask him how he had gotten in. His large form blocked the doorway, forcing me to acknowledge him.

"I hope you're not here for a lesson. I have somewhere I have to be," I said, oddly disconnected from my annoyance. I sensed the emotion welling within me as though it were a presence in another room I had yet to search. I was in no mood to deal with him. I wasn't in the mood to deal with anyone, but I knew I didn't have that luxury. Half of Canto likely thought I'd killed my own mother. I guess they weren't entirely wrong, but not showing up to the funeral was not an option.

"Miss...Inez, I'm not here to reprimand you. I wanted to ask you a question before you lock yourself away again," replied Rowley. He remained in front of the door, blocking my escape.

"Hooray, questions. I have a question. Why are you here? If you think I'm still going to help you, you've come on the wrong day," I said. I'd meant to be glib, but my tone merely showed disinterest. He cocked his head to the side, his eyes narrowing.

"My question is, how have you not incinerated the house?" he asked with utter calm. "I can only imagine your emotional state, yet you've found control. Would you like to know why?" he asked but I knew the question was only a formality. I crossed my arms, waiting him out, not willing to offer him anything. The incident in the shower came to mind and I had to admit I'd wondered myself, but I wasn't going to admit that to him.

"I've been studying your progress and from what you've told me about your time in the past. I think it's tied to your sacrifices," he continued. "There is a school of thought that says using great Powers requires a substantial sacrifice. That same notion holds when the sacrifice is truly significant, the astral mind takes over, cutting the mage off from their emotions and allowing the mage to wield more magic," he said. Then he paused as though considering his next words carefully. Rowley's features softened and he rose from his spot. "I can think of no greater sacrifice than your mother."

"You're saying my mother was some virgin sent up to appease the volcano? *Did I have to lose my mother to control my Power?* Well, that's something to celebrate. Let's have a party... I'm already dressed up and everyone's waiting. We can tell them all. 'Welcome everyone, I killed my mother, but it's a good thing because now I won't destroy the town.' Thanks Rowley," I said, the words having more bite than I truly felt.

My mind tentatively sought out that place within me where my emotions were hiding. All I felt was a gnawing cold and something approaching fear to see behind the ice wall I'd erected. I suppressed the urge to venture too deep, knowing it would undo me. "Is that all? Because I have somewhere to be." I said. Without whispering any words of Power, I lifted Rowley with my astral mind and set him on the stairs behind me. It was as easy as that.

"I think you've just proved my point. You've already made the sacrifice," he said, walking down the stairs.

"And control is my reward?" I asked, but it wasn't a question I expected him to answer.

"Make use of what you're due. Canto is still in danger and—"

"And what? I'm going to use my Powers to help...the same Powers that killed my mother? I hope you enjoyed that parlor trick. It was my last. Now, I have somewhere to be," I repeated for the third time and left him there as I headed for the door.

"Your mother came to you that morning to show her support, to show you she believed in you. Don't make a liar of her now," he shouted.

"My mother... My mother is gone! My magic did that. Now you can all burn for all I care," I said and left.

THE CEMETERY WAS ABUZZ with gossip. I was able to stand behind the statue of its namesake and listen to people speculate about how Filomena Garza was gone, and the only witness was her daughter. Some said it with sympathy, but others said it with perverse relish. All of them speculated about who would inherit her ducal title and the estate of Árbor Real. My status as daughter of a noble with no title of my own wasn't common knowledge and with the engagement to Zavier, it was murkier. I already knew the house was mine, but I didn't care about the title. Not today.

Lots of winks and nudges were exchanged and then Zavier appeared, parting the crowd. He took my listless and feeble hand into his stronger ones and led me to the front of the chairs.

It was odd, looking at the grave—a space which was supposed to represent my mother—and knowing she wasn't there. I'd had an irrational thought of bringing the shell imprisoning her and placing it in front of the large painting for more authenticity. The cold had not abated and others coped by milling about for warmth.

I let go of Zavier's hand and sat down with my back straight, ignoring the comments buzzing around me. Staying as remote as possible. I didn't want to invite sympathy for fear it would attract others to speak. Sadly, my approach didn't work with everyone.

"Inez, I am so sorry for your loss. I know it's hard to imagine now but it will get better. If you ever need anything at all, feel free to ask," said Betlindis. Her hand patted my shoulder, sympathetically, unintentionally raising my protection spell.

"Ouch, static electricity."

Toman and Meiri flanked me all of a sudden, keeping away any other well-wishers. Zavier and Mrs. Haro did their best to convey my thanks for the attentions. In my mind, I entered that room where all my feelings resided.

I'd thought of them as hiding, but in truth they were more like caged creatures, prowling hungrily in their confinement. I turned from them and brought my attention to the cold outside rather than in. Lita would be appalled and Mamá would expect better from me, so I shook off my protectors and climbed the makeshift dais. The crowd hushed as I looked at my mother's portrait. Taking courage from her strength. I faced the crowd.

"Hello. Thank you for coming. My mother is...was a lot of things to a lot of people," I began, then cleared my throat. "She was head librarian, official Canto archivist and founder of the historical society. She was also an outspoken member of the Royal Council and an advocate for magic here and in all the Enchanted Isles. My mother was a lot of things, but to me she was just Mamá.

"When I was little she was the person who kept the monsters at bay and made the best oatmeal. I also thought she could leap tall buildings. As I got older I didn't worry so much about monsters and oatmeal, and maybe I took her for granted. She always wanted me to be patient and thoughtful and...well...I guess I have to take care of my own monsters now.

"I still don't know how to make oatmeal. I should have paid more attention to that. I should have... Thanks again for coming," I finished in a whisper. A small curl of cold that had wrapped itself around my insides eased slightly.

Getting that off my chest made me feel oddly better, like a confession. I smiled at her portrait and left the dais, hoping that wherever she was she had heard me. Then I remembered where she was—in a shell, which I had left with Viktor. The alarm bells that should have gone off with that realization were muffled.

ZAVIER WALKED ME BACK from the funeral. I wanted to be alone, but the prospect of the empty house that now belonged to me was daunting. His hand around mine was warm and solid, and he understood that I wasn't in the mood for conversation. Still, he kept taking quick glances my way.

I think he was worried because I still hadn't cried. If I was honest with myself, I was worried too. Rowley's revelation that my control was tied to the loss—I wasn't ready to say death—of Mamá was starting to make sense.

Why wasn't I angry? Sad? Guilty?

I felt nothing after just leaving my mother's funeral, sham though it was. I didn't want to feel any of those things, but I knew to feel them was more normal than what I was currently lacking.

We approached Árbor Real, an estate I now legally owned even if my mother's title was likely lost. When I'd learned I couldn't inherit the title years ago, it hadn't bothered me. The house meant more, but that was at a time when it was full of people I loved and who loved me in return. I'd always considered the house a reflection of me even before it was mine. The herbals room, my knowledge. The kitchen, my instincts. My room, my messy personality. And my heart...

The house looked as it always did. I could fool myself into believing she was on another work trip. Another meeting for the historical society: "Just wanted to let you know, so you won't think I disappeared."

Not letting go of Zavier's hand, I led him into the sitting room, my current retreat from reality. His shoes crunched on a piece of paper protruding from under the desk. It was a note from my mother.

Nena, please clean up. What if someone came to visit? – Mamá

I almost laughed at the thought. I don't have to clean my room if I don't want to, I thought rebelliously. Zavier took the note from my hand as I turned from him, finally breaking our link.

"Do you need anything?" Zavier asked, stroking my back. I shrugged him off and faced his concerned expression.

"Your being here is enough for now," I replied absently.

Only it wasn't true.

My half-hearted smile didn't fool him for a minute. His hug was sudden and fierce, crushing me to him. I thought I would cry, but the tears didn't come. Instead, I idly considered the hard buttons of his coat pressing against my chest.

"I'm here if you need me," said Zavier cupping my face in his hands.

"I know," I whispered and kissed him. It started as a harmless peck, but grew in intensity. The cold that enveloped my chest eased a fraction. *Is Rowley right? Am I protecting myself from feeling with magic?*

I tentatively reached out to feelings as though they were a separate entity. I thought about Mamá and how she was the person I would have brought this problem to, but she was gone. I remembered her being thrown across the room by my magic.

I stepped back from those feelings, too large and raw and making my fingers tingle. Instead, I focused on the man in front of me. My emotions for him were simpler, and I welcomed being able to feel something safe.

Lust.

I now knew what I wanted: to experience something other than this gaping hole of loss.

Pulling him with me, not breaking the kiss, I leaned against the desk. My hands easily unbuttoned his coat, sliding beneath the heavy fabric. I pulled his body closer, seeking his warmth. My hunger was unexpected to us both, and he resisted my fumbling attempts with his shirt.

"Inez, I know you're upset, but maybe you should—"

"Zavier, you're not my mother! I don't need anyone telling me what to do. No one can do that anymore. I want this," I said, gripping him tighter. His hands grabbed my wrists, and tightened as I struggled.

"Inez, I love you..." His grip lessened and I took advantage, releasing myself.

"Then...?" I replied kissing him again. I barely registered the concept. I was too busy trying to undress him. When he resisted, I changed tack and began to undress myself. I loosened the buttons of my gown and let it slide down my body, discarded on the floor between us.

That got his attention. He stared with taut control as I stood in my undergarments. No man is that noble and I watched the war of decency battling with desire cross his face. Guiding his hand back to my hips, I knew decency was wavering.

The icy coolness that had settled in my heart since I lost Mamá at the bay was thawing.

Zavier's arms wound themselves around my waist. He was willing—I could feel that despite layers of winter clothing—but he wasn't eager. There was still his reticence I had to overcome which I addressed with more temptation. My lips parted beneath his as I pulled the hem of my underskirt above my knees. His hands stopped me as I reached mid-thigh and broke the kiss. I knew whatever magical protection had kept me from my emotions was wavering because I was annoyed.

"Zavier don't presume to know how I need to feel right now. I—love you, too," I said, still detached from the sentiment, but I knew it was true. I was surprised by how it warmed me and so repeated it with more feeling. With infinite gentleness, Zavier kissed me and I finally felt his passion ignite.

This was going to happen.

And never again would there be someone to stop me.

Chapter 40

There was a rite of passage throughout the Isles. When a child turned fourteen, they were given what most people called olí, for short.

"The formal name is citrus aurantium variation amara," Lita had said. Her back had been to Mamá and me while she worked on some tincture. I remembered the smell of raisins mingled with citrus of the fledgling plant. It still didn't erase the discomfort I felt having this conversation with my mother and ostensibly with my grandmother.

"Knowing the Latin name doesn't help," I'd responded and Mamá smiled at Lita's bemused expression.

"*Con no se, no se escribe*," Lita replied. You're never hurt by knowing more. Listen to your mother.

"As I was saying..." Mamá continued. "You're a young woman now and before you know it you'll have someone in your life who you'll want to share—intimate time with—"

"We've talked about sex before, Mamá," I interrupted. It wasn't a new topic, but the plant made it official.

"And knowing that, you should be prepared for the responsibility," she continued as though I hadn't spoken. "You must tend this plant daily for a year. If it doesn't die it will bloom white cup flowers." She handed me the terracotta pot with a small green sprig in the center. I'd heard stories of parents tricking their children with pots of just dirt to keep them from growing a plant that would allow them to have intimate relations without adverse effects—so they would wait until marriage.

"The liquid in the flower cup is bitter, but only for a moment. You can store its contents indefinitely in these glass vials." Lita handed me a dozen thin vials; each could hold up to a tablespoon of liquid. Mamá handed me a box with spaces for the vials.

I'd tended the plant for the proscribed year and then harvested the flowers for years thereafter, but I'd never used them.

I knew the moment Zavier gave in.

He led me to the sofa although we remained standing. His mouth sought mine, lips parted, and I sighed as the iciness within me continued to melt away. Zavier's hands and lips roved my body deliciously. All his hesitation was gone and all that remained was a growing hunger that reached out to me. And he did reach me.

Zavier was bringing more than my body to life. It was as though the house had been closed for too long and then someone lit a fire. My feelings sparked and grew, igniting us both.

My awareness wasn't absolute. I couldn't for example, remember how we ended up on the sofa with all the pillows removed making a nearly comfortable space for two.

"Should we go upstairs?" he asked, and I froze. Besides my room being a mess, I couldn't go up there yet. *Will I ever be able to face that empty room at the other end of the hall?* What I was doing now felt small in comparison.

"No," I said quickly, pushing down the emotions I wasn't ready to address yet. Instead, I unbuttoned his shirt, discarding it and his coat. My corset was ridiculously difficult for him to remove and in the end I did it for him. It was both a nuisance and a relief knowing that Zavier hadn't spent time perfecting the removal of women's undergarments.

Zavier's pants had been frightfully easy to discard after which his kisses changed from insistent to tender. The change startled me, and I briefly wondered if he'd changed his mind.

"Are you sure you want this?" he asked, his voice a breathless rush. "I would understand—"

I stopped his questions and ended any doubt with my own searing kiss. We were laying down and facing each other, bodies pressed together. He pulled back slowly, his eyes dark with longing.

"Then don't we need...?" He let the sentence hang for a moment as I realized what he was asking. It was one of the few things I'd put in the room without Mamá's knowledge.

I reached under the sofa and removed a box from the hidden compartment. I opened the box to reveal twelve vials and removed two.

"And here I thought it was the KM who were always prepared," he replied with a small laugh, trying to ease the tension. He lifted me from the ground back to the sofa, calm and sure. I tried not to think of how many times he might have done this before.

A handsome, capable man and a prince to boot. Women must have been throwing themselves at him for ages. It was for the best that he knew what he was doing. At this point we needed someone with experience, and it clearly wasn't me.

Zavier's weight on top of me was reassuring. His mouth found mine as his hand traced the sides of my breasts. My next act of bravery was moving his hand from my chest to my thigh hoping he would understand the meaning. His response left me in no doubt as my body responded to his fingers on the delicate flesh between my thighs.

It was almost enough, but I needed more—so much more.

"Zavier..."

"Okay, you're sure because we can still stop right now," he said breathlessly, but his face mirrored my desire. He probably would have stopped for me, but it really was too late to stop this.

I didn't want to stop.

Zavier uncorked his vial and downed the contents in one swig. My legs willingly parted as he positioned himself above me. I opened mine and smelled the citrus perfume within, suddenly reminded of that long ago day when Mamá, Lita, and I had "the talk" to prepare me for this.

I drank it quickly, but not quickly enough to avoid the bitter taste. And yet just as quickly the flavor evaporated.

"This will give you twenty-four hours without the possibility of pregnancy," Lita had said, "but every hour from the taking makes it less efficacious," she'd added.

Zavier took his time then and I marveled at how much feeling I had missed under the protection spell. I gave myself over to his loving intensity, calling out when he finally entered me. We both reveled in the sensations and it was then I knew the protection spell had faded away to nothing. A blaze burner at the corner of my vision sent a plume of fire straight up and just as quickly returned to normal.

I felt a dam break in me and now I was crying out in pleasure, unable to stop. He followed, whispering nonsense in my ear. I couldn't stop moving—not wanting the feeling to end. He kissed me again as my rocking hips settled, and I finally stilled.

"I love you," he said.

The joy of Zavier's and my joining, the grief of the past few days overwhelmed me. Then I laid my head against the hollow of his throat and finally cried.

Zavier's arms enveloped me.

I MUST HAVE CRIED FOR a while and then dozed off because the next thing I knew, it was evening. A soft throw, which turned out to be Zavier's coat covered me. He was looking down at me with tender eyes filled with concern. I was more self-conscious now than I had been when I stood naked before him. But I needed him to know that I hadn't cried for what we had done.

"I'm sorry. I hope you know that wasn't because of..."

"Don't apologize," he said, then leaned over to kiss the top of my head. "When my parents died, I was young, so I spent a lot of time breaking things and lashing out. Especially at my brother who seemed to be trying to take their place. *This* was probably healthier and better for the walls," he said with a chuckle.

"I don't want you to think I regret this. It was just... A few days ago Mamá was saying how I should wait, and I just wanted to make love with you without my mother finding out. Now I have this irrational need to tell her about it, and...and I can't. It got to me, that's all, and now I realize I wish it was a few days ago when I had to sneak around, but still had a mom," I said, feeling the tears welling up again. He lay down and took my in his arms. My tears were spent, but I needed to change the subject. The emotions I'd finally accessed were too raw.

"So how did we do? I don't know a lot about the subject, but I'm guessing you do?" I tried to sound casual, but he understood what I was asking. He sat us both up, tucking me against his side and turning my face toward his.

"Do you think I've done this before?" he asked, his hand still under my chin.

"Well—you were so—capable," I said. We both laughed at that, and it broke the tension I felt in my stomach.

"Inez, I knew how, but that wasn't from practice. And for the record, it was amazing."

At that moment I knew I should be sad, thinking about all I had lost, but instead, I felt I would burst from happiness. Telling him wasn't possible, but my kiss said it all.

MY BODY STARTED TO betray me.

I was sore from sleeping, scrunched up on the sofa and needed a shower, but I also felt braver having finally cried. Outside night had claimed time, and a soft snow started to fall. It was time to go to my room and face that the bedroom down the hall from mine was empty.

Sadly, that meant going upstairs and sending Zavier home. I thought I would deal with the latter first.

"Aren't you due on patrol?" I asked, aiming for a casual tone.

"Getting rid of me? Well, no such luck. I'm not going anywhere tonight. Let's go upstairs," he said. He must have seen the look of panic on my face, but he misinterpreted. "Unless you want me to— We don't have to..."

"It's not that. I haven't been upstairs since it happened," I said, looking away. I had hoped to go through the painful and potentially embarrassing process of taking the steps one at a time alone. He turned my face to him, giving me a light kiss.

"You can't avoid it forever and you're not alone."

After collecting clothes, we made our way upstairs. I was a little stiffer than I thought, but the slight pain I felt blocked out a deeper one.

Concentrating on the minutiae of small things helped. I took the steps at a normal pace, but never looked up. I couldn't face the empty room at the other end of the hall...a reminder that she wasn't coming home. I reached my door without incident and counted that a small victory. My room was a mess—as usual. I tried to clear a path, all the while hearing Mamá's voice in my head. Mamá would have been mortified by the state of my bedroom while entertaining company.

"Don't clean for me. Oh, hello Cochi," he said, scratching under her chin. She was a lot more polite to him than me.

"Aren't men supposed to be slobs? I've seen your rooms—you're ridiculously neat," I said. I wondered if all joy had to have a twinge of pain to be truly felt. Speaking of pain...

"Can I leave you in my mess while I...go and clean up?" I said, putting my bundle of clothes on a chair. On the dresser was Beval's nightshirt, which I took with me.

"Your chinchilla will keep me company," Zavier said.

"The traitor. She always liked you more," I said.

THE SHOWER DID WONDERS for my aches. My other pain was dulling slightly. I cried a little, but it wasn't the torrent of a few hours ago. I had been too young to appreciate the loss of Lita and Beval. Grief wasn't a constant thing—it was more undulating waves. Sometimes it was gentle and receded without disruption, but other times it was a breaker that crashed over you.

Right now, it was more of a patient tide, waiting for its time to return. Zavier was still petting Cochi when I came back. She was practically purring! She'd never been that sweet with me.

I couldn't blame her; his hands were magic.

"Nice choice," he said. I was wearing Beval's nightshirt, my preferred sleeping attire, which went well past my knees. I was suddenly self-conscious. What did one do after an experience like that? Should I offer him something to sleep in other than his undergarments? My ambivalence must have shown and Zavier took both my hands in his.

"Are you hungry? We could go out," he said. I hadn't eaten since this morning, but my appetite was non-existent.

"Can we just go to bed?" I asked, not knowing where that would lead. Zavier was only wearing his underwear and I had nothing on underneath the nightshirt.

Getting into bed together felt warm and comfy, yet still a tad awkward. I didn't know how to behave, and Zavier was being very careful with me. I tentatively touched his bare chest, tracing lines over the firm plains and the sparse patches of hair. There was a scar on his shoulder I hadn't noticed before and a small birthmark on his collarbone.

Zavier's right hand was resting on the small of my back while the other smoothed my hair off my face. He stroked my cheek and crooked a finger under my chin. The kiss that followed was soft and unhurried, demanding nothing, but my body responded all the same.

My hand slowly made its way from his chest down his taut stomach to the other tuft of hair by his belly. The hand that was on the small of my back was now on the back of my bare thigh inching its way under my nightshirt. Feeling bold, I let my hand stray inside his own night attire. The heat rolled off of him.

He moaned, still kissing me and my body responded again. I knew he could feel the heat coming off me even through the long nightgown.

Zavier pulled me on top of him, trapping his length underneath me. It felt too good to stop, but I was at a loss again. I wanted to be underneath him, safe and familiar. Up here I was exposed, despite the clothes.

"If you're on top, you can control it," he said, reading my mind. "I can't do all the work." His hands were fixed on my hips holding me there. The only way to proceed was to take it as a challenge.

And I never back down.

Summoning my courage, I sat up and pulled off my pajamas. His sharp intake of breath was nothing to his other bodily response. I leaned over and kissed him slowly and deeply. Zavier's hand found a way between us, easing his underwear down.

I rolled my hips slowly and gently, hoping not to hurt him. His breath became more ragged as he held my waist.

"You're going to kill me," he said haltingly.

"What do you mean?" I stopped, wondering if I'd hurt him.

"I'm reciting regulations from the KM handbook in my head, but I'm going to run out soon," he said through gritted teeth. It made me smile to know I had this effect on him.

"You can stop the recitation," I said.

"You'd be surprised how long I have to do that. I'm up to the code of conduct," he said, pulling me in for a kiss... This one was not gentle and betrayed how far gone he was.

Zavier had to position himself, and I braced myself. I sat up, sliding myself over his length easily, though he still made me stop so he could catch his breath.

When his breath and mine eased a little, I started to move in lazy circles reveling in the feel of him. His hands stayed on my waist, his eyes watching me through half-closed eyes. My eyes closed completely when I felt the now familiar coiling of sensation in my belly spreading throughout my body.

Zavier's hands moved to my hips, speeding my movements. I cried out a little at the change in rhythm. His eyes flew open, momentary concern reflected on his face. When he felt me pick up the pace, his face smoothed back into a look of joyful concentration. His breathing changed, and I knew it would be soon.

"Inez—I can't—Oh..."

"Zavier—now!" I felt his explosion send me over into my own. I almost fell backwards with the force of it, but Zavier's grip was strong and firm.

I'd never felt so good, and when he said, "I love you, Inez," I said, "I love you, too."

Chapter 41

A dark and forbidding forest unfurled before me. It was familiar in a surreal sort of way. I was aware of the dream while being in it, but it was more than just a dream. The trees were ones I had seen before, and the air had a freshness to it I wasn't used to in Canto. Off in the distance light peals of children's laughter were a descant to a more deliberate melody. I hummed to myself, relaxing into my new surroundings, but the music I made was oddly hollow—like a sound heard through a tunnel.

I stopped abruptly, not liking the sound.

"We're disappointed with you," said a familiar voice in rhythm with the far-off music. I turned to find Lita and Beval standing behind me. Their faces were set in determined lines with frowns and they faced me with crossed arms.

The happiness I had felt was blown away on a chilly wind and I remembered everything. My mother, locked in a cowry shell. Using the augmenting lens after being told the risks. Getting instruction from Viktor, knowing she couldn't be trusted.

I read the displeasure in their eyes. My shoulders hunched more with each realization.

"I'm...I'm so sorry. I didn't mean to trap Mamá and I—"

"That was a risk your mother took and the consequences, though terrible, were inadvertent. On the other hand, deciding to turn your back on your magic—on Canto—isn't," said Beval with a shake of his head. His tone was disapproving, but gentle.

For a moment I was confused. The last time I'd visited this afterlife glade I'd been near death and neither Beval nor Lita could hear me. What did it mean that they could now?

"Too many people have sacrificed to get you to this point, and you repay their memory with petulance," intoned Lita. Her look bordered on disgust and hurt most of all. "The women in this family are made of stronger stuff than that. We grieve, but we move on."

"But my magic made this happen. I almost killed Toman. Mamá...Mamá is gone," I replied wretchedly. "Is she here?"

"Your mother is where you left her. In a shell, in the hands of Viktor Lake," said Lita. Her tone was like a slap in the face, a bucket of cold water. I felt hot, angry tears start to form.

"Rina, she's very young," said Beval in a more conciliatory tone. Only Beval called my grandmother Rina and he only used the nickname when he knew she was truly angry.

"And she shows it by dallying with some boy instead of— "

"Enough. She needs our help not our condemnation. She just lost her mother," he said with a tone he'd seldom used in life. Beval had never been forceful with Lita, but he had his way of getting his point across.

She subsided and sniffed loudly.

Beval continued. "I know this is hard. It was hard for your mother when she realized what you were to become, but she was brave for you. Now you must be brave for her, for everyone."

"Inecita, you have to understand; everything until now was a part we all had to play to get you to this point," my grandmother said more gently. "As of now we're working with our eyes closed because no matter what you were told, the future isn't written yet. Every choice you make takes us down unexpected paths. But that doesn't change your duty. Don't squander your gifts. Start by getting the shells back."

The tears never came, but the sorrow of being alone remained. Beval and Lita were gone. Mamá was gone. The responsibility was all mine. It was a palpable thing. No one could hug me and tell me it would all be okay. The truth they had shared was too sobering. It would only be okay if I made it so, and it was like being buried alive. I was on the precipice of being a true mage and it was the loneliest place I'd ever been.

I remembered Beval's story of the Heart Render and her search to find someone to share the burden of her magic with. But she didn't. No more soft words and reassurances. No more "there, there" and a bowl of oatmeal. I didn't feel strong, but I had to be anyway. Not for the first time I wondered if adulthood was just a show?

The forest was starting to fade and I couldn't hear the music anymore.

It was yet another ending that I wasn't prepared for, and I had a choice to make: to let it beat me, or push through. *We grieve, but we move on.*

In the place between waking and dreaming I heard Lita and Beval whisper, "We love you."

I AWOKE IN THE PREDAWN, Zavier still sleeping by my side. The warmth of his body made me want to burrow further under the covers and block out the world, but I knew that wasn't a luxury I could afford. My conversation with Lita and Beval was still echoing in my memory, reminding me that I had a purpose.

I slid out slowly, careful not to disturb Zavier. The floor was cold, a bracing reminder that keeping this house warm was now my responsibility.

Without hearing the voice in my head, I swept my hand over Zavier's forehead and whispered *SWEP,* pushing him into a deeper sleep.

Making my way out, I stole one more glance at him. I smiled, remembering how happy he made me, and I tucked that joy away like a treasure to revel in later.

The herbals room was pulsing with energy, as though it had been on alert, waiting for me. I sat in the middle of the room thinking of all the times I had come in there. Lita, Beval, and Mamá always said the time would come when it was mine alone and now that time was here.

Would I be enough? The memory of them loomed like giants that dwarfed my intentions. I no longer had the benefit of the augmenting lens, but I still had my words. "*GWEM,*" I chanted and focused all my will on the shells. *Gwa Tkei.*

They were hazy things, suspended in my mind's eye. As I called their details into focus, their brilliance, and the intricate patterns on their surface, the box which held them, they became clearer, more real.

With my eyes closed and my hands outstretched, I reached for them through the ether. Smooth wood grazed my hands and weighed down my arms. They were here, now. I had done it! I opened the case. Four shells—three with swirling patterns and one strangely dull—sat in their niches. With a new awareness, I put them back in their hiding place behind the table inside the wall: My magic had grown.

The horn, I knew would not be as easy. Water was still too strong—a barrier to subdue my call from so far away.

I returned to the bed where Zavier's prone form still slumbered peacefully, unshaken by my cold feet. It was another moment to tuck away for later contemplation.

My real battle was about to begin.

Chapter 42

Getting rid of Zavier was harder than I thought. He was reluctant to leave me alone and I was reluctant to be left. More than I had anticipated. He still had duties, but nothing would have made me happier than to have him abandon them for the day and spend it with me. But I knew he couldn't be there for what was to come.

We procrastinated until lunchtime and then I gently kicked him out, making sure he used the mirror instead of walking or calling for a horse. After the ultimatum The Cat had given me, I didn't want to risk Zavier getting caught unawares. Meiri was under house arrest again and Mamá...well, she was safe from The Cat at least.

As it was, the deadline had come and gone, and The Cat was eerily quiet.

I promised myself if I survived the encounter, I would confess my magic to Zavier. Even if it meant our relationship would end, he needed to know that all this had been caused by his sister-in-law's maneuvering with Mythos' interference.

In the shower, I practiced making abstract forms with the water streams. "*Akwa pleu...wed gel...aug...leu.*" I stopped the flow, started it again, and even looped it above my head like a halo. My confidence in my new skills was growing, but I knew I had something else to do before I found that horn. I still knew my control came at a price and defeating The Cat could cost me my life. It was something I had to consider. And I had another promise to keep before I considered anything else.

I LEFT THE HOUSE, HEADING in the direction of the palace and was more than a little surprised when I saw a rider coming toward me. She wore the livery of the royal house and her satchel marked her as a messenger, although I'd never seen her before. For an irrational moment I considered running the other way because I knew that if the messenger wasn't from Zavier it could only be from one other person.

"Queen Hortensia requests your presence," said the rider and her lack of an actual letter further disquieted me. *Did she know what Zavier and I had done?* He hadn't gone home after the funeral, but it wasn't strange that he'd been reluctant to leave me. I shook myself from the thought of Hortensia taking me to task for sleeping with her brother-in-law. Zavier and I were both adults. Then again, I remembered Mamá warning against having sex with Zavier before the wedding because it was just the sort of thing Hortensia would use to make the engagement unpleasant, if she didn't outright refuse her consent.

The messenger hadn't moved, and I realized she expected me to come now. I never liked horses but riding one with a messenger was even less appealing. I sighed and nodded.

"I can come now," I said and reached for the reigns. I was saved from embarrassing us both with my lack of horse riding skills when the royal carriage trundled up. This was a surprise. I appreciated the gesture, but I had a feeling it had more to do with Hortensia's belief that I would ignore the summons. The rider trotted away as I climbed aboard the carriage.

The trip was ridiculously short considering I lived less than half a mile from the palace. It was clear that she had sent the carriage to make sure I didn't bolt from the messenger.

A patrolman waited at the water elevator to bring me to the queen. He was silent and it gave me time to think of what I would say if I really was there to explain why Zavier and I had slept together.

That was the least of my concerns.

Last time I was here was when Zavier was recuperating from his beating at the riot, the one I still thought was instigated by The Cat and his mind-controlling fiddle. Since then, I had studiously eschewed the palace hoping to avoid the very person I was now there to see. No one could refuse a summons to the palace from the queen.

The cloud palace—literally made of clouds—was never the same twice. It tended to take on the characteristics of the weather outside. Today the palace was chilly despite clouds being a natural insulator. The air had a raw quality to it that made me rub my hands together, hoping that by doing so, I'd bring feeling back to the tips of my fingers. My escort gave me a sympathetic look and began to remove his gloves.

"Thank you, but I'll be fine. You're the one who has to walk these halls for hours. I should be out in a few minutes," I said, hoping that was true. How much time did a dressing down about pre-marital sex take?

The guard looked skeptical, but tugged his gloves back on. He led me to a door that looked far too ornate and heavy to safely reside in a palace made of clouds, and knocked. He nodded deferentially, like I'd seen the palace guard nod to Zavier and I realized it was the first time it had happened when Zavier wasn't around. I wondered if my position as the prince's almost fiancée had caused the change or if Zavier had spoken to the guards. My musings were cut short by the muffled voice of Hortensia.

I was escorted to the queen's private study, which was a first for me. Her private rooms were much like the rest of the palace. Large blaze burners spaced four hands apart lined the walls. The light danced without a discernible breeze and gave off warm light, which was a welcome change to the long hallway. There were trunks and chests of various sizes being used as tables full of loose papers and large envelopes. I appreciated and recognized the controlled chaos as my own room was rarely in order.

Hortensia sat behind an ornate desk made of blue glass on a chair made of some diaphanous material I couldn't name. The only other chair, also made of the same material sat on the opposite side.

The patrolman didn't announce me, he simply left the room and closed the door. A flash of cold bubbled in my core, the beginnings of my protection spell, but I was able to quash it. Queen Hortensia took her time looking up from the papers she perused on her desk. My eyes alit on a page with the seal of Mythos, a craggy cliff overlooking an endless sea. Even reading upside-down I saw Zavier's name mentioned many times. When our eyes finally met I saw cold calculation and something else I couldn't define. She pursed her lips and slowly stood.

"Inez, I wanted to personally convey my deepest regrets at the loss of your mother," she began. For a moment she seemed perfectly sincere although I couldn't remember her being at the funeral. I waited for her to continue, but she seemed to be waiting for an acknowledgement of some kind.

"Thank you, your Majesty," I said and was proud of how neutral my tone was. It was the first real condolence I had accepted and it felt odd that it came from the queen, who I knew didn't like me or my mother.

"I know this is a trying time and I'm glad the prince took the time to console you. It's important to have friends at a time like this," she said, and took her seat again. She motioned to the other chair, and I sat reflexively biting back my comment that Zavier was more than my friend. "And I'm equally sure it's important to hold onto something tangible to feel safe and secure."

I didn't know where she was going with her speech, but it felt as though I was supposed to admit to something. I thought it best to wait her out the same way I did with Áliz when we were locked in heated negotiations. The last thing I would admit to was Zavier spending the night in my bed.

"I remember when you were first brought to court and having to turn down your mother's request to formally acknowledge you as her heir and I've felt remiss about that day, especially now."

I kept my face blank and resisted the urge to lean in closer because I had a feeling I knew what Hortensia was offering. Looking eager with Áliz usually got me a few coins short of the deal I wanted to make, and this was worth a lot more than money.

"Inez, I want to give you your mother's title. By rights you are the duchess of Árbor Real and would be free to pass it on to your own children in the future," she said and smiled in a way that almost made me believe her. Almost.

"That is wonderful to hear, your majesty. I hadn't thought about the title or the lands that come with it, even if the house there is in my name," I said not knowing what else to say.

"I'm glad to give back even a small piece of your family, if I can," she said and stood reaching out her hand as if to shake mine. I hesitated for a moment, but I knew refusing the hand would be churlish. Before I took my hand back, her other hand covered my own. "I just need you to separate yourself from the prince."

And there it was. I knew Hortensia wasn't as generous as to allow me my ancestral seat without paying some price. It was the one hand she hadn't played yet and I was surprised it had taken her so long to consider it—my mother had only been officially dead for three days. Although I was glad the protection spell that had shut down my emotions had dissipated, I would have liked to have it back at that moment. My mother's loss was still a raw nerve and Hortensia casually using it as a way to manipulate me into leaving Zavier was cold even for her. I didn't like her, but I wouldn't dangle her inheritance from a dead relative over her to get her out of my life. I decided that a little anger wasn't out of the question.

"Hortensia, are you seriously asking if I want my mother's title over Zavier?" I asked in an angry whisper. I'd made my peace with the loss of Mamá's title long ago, but it still rankled. A tingle of magic edged its way to my fingertips and for a moment I saw real fear in her eyes. She pulled away and lowered her eyes to the desk, her hands rifling through a stack of papers.

Hortensia handed me one: the deed to Árbol Real. The signatures of Lady Sabrina and the late king and queen were emblazoned on the bottom.

"The only proof you have that the house is yours is a document signed by three dead people and there is the matter of how your mother died," she said, her manner flustered. I smiled and silently thanked the Goddess for all those verbal sparring matches with the Jabberwocky.

"Hortensia, you have a real problem now. You keep antagonizing the future queen of Canto and it makes no sense to hope that I'll forget it when I am queen. Zavier chose me and even better I chose him in front of many living people *and* the Mythosian envoy. Keep the title—I have a better one coming," I said and left, not daring to look back.

THE UNDERSIDE OF THE palace was deserted. Even the horses were staying silent save for their quiet munching of oats. I walked noisily to the door, wanting to disturb the trance-like calm.

My feelings toward Hortensia aside—and they were far from cordial—I never would have thought she could stoop to this level. She had essentially threatened me with homelessness if I didn't give Zavier up. And that was only after trying to bribe me with Mamá's title. Hortensia's cold calculations had led her to believe that either one of those proposals would sway me. It was a good thing I was learning control over my Powers or there was a serious possibility I would have made the cloud palace fall out of the sky.

I was still angry as I stood in front of Toman's door. My hand stilled, poised to knock. A small voice inside me, not the spell voice, said, "Maybe you should take her offer."

I knew two things: I loved Zavier and I was lying to him every day. Didn't he deserve my honesty? Or was that being unfair to him? If I told him about my magic he had to weigh his sense of duty to the Crown against his love for me. Was I scared that he wouldn't choose me or scared he would? I lowered my hand in frustration. All this time I'd known being with Zavier meant taking everything that came along with it—the royal obligations, the intense scrutiny, Hortensia—but I'd known all of that before our dance at the Egalitarian Ball. Zavier being with me meant accepting my magic and I still hadn't given him the chance to make that decision on his own—with all the information. Maybe it was time to give him the benefit of the doubt.

Maybe I could wait until after I faced down The Cat. After all if I died because of The Cat what would I have gained by telling Zavier about my magic beforehand? With that settled I focused on what I was considering doing for Toman now.

When we'd been in the past, Toman had nearly died and would have if not for my magical intervention. When I hadn't been sure that we'd all make it back, Toman had asked me to take care of his mother. I knew at the time he meant for me to visit, but with my new-found control, I wanted to give him more. My knock on the front door was answered promptly by PJ. How much time was he spending with Toman?

"Hi, is Toman around?" I asked awkwardly. It hadn't occurred to me that he would be here when I made my offer.

"In the back with Dottie. Um...sorry about your mom," he said hesitantly with a clumsy turn of his mouth as if the words he had formed were not the one's originally intended. I nodded, still unsure how to answer this offer of condolence. The urge to correct everyone was so strong I had to bite my tongue before automatically blurting out *she's not dead.* But how would I present that truth? I wasn't so sure what to call the state she was in now.

Walking past PJ, the smell of stale air assaulted my senses. It was the smell of deep winter, when no windows are opened, mingling with something more unsettling. All the deaths in my family had been sudden. Was this the smell of a slow decline?

Toman was sitting next to Dottie's sleeping form, his forehead resting in his hands. His hunched shoulders spoke of exhaustion and despair, but straightened as I closed the door. He glanced at me with a familiar look of desperation, one like Betlindis gave me whenever she asked about her father. I couldn't help her, but Toman was all the family left to me and I couldn't turn him away.

"I'm sorry," we said simultaneously. Toman rose from his seat, and we hugged intensely, but with dry eyes. This wasn't uncomfortable pity—it was mutual understanding. After a minute or two, Toman broke the embrace. I looked down at the once vibrant Dottie. She was considerably younger than my mother, diminutive with a buoyant personality. Now she looked haggard and the leeching of her color reminded me of a painting left out in the sun too long. Her shallow breaths were labored and painful to watch, the pain of which I couldn't keep from my face. Toman pulled me to the far side of the room.

"How long has she been like this?" I asked, still taking quick glances at the bed. Toman shrugged.

"Since before your mother... For a bit," he said with a wry smile. "I'm surprised she's still here, to be honest." His eyes were still trained on the bed.

"I can fix that, Toman. I promised I would and—"

"No, Inez. After...after we came back from the past I spoke to Rowley," he said, lines of worry creasing his brow, "and he told me what healing magic does—why it's so dangerous. I can't let you."

"I'm not asking your permission," I said more fiercely than I intended. How could I explain to him what it was to lose the only family you had? Dottie was slipping away and despite the pain it caused him, she was still here. Losing her would be ten times worse and it was a feeling I didn't wish on my worst enemy, let alone my best friend.

"I don't want you to be alone." Toman's face changed, and I turned quickly to the bed, not wanting him to see the truth in my eyes. Dottie's chest was still rising and falling.

"We are not alone, Inez. We have each other," he said and embraced me again. I couldn't speak for fear of dissolving into tears. How could I tell him I might be gone soon? I knew I was strong enough to stop The Cat for good, but I didn't know if I was strong enough to survive the amount of magic I'd need to use.

Even if I told Zavier about my magic and my plans, and he accepted it, what would it accomplish? He'd insist on helping, but that was a conversation for another day. I was so moved, but as much as Toman was like family it wasn't the same as having someone there no matter what, who knew you more than was comfortable. That was something I couldn't share. I pulled away.

"I know, but I...I have to," I said, not wanting to admit that this was the closest I could get to saving my own mother. "Keep PJ busy and don't let him in here." Toman was about to object, but I pushed him toward the door. He spared another look toward his mother and then left with still-stooped shoulders, but a glimmer of hope lit his eyes.

"Toman? Is that...?" Dottie whispered with a hoarse voice. I took Toman's seat by the bed and set my bag on the nightstand.

"Hi Dottie," I whispered with a forced smile. "Toman had company and should be back in a minute, but I wanted to give you this. It's one of Lita's recipes." I opened the canister in my bag with still warm Dreamless Sleep in it and poured it into a cup sitting on a table beside the bed.

"Oh, Inez. I was just thinking of the first time I met Filomena. Your mother and I were so different, but we had so much in common. I'm so happy you and Toman have each other. When I'm gone make sure you keep each other safe," she said weakly.

"You're going to be fine. Just drink this..." I said, trying to lift her head to the cup.

"...so happy you have each...other. Can't be with his family. Wouldn't underst..." she babbled, spilling most of the tea onto the quilt under her chin. I tried again, this time getting more in her than on her. Another cup and I laid her head down back on her pillows. But her eyes looked around the room, suddenly frantic.

"I have to tell...look under the bed," she said her voice fading. "Please." Despite her fog, she was so insistent that I relented. I found a small hatch and within was a box. I brought it up and she mouthed for me to open it. Inside were letters tied with ribbon and underneath was a picture of Dottie holding a newborn and behind her with his arm around her shoulders was the old king, both smiling down on the child.

"They might try to take away...away his home. Only one he knows. Don't tell Toman," she said with pleading eyes. On the back of the picture was a note that read:

Our beautiful family

Beside the note was a date I knew so well. Toman's birthday. Was Dottie trying to tell me that Toman was the old king's son? I wanted to shake her awake, but she had already succumbed to Lita's powerful potion. I shoved the box in my bag with what was left of the tea.

Could Toman be a royal? I had the irrational need to tell him and have a good laugh over all the times he made fun of them, but Dottie didn't want him to know. Why? Was she ashamed of what she...*they* had done? Or was it something sinister? Would Toman be in danger if he knew?

Another claimant to the throne would have too many implications. A source of scandal for the Royal House. Perhaps a rallying point to the rest of Canto who felt the Royal house needed some shaking up.

How would Toman take it? More importantly, how would the royals take it? All the possibilities swirled in my head in an unending loop of questions and worries. *Can I really keep this from him? Can I really keep it from Zavier?*

There were already so many things I couldn't share with him, but this concerned his family. I looked down at Dottie, sleeping peacefully and envied her. Why had she thrust this on me? When had I become a receptacle for other people's secrets?

It didn't matter. I had to set that aside for the moment and get Dottie better. Then I could ask her what I needed to know and maybe convince her to tell Toman. I had enough burdens without carrying around the secret of my best friend's possibly royal father.

To be sure I wouldn't be interrupted, I put a lock spell on the door and spoke the word of deep sleep over Dottie. My time keeping the world out after my accident with Mamá and the shells had given me ample practice. The word of Power, *syu*, to bind, was barely a whisper but the spell rose quickly.

I shut the blinds, making the room look cave-like. I didn't have the sense of urgency I'd had in the past when I used healing magic and was suddenly at a loss as to how to activate it. With Toman I knew exactly what was the problem and resolved it. Dottie's illness was still a mystery that had to be solved before I could fix it. My mind went blank and I let it wander, noiselessly searching for the right word to say.

My mind fixed on one word, glowing dimly in a dark corner. Somehow I knew it meant, to see...*weid.* See what? I asked the distant voice in my head. The voice answered firmly, *ghosti*...stranger. I'd never taken the time to analyze the voice, just thinking it a subconscious extension of my own.

Listening to it now, I recognized a small lilt that I'd dismissed before. It was the combined voice of Lita and Beval with mine as a sort of song. It raised all the hairs on my arm to know that. It boosted me and reinforced Toman's words. *We are not alone, Inez.*

I chanted the words silently, *weid ghosti* and felt my hands go numb before I felt them prick with the familiar sting of Power pushing its way through my blood. No, it was more magic overpowering my own magic, making its presence felt because it was always there quietly thrumming within me.

I placed both hands over Dottie's fluttering heartbeat, forming a triangle.

An image appeared in the darkness above it of Queen Hortensia putting an object in Dottie's hand. It was a locket of some sort, and I could see Dottie opening it and her eyes lighting up after seeing what was inside. I couldn't hear their words, but both women were smiling.

Uncovering Dottie's neck, I found the locket. Touching it was like touching ice and fire at the same time. It didn't want to budge, no matter how much I pulled. *Ag gleubh,* I chanted...*move apart.* It began to slowly dislodge, like a scab scratched off too soon. Underneath, the skin was chaffed and puckered and the color of a bruise.

I ripped the chain off her neck, my hands not wanting to hold it. I opened the locket and found a picture of the old king and queen. Did Hortensia know or was this something that had been left to her by them? It was clearly cursed, but I put it in the bag with the tea and letters to puzzle over later.

Dottie's color was still sallow but brightening. No one would have suspected something as innocent-looking as a gift from the queen had anything to do with the decline in her health. Why would she go to such lengths to get rid of Dottie? 'They might try to take away his home,'" Dottie had said. I thought she meant the cottage, but would Hortensia banish Toman without his mother's protection? More was at play than I had realized.

Dottie was still sleeping peacefully and her breathing was returning to normal. The locket stain was fading to nothingness without any help from me. I whispered "*weid*" one more time and let my eyes sweep her body. I found no sign of illness or malignancy. With the combination of the tea and the sleeping spell, she would probably sleep until tomorrow and despite all my burning questions, I was reluctant to wake her.

Toman and PJ were sitting on the couch having the whispered conversation of those who found themselves in a sick house. Their hands intertwined, they looked up at me with questions in their eyes. I gave them a small smile.

"I think Lita's recipe helped. Toman, here's some more, which you can give her when she wakes up," I said, handing him the canister. I winced, feeling the locket graze my hand.

"What did you give her?" asked PJ, his stance oddly defensive.

"Just something Mamá found in Lita's journals. I...I thought it might help," I replied cagily.

"But what's in...?"

"PJ, can you check to see if we have more quilts for Dottie?" interrupted Toman. PJ looked put out but shrugged and went to look.

"Did it work?" he whispered.

"It did," I said slowly. I struggled with how much I should tell him. The explanation about the locket would bring up all sorts of questions that only Dottie could answer. I couldn't betray her confidence without her permission. So I remained vague. "Something was wrong with her heart."

"Her heart? Like what?" he asked, incredulous. "You don't look as tired as you did after you brought me back."

"Maybe I'm just getting better at it. Check with the healers if you want to know more. I should go," I said, shrugging his questions away. Meeting his frank eyes was more than I could handle. I knew PJ would have more questions and I didn't have any answers for him either.

"Inez, stay for dinner," Toman said, trying to take my bag. "PJ has to go back to the tavern anyway."

"No, I'm... I have an appointment and he should stay here in case... In case Dottie needs him," I said, looking at Toman pointedly. I hoped my intent was conveyed but being any more specific would lead to another set of questions. I clutched my bag closer. "If anything...I'll talk to you later."

I left abruptly, wondering what would be harder, getting the horn, defeating The Cat or lying to Toman until his mother woke up.

Chapter 43

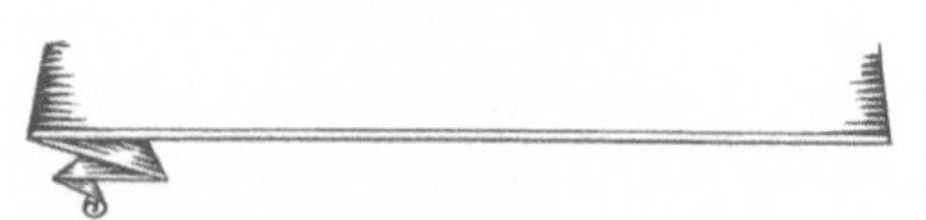

A flurry of snow fell on the dingy quilt of old snow, making everything seem new. The air was crisp, with winter's cold showing the steady rhythm of my breath. I was well clear of the palace before I allowed myself to stop moving. Dottie's revelations were muddying my thoughts and without the protection spell, my emotions roiled.

Keeping my magic a secret from Toman had been hard enough, but it had been my secret to tell or not tell. I had gone to Dottie, prepared to give up a little of my life to save her, but I hadn't been prepared to betray my best friend.

How could I face him again and not tell? Would I blurt it out; say "You're Zavier's half-brother?" Or would it be a casual slip like, "Sorry I stole your mom's locket with the picture of your father in it, but it was cursed by the Queen who probably knows you're the old king's bastard?" Well, that wasn't very casual, but even now it was on the tip of my tongue, wanting to be loosed on the next unsuspecting victim.

I kept moving.

Why had Dottie done this to me? Why had she done it to Toman? When I found out about my own father I had been surprised but mostly indifferent. I'd been curious, but it hadn't affected my identity. Toman, on the other hand, seethed about Dottie's treatment at Hortensia's hands. He wasn't fond of most of the royal court and now he could learn he was apart of them.

Dottie had always been vague about Toman's father, but alluded to a grand romance that ended tragically. It fed into Toman's need for drama. Would finding out his father had been the king be welcome news?

I'm sure a part of him would love it, but his anti-royal streak might rebel after years of slights from Hortensia. I'd be a bothered if my mother and I were living next to a stable, working constantly, when in truth he could have been living a life of luxury and leisure inside the Cloud Palace. No, finding out would likely be more complicated than I could even imagine.

The bay was still frozen around the edges, but I could see where the ice had become flimsy and breakable. Thawing was not going to be a problem, but that had never been my concern. Playing around with the shower jets in my bathroom was a game compared to the body of water before me. Its depth and breadth felt ponderous, immoveable. I put down my bag heavily, the weight of my current situation making my shoulders droop.

I took three deep breaths, grounding myself to the earth. The cool, glassy surface of the water viewed my preparations with disinterest. Three more breaths and my bond with the ground firmed, silently tracing my thoughts with the surrounding trees.

I spared a stray thought for the tree that had steadied me when Toman, Meiri and I had traveled to the past. I wondered if it sensed my presence or if some descendant of it recognized my call. Air rippled the bay, making wider bands against the water's resistance.

Closing my eyes, I took three more deep breaths and exhaled the last with a word...*SPEK*—to observe and flow.

My perception changed. Although my eyes stayed closed, the vista behind my eyes was the bay. The spell tinged the water before me, a murky blue. I scanned the horizon with my new vision and saw an indistinct shape the color of violets. It was no bigger than a small crate.

I moved forward into the shallows of the bay, my boots keeping a fraction of the cold from me. I couldn't risk using the warmth spell while attempting such difficult magic.

The lit shape, now more distinctly a rectangle, was further out than I could wade. Swimming in the icy water was madness and I searched my memories for a word of Power that would suit. For a split second, when my concentration was overcome by excitement, I lost the light. My hands formed tight fists and I gritted my teeth. I redoubled my efforts. The cold water now waist deep, caused my teeth to chatter.

The bright light returned, and I remembered. At the top of my lungs I yelled *SKEUD*, shoot. The water in the area of the light blasted into the air in a fountain of spray and hovered over the spot. It was too far out for me to swim even if I could maintain both spells at once. Plate spinners had less to worry about than I did at the moment.

"Perhaps... Perhaps I could be of some assistance?" said a voice behind me. I twirled in an instant, my eyes open and my hands tingling, at the ready. The king stood inches away from me looking benign. He didn't cower when I flexed my hands, but he looked at them intently like a deer wary of a wolf. I searched the shore with my eyes, wondering if he had come alone. It appeared he had.

"What are you doing here...your Majesty?" I said as an afterthought. I let my hands fall slowly to my sides though I still felt the errant twitch of Power ready to respond at a moment's notice.

"The same as you. I was looking for the horn, but you are clearly capable of finding it yourself. There was a family in the past entrusted with the secret of its location and they shared it with reigning royal of the blood. My father told me, and I'll tell Zavier one day," he said, wistfully.

I wondered if the family Xander spoke of was Sebastian. In the past he was the only one who saw where the horn landed with certainty, and I could believe Sebastian would try and help by securing the horn in the past. I gave the king what I hoped was a neutral look.

"I know how hard water can be, but sometimes it can be overcome with two people working the same spell," he said matter-of-factly. "What spell were you using?"

"I...I don't know. Just... You know about me?" I asked, wary.

"I wasn't sure, but I suspected as much. You're amazing. I guess I wasn't to be the one, after all," he said with a note of regret despite the small smile he made with the words. He reminded me of Zavier so much at that moment, I smiled back, completely disarmed.

"I won't pretend I'm as good as you at this, Inez, but I would like to help if I can. Shall we?"

It was so incongruous. I was standing on the bank of the bay with the king. Two war criminals discussing our illegal use of magic as though we were exchanging ideas about the weather.

Fell said the king was dangerous, but he didn't feel dangerous at the moment. However, when he used magic, I'm sure it was another story. I remembered him saving Zavier and the ragged disjointedness of his mind reaching out. But he already knew my secret and I knew his, and I'd worked with worse people in the past.

He walked toward me, and we stood shoulder to shoulder in the freezing bay. We stood for a moment, allowing the water around us to still. I took his hand in mine, so familiar to me, yet so foreign. He closed his eyes and I followed, lending him my altered vision.

I felt him startle then quickly recover. His hand was slightly cool and clammy, but I could feel the warm surge of magic coming to the surface. It was still jagged, an interrupted flow, like a hose someone steps on, releases and steps on again. His magic sought my own and when they touched I felt the jerk of his hand in mine.

My magic helped even out his magic, smoothing out the rough edges, sealing the cracks. I couldn't see his face, but I knew somehow that he was smiling. He released a contented sigh. That strengthened my resolve and I knew I wasn't in this alone.

The violet shape reappeared over the surface of the water, skimming the spot where the horn lay. I chanted *akwa bheid* softly and heard Xander repeat it along with me. Soon we found our rhythm and the resistance of the water lessened perceptibly. The water under the light rippled faster and faster, creating a whirlpool effect.

While Xander continued the chant, I pushed farther, awakening my astral magic. In my mind I formed the word *gwem,* come. Beside me Xander had gone silent, and my eyes flew open. I watched his neck tip back and his jaw go slack.

My eyes followed his line of sight. The horn shot to the surface in a spray of water and light. When the horn landed on the shore behind us, we both dropped hands, splashing out of the shallows. We stared at the horn and at each other in awe. It was a wonderful moment.

Which lasted a whole minute.

Then I saw the change. His eyes clouded over, and I could see the insanity creeping up, as though it were replacing the flow of magic from a moment ago. I grabbed the horn, not knowing what he would do next.

Xander fell to the ground rolling in the snow as though he wrestled with an unseen enemy. Maybe he was. Maybe he could see the crazy coming at him and wanted to fight it off.

I didn't wait to see who would win. I grabbed my bag and the horn and ran toward the tree line. An invisible target pricked between my shoulder blades, and I fell, throwing both my bag and the horn far out in front of me. I heard the heavy footsteps closing in as I spit snow out of my mouth. I wasn't surprised to see some blood. Painfully, I rolled onto my back, not trusting myself to stand in time. Xander pounced on top of me.

"You're like her, seeing too much—and look what happened," he raved, grabbing my hands behind me. The tingle of Power, usually a gradual thing, was a sudden jolt, making me cry out as it grabbed at his magic again. This time his magic fought back, knowing it wasn't symbiosis his Powers sought, but oppression.

I remembered Rowley's words about how in a magical fight it's your will or someone else's fighting to survive. His knee dug into my chest, making it harder to breathe. I reacted, croaking out the word *skeud*.

He flew back a few feet as I gulped for air and coughed. I scrambled back, bracing myself against a tree and the odd sense of déjà vu overcame me. Shakily I stood, hands at the ready, but all I heard were wrenching sobs.

"I...I'm sorry. I should have known. Sometimes it just leaves me tired, but...but other times... Are you hurt?" he asked still prone on the ground. I shook my head and then realized he couldn't see that.

"I'm all right. But stay over there for now," I said with a sore throat. I coughed, the air too cold after our brawl. Then he started to laugh, hysterically, manically.

"It was you all along. All those years wasted with them thinking *I* was the one. Bye Mommy. Bye Daddy. Power requires sacrifice, you know," he said, before erupting into another fit of laughter. Xander sat up suddenly, his eyes full of wonder again, but it wasn't wholesome. My sense of dread warred with my disbelief. I somehow knew what he was implying, but I didn't want to accept the possibility.

"Did you know that? Your dead mother made you stronger. Even more so if you did it. It just made me unbalanced...or maybe that was my father."

The tree against my back was a comfort and a crutch after the blow. Was King Xander saying what I thought he was saying? Did he kill his parents with his magic? How was that even possible?

As I asked myself the question, I pictured the moment when I trapped Mamá in the shell. I knew exactly how it could happen. Had someone seen Xander kill his parents? Did anyone know that he had done it with magic?

I'm like her...and look what happened. Lita. Lita had seen or learned of how the old king and queen had died at Xander's hand, with his Powers, and that kind of secret coming out to Canto, to Mythos, would end the royal family's dynasty. Mythos would have to intervene, and Canto would cease to be sovereign. Any chance we had of returning magic to Canto would end. The last time Mythos interfered in Canti affairs we'd lost our magic. Who knew what we'd lose if they took over.

Even as I grappled with that, my magic sought his again. The words came again unbidden. *SYU*—to bind. His magic, at its breaking point, slowly collapsed in on itself. Not gone, but dormant. It would have been so easy to speak the next word. To have done and kill him with a flick of my wrist. He was a broken man, useless and crazed. And would someone have to do the same for me one day?

On my scariest days I wondered if magic would drive me mad—if I would end up like Austra, her mother, or now, King Xander. I had already hurt people I loved.

"Thank you," he said in a small whisper.

"Yes, thank you," another voice purred, picking up the horn.

"YOU ARE VERY LATE FOR our appointment, but because you've brought me such a lovely gift I'll overlook it," said The Cat caressing the horn. Strapped across his back was the fiddle. "Where are my other treats? Come on, I asked for them so nicely."

"What makes you think I would give them to you?" I replied fiercely. The king was still sitting on the ground, but was more alert.

"Oh, maybe because I brought you a gift, too. Here, doggie, doggie," he said mockingly and whistled. Rowley stepped out from behind a tree, his face blank and his tongue lolling about the side of his muzzle.

Instinctively, I took a step toward him.

"No, no, no. And who's your friend? Oh my, you are full of surprises. The king?" He executed an elaborate bow, never taking his eyes off me. Why had I bound the king's Powers? I could have used some of his crazy right about now.

My stomach was in knots and I felt weak. Astral magic took so much more concentration and strength. Even now I felt myself wavering with all the magic I'd already used. I couldn't focus my Powers with so many moving pieces in play. It was more than that. I recognized this feeling of being hollowed out. I couldn't see it, but I knew. I knew The Cat was working some spell to drain me.

"You're looking a little green. Sorry about that. My new toy is a little demanding of attention," he said and pulled out a box from his boot. A box that contained the augmenting lens. I saw him wince and wondered if it was working on him, too. I needed to distract him.

"Okay, they're in there," I said, motioning to my bag. He moved to pick it up, but thought better of it.

"No, you get them out and don't try to be cute," he hissed. I grabbed the bag and rummaged through, looking for it. My hand stung as it closed over the metal oval. Then with the other hand I pulled out the box of shells. I set that on the ground and swiftly threw the locket at The Cat, who caught it deftly in his paw. He purred in amusement. "Didn't anyone ever tell you about cat-like reflexes?" He brought in his other paw with the lens to the paw holding the locket to take a better look. "What the—?"

The lens was so enthralled by the Powerful magic in the locket, the lens stopped concentrating on me. I'd hoped for such a reprieve.

The oppressive spell The Cat had worked began to lift, giving me back my strength.

Tingling back to life, my hands thrummed with renewed power. The Cat tried to release the lens box and the locket, but both were fused to his hand. He hissed and spit to no avail, outdone by his own greed.

I spoke the word, "*sengwh,*" hoping my magic could overcome the fact that the horn only answered to someone of El Niño Amoratado's line. I vaguely felt a presence behind me.

"The word of Power is '*bhel*,' Inez," said Xander. I didn't question it, knowing The Cat would find a way to extricate himself from the locket and the lens any minute. I concentrated the last of my strength and magic into the word, both verbally and with my astral magic.

The horn sang out, ripping through the noise of The Cat's protests. Its piercing cry, combined with The Cat's screeching hiss, made me cringe, sending up my protection spell. All I saw was metal and fur battling. Metal had the upper hand, but fur was desperate. It was futile, nonetheless. The horn sucked up The Cat and the fiddle leaving only the lens behind. The locket was gone.

Rowley shook himself furiously, dazed, but looking more aware. Seeing the augmenting lens and the horn he barked loudly and started digging. With his large paws it took little time for him to make a hole for both, but I stopped him before he could deposit either.

"I think I know a better place," I said.

ON THE EDGE OF ÁRBOR Real, where an old shed used to sit, I found the tree that had helped me in the past. It looked weathered, but sturdy, with more branches and roots. I opened my parcel and found a knot hole hollow in its trunk.

The horn and augmenting lens box fit perfectly in its hollows and with both hands on the bark I spoke my question. As both items were swallowed up in the darkness of the closing hollow, I felt a response. It wasn't words, just an agreement.

The king was waiting in the shadows, avoiding anyone's notice. His resemblance to Zavier wasn't remarkable—they were brothers—but the similarities were just enough to make me want to trust him. He's what I imagined Zavier would look like in twenty years if Zavier faced a lot of disappointment. Or had uncontrolled magic.

Correction, he'd had uncontrolled magic and I'd somehow bound it. It may have been my hope, but the king's eyes looked a little less haunted now. He offered to walk me to my door, but I declined, wanting some time to myself. I wanted to think about the best way to approach Zavier, to tell him about my Powers. Yet another brush with mortality and my constant risk of exposure made me realize I couldn't keep my magic from him any longer. I felt a lightness at the thought of total honesty even as I dreaded the conversation.

"Before I go, I have to say this," he began.

"I know, but you don't have to worry. I'll keep your secret and I intend to tell him about mine," I said weary from the day.

"Thank you, but no. I need you to let him go," he said calmly.

"Let him go? Do you think—?"

"I think it's very easy to get caught up in a moment and then want to share. I know even more the burden of so many secrets and not wanting to carry the burden alone. Zavier is clean of all this...this magic... Of all the lies. He deserves a chance to stay clean. You don't have to do it now, but I expect you to do it soon."

"Hortensia knows about your magic," I said in a whisper. It was the first time someone was telling me not to confide in Zavier and it was Zavier's brother.

"And she carries the burden of knowing. Every day she has to keep that secret and not just from my subjects, from Mythos. The things she's had to do to keep me safe..." He didn't finish the sentence, but his face told a tale of anguish and regret.

If I told Zavier about my magic, it would be the same for him and Zavier was more dutiful than Hortensia. She thought of her own interests, while Zavier thought of everyone's interests. And yet what Xander had said rang true. I did want someone to share the burden of my secret and it wasn't Toman or Meiri, even though I knew they loved me. I needed to tell Zavier.

"And if I don't?"

"The Mythos overseers are just a walk away from the palace. It wouldn't be easy to prove you have inherent magic, but the Mythosian authorities assure me there are methods for doing so and on the word of the ruling house of Canto they would look into it," he said.

"And what's to stop me from exposing you?" I asked.

"Miss Garza, you are all that is left of your family and if I turned you in the investigation into inherent magic in your line ends with you. If I'm investigated, all my blood relations would be examined, thoroughly. Think about it," he said and then left me in the gathering darkness.

It wasn't hard to believe that a man who killed his own parents would ever hesitate to threaten his only brother. I may have saved Canto, but Zavier was still in danger because of my magic.

Chapter 44

I tossed and turned that night, not wanting to give in to Xander's demands. I should have told Zavier everything from the beginning and then I wouldn't have this hanging over my head. *Is he right? Should Zavier have a less complicated relationship with someone who could share all her secrets?*

I wanted that for Zavier as much as Xander did and probably with better reasons than a concern that your little brother will discover you killed your parents. Zavier would be king one day and he needed a consort that didn't hide in the shadows. Or worse, would he have to turn into Hortensia, cleaning up his deranged partner's messes?

The morning brought me little insight and Mamá wasn't there to confide it. But I wasn't alone. I sent a message to Toman, hoping to talk it out with him.

Toman arrived without his usual spring. I worried that his mother had taken a turn, but he was quick to reassure me. He wouldn't come in.

"Inez, what happened in that room when you were there with my mother?" he asked tentatively.

"All you need to know from me is that Dottie is better. Anything else you'd have to ask her," I replied, not wanting to rehash this.

"I did and she told me I should be careful being your friend," he said quietly. It was like the air had been sucked out of the room and all I could do was stare at him with my mouth hanging open.

"She told me that you only saved her so I wouldn't be alone after you married Zavier. 'She won't have time for commoners after she becomes a princess. It's for the best.' Is that what you said?"

"Toman, does that even sound like me? I would never... I could never—"

"Then tell me what happened," he demanded.

"I...It's not my secret to tell," I said lamely.

"Secret? Dottie doesn't have any secrets. How many times have you said that Dottie could make gossip her full-time job if she ever stopped working at the palace," he said with a sneer.

"Toman, I never meant—"

"Now I know what you meant. Thanks for bringing Dottie back—now you have no obligations to me," he said before storming off.

"Toman? Toman!" I called, but he didn't come back. I considered chasing after him. He'd been my closest friend for years. I closed the door and turned back to my empty house. The loneliness invaded me like an intruder, demanding everything.

All my support was gone. Meiri would always be beholden to her mother. Toman had no reason to believe me over the word of his mother, and only Dottie could tell him the truth about her being the old king's lover. With Mamá gone, Toman's repudiation, Xander's ultimatum and implied threat to Zavier if I didn't end our relationship, I had nothing to keep me in Canto.

THE PALE LIGHT OF COMING dawn was the only illumination I needed to climb the sturdy vines on the side of Green Gardens manor. It had been too long since I'd had to slip into a home to steal for the hidden market, but it was the first time I was sneaking around to leave something behind. My bundle shifted in the makeshift harness on my chest. Cochi's long back paw kicked out as she dreamed of whatever chinchillas kept in their sleeping minds. Her travel cage was strapped to my back because her three-story home was too unwieldy for the ascent. I'd considered taking her to Jacque, but I didn't know if he still had his illegal griffin cub wandering his new house. I imagined Cochi was about snack-size and Jacque was a permissive pet owner. He was also a smuggler, so dropping off Cochi and bolting wasn't an option. I'd get caught and then there'd be questions I didn't want to answer.

I looked down below. Compared to scaling the palace, Green Gardens manor was simple. It was laughable that a guard stood watch at the front of the building, but no one patrolled the back. Lucky for me, that's where Meiri's window was located.

I pushed through the window, which was made of translucent plant matter, and landed on quiet feet. Jacque couldn't have managed a better landing, but I still looked toward the closed door on the opposite wall. Green Gardens manor, like most manor houses, was a series of apartments. Meiri's "room" was really more like four with a sitting room, bathroom, wardrobe and her bedroom. I'd landed in the wardrobe and gently placed Cochi's cage on a chest of drawers. I exited as quietly as I could and crept to Meiri's bedroom.

The door opened soundlessly, which was a feat considering the hinges were made of wood. Meiri lay sleeping in a bed shaped like a flower, and I wasn't entirely sure it wasn't one. Her breath stayed even, but still I didn't want to take any chances.

"*Swep*," I said in a whisper and her brows furrowed before smoothing completely and her mouth went slack. Her snoring startled Cochi and under other circumstances Lady Meiri's snoring would have been hilarious. As it was, I was fighting back the urge to wake her in the hope she would convince me to change my mind. Instead, I left a note on her nightstand and slipped out as quietly as I had come.

Back in the wardrobe I lifted Cochi out of the harness. Where her warm little body had slept, now a cold spot formed which had nothing to do with her bodily loss or a protection spell.

"Well, I think Meiri will take good care of you," I whispered to Cochi as I placed her in the cage. She settled into the bedding but kept her dark eyes on me. Her unusually intense stare made me look away and my eyes alit upon a coat completely made of fur. I looked back at Cochi. "Don't mind her furry clothing—I know she wouldn't make you into gloves or a muff."

Cochi blinked at me and for a moment I thought she understood everything I was saying. The idea that my nocturnal monster might miss me when I was gone suddenly constricted my throat. She continued to watch me, blinking occasionally as I sobbed.

I looked up at the broken window and worried about the cold air seeping in. I grabbed one of Meiri's many coats and draped it over the back of Cochi's cage. "I'll come back for you, I promise," I said and reached through the bars of her cage to scratch under her chin. For once she allowed it and I knew it was time to leave.

The window closed after I exited and whispered "*yeug teks*" to weave the plant materials back together.

I WAS ALL OUT OF TEARS as I trudged through the woods again. The backpack was heavy, but kept my back warm from the stray winds up on high. Looking back, I could almost see the window of my room in the distance. I hoped finding Cochi in *her* room wasn't too big a shock for Meiri. The note I left would explain everything... Well, most things. There were some things I still couldn't wrap my head around. It didn't really matter, but my chinchilla was the last one I had to worry about.

I'd made the decision abruptly and I didn't want to question where it came from. I just started packing, knowing I couldn't go on being so careful and expecting, without it unraveling every now and then. Too many secrets, too many lies and too much hurt couldn't be suppressed indefinitely. I couldn't fight the people I loved anymore, so instead I would learn all I could so I could be a help instead of a danger.

I'd wondered what to say to Zavier and knew another lie wouldn't help. He would move on eventually and find a better queen. I wasn't meant for palaces. Still, a lump formed in my throat, thinking of his face as he realized I'd left.

The path became steeper, so I concentrated on that instead of wallowing in self-pity. *Who am I kidding?* None of them would understand, but I didn't have to be there to answer any of their questions. I had my own to answer and as I looked up at the craggy mount, I knew the other side of Fae Range was a good place to start.

In the distance I heard a dog howl. Rowley couldn't follow me.

No one can.

THE END

Read the exciting conclusion of the Enchanted Path series

A Mage's Path

Coming Soon!

Acknowledgements

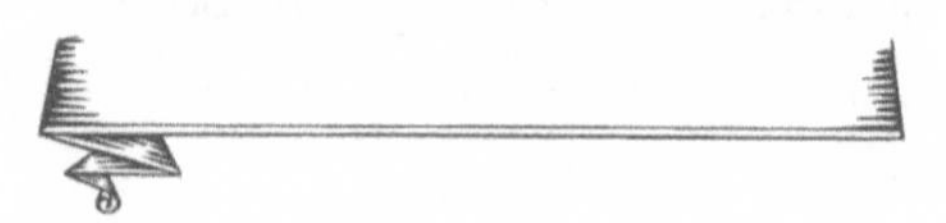

This book, like all my other projects, couldn't have been completed without lots of help. I want to thank my husband for his love, support, and all-around best beta reader. To my mother for buying all those blank books and never saying no to another bookstore splurge. Pat, my editor, thanks for being so patient with me when my inspiration took a holiday. Jack, my cover artist, who can read my crazy ideas and make them into art. To the tons of bloggers and readers thanks for making my past books successful. And to thousands of cups of tea, streaming services, video games, and all the books that got me through the past two years without losing my mind.

Cast of Characters

Inez Garza, smuggler and disinherited heir to Árbol Real

Lady Filomena Garza, Duchess of Árbol Real, Inez's mother

*__Lady Sabrina Garza__, Duchess of Árbol Real, Inez's grandmother, aka "Lita"

*__Beval__, Inez's grandfather

Izar, Garza family mirror

Rahd, Inez's father from Mythos

Lady Meiri Green of Verdant

Lady Eugenia Green, Countess of Verdant

Lord Archibald Green, Count of Verdant

Sir Archibald Green, aka Archie or Arch

HRH Prince Zavier Cole of Canto

HM Queen Hortensia Cole of Canto

HM King Xander Cole of Canto

*__HM King Yann__, king of Canto, father of Xander and Zavier

*__HM Queen Gaetane__, queen of Canto, mother of Xander and Zavier

Dr. Fell, royal healer

Piotr Podkin, Captain of the King's Men

Cleph, a King's Man

TOMAN TOOKMON, aka Tommy Tucker (stage name)

Dottie Tookmon, Toman's mother, employed at the palace

Pablo Gaitero, Jr. "PJ", owner of the Pickled Pepper

***El Niño Amoratado**, pirate and wielder of the blue horn

***Sebastian**, a King's Man

***Theodore Podkin**, A King's Man and ancestor of Captain Podkin

***Esmeralda**, "Alda", Inez's ancestor

JACQUE LESTE, smuggler and stuntman

Áliz aka the Jabberwocky, runs the hidden market

Viktor Lake, only legal mage in Canto

Rowley, leader of Birthright and a Labrador Retriever

Mathilde, First Teacher at the Academy

Chavah Deena Haro, proprietress of the Cup & Board

***Squirrel**, a smuggler

Betlindis Hart, researcher at the Canto library

***Rex Hart**, Betlindis' father

AUSTRA HUMPHREY, daughter of Delaware Humphrey, Queen of Somnambulam

Flora Merriweather Humphrey, mother of late Delaware Humphrey & CEO of Humphrey Farms

***Delaware Humphrey**, father of Austra, son of Flora & Orpington and former fiancé of Filomena

Diarmaid, deaf/mute butler of Humphrey Estate

***Queen Celeste** of Somnambulam, mother of Austra from Faery

*__Donata__, the Candlestick maker and founder of Faery

*__Beata__, the Baker and founder of Canto

*__Amata__, the Butcher and founder of Mythos

The Cat, feline mage from the past

*Deceased at time of present story

Words and Phrases of Power

Ag: move, draw or drive

Ag gwa tkei dem: bring my desire to me

Akwa: body of water

Aug: increase

Bheid: split

Bheid gwhen: deep cut split

Bhel: blow, swell; shine, flash, burn; white, various bright colors

Bher: carry

Bher uper reidh dgyes yer: carry me back through time

Bheu: grow

Gel kerd: pause the heart

Gleubh: to tear

Ghosti: stranger

Gwa reidh:

Gwapehwr: bonfire

Gwa tkei:

Gwei: live

Gwhen: kill or strike

Hepgwa akwa: boil water

Magh: be able to; have Power

Sengwh: sing, incantation; raise Power

Skeud: shoot, chase, throw

Sreu: flow

Swep: sleep

Syu: bind
Weid: see
Wrad: branch, root

Other Books by I.L. Cruz

The Enchanted Path Series

A SMUGGLER'S PATH: Book I

A Noble's Path: Book II

A Mage's Path: Book IV (coming soon)

NOVELLAS

The Cemetery Circle

The Cemetery Circle: Funeral Bells (coming soon)

Praise for A Smuggler's Path

An epic, rewarding tale sure to garner fans ready for sequels. *-Kirkus Review*

A DELIGHTFULLY CREATIVE adventure, *A Smuggler's Path* by I.L. Cruz stands alone in a very crowded fantasy genre, boasting a youthful, energetic spirit and a wonderful new world to explore for readers of fantasy. *-Self-Publishing Review*

...I DID ENJOY THE BOOK and I think more people definitely need to check it out. *-Rosina, Lace and Dagger Books*

...I ABSOLUTELY ADORED the main protagonist Inez - she was strong, and independent, and yet we experienced her struggles, the choices she was torn between. Would highly recommend this book. *-Rowena Andrews, Beneath a Thousand Skies*

THE WRITING WAS LOVELY and easy to read...The protagonist is a strong, fierce Latina who comes from a long line of strong, fierce

About the Publisher

Bosky Flame Press, A name and a memory

As a child I spent part of my summer at my great aunt's house in Puerto Rico every year. When I was left to my own devices, I would sit in her front yard under the expansive tree with bright red flowers and massive seed pods that made music when I shook them. I sheltered from the sun under its bows and created little stories that I whispered only to the tree. The tree was the *Flamboyan*, but it's also known as *flame of the forest* or *flame tree*. When it came time to name my imprint, which would feature Latina protagonists, I wanted it to feel like a cherished memory. That's how Bosky Flame Press was born.

Lightning Source UK Ltd.
Milton Keynes UK
UKHW010655051022
409964UK00006B/576

Latinas, and I loved it...What I particularly enjoyed was that the women were strong and empowered, but not to the detriment of the men. *-Sammie, The Bookwyrm's Den*

...I LOVED THIS BOOK, the characters were well-developed and I really enjoyed the world that was created...I am looking forward to reading book two! *-Ari Meghlen, The Merry Writer*

Praise for A Noble's Path

A charismatic heroine propels this kinetic and imaginative fantasy sequel.

-Kirkus Review

...*A Noble's Path* is a magical melee packed with honorable heroes that touches on a number of relatable and timely themes. *-Self-Publishing Review*

...I WILL KEEP AN EYE out for more books written by I.L. Cruz, and if you enjoy fantasy, you may want to check this book out. *-Jéssica*

I WOULD RECOMMEND THIS book to lovers of fantasy novels, which focus on people, their secrets and their reputations. *-Ellie Mitchell, Bookish Beyond*

...THIS BOOK WAS AMAZING to read and I can't wait for the next one. I want to know more, see more and go through more adventures...I do recommend this series to everyone who likes Fantasy with great and real characters. I am sure you're going to love it. -*Galit Balli, Coffee n' Notes*

THIS SERIES OFFERS a really good mixture of adventure, mystery, fantasy and romance for teens and adults alike, and I absolutely need to know what will happen next on Inez's 'Enchanted Path'. -*Steph Warren, Bookshine and Readbows*

Get email notifications, learn more about the world of The Enchanted Isles, and other stories on www.booksbyilcruz.com

THANKS FOR CONTINUING to support my writing. If you liked *A Rebel's Path* (and look forward to the next and last book in the Enchanted Isles series!) please leave a review wherever you purchased this copy—it's the best encouragement a writer can get to keep sharing her words and ideas—and tell you friends, family (and complete strangers if the mood hits you) about The Enchanted Isles novels. Thanks again!

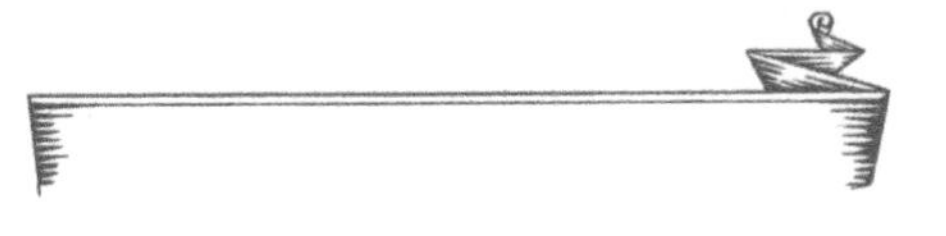

About the Author

I.L. CRUZ HAS BEEN writing from the moment she discovered a blank notebook was just a book in waiting. She decided to make writing her full-time career during the economic downturn in 2008. Since then, she's used her BA in International Relations to sow political intrigue into her fantasy worlds and her MA in history to strive for the perfect prologue. When she's not engaged in this mad profession, she indulges her wanderlust as often as possible, watches too much sci-fi and reads until her eyes cross. She lives in Maryland with her husband, daughter, and a sun-seeking supermutt named Dipper.